Praise for R

'I was impressed by *Th*
pleased to find myself ra
the strange world Rober
captures the sense of living in a state where terrible things
can happen to your neighbours. A fine start, and I look
forward to reading more from him.'
A Common Reader

'Imagine Brighton in chaos. Communities are divided –
socially, economically and physically. The council is
all-powerful, inconvenient people are "dealt with",
children are controlled and tolls strangle the transport
system. In *The Noise of Strangers* Robert Dickinson
creates a world that only vaguely resembles our own. This
intriguing story brings the issues of political influence,
red tape and corruption to the fore – if only by making us
relieved that it seems improbable it could come to this.'
Liverpool Daily Post

'I recommend it to those who like complex fiction,
who enjoy the demands of reading material that makes
them think, and those who have a dry sense of humour
– at the heart of this bleak, dark and all-too-believable
novel of a near future we should fear to live in is a joke
so mordant and black, and so beautifully constructed and
clever, that it will make you laugh out loud.'
Kay Sexton

'I loved the structure of *The Noise of Strangers* – it
flits between standard narrative, transcripts of phone
calls and meetings, inter-departmental memos,
sinister notes, and articles from an underground
newspaper. As a satire, it works well, and is
completely believable as a "nightmare present"
scenario. I admired its imagination.'
The Bookbag

'Dickinson's poems deliver the impact
of myths in styles which combine craft,
intelligence and humanity.'
Jackie Wills

'Dark and playful and self-effacing,
Dickinson is a strong poet.'
Guardian

'Robert Dickinson's poetry crackles with energy
and wit; utterly clear-sighted, it's also compassionate,
exploring the emotional territory of those on
the margins. Sensuous and surprising, these
poems are constantly probing the possibilities
of language – and the question of what it
means to be human.'
Catherine Smith

'A collection which takes the small, cramped details
of our lives and builds them into pictures of lasting
beauty and real insight. The result is invigorating,
exciting, occasionally bizarre. This book is full of rare
achievements: intellectually satisfying, it is also accessible;
wryly funny, it finds time to be moving; sweepingly
ambitious, it paints a world in the cramped writing of
a Parkinson's sufferer. Read it, you'll see.'
Ink, Sweat and Tears

*To read an extract from The Noise of Strangers,
turn to p.295*

About the author

Robert Dickinson is the author of *The Noise of Strangers*. He has also published two volumes of poetry, *Micrographia* and *Szyzgy* (with Andrew Dilger), and he wrote the comedy drama *Murder's Last Case*, and the libretto for Joby Talbot's choral work *Path of Miracles*. He lives in Brighton.

THE SCHISM

ROBERT DICKINSON

Myriad Editions

Published in 2013 by
Myriad Editions
59 Lansdowne Place
Brighton BN3 1FL

www.myriadeditions.com

1 3 5 7 9 10 8 6 4 2

A CIP catalogue record for this book is available from the
British Library.

ISBN: 978-1-908434-22-7

Printed on FSC-accredited paper by
CPI Group (UK) Ltd, Croydon, CR0 4YY

Now has come the last age of the song of the Cumae...

One

When I started at Elding Collections there were five of us: Brian, who'd told me about the job, Tony and Hameed, who worked north of the river, and Piers, the office manager, who did the paperwork and took the calls. We had one room, and a toilet on the next floor up that on winter days had been known to freeze. We had three desks and four chairs, some phones, a kettle, teabags, powdered milk, and wall calendars from three different banks (Tony also had one from the *Sunday Sport* which Piers made him keep in a drawer). Our office was over a shop that, in the time I was there, had sold everything from office stationery to discount kitchenware. Every few months one business would fail, the shop would be empty for a week or two, then another lot of short-lease optimists would move in and start losing money.

Elding Collections was the only thing that never changed, but then Elding Collections thrived on failure. Back then we collected credit cards, cheque cards and debit cards from subjects who'd overspent. We had strict rules. We weren't interested in money or furniture, only plastic. We were definitely not bailiffs. We carried business cards that identified us: *Elding Collections, A Discreet and Professional Service.*

This wasn't entirely honest. We were not discreet. If we couldn't find the person we wanted, we went straight to their neighbours and told them who we were and why

1

we were there. The neighbours were usually happy to help. As for 'professional', all that meant was that we were paid for the work. Criminal record? We don't care. No previous experience? Not a problem. Odd gaps on your CV? Step right up. They were no exams to pass, no minimum standards to meet. All the job required was basic literacy and a *London A–Z*. You didn't even need a car. Discreet and professional? I would have been happier if the cards had said: *Elding Collections, We're Not Bailiffs*.

People assumed our job was dangerous, that it brought us into daily contact with the underclass, that we had to go from door to door in gang-controlled estates where the inhabitants stopped abusing their children only when it was time to defraud the DSS. Sometimes we'd explain that the underclass didn't have credit cards – unless they'd stolen them, in which case they weren't our concern. But sometimes we'd pretend the work was more dangerous and interesting than collecting pieces of plastic from people who had been told we were coming.

It was an odd job. It wasn't what any of us had thought we'd end up doing. We were all treading water, waiting until we had a better idea. And it had some advantages. I wasn't stuck in an office, I could work to my own timetable, and, above all, I got to wear a suit.

In those days I liked suits. I liked them so much I wore them at weekends. I had a suit for the pub, another one for restaurants, and one for staying at home, watching television.

Shona, my old girlfriend, used to say it was because I was a control freak. That was her joke about me: 'You're a control freak, Pat.' It wasn't a complaint; it was why she liked me. The first time she saw my flat she'd said, 'It's a bit... *sparse*, isn't it?' I didn't have any ornaments or trophies, there were no posters or photographs, and everything was in its place.

'I prefer to think of it as tidy,' I'd said.

She'd laughed, which I treasured because she didn't laugh often. 'But do you actually *live* here?' She walked around the room, careful not to touch anything. 'Don't get me wrong,' she said, 'I like it.' She really did. She liked it enough to move in for a while. She didn't stay long, but when she left it wasn't because I was too tidy. No, when she left it wasn't personal.

I stayed in my spotless flat. I'd sit on my immaculate sofa in a suit and tie, and feel relaxed, or as close to relaxed as I ever feel. The only times I didn't wear a suit were when I ran in the mornings. My brother had been a schoolboy boxer, a promising welterweight; I had been a runner. Good enough to be chosen to represent the school; not good enough to win a race. My one talent was persistence. Every morning, if it wasn't raining or snowing, I still ran. I ran from habit, automatically. There were mornings when it was as if I'd woken up to find myself a mile from home and running already. I *dreamed* of running. Not of chasing or being chased, just running, and along the same streets I used when awake. The only difference between the dreams and reality was that in the dreams my brother would be running with me, a few yards behind, breathing heavily. I'd wake up with a sense of loss, check the weather, put on my running gear, and run. Later, I'd put on a suit and go to work, or, if it was the weekend, I'd put on a suit and go to the supermarket.

I didn't know why I dressed like that, and still don't. I wore shirts with collars half an inch too small because I liked the feeling of tightness at my throat. It wasn't a sexual pleasure, except maybe in the kind of deeply buried way that's so deeply buried it doesn't count.

At Elding Collections the suits were mandatory. We were supposed to look official, as if we meant business.

It was one of those rare mornings when everybody was in the office at the same time. Piers was sorting the papers on his desk into even neater piles; Brian was leafing through

The Ring Magazine; Hameed was thoughtfully picking long blonde hairs from the sleeve of his jacket. I was staring out of the window. It was eight o'clock and raining, and the only jobs we had that day were tracers.

In theory the card companies put out tracers to find a subject who owed them money. In practice all they wanted was for us to confirm that their debtor had moved. It was a formality, a box to be ticked before they could write off the debt. If they'd really wanted to find someone they wouldn't have asked us: we were rubbish. We'd visit the last known address, telephone the last known employer, and then give up. We only found the ones who hadn't actually moved. According to Piers, that gave us a success rate of fourteen per cent. Tracing was easy work, but dull.

That morning we had sixty-eight requests and were reluctant to start.

'Bloody rain,' said Brian, for the fourth time.

We could hear the crashing from the staircase that meant Tony was on his way up. He burst into the room, panting. 'It is pissing down out there.'

Tony swaggered like a heavy in a TV procedural. He was thick-set, with a square head and bright blond hair set in a dandified little quiff. The hair was ridiculous, deliberately ridiculous, like a provocation, daring you to laugh at him. It was supposed to grab your attention while telling you he was so tough he didn't care what you thought. It didn't fool us.

He stood in the doorway, flapping his hands. He was drenched, the quiff smacked flat against his forehead, his face shining, though that might have been sweat. 'Car's packed in again,' he announced, gasping. 'Mile down the fucking road. Look at this.' He raised his arms like a man held at gunpoint. His suit was two distinct shades of dark green. 'How am I supposed to work in this?'

'You should have brought a brolly.' Hameed could always be relied on to say something sensible.

'Didn't have the time. I had a heavy session last night...' And then Tony was off on one of his stories, all whisky chasers, violent misunderstandings and half-hearted punch-ups in car parks, usually with a girlfriend I suspected didn't exist.

We'd all heard these stories. They were part of office life, like the bad heating and the frozen toilet. The details – the name of the pub, the amount drunk, the number of witnesses – might change, but the stories followed the same pattern, as formulaic as the shipping forecast. We never knew how much of each of them could be believed. I suspected not much. I suspected most nights he sat in a pub by himself dreaming up these altercations, if he went to the pub at all.

On the other hand, Tony had two things which set him apart from the rest of us: a criminal record and a degree. Piers had a degree as well, but he was the sort of person – middle class, professional – you'd expect to have one. Tony presented his academic career as a blip, a kind of lost weekend. He gave different accounts of his arrest. In one, he'd beaten up his ex-girlfriend's future husband during a heavy drinking session after taking his finals. Others would hint at armed robbery or drugs, or whatever else was in the news that week. Tony was proud of his record, touchy about the degree, and vague about both. Like the rest of us, he was working for Elding Collections until something better turned up.

Piers handed him a worksheet. Tony glanced at it while still talking. It was a gift: he could read and talk at the same time, as if his story was pre-recorded. He had to wait until it finished before he could respond to the worksheet.

'More bloody tracers? What's happening to people? Oi, Piers, you know how many I had last week? Course you do, stupid bloody question.' Tony paused, expecting laughter. We couldn't be bothered. This didn't stop him. 'Place I looked at yesterday. Fucking weird. Fucking weird. Another runner. Piddling amount. Tower block. Rang the doorbell. Flat

5

battery. Farty sort of noise. Nobody's going to be in anyway, so I bang on the door a few times. Fuck me if it doesn't open. Some tart inside. Turns out to be our man's sister. She's looking for him too. You should have seen the state of the place. The walls had been painted black. Usually it's just dirt, or they've smashed the place up. This one had been fucking *redecorated…*' Some people took offence at the way Tony spoke; it was what he wanted, part of his act. At unguarded moments his voice changed – he'd sound like a Radio Three announcer, or Piers.

Hameed had a similar story. A shared flat, the absconder's room painted black… Tony drew the conclusion. 'Maybe they're Satanists. Maybe they hang crosses upside-down. Farrell, you're the Catholic boy, what do you reckon?'

'Don't ask me. I'm lapsed.'

'You? You're the most Catholic Catholic I've ever met. If Armani did hair shirts you'd be in your element.'

Brian stood up, shaking his head. 'I can't stay here any longer. Patrick, shall we make a start?'

Out in the street, we split up. I didn't have a car, so when I worked alone my range was limited. Fortunately our office was in the middle of the defaulters' area of choice – Piers had once explained the economic reasons – so there were always subjects within walking distance. More than once I'd had to go no further than the shop downstairs.

According to the charge sheet the first subject owed about eight thousand pounds, most of it on a credit card he was still using. He was, we'd have said, typical. I went to the rat hole where he was supposed to be living, one of those divvied-up tenements made shabbier still by waves of students. We hated students at Elding Collections. Freeloaders, we thought – pigs in shit. Even Tony hated students, and he'd been one. I was ready to dislike this one more than usual because he'd made me walk through the rain.

The door was opened by a thin kid with a straggly beard. I knew straight away he was the subject. His cheeks were stained with patches of vivid red and black, as though he'd recently been involved in a lab accident. It was a dark morning, but he still blinked as if the light was too strong. Eight thousand pounds in debt, and whatever he'd spent the money on hadn't involved fresh air or personal hygiene.

As soon as I saw him I expected hostility. It was the way his mouth was already open. Not in the slack-jawed way of some of our subjects, but as if he'd been about to say something and I'd interrupted.

I went through the formalities. 'Is Joshua Painter in?'

He half closed the door. 'Who wants to know?'

I showed him the business card, explained what I wanted. He looked hard at me for a second or two, then declared, 'I can't let you have it back.'

'You don't have a choice, Mr Painter.'

'Are you threatening me?'

'No, Mr Painter. I just want the card.'

I expected him to slam the door in my face, which would mean I'd have to come back the next day and at random intervals after that. As we charged our clients for each visit, this wasn't so bad. But instead he opened the door wider, stepped forward, and pushed his face up to mine.

'Don't lie to me. Your coming here is a threat, understand? But you don't frighten me.'

His breath was like the dustbin behind a pizzeria. I took a step back. 'We don't make threats, Mr Painter. I've just come to collect the card.'

'I have a *right* to that card.'

Another subject who hadn't read the small print. I wondered what he was supposed to be studying. I explained why he did not have a right to the card. It's a standard speech, and comes as a surprise to some people. It was a surprise to Joshua, though he tried to conceal this by nodding impatiently.

'I know all that.'

'Then can I have the card?'

He pointed at me as if he was picking me out of a line-up. 'I'm going to get the card. I'm going to my room to get the card. Stay here! I don't want you coming in. I know what you people are like. You step through that door and I'm calling the police.'

He disappeared into the black hallway. It wasn't worth following him. An old woman on the other side of the street watched me, attracted by the raised voice and the prospect of an argument. I smiled at her until she walked on.

Joshua came back, stamping down the stairs. He threw the card on to the wet pavement behind me. 'There. Take it.'

I bent to pick it up. 'Thank you, Mr Painter.'

'I bet you're proud of yourself. I bet you're really proud of yourself. I bet you really fucking get off on this.'

I pocketed the card. A lot of subjects, once the plastic's out of their hands, try these public displays of scorn. It gives them something to tell their friends afterwards. *I really let him have it*, they probably say. *You should have seen his face.* We provide a discreet professional service, so we're not supposed to say anything back. I didn't even say goodbye.

He spat, missing me by several feet, and closed the door. I thought I'd seen the last of him.

The next two subjects were an ex-machinist and a store manager. The ex-machinist was a lamb. A woman I took to be his mother let me into his dingy flat and pointed out the card on the oak-effect coffee table. The subject himself was in a dressing gown, watching television. He didn't protest or even seem to notice I was there. Afterwards, when the woman showed me to the door, I said I hoped her son would find work soon. It's the kind of meaningless courtesy that usually goes down well. She took it badly. 'That's my husband.'

The store manager wasn't at home, so I went to his shop.

He tried to make an argument of it, accusing me of driving away customers. I'd been in the shop for half an hour without seeing a customer, and said so. He offered me a discount on some Venetian blinds. I told him I preferred screen blinds, but he didn't have any.

A typical day. And then I visited my brother.

I went to see Mike every few days. The visits were as predictable as Tony's stories. I'd close the door behind me and sit on the end of his bed. The mattress was old, sunk in the middle as if an invisible man were sleeping there. His room had a single bed, an old wooden chair, and a small, high window. No radio or television, no newspapers or books: the window gave him all the entertainment he needed. He could spend whole days standing on the chair, looking out at a few hundred yards of untidy grass, and, beyond that, the trees that hid the wall. 'Mike,' I'd say. 'How are you, Mike?' He would stay on the chair, his face pressed so close to the window that his breath would keep misting the glass. The chair had uneven legs and every time he wiped the windowpane with his sleeve it would rock and I'd lean forward slightly, ready to catch him. He never fell. He'd spent so long on that chair, he knew all its movements.

Sometimes he'd say something like, 'There were three of them here today.'

'Yeah?' I'd say. 'Three of them?' I often wondered if he was aware who was in the room. As far as I knew, I was his only visitor. Our parents never went and he'd never really had any friends of his own. 'Where were they, Mike?'

'They were walking on the path. They didn't see me.'

'Yeah?'

'On the path. They were waiting.'

'Yeah?' I'd try to make it sound like a conversation, as if there was a third person in the room I was trying to impress. *See how normal we are.*

9

'Yesterday there were two of them.'

'Two?'

'They stayed over by the trees. They didn't think I could see.'

After a few minutes a nurse would come to the door. The nurses would change but somehow they all had the same hesitant speech and sleepy expression as the patients.

'Would you – er – like me to bring you some tea, sir?'

They always called me 'sir'. It must have been the suit.

'No, thanks. Bring one for my brother, though.'

I'd learned to refuse the tea after the first few visits. It took too long to prepare. I'd forget I'd asked for it and then, just as I was about to leave, the nurse would come back with a chipped institutional mug of something cold, which I then had to stay to drink. They meant well, the nurses; they wanted the best for everybody. But the dull glaze on the cups, like the long grass outside, like the old chair, like the old mattress, was just another reminder that you were in a place where things were wrong.

The nurse would leave. Mike would stay on his chair, looking out of the window, while I told him about my job or the latest about our parents. There was never much news about them. 'They've got new carpets in the bedrooms. Mum says they'll have to get new wardrobes now, but Dad's happy with the old ones…' It was all at that level. I'd pass on whatever gossip I had about people he used to know. Sometimes, if there was nothing to tell him, I'd invent things – small, credible accidents, say, or plausible visits from relatives – and out of some vestigial politeness he'd say, 'Yeah?' or 'Really?' before returning to the one subject that interested him: 'They let anyone in here. People walk in off the streets.' And then I'd start again, with a story about Dad redecorating the guest bedroom or the latest about Paul Kavanagh. I didn't know how much he understood but I'd tell him anyway, as if my scraps of news could make a difference, as if hearing

10

about Dad's DIY for the thirtieth time could bore him into sanity. I sometimes had the idea that it wasn't really my brother standing on the chair but someone who'd taken his place, a changeling who might bring back the real Mike if I pretended I hadn't noticed. The real Mike had been fit, a promising amateur welterweight who might, if all else failed, have become a decent professional middleweight. But all else had failed: the man on the chair seemed to be in his thirties, too old to be Mike, and flabby and pale.

After half an hour I'd have run out of things to say. 'Well, Mike, I'd better be going.' I'd stand by the bed for a few seconds longer. Sometimes he'd say goodbye, sometimes he wouldn't. He never turned away from the window. In the hall I might pass the nurse coming back with the tea.

'How – er – is your brother, sir?'

'No different.'

'Ah.' And the nurse would nod sadly and take the tea through to my brother's room. I'd cross the TV lounge as quickly as I could, and then go back to work.

That day Brian picked me up outside. 'How was he?'

'Same as ever.'

'Bloody shame.' He showed me the worksheet for the afternoon. 'Might as well get cracking.' Even allowing for the sclerotic London traffic we calculated we could get most of the work done before four if we worked together. Thirty house visits, most of them in the same area, then back to the office for the phone calls.

The first half-dozen were easy enough. No answer, or someone telling us our subject was gone. We pretended to believe them. We weren't interested in actually finding anybody. A successful trace meant paperwork.

House number seven was another divvied tenement. Brian sat in the car while I sprinted through the rain to the door and found the bell for the flat.

To my surprise, Joshua Painter answered. He looked just as surprised to see me. 'You again. Are you following me? I gave you the card, right. What do you want now?'

I took a step back. 'I'm not interested in you, Mr Painter. I'm looking for Peter Bedding. Does he live here?'

'Why should I tell you?' He stepped forward. Angry subjects do that: they're so intent on what they want to tell you they'll follow you right out of their houses and not notice until they're in the street. The rain stopped Joshua. He glared at the sky and retreated into his hallway. 'Why should I do anything to help you?'

'Does that mean he lives here?'

He looked thoughtful. I wondered if he was preparing a speech. 'He's moved. He doesn't live here any more. Are you happy with that or do you want to search the place?'

'I'm happy with that.'

This surprised him. It didn't give him the chance to say what he'd intended to say. He settled for something else. 'Do you know what you are? You're scum, that's what you are.'

'It's just a job.'

'That's what they said in the gas chambers.' He slammed the door in my face.

'What happened?' Brian asked, back in the car. 'He looked cross.'

'The usual. The sub's not there any more, and I'm scum. I'm a Nazi.'

'Someone who knows you, then.'

'Actually, yeah.' I told him about the earlier meeting.

Brian thought about it. 'So what do you think he was doing there?'

I said, 'Who knows what these people do?'

Sixty-eight people were missing that month. We weren't concerned. It wasn't as though it signified the collapse of society. Our runners left for the traditional reason: to avoid

12

paying debts. Whether these were accumulated through carelessness or bad luck didn't matter. Tony liked to say the subjects were either losers or shits, and it didn't matter which because we treated them all the same. They were names on a list, paperwork. There were other people who disappeared, of course, the ones whose out-of-date photos were taped in shop windows: 'Not seen since...' We weren't concerned with those.

We knocked on doors, made telephone calls, then went home and forgot, knowing our runners, economic fugitives, would have to turn up somewhere. Anything else that happened to them had nothing to do with us, nothing at all.

At around visit number sixteen we began to get fed up. We'd had three abusive answers in a row, and the rain still hadn't stopped. We sat in a parked car at the edge of a housing estate, one of those places supposed to be rough. That was how we spent a lot of our time: sitting in cars, waiting for the rain to stop. Brian looked at a drenched poster stuck to a dirty grey wall. I looked up at the sky, the big dramatic clouds bunched over the maisonettes. It was three in the afternoon and there were no pedestrians.

'I beat him once,' Brian said.

I had been thinking about my brother, the way I often did after a visit. 'Beat who?'

Brian nodded to the posters covering one wall. A forth-coming contest, local boy challenging for a national title. 'Him.'

'I'm not surprised. He's a welterweight.' Brian had fought at light-heavy.

'Not him. On the undercard.' You couldn't tease Brian. I'd never seen him lose his temper. The unruffled calm might have made him good at Elding Collections but it also made him the dullest successful fighter in a dull division. Eight professional victories, so tedious no promoter would touch

13

him. I'd seen his last match. It had gone the distance – all his fights went the distance. I'd soon given up trying to watch. By what felt like the thirty-fourth round I was examining the lights or attempting to flirt with the card girl's sister. All around me people were pinching themselves or miserably studying the programme, while in the ring, oblivious to the catcalls and cries of derision from his own corner, Brian plodded to victory as casually as a man painting a fence on a hot afternoon. Afterwards he had been able to give a blow-by-blow account. He remembered every detail of all of his fights, amateur and professional. Probably he was the only person who cared. None of his opponents ever became successful. Here, five years later, one of them was still on the undercard.

Prompted by the poster, Brian started telling me everything he could remember about their old fight. It took nearly half an hour. 'I might go and see him,' he concluded. 'See if he's got any better. Want to come? It's not as if you have anything better to do.'

'Maybe.' I'd been keen on boxing once, mainly because of Mike. I knew Brian through Mike's old gym. Shona had trained there as well. If I followed the sport now, it was because of Brian: it gave us something to talk about, and involved memorising fewer names than football.

'Good. I'll see about the tickets.' Brian looked up at the sky. 'Bloody rain. You know,' he added, as if it was hardly worth mentioning, 'I'm seeing Sue tonight for a drink. You should come.'

'I don't want to get in the way.'

'You won't be. You should get out more. It'll do you good.'

'I do get out. I run.'

The rain slackened and stopped. Brian yawned. 'Sue thinks you should come. Let's go back to the office.' He started the engine. A pedestrian, the first we'd seen, ran across the road a little ahead of us. 'There's your friend,' Brian remarked. 'Coincidence.'

I was thinking of Mike again and hadn't really noticed the thin man in a large black coat. He turned as he passed, though he didn't look in our direction. It was Joshua Painter. He stood for a while in the middle of the road, staring up at the sky, then wrote something in a notebook and walked on.

'No friend of mine.'

'Too many drugs.' Brian sounded philosophical, as if taking too many drugs was something anyone might do, by accident, say, or through sheer absent-mindedness. 'Too many psychotropics.' Brian, in his slow, methodical way, was keen to expand his vocabulary. From the way he said it, I knew 'psychotropics' was a recent acquisition and that I would hear more of it in the next few weeks. We'd gone through the same process with 'anomaly' and 'dyspraxia'.

We drove back to the office.

We found Tony on the phone. 'So you haven't seen him since then? No, no, thank you for your time.' Tony sometimes used his middle-class voice on the phone, though he pretended it was put on. He always swore as soon as he put down the receiver. 'Fucking lying cunt, he was there last week.' He pretended to notice us. 'You tossers find anybody?'

'Nobody.'

'Same here. Where does that leave us, Piers?'

Piers didn't even look away from his monitor. 'In one day our monthly average has dropped to two per cent. To one point eight seven per cent, to be precise.'

If Elding Collections had been a space opera, Piers would have been the alien who didn't understand human emotions.

'Getting close to that magic number.' Tony signed a report with a flourish, as if it was an important treaty and the world was watching. 'What happens when we reach no success at all? Or negative figures? What would that be?'

'Finding people we're not looking for,' I suggested.

'No.' This was the kind of question Piers found interesting. 'It would be not finding people who are there.'

We debated the point. Brian didn't take part. He sat at his empty desk and looked at us tolerantly.

To kill the last hour we started making calls. *I'd like to talk to... Could someone in personnel help?* If it was a small company, a garage or a shop, we said who we were. If it was a big company we'd pretend we were friends. *Not there any more? Not to worry, I'll catch him at home later.* We tried to vary our voices, except for Piers, who only had one. Tony had the full range, from upper middle to dead common, with a few provincial accents for relief. We asked the same questions, were given the same answers.

'Christ, this is dull,' Tony said towards five. 'Jesus fucking Christ, this is dull.' He threw a paper dart at me. I unfolded it. He'd written, *At least we're not selling double glazing.* I screwed it up into a ball.

Brian finished his own call.

'Don't complain,' he said thoughtfully. 'At least we're not selling double glazing.'

Tony slapped his desk in triumph, then glared at me. 'Laugh, you bastard.'

I threw the ball of paper into his face. 'I can't. It's not as funny as it was the first six times.'

'What is it with you? Jesus, you're uptight.'

'There's nothing wrong with me.'

He slapped his desk again. 'Oh, yes, there is. You are screwed so tight something's going to snap. You don't relax a bit, mate, you're gonna end up in the cackle factory.'

'Careful,' Brian said, but Tony was on a roll. He knew about Mike, they all did. But Tony got carried away. He said things because he liked the sound of them.

The office had a lot of telephone directories. I picked one up from the floor, balancing it on the palm of my hand.

'Still,' Tony said, 'least it's somewhere they know you. Fuck, they'll probably let you share a room. They could rename it the Farrell Wing – '

'Don't,' said Brian. Too slow. Tony caught the spine of *E–K* square in the face. It almost knocked him off his chair. Almost: I'd thrown it sitting down and didn't have the leverage. Tony cupped his face in his hands and turned away howling.

'You shouldn't have done that,' Brian said mildly.

'I know. I should have stood up.' I vaulted on to my desk and took a long step on to Tony's. He might have had a weight advantage, but I'd hurt him first and he didn't see me coming. I put my foot against his back and pushed hard. The chair was on castors and went down with him. He hit the floor heavily, with a hoarse gasp. His face was bright red, and there was a black line across the bridge of his nose. He put his hands up for protection, untangled his legs from the chair, and tried to roll away. There wasn't enough room. He was trapped between his desk and the filing cabinet. I jumped down from the desk, got in two sharp kicks, then jumped clear of his stabbing feet.

Piers didn't say a word. He'd seen it all before.

Tony pulled himself back up, then righted the chair. He stood leaning against his desk, one hand over his nose, the other pressed against his side, just under the ribs. He couldn't talk, and his white shirt was grey with sweat. Brian laughed gently. I moved back behind my desk. Tony was too out of breath to hit me, but he might have thrown something. We watched him. Gradually he stopped rubbing his side and experimented with taking his hand away from his nose.

Hameed came in with a worksheet. He looked at us looking at Tony, handed the sheet to Piers, and left. Piers glanced through the paperwork. 'Our monthly average is now two point one eight.'

'Ham had a good day, then.' Brian was beginning to get tired of watching Tony. 'That's good.'

Tony finally spoke. He was still out of breath. 'What's good about it?'

Brian shrugged.

Tony glanced at me, then stared at his hand, looking for blood. There wasn't much: a little thick, dark seepage from the top of his nose.

'You're a mad cunt, Farrell,' he said, admiringly. 'Don't think I won't hold this against you.' He pulled at where his damp shirt clung to his stomach. 'I've had enough. All I've had today is aggravation.'

He picked up some papers from the floor, threw them on to Piers's desk, folded his jacket over his arm, and left.

Tony should have been used to aggravation. He was, as Brian used to warn me, a wind-up merchant. The only one of us who hadn't taken a swing at him was Piers, and that was only because Tony would get bored long before Piers showed any signs of getting angry. I'd hit Tony before; Hameed had nearly broken his arm; Brian had allegedly once knocked him cold (he was supposed to have done it impersonally, on behalf of somebody else). Tony accepted it as proof he was tough. I sometimes thought he'd have been disappointed if I *hadn't* hit him. Now and again he'd hit back, but his heart wasn't in it. For all his swagger he wasn't very good at fighting. His retaliation was mostly verbal.

'Those kicks were a bit unnecessary.' Brian, as a fighter, had always believed in doing just enough to win. 'You should relax a bit more. Maybe try some psychotropics. Let's go to the pub.'

A typical day.

Two

Sue had been Brian's girlfriend for over a year. She was sunbed-orange, thin in a way that suggested punishing diets, and wore bright clothes designed for teenagers. She wasn't my type, and I was surprised Brian thought she was his. I kept waiting for him to realise his mistake and grow tired of her. He never did, which showed how little I knew about him.

We'd got off to a bad start. The first time we'd met she'd asked the date of my birthday. She not only identified the star sign, she added that I shared the day with Jacques Cousteau and Lynsey de Paul. She seemed to think I'd be impressed. I was, in a way. Brian might think she was clever and charming, but I didn't like the way she looked or what she talked about or even her choice of perfume – and she wore lots of perfume. That night, for instance, I could tell she was in the pub even before I saw her waving across the room. Sue always behaved as if she thought meeting you was the highlight of her day, which, if you wanted to see her, might have been endearing. She was with another woman who had her back to us. *Shit*, I thought, *she's brought a friend*. I almost walked out.

I didn't. I needed a drink, if only to dull the nagging sense that I'd overreacted at the office. The alternative to drinking with Sue was drinking alone, and, annoying as I found Sue, my own company was worse. I steeled myself for an evening of polite boredom and joined them while Brian went to the bar.

The other woman was not like Sue. She was younger, had straight dark hair, pale skin, and was dressed in black. When I sat down she looked at me warily. Not Sue's friend, I thought, but somebody who worked with her; somebody who'd agreed to come out of pity and was probably now wondering what she'd let herself in for. I could sympathise. I preferred her reserve to Sue's gushing, 'How are you, Patrick? Is that a new suit? It looks good on you. Don't you think it looks good on him?'

I knew I was unfair to Sue. She had good intentions, and she probably meant everything she said, at least while she was saying it. She was a good-hearted, salt-of-the-earth type. Still.

She finally got round to introductions. 'What am I doing – you two don't know each other, do you? Patrick works with Brian – but I've told you that already! Patrick, this is Jane. Jane's my sister.'

Looking back, it's hard to disentangle my first impressions from what I learned later. Jane was to become such an important part of my life that it's difficult to remember a time when I didn't know her. I remember thinking she was attractive. I remember wondering if she had a boyfriend. I wouldn't have guessed she was related to Sue. They seemed to have nothing in common. Jane even spoke differently, as if she'd been raised in a different household. Sue had a kind of breathless enthusiasm: she overreacted to everything, laughed at every joke and was astonished by every anecdote. Jane was dry, deadpan. I had the feeling she'd spent most of her recent life trying to live down her well-intentioned but embarrassing older sister.

'Jane's a computer programmer,' Sue told me, with awe.

Jane shrugged: she knew what the world really thought about computer programmers. 'It's only temporary.'

'No, I think it's good.' Sue wouldn't let her sister sell herself short. 'It must be really difficult, all those *numbers*.' She said *numbers* as if they were obscure scientific phenomena she'd heard of but never encountered. 'I couldn't do it.'

'It's not so difficult,' Jane said, still looking at me. 'Once you get the hang of the basics it's just common sense.'

'Jane is really clever,' Sue insisted. 'Not like me. She showed me one of her books once. I couldn't understand any of it. I use computers all day at work but I don't understand how they work.'

Brian arrived with the drinks.

'Hello, babe,' Sue crooned, as they leaned in for a kiss. Jane averted her gaze at the same time I did and our eyes met. She grinned. When Brian finally disengaged from Sue he turned to Jane.

'So, what's the news?'

He showed no surprise at seeing her, but then Brian never showed surprise. His unruffled calm had more than once been mistaken for concussion. I wondered if I'd been set up. Jane later told me she was wondering the same thing.

'I've moved,' she said, giving me a sidelong glance. She still didn't know what to make of me. I realised this was because I hadn't yet said anything.

I didn't get a chance now. Sue swooped in. 'You haven't! Really? Your stars said there would be a change.'

'Really.' Jane noticed that I had winced. 'You don't believe in star signs, do you?' she asked.

Sue squealed in protest before I could answer. She took astrology seriously. She also believed in psychics, would not risk walking under ladders, and thought it was bad luck to scratch her nose when it itched. Sue never gave any of her beliefs much thought: they just accumulated, like lint in a pocket. Later on she'd find she believed in feng shui and the healing power of crystals.

But I was no better. If I thought astrology was crap, it was only because people like Sue believed in it. I didn't have a rigorously worked-out position.

21

I still didn't get a chance to say anything, as Sue was more excited about Jane's new flat than I've ever been about anything, ever. 'So where is it? Who's your new landlady? What's she like? Is she better than your last one?'

Jane laughed. 'Cissy wasn't bad!'

'Oh, she was, Jane, she was strange. Go on, tell them about her.' Sue turned to me. 'The woman she used to live with was really strange.'

'She was not. She just liked watching musicals.' Jane seemed torn between amusement and exasperation. 'She worked for Deutsche Bank. She had a good, sensible job. She wasn't strange at all. She just really liked musicals.'

'But you said it was all she watched.'

'It was, pretty much. Occasionally she'd watch the news, but the rest of the time it would be *Show Boat* or *Singin' in the Rain* or *It's Always Fair Weather* or *The Pirate*. I've been there for four months and I know *Singin' in the Rain* by heart. And *On the Town*...' She waved away the memory. 'There was nothing wrong with Cissy. In some ways I'm sorry to leave. Honestly, I was beginning to like *Show Boat*.'

'I can't stand those old films.' Sue clearly thought this was an uncontroversial opinion. 'They're such rubbish. I can't stand anything in black and white.'

'They're not rubbish. And you can't talk. You like Bruce Willis.'

'He's good-looking. And at least his films are modern.' Sue pouted. 'Besides, you liked him in *Moonlighting*.'

'Only the first season,' Jane conceded. 'After that he went to seed.'

Sue was defiant. 'Bald men are sexy.'

I didn't know what they were talking about. I watched television most nights in a kind of trance. News and sport, crime dramas. I hadn't been to the cinema in years.

'Anyway, I've now got a new room with someone who isn't interested in musicals, so hopefully I'll never have to sit through *Dubarry Was A Lady* again.' Jane turned to me, determined this time to make me talk. 'So how was your day? Repossess much?'

From her tone I guessed Brian had already given the we're-not-bailiffs speech and she was joking. I told her it was a typical day, dealing with typical subjects. I didn't mention kicking Tony. I didn't want to look bad.

'You're as coy as Brian. What's a typical subject?'

'There's a bloke at work who divides all our subjects into losers or shits.'

'Tony,' Brian explained.

Sue shuddered. 'I don't like the sound of him.'

Jane wasn't interested in Sue's opinion. 'Give me an example.'

'You must realise I'm not supposed to talk about them.'

'You don't have to give me names.' She smiled, a fellow conspirator. 'Come on, Patrick. Brian here never tells me anything.'

'OK.' I liked the way she'd used my name. As an example of a loser I told her about the man who was married to the woman I'd mistaken for his mother.

Jane nodded. 'And why do you say he was a loser?'

'Because he'd stopped caring.' I tried to describe the feeling of terminal despondency that had filled the room. 'He didn't try to argue. He didn't even look up when I walked in the room.'

'You know,' she said, 'he could have been depressed.'

I realised she was probably right. I'd blithely dismissed a mental illness as if it was a moral failing. I felt, briefly, as if I'd been caught stealing from the poor box. Sue was baffled by Jane's comment ('So what if he was? That's no reason for sitting around on your arse all day...') but I saw it as a good sign: Jane didn't make that kind of snap judgement. She knew things her sister didn't. She was a *better person*.

'So...' Jane pressed on. 'Now describe a shit.'

I described the student. I described his appearance. I repeated some of the things he said.

She interrupted. 'And he compared you to a Nazi? I think I know who he was. Was his name Joshua Painter?'

Sue laughed. 'One of your friends, Jane?'

'He's more a friend of Adam's.'

Adam, I thought. Boyfriend. I should have known...

Sue sounded dismayed on my behalf. 'So who's this Adam, then?'

Jane glanced at me. 'Just a friend. Someone I used to work with.'

'Jane's got a lot of strange friends,' Sue told me, as if I was supposed to rescue her from them.

'Adam's not so strange when you get to know him.' Jane, hearteningly, seemed to care what I thought. 'So, Joshua's still pretending to be a student?'

'Final year.'

'Still? He'll never finish.'

Sue said that in her opinion all students were scroungers who wasted their money on drink and drugs. Jane appealed to me. 'Can you see why I left home at sixteen?'

'Nineteen,' Sue corrected.

'Nineteen was when I left for good.' Jane seemed keen to change the subject. 'I'm not surprised Joshua's in trouble. He was always bad news.'

'Really? What sort?'

'All sorts. Drugs, mostly.'

'Typical student,' Sue said.

'But you're right about him.' Jane ignored her sister's comment. 'He is a shit.' She seemed determined to be friendly towards me, to take my side. I wasn't sure if this was because she liked me or because she just wanted to rile her sister.

She told me later she couldn't understand why I hung around with Brian. 'You're cleverer than he is...' I'd tried to explain that Brian wasn't stupid, but she wouldn't believe me. He was Sue's boyfriend, after all. What more evidence did she need?

That night she asked questions. What did I think of Major? Who had I voted for at the last election? Did I believe in God? They were serious questions, but Jane made it sound like a game. I wondered if she'd once been asked the same questions herself, in the same playful tone. No, I'd never joined a political party. No, I didn't go to church.

Sue listened with a mix of outrage and astonishment. 'You can't ask him that! Leave the poor man alone! No, Patrick! You don't have to answer that!' I wondered if Jane asked these questions *because* they upset her sister. Sue's usual strategy was to agree with whatever people told her; she became nervous in the presence of disagreements. I think she was frightened Jane would turn on her next. The last book I'd read had been *Empire of the Sun*. I'd never wanted to join the army. I'd been abroad only once.

'Only once?' This surprised Jane. 'Even Sue's been more than once.'

'That's just how it worked out.' A stint in Tenerife as a travel rep. I'd pulled out after a month because I couldn't bear the thought of Mike not having a visitor. I decided not to tell her about Mike. Not yet, not in front of Sue. 'Is that it? Do I get the job?'

'I'm still undecided.' Jane said it lightly. One of the things that attracted me was the difference between what she said and the way she said it.

She had to go soon afterwards – there were clothes she needed to collect from her old flat. Before she left, while Brian and Sue were at the bar, I said I'd like to see her again. 'When you've had a chance to assess my responses.' She seemed surprised I thought I had to ask.

So I saw her again. Jane wanted to meet in a pub called the Half Moon. It was a small pub I'd passed a few times

25

without ever going inside, a poky little place with a few customers in jeans and T-shirts, fresh from their building sites. Country and western music was playing. There were signed photographs on the wall: middle-aged men smiling in dinner jackets, women clutching bouquets. I didn't recognise any of them.

I was the only person there in a suit. I wondered why Jane had chosen this pub. I suspected it was because none of her friends would use it. She didn't want to be seen talking to me.

She arrived, once again dressed in black: a short dress, leggings, a smart jacket. Her hair was tied back, as if she'd come straight from a job involving dangerous machinery. She seemed pleased to see me.

We asked about each other's days and quickly established that our jobs weren't important. 'Most of us don't live up to our potential,' Jane said. She quoted that line about most men living lives of quiet desperation. 'What we do for a living is meaningless. What we do outside is what matters.' From the way she talked about *meaning* I had a momentary fear she'd turn out to be a Jesus freak or a Scientologist. I said I wasn't sure what a meaningful life would feel like. I didn't want that kind of responsibility.

She laughed. 'I don't mean a higher purpose or anything like that.' She said she had her friends. What did I do?

I told her my brother wasn't well. That took up a lot of my time. 'Actually, it doesn't,' I corrected myself, 'I only see him once or twice a week, but I think about him a lot.'

She looked concerned. 'Can I ask what's wrong with him? That's if you don't mind talking about it.'

Normally I would have minded. I'd have said Mike was unwell and left it at that. But I had the sense that I could trust Jane, that she wouldn't be horrified like Sue, or amused like Andy Longman. I told her Mike's diagnosis and where I visited him. I described a typical visit. When I'd finished she said, 'It must be hard. I know it's difficult to talk about those places.' There was nothing glib about her. I was touched, the way you sometimes are at an unexpected kindness. She ended with, 'I can understand why you do it. But you still need a life of your own.'

'I have a life.'

She smiled. 'You need one that's a bit more fun. You need to look forward to something.'

'I looked forward to this.'

She winced. 'Look, some friends of mine meet up sometimes. You could come. If you're interested.'

I was interested, if only to find out more about her friends. 'As long as they're not like Joshua Painter.'

She laughed. The man was becoming our private joke. 'They're nothing like him.'

'What are they like?'

'They're like me.'

Which gave me an excuse to ask her questions. I learned she'd worked as a programmer since finishing college. She helped build financial applications. 'It's pretty dull. But the pay's not bad.'

I told her I'd never used our office computer. She was surprised. 'How do you access your records?'

'We have a filing cabinet. And Piers.' I told her about Piers.

She was amused. 'You're in the Dark Ages.'

I was surprised at how relaxed I felt in her company. It was only later that I realised how cleverly she'd deflected some of my questions. At around ten she said, 'Do you want to come back for coffee?'

'Will your landlady mind?'

'She's out tonight. I wouldn't ask you otherwise.'

'Does she disapprove of visitors?'

'Not really. Ros is… she has her own ideas.' Another non-answer. 'I get on quite well with her. Do you want a coffee or not?'

Her flat was a surprise. I'd expected untidiness, but Jane led me into a room as neat as a show home. The chairs were symmetrically aligned; the television screen in the corner was at a precise forty-five-degree angle to the wall. There were no ornaments, no magazines left under chairs, no unfinished mugs of tea on the table. Apart from having a wall chart and a computer, it was like somewhere I might have lived.

Jane went to the bright, spotless kitchen and switched on the kettle. I could hear her opening and closing cupboard doors and moving packets and tins. At first I thought she was making a lot of noise just to show me the trouble I was putting her to. Then I remembered she was new here and probably didn't know where anything was kept.

I stood at the kitchen door. 'Jane, are you sure this is your flat?'

'I think so.' She found two mugs and held them up. 'I've only been here a week. It's Ros. She's always tidying things up.'

'Ah.'

'And I think she disapproves of coffee. She hides it.'

'Sick woman.'

I didn't want to make her uncomfortable so I turned away and studied the chart over the computer. It was a home-made effort, printed across twelve sheets of A4. It showed four concentric circles divided into a dozen or so parts. It looked like something that might be used at a business seminar – a flip chart of market segmentation, say, or a breakdown of last year's costs. At each intersection of a line there were numbers, some printed, some pencilled in. I couldn't make sense of them.

'What's this chart about?'

'That's Ros's.' Jane had found a jar of coffee. 'I've found some instant. I don't know where she's put my stuff.'

'If she doesn't like coffee, why does she have instant?'

'It was in the back of the cupboard. Maybe it belonged to her last lodger.'

'Maybe she drinks it secretly. It'll be fine. It's what we have at work.'

'I'd have thought your work was stressful enough.' She brought the mugs through. We sat on facing chairs. She pulled off her sweater and threw it on to the floor at her feet in a matter-of-fact way. Underneath she wore a black vest that left her shoulders bare. Her pale skin reminded me of Joshua Painter. I couldn't see how she knew someone like him, however indirectly. But then I didn't understand how Sue could be her sister. 'So, what's this Ros like?'

'She's very particular.'

'I guessed that. What does she do?'

'She has her own business.'

'Computers?'

'Once. Once she was just another code monkey. That's how I came to know her. Stroke of luck really – I couldn't have stayed with Cissy for much longer. You can only watch so many musicals.'

'You said you were beginning to like *Show Boat*.'

'That's why I had to leave.'

'I've never seen it.'

'It's actually pretty good. You think it's going to be some cheesy old song-and-dance thing and – '

We heard the front door unlock.

Jane glanced down at the sweater she'd left on the floor. 'That's Ros.'

I was curious about Ros. From the look of the flat I imagined someone forceful and chic. She'd be wearing a suit and her first words would be about the terrible day she'd had.

Wrong on all counts.

Into the room stepped what seemed to be a little girl dressed in generic East European peasant costume: shapeless heavy fabrics in different shades of dark brown. Ros was about five feet tall. My first thought was that she was a mature twelve-year-old, then I saw the faint lines around her eyes. Like Jane, she had straight black hair. Unlike Jane, she had the remains of a suntan and a stud in the side of her nose. She was pretty, and gave the impression she didn't think this mattered – the sort of woman Sue would tut over and wonder why she didn't make more of herself.

She was in a bad mood. She stood over the sweater and frowned. 'Christ, Jane, I leave this place for one evening and you turn it into a tip.'

Jane picked it up quickly. 'It's only a sweater.'

'You can still put it away.' She pointed at the coffee mugs, which were still full. 'And what about this?' She moved through to the kitchen. 'And you've left the coffee out. Again.'

Jane whispered, 'I've never left the coffee out.'

Ros came back into the room and stared at me. I half expected her to say, *And what's this?* Instead she held out a hand. 'I'm Ros.'

'Patrick.'

'What do you do, Patrick?'

Jane picked up the mugs and took them through to the kitchen as if she didn't want to be there when I answered.

I told Ros I worked for Elding Collections. Ros frowned again. 'Aren't they bailiffs?'

I issued my usual denial. She didn't look convinced.

'So what do you do for them?'

Jane tried to be conciliatory. She called, 'He met Joshua Painter the other day and confiscated his credit cards.'

Ros wasn't amused. 'Don't talk to me about Joshua Painter.' She walked up and down, looking for further signs of disorder. 'I never want to see him again.' She said it as if she meant it.

I asked, 'What do *you* do?'

She stopped to look at the chart on the wall. It seemed to calm her down. 'I'm an astrologer.' She marched to the bathroom.

I went into the kitchen where Jane was noisily washing the cups. 'An astrologer?'

Jane didn't turn around. 'She's a good one, too.'

Ros came out of the bathroom. 'I hope you're planning to put those cups away.' Then she changed tack. 'Hey, I've had it done.'

Jane was immediately interested. 'Really?'

'Yep. That's phase one.'

'Show, show.'

Ros took off her waistcoat and lifted the front of her top. There was a small gold ring in her navel. She smiled at us proudly. 'And next week the nips.'

Navel rings weren't so common then. These days everybody under twenty-five seems to have something pierced. Back then, I gaped and repeated, 'The nips?'

'Nipples,' Jane said, as though it was obvious. 'What did you think she meant, the Japanese?'

'I don't get it,' I think I said, though it's possible I just stood there with my mouth hanging open.

Ros gave Jane a questioning look. She said, 'It's my body.'

'Fair enough.'

'I don't have to conform to any socially imposed ideal of femininity.'

'Of course not.' After all, if the socially imposed ideal meant someone like Sue...

Ros finally lowered the front of her shirt. 'What I choose to have done to my body is my decision, and you can't – '

'Ros,' Jane said. 'He *is* agreeing with you.'

'I'm not going to argue the point.' Ros turned to her. 'Did you get it?'

'No.'

Ros sighed deeply. 'Never mind. You'll have to get some tomorrow.'

I didn't ask what she meant. Bread? Toilet rolls? Tranquillisers? I said, 'I'd better go now.'

Ros put her hands on her hips and glared at me. 'So soon?'

Jane saw me to the door. 'Sorry about that.' She spoke softly, not wanting to be overheard. Her tone reminded me of a teenager apologising for some gaucherie committed by a parent. 'Not everyone can get on with Ros.'

'I noticed.'

'She's not really a bad person.'

'You say that when someone is. Can I see you again? Somewhere less tense?'

'Same place? Tuesday?'

We agreed on a time. Then, almost furtively, she pushed a thick paperback into my hands. 'Read that.'

'By next week?' I put it in my jacket pocket. I'd look at it later. 'Will there be a test?'

Ros peered out of the lounge. 'Jane, what have you done with my notebook?'

Jane sighed. Her expression said, *See what I have to put up with?* 'You don't have to read all of it. But I think it explains a lot.'

She closed the door before I could say anything else.

It was abrupt, but I wasn't dismayed. If Jane was in a bad mood it was because of Ros, and Ros looked as if she could put anybody in a bad mood. The good thing was that Jane wanted to see me again. And she'd lent me a book.

I didn't look at it until I got home. It was *The Fourth Science* by Erin C. Burke, published by the Occulta Press at $12.95. The first three sciences, according to what Erin C. Burke called the Introit, were chemistry, biology, and physics. The fourth science was 'that which used to be known by the derogatory title of "magic"'.

I wondered what it was supposed to explain.

Three

It's odd that I met Joshua and Ros in the same week, but I don't want to start reading significance into these things. One of them was a subject, the other was the friend of a friend. I'd have met them both sooner or later. The fact that they knew each other wasn't significant either. Even Joshua, who saw a pattern in most things, didn't make much of our first meeting. He wrote about it in his diary only because it was a financial setback. That's how he described it: *Financial setback. Agent very negative.* He'd underlined *very*, but then he underlined lots of things: the weather, the length of the queues in the post office, important numbers. I know this because some time later I broke into his flat and stole the diary. I still read it from time to time, trying to make sense of what happened. It isn't much help. For one thing, Joshua didn't use the standard calendar; according to his system the financial setback happened on 5/24/7021.

The Fourth Science was hard going, and not just because of the Latin chapter titles. I couldn't tell if it was serious. When Erin C. Burke described physics as a 'typically masculinist destructive science' with findings that were 'meaningless to the average person' I was surprised. Was that what educated people were saying? Was the periodic table really a 'social construct'? I didn't know enough about science to argue, but there were a few things in the book that sounded wrong. Were witches really burned because of the Enlightenment? Was Aquinas a lifelong practitioner of magic? (At least I'd heard of Aquinas.) There were sentences I simply didn't understand: 'The new quasi-Aristotelian paradigm objectified the self as Other...' And then there'd be stuff about 'the transgressive heuristics of apraxis' and 'the societal (de)construction of implicit fabula.'

I was in the office on Tuesday morning, waiting for Brian and frowning over a chapter that was either clever or a waste of time – I really couldn't tell – as Tony was yammering on about black rooms and Satanism, which was becoming an obsession with him, so I said, 'Well, how about this,' and read one of the sentences I did understand. '"We have to distinguish between devil worship as the survival of earlier religious practices and Satanism as a deliberate perversion of Christian doctrine."'

'Don't take the piss.' Tony snatched the book out of my hand. 'Oh, fuck, the occult. Your standards are slipping.' He opened it near the middle and skimmed a few pages. 'The occult *and* critical theory. Where'd you get this?'

'A friend lent it.'

'Girlfriend, yeah? It's always tarts that read this kind of bollocks.' He handed it back quickly, as if it might be contaminated. 'And you're trying to get into her knickers, I bet.'

'It's not like that.'

'It's always like that.' And then he told one of his stories, this one ending with a misunderstanding in an IRA pub. The moral seemed to be that if Tony fancied a girl there was no belief he wouldn't renounce if it might persuade her to sleep with him. His story annoyed me, and made me uncomfortable. I didn't think I was like him, but here I was, struggling through a book I couldn't understand. If Sue had given it to me I'd have known what to think. But Jane was different. She was cleverer than Sue, wasn't she? So did that mean this book was clever? It *sounded* clever. There were words I didn't know, and some sentences I could understand and not disagree with. Tony might say it was bollocks, but what did he know? His pose was that he didn't read books. Tabloids or the *Racing Post* maybe, but never a book. And what did Jane make of it? Did she think it was half right, sort of OK, or was it the book that had changed her life?

Later on, as I sat in the Half Moon, waiting for Jane, I kept going over these questions. I was about halfway through the book by then and still didn't know what to think. I wasn't even sure if Erin C. Burke actually believed in magic, or was just using it as a stick to beat science with. She might talk about the persistence of belief in magic as evidence that 'the natural wisdom of humanity is to personalise the cosmos', but she never gave any indication that she believed any of the spells and rites ever worked. I was puzzled. If this was the book that was supposed to explain things, what did it tell me about Jane?

Jane arrived. She seemed pleased to see me. She noticed the book but didn't say anything. We caught up on each other's news. I told her I'd visited Mike. She was grave. 'How was he?'

'OK.' It was as much as I could say. Mike didn't change. Visiting him was like visiting a local museum, the sort that has no new exhibits and might soon close for lack of interest. I changed the subject. 'How's Ros? Cheerful as ever?'

'Ros is *OK*.' Jane was as defensive about her as I was about Mike. 'She likes things to be perfect, that's all.'

'That's not a sign somebody's OK.'

Jane didn't smile. I realised I'd crossed a line and tried to make amends.

'Is there really any money in this astrology business?'

'Enough for her to do it professionally.' Jane was guarded. Did she think I might laugh? 'She's good at it.'

'I once had to take some cards back from a medium.'

She shrugged. 'Everybody knows mediums are fakes.'

'And astrologers?'

'It's not the same.' She explained: newspaper astrology, the sort Sue read so eagerly, *was* rubbish. The important thing was the position of the planets at the time of birth. A French scientist had proved that Mars had a significant effect on the development of character. It was real, serious research. There were books about it, papers. And, if that didn't convince me, all I had to do was ask Ros to cast my horoscope. All she'd need was my exact date and time of birth and £250.

'How much? Don't I get a discount?'

'That's *with* a discount. Usually it's three hundred.'

'And people pay that much?'

'Why not? As I said, she's good.'

'But what do they get for it? She taps some numbers into a computer and it prints out their personality and prospects…' I was trying not to sound sarcastic.

She told me how the computer merely produced a chart, and that the difficult bit, the bit that required the skill and experience, was the interpretation. She made it sound reasonable. By the time she'd finished, £250 seemed a bargain.

She asked if I'd read the book.

I was cautious. 'About half.'

'What do you think?'

'I don't know what to think. There were parts I didn't understand.'

'The jargon can be a bit dense,' she conceded. 'But what about the bits you did understand?'

I tried to think of something uncontroversial. 'Some of what she said about physics seemed interesting.'

'The false paradigm.' Jane nodded approvingly. 'It was something I'd thought for years.'

'Yeah?' It was something I'd never considered. For me, physics wasn't a paradigm, it was a class I'd never taken at school. 'Mind you, I think she's wrong about Aquinas.'

This amused her.

'Right. And *you'd* know about Aquinas.'

I let the point go, though in fact I did. At St Augustine's there'd been a choice between football and Dogmatic Theology. I ran in the evenings, or sparred with Mike. I didn't need football. Instead I sat in a quiet room with Joseph, who was clubfooted, Dean, who had one lung, and a third boy who was just stupid. Mr Sullivan, known as the Perv, took the class. He was keen on medieval scholasticism and changing rooms. I liked the class. I liked the way words had different meanings there. Even today, when I come across words like *essential*, *accidental* or *sensible* I sometimes hear Mr Sullivan's voice, a voice so effeminate there were boys who claimed he was really a woman in disguise. I knew about Aquinas all right. I could still remember his Five Proofs for the existence of God, and had once surprised Piers by reciting them.

'But the details aren't really important,' Jane said. 'I know a lot of it sounds weird, but I think there might be something in it.'

'It does sound weird.' I didn't know where the conversation was going. 'How long have you been interested in all this?'

'Not long.'

'Is it because of Ros?'

She looked at me scornfully. 'I was interested in this before I met Ros. I heard of that book through Adam. I know Ros through Adam.'

Adam again. Ex-boyfriend? Guru? I felt a twinge of jealousy. 'The man who knows Joshua?'

She nodded. I could see she was wondering how much to tell me. Maybe she thought I'd laugh. It's OK, I wanted to say, my last serious girlfriend was interested in kickboxing – as a *participant* – and I didn't laugh at *her*. My brother spends his days standing on a chair convinced there are people looking for him. Why should I laugh at magic and astrology? True, Sue was not a good advert for astrology, and everything

I knew about magic came from horror films or the Sunday papers or a few obvious nutters I'd seen on television. But I could easily have the wrong idea, the way I'd had the wrong idea about computer programmers.

'It's just...' She hesitated. 'I think Adam might be on to something.'

'What sort of thing?' I was practically inviting her to convert me. 'What does Adam do?'

'It's a kind of research.' She frowned. She was, I thought, embarrassed, as if confessing to a secret and childish vice. 'I didn't think there was anything to astrology until I met Ros. She convinced me. Not of everything. A lot of it's just symbolic bullshit...' She trailed off again, then shook her head.

'But some of it's serious?'

She gave up. 'Look, there's a meeting tonight. Would you like to come along?'

I was intrigued. The Half Moon was getting noisy. The country and western had been replaced by a looped sequence of ballads about the old country.

'As long as I don't have to swear an oath.'

I was curious about her friends. Or rather, I was curious about Adam.

They were meeting a short walk away, underneath a pet shop in one of the streets I ran down in the mornings.

'They get together every couple of weeks,' Jane explained on the way. 'Just to talk things through. They're good people.'

'How do you know them?'

'Work, mainly.'

'They're computer people?'

'Mostly.' She was suddenly defensive. 'What's wrong with that?'

'Nothing. I just couldn't see the connection.'

'There isn't one.' She softened. 'Mind you, Adam does have some theories… This is the place.'

There was an unnumbered door next to the door of the shop. Jane rang a bell and muttered into an intercom. The door clicked, and I followed her into a dingy passageway, then down a narrow flight of stairs. The carpet was frayed, the walls were bare. It was like going into somebody's cellar. I half expected to find a boiler, a few cardboard boxes, an old bicycle… Either that or a room the size of warehouse filled with computers and surveillance equipment, and a man in a white coat saying, 'Agent Six, you're late…'

Jane opened the door at the bottom of the stairs.

The room we stepped into was dim, but still brighter than the staircase, and contained about a dozen people, male and female, who seemed to have been interrupted in mid-conversation. The space seemed wider than the shop above; I wondered if two neighbouring cellars had been joined together. The walls were bare brickwork and the furniture consisted of half a dozen sofas that might have been rescued from skips, arranged facing inwards in an oval shape. The light came from two fuzzy fluorescent strips. The first thing I noticed was how much the people looked like each other. It wasn't just that they were all in black. The women were all a similar age to Jane and they were dressed in the same way, like understudies for the same role. So these were the friends Sue had found so strange. They didn't look a threat to anybody.

Ros was on one of the sofas. She smiled at Jane before glaring at me.

A man got up from the arm of the sofa nearest the door and came over to us, smiling intently. He was tall and thin with long, mousy hair tied in two plaits, a style I'd never seen on a man. There was something fixed about his smile, as if it was the result of having too many teeth rather than real friendliness. He greeted Jane with a hug, which she accepted stiffly.

Jane said, 'This is Adam.'

He shook my hand. 'You're Patrick, right? Jane told me all about you. At last we meet.' He led us over to the sofas. I wondered how much Jane could have told him. A few political opinions and the last book I'd read? 'And you've come in just as things are starting to get interesting.'

He introduced us to the others. There were nods, smiles. When we sat down, one of the women handed us plastic cups of red wine and the discussion resumed. They talked in serious, low voices, careful not to disturb any neighbours.

They talked. Adam gave the impression of being in charge. He interrupted, finished other people's sentences, and began his own with phrases like 'What you mean is...' just like someone fresh from a seminar on effective management techniques.

'The best day for that has to be next Thursday.'

'That depends on the calendar.'

'I can't make Thursday.'

'I'd need to see the latest charts.'

'But we have to take the angles into account. Sarah?'

'It's not the angles that are the problem...'

I couldn't understand what they were talking about and nobody offered to explain. From time to time I noticed Ros looking at me resentfully, which would have been more wounding if she hadn't looked at everybody else in the same way. She didn't say anything.

Jane didn't say anything either. I sipped the wine, conscious of time slowly passing. Why had Jane brought me here? Was this a test, like her list of questions? She seemed to have forgotten me, and listened carefully, as if at any moment she expected the talk to become interesting. Opposite her, Ros leaned forward, her arms crossed on her knees, like a small child impatient to be somewhere else. I couldn't blame her. From time to time Adam would glance in my direction and raise his eyebrows to show he recognised how boring this appeared to outsiders. He would try to guide the group towards a decision – any decision – only for someone to raise an objection or change their mind.

Beyond the business with the eyebrows, Adam showed no signs of impatience. 'I see your point, but Sophie has already suggested a solution to that. Sophie?'

'I don't think we can go ahead if Sarah's not happy.'

'Sarah?'

'If Sophie has concerns about this…'

And so on. I found myself wondering what they would be like to work with, and whether any of them were potential subjects for Elding Collections. I decided they all had well-paid, dull jobs and were careful with their money.

Adam made an effort to include everyone. 'Ros, what's your input on this?'

Ros looked at him with cold fury. 'Do you have a subject?'

My ears pricked up at that. *Subject* was our jargon.

'That isn't a problem at this stage…'

'If you don't have a subject, this whole thing is a waste of time.'

'I appreciate your concern.' Adam wasn't fazed by the hostility in her voice. 'But that's not the real issue.'

'Have you or haven't you?'

'Ros, it really isn't a problem.'

One of the women chipped in, 'There are procedures we need to establish…'

It was nearly midnight. They seemed to have been talking for hours and gave every sign of being able to talk for hours more. I nudged Jane. She sighed and nodded. I sensed she had only been staying because she had been told to expect something important. When somebody said, 'I think we need to go back to the beginning on this,' she finally lost patience. She stood up, almost pulling me to my feet.

'I've got to go. Let me know how this turns out, OK?'

41

Ros looked up at us, startled.

Adam was equally surprised. 'Sure, Jane, whatever you say.' His expression suggested that she'd decided to leave just as things were getting exciting.

Once outside I asked, 'So what was that all about?'

She shook her head. 'It's something they're planning for the end of next month.'

'Yeah? It's not going to happen.'

She laughed. 'I don't know. There'll be something. Even if it's only symbolic.'

'Yeah?' I tried to imagine what this could mean. 'I didn't understand a word.'

'You should have said. Adam would have explained. He likes explaining.'

'That's *why* I didn't say anything.'

'They are usually more fun.'

I had been ready for her to say they were useful, professional contacts. I hadn't expected her to claim they were *fun*. 'More fun? Is that possible?'

'They weren't at their best.' Jane must have felt she'd said enough.

We reached the door of her flat without saying another word. Until: 'Listen, I'm going to be very busy for the next week…' There was a big project for an insurance company, a deadline, and a lot of work that hadn't been done properly the first time. She ended with, 'Want some coffee?'

'OK.'

We went up to her flat for the second time.

The living room hadn't changed. Everything was in place, everything was clean. Jane found the mugs more quickly this time. Despite her reassurances, I wasn't sure about the group in the cellar. They had seemed friendly enough, but somehow laughable. I thought Jane deserved better.

'What time will your friends finish?' I asked.

'Why?'

'I want to be out of here before Ros gets back.'

'Ros isn't so bad. Anyway, she's staying with Beth and Margaret tonight.' She said *Beth-and-Margaret*, as if it was a single word, the way you'd say *law and order* or *rhythm and blues*.

'Margaret and Beth. Which ones were they?'

'They weren't there.' She said it as if it should have been obvious. 'You wouldn't see them at one of Adam's things.'

'Why not? Don't they get on?'

'They used to. There were disagreements.'

'But they still like Ros.'

'They respect Ros.'

'*Respect*. Does that mean they're afraid of her?'

While Jane waited for the kettle to boil, I looked at the chart over Ros's computer. Knowing what it was didn't help me to understand it. 'So tell me about Beth-and-Margaret. Are they astrologers as well?'

'Well, not really. Beth reads the cards and Margaret's a priestess.'

'A woman priest? Church of England?'

'They call it the Old Religion.' She handed me a mug. 'And it *is* priestess.'

'Right. What do *you* think of them?'

'Margaret's OK. Beth isn't so bad.'

'Do you believe in it? The Old Religion?'

'Not really. I'm more with Adam. I think there's something there, but it's not what they think. Do you know the definition of religion as the belief that there's a hidden order to the world? I think there's something beyond all this – ' she gestured at the furniture ' – materialism. Don't you?'

'Sometimes.'

She told me she'd become disillusioned with religion in her early teens. But she had never lost the sense that there was more to life than what Mr Sullivan used to call *sensible phenomena*. 'I mean, there has to be more than just making money for other people. And Adam – some of his ideas sound strange at first, but he does make a lot of sense…' She was awkward, as if she wasn't used to talking about this, perhaps conscious how easy it would be to laugh at her piety, her unexpected seriousness. But I couldn't laugh. I could see what she meant when she described her friends as good people, because Jane herself was a good person.

We went into her room. I saw the arty clutter, the clothes on the floor, the unmade bed. There was a little desk with her computer, and a bookcase stuffed with manuals and slim paperbacks. She dropped on to the bed. 'See?' She gestured at the Oriental rug hanging above the headboard. 'This is my space.'

She relaxed. She pointed out some of the ornaments she considered important, and made fun of the way I undressed. 'Why do you fold everything? There's nowhere to put any of it.' She was right. There wasn't a chair or a dressing table, only a bedside cabinet already taken up by a lamp. Her own clothes had been tossed on to the floor, along with everything else she'd worn that month. I made a small clearing and left my own clothes in a neat pile.

Disturbing her tangled stockings and skirts released an unpleasantly sweet smell, as if she'd spilt a bottle of cheap perfume. I reeled back. 'What is that?'

She was now under the sheets and still looking pleased with herself. 'Incense.'

'You mean this is sacred ground? Your bedroom is your temple?'

'It's my personal space.'

'Incense. Must be easier than cleaning the place once in a while.'

'You're beginning to sound like Ros.'

'Yeah? Perhaps I should ask *her* out.'

'She won't like you.'

'Why not? What's wrong with me?'

She paused to think about it. 'You're not bad...'

'Thanks a lot.'

But I didn't mind. I thought I'd got off lightly. 'Not bad' is the story of my life. It could go on my headstone: *Patrick James Farrell: He Wasn't Bad*. Even the thing I'd been best at, I hadn't been *good* at. Middle-distance running wasn't as glamorous as the sprint, or as single-minded as the marathon. I was good enough for St Augustine's but never made it to county standard. At inter-school events they called me Lazarus because I always came fourth – a rotten joke of Andy Longman's revived at every track meeting. I ran well, but not well enough. It was the same for everything else. School, work, life, you name it. Competent, but not praiseworthy. Could do better. Not bad.

As she turned away from me, I noticed there was a small tattoo on her right shoulderblade. Circles within circles, just like Ros's astrological chart, with neat little symbols inside each ring. I traced its outline with my finger, half expecting it to smudge.

'When did you get this?'

She stiffened, like a cat. 'Years ago.'

'Why?'

'I liked it.' She rolled over and faced me. 'Don't you?'

'I don't know. You're not going to get anything pierced, are you?'

'Like Ros? You don't like it, do you? Now you mention it, I might get something done.'

'You'd regret it later.' I reached round and traced the tattoo on her back. 'You might regret this one day.'

'It's just a pattern.'

I didn't believe her. 'I bet Ros would say it's more than that.'

'She would. But it's a pattern as well.'

'Are you going to have any more?'

45

'I might. I wouldn't go as far as Ros, though. She has plans.'

I didn't ask what they were. I didn't care about Ros or her friends talking endlessly in a cellar. They could do what they liked, as long as I was with Jane.

Four

Mike still mattered, of course, but he was safe in his room in the Lilac Wing. The people around him might change – the nurses, the orderlies, the other patients – but Mike and my visits would always be the same. I'd nod to the woman at reception and then walk through the TV room, where the patients who could bear each other's company stared at a television with a blurred picture and the volume set too loud. These patients frightened me, not because of any threat of physical violence – the dangerous ones were in the Marigold Wing – but because of the way they moved: either not at all, or strangely, repeating the same gestures – a half-wave at nothing, a nod of the head – as if something important depended on it. They all looked about forty-five, not exactly old but not young either. Whatever their calendar age, they all had the same shabby, washed-out look as the carpets and furniture, a kind of protective coloration.

Sometimes, because I wore a suit, they would stop me and ask questions. Suits, for them, meant officialdom, authority, answers. There was one man in particular – one of the older ones, a lifelong case – who once begged me to get him out; he didn't want to die in there. When I told him I couldn't help he started crying, which only made me feel worse. I used to cross the room as fast as I could without actually breaking into a run.

One day, after seeing Mike, I marched through the room, and was almost at the door when someone – one of *them* – said, 'Christ, it's Farrell.'

47

The voice was familiar. I turned. The old man was in a scuffed armchair under the window, head back, mouth open, asleep. The usual early afternoon rubbish blared out of the television. One of the others had stood up and was walking towards me, right arm outstretched, as if it was broken and he was offering it for treatment. He moved stiffly too, like someone just woken from a deep sleep. 'Patrick, what are *you* doing here?'

With a jolt, I recognised him. Kevin Taylor. We'd been in the same year at St Augustine's. I said, 'Hello, Kevin.'

He came right up to me, smiling warily, and put his hand on my shoulder. He had the undernourished look of a long-timer, and his clothes, a faded sweatshirt and jeans, were almost the standard issue. My brother wore the same.

'Close. I'm Jerry, the brother. You visiting as well?'

I nodded. Kevin Taylor had been Paul Kavanagh's friend rather than mine. I'd never had much to do with him. I'd once taken Mike to a party at his house. Kevin had been planning it, or talking about it, for months. Only six other people had turned up. Kevin spent most of the evening saying he couldn't understand what had happened and insisting more people would arrive soon. Nobody had. Mike had laughed about it for days afterwards. The Kevin Taylor I remembered had been all talk, and silly talk at that. Paul Kavanagh must have tolerated him because he'd been good at darts or had an interesting record collection, or for some other reason. I'd never liked him enough to find out. I was certain about one thing: Kevin Taylor had five older sisters. That was common knowledge, Kevin Taylor and his five ugly sisters ('If they were the last women alive,' we'd ask each other, 'and you had to choose one, which one would you have?'). Nobody had ever mentioned him having a brother.

I told him I'd been to see Mike. 'And you?'

He looked around the room. There were lines around his eyes and mouth, and his hair was almost white. He was twenty-five, my age, and he looked like a well-preserved older man. For a moment it seemed possible this really was Kevin's brother – one of those dizzying moments when you doubt the order of the months or the correct spelling of your own name. It didn't last. This *was* Kevin, whatever he said, and he wasn't there to visit.

He shuddered. 'Michael, yeah. I heard about that. Terrible thing when that happens.'

I felt sick. This was worse than the usual appeals for help. I took a step back, wondering who else I was going to meet. Paul Kavanagh? Andy Longman? Everybody I'd ever known, waiting in the corridor for me to join them?

Kevin seemed to expect me to say something. I took a chance. 'Is Kevin around?'

He winced, and looked down, muttering. I was ready to run. Then he looked up again, and managed a smile. 'You're looking smart, Patrick. You working, then? Successful?'

The suit gave me an excuse. In the armchair under the window the old man was beginning to stir. 'I don't know about successful. Busy, though. I've got to go.'

Kevin looked at me as if he understood. The old man suddenly woke up and stared in my direction, probably trying to remember who I was. Kevin finally let go of my shoulder. 'See you around? We'll go for a drink some time, yeah?'

'Yeah,' I said. 'Sure.' I walked out, determined not to stop for anyone. By the time I reached the street my eyes were stinging.

After that I started seeing Kevin more often, and not only in the TV lounge. He became a familiar sight in the streets near my flat, where I'd pass him on my morning run. He'd be standing at the corner of the high street like someone waiting for the shops to open, wearing his jeans and trainers and an old coat that looked as if its last owner had been savaged by dogs. Sometimes he saw me coming and would nod cautiously. At other times he kept his gaze fixed on the pavement. Later, as I walked from my flat to the office, I might meet him again.

At first he was nervous. I'd say his name and he'd back away, mumbling. After a few days he realised I wasn't going to hit him. He'd walk alongside me, talking and hugging his chest to keep his coat in place.

He told me his life story, what he could remember of it. It was different from the one I'd heard in the TV lounge. Kevin knew he was Kevin. He also knew he was sometimes Jerry. Jerry didn't know he was Kevin. That seemed to be the only difference.

He slept in a lock-up on the unmade road behind the shops. He'd had problems with drink, he told me, and his family no longer wanted to know. They'd put up with it for years, and then, to his surprise, chucked him out. They hadn't arranged for him to go somewhere else, just given him two carrier bags of clothes and told him to leave. He hadn't known where to go, so he hadn't gone far. The clothes had been stolen on his first night, or he'd lost them, or given them away – he couldn't remember which. He saw his sisters occasionally, as they crossed the street to avoid him or ducked round corners, their hands covering their faces. Kevin accepted this treatment as no more than he deserved. The only thing he resented was his illness.

His illness. He made it sound ordinary, like asthma. Except his illness called itself Jerry and was an outpatient in the same place as my brother. Mike sometimes complained about people walking in off the streets; Jerry was one of them. He wasn't even a proper outpatient; he just turned up from time to time and sat in the TV lounge. He wasn't treated or tested or on anybody's records, but the staff there knew his face, knew he was harmless, knew all he would do was watch television, drink a few cups of cold, sweet tea, and leave before they started locking the doors. Jerry really believed that Kevin was his younger brother. If I asked him what he was doing there he'd say he was visiting Kevin, and show real surprise when Kevin wasn't in the room. Kevin, though, could remember most of what Jerry did. Fortunately for him, Jerry never did very much. His main characteristic was good-natured confusion. His idea of antisocial behaviour was to eat *two* biscuits.

Once or twice a week I'd find him two turnings away from my flat, waiting. He'd walk almost to the door of Elding Collections, telling me what he'd done since I last saw him. He was cheerful. You'd have thought he enjoyed his life. He'd start off with, 'Haven't seen you for a few days,' and move on to his latest little triumph: a few quid here, chance of a job there, a sleeping bag found on a skip somewhere else, nearly new. He never asked for help, though I usually gave him a few pounds' conscience money before walking away. Sometimes he talked about his illness. Most of the time, though, he talked about the past. 'Do you see much of Andy Longman these days?'

'No.'

'No? Can't say I blame you. Saw him two weeks ago. He hasn't changed, yeah? Gave me a fiver. Do you know what he told me? Told me to fuck off. Laughed, yeah? He was with his mates.'

'Sounds like Andy.'

'Yeah. Do you remember…'

And off he'd go, into some anecdote that ended with another one of Andy Longman's jokes. Kevin's memory for details about Andy Longman and Paul Kavanagh was photographic, though he wasn't always clear about what had happened the previous week. Kevin assumed I'd been present at everything he had: this party, that nightclub, the pub, what was it called, where Andy's girlfriend emptied a pint and then an ashtray on his head…

I didn't remember it, or any of his stories. I'd probably been out running or sparring with Mike, or at a gym holding the focus pads for Shona. Why waste time with Andy Longman's crowd? I had been drifting away from them even before what Kevin referred to as 'that night at Charisma'.

That was one I did remember. Back then, Charisma was *the* cheap late-teen nightclub. It had pink lights, a terrible DJ, an unreliable sound system, surly, incompetent bouncers, and a bar that regularly ran out of beer. It should have failed after a week but was kept solvent by underage drinkers who went along just to see what would happen next – a punch-up maybe, or a power failure. The place was a joke, and we ended up there most Friday nights along with all the fifteen-year-olds and the thirty-somethings barred from everywhere else. It was at Charisma that Andy Longman had made a crack about my brother, and we'd almost had a fight.

I can't remember what he said, only that at the time it sounded unforgivable, and that I said so. Seconds later we were squaring up to each other at the edge of the dance floor, steadying ourselves for the first head butt or stamp. The dance floor was packed, and the bouncers didn't notice a thing. We watched each other, both of us sweating heavily, our arms almost pinned to our sides by the press of the surrounding bodies. Andy drew his head back fractionally, and lunged forward. Easy, I thought. I sidestepped, kicking his feet out from under him. He fell heavily: I remember being surprised that there was room for him to fall, among all those dancers.

Once Andy went down, the dancers seemed to close in around him. They didn't care. People fell over a lot in Charisma. Most of my friends had their first experience of public drunkenness there. I had to push people aside to kick him again: a good hard stab to the midriff. Andy grabbed my ankle and tried to pull me down. I stamped on his elbow with my other foot until he let go. By then, even the bouncers had realised we weren't dancing together. Glancing up, I saw one of them making his way through the crowd. I decided to give Andy one last stamp on the back of the head and then run.

Before I could do it someone had seized my arms and pulled me away, into one of the darker corners. It was Shona. 'Christ, Patrick, this is so tribal.'

That was the last time I went drinking with Andy Longman, and the last time I ever went to Charisma. I wasn't barred. The bouncers never caught me. They never caught anybody. I didn't *want* to go back. Andy still went faithfully every Friday, and only stopped when they changed the name to Innuendo and started having gay nights.

I still had some friends: Paul Kavanagh's crowd, with Kevin Taylor at the margin, and Brian and the others from Mike's old gym. I went out drinking with them and on the surface everything was OK, but what had happened to Mike soured things, and what I had done to Andy Longman scared them. I began to have the feeling they were talking about me behind my back. Of course they never mentioned Mike while I was there. What could they say? Our friendship was based on banter, our willingness to be made fun of, to tell hard jokes about each other. What had happened to Mike was serious in the wrong kind of way. If he'd died, the way Paul Kavanagh's brother had died, it wouldn't have been so difficult. A few weeks' silence, then the occasional respectful mention. But Mike was still alive, and I was there, listening carefully. If it had happened to anybody else's brother I would have been as ruthless as any of them, and as ready to complain if our victim seemed to lose his sense of humour. But because it was *my* brother I was angry at any remark that didn't sound properly respectful, and suspicious of any that did. I saw insults everywhere.

The result was that Paul Kavanagh's crowd stopped asking me along on nights out, and when I invited myself I soon realised I was unwelcome. After a few months I stopped going. Soon, all I had left was the regular ordeal of visiting Mike, and Shona. Sod 'em, I'd thought, Shona was enough.

That didn't last either. Another story.

Kevin had lost touch too, for his own reasons. He talked about the days when we had all been friends as though they were the Golden Age. Each time I saw him he looked shabbier, a little paler, a little sicker. There was a rash that started under his left ear and began to spread across the side of his face. I worried about him, without doing anything to help. There was a spare room in my own flat, but it never occurred to me to let him use it. I'd listen to his stories, give him some cash, wish somebody would do something about him, and then forget him as I made calls on defaulters or confirmed people had moved. Kevin Taylor wasn't my problem. I didn't mention him at work. I didn't even tell Jane. I wasn't ashamed of him; I just didn't think he mattered. He was a reminder of a world I'd left long ago. Jane was my life now.

Ros occasionally spent nights with Beth-and-Margaret. 'They drink wine and talk about alignments…' was how Jane put it. On those nights we'd stay at her flat. Jane was more relaxed when Ros wasn't around. She didn't wash up, left discarded clothes on the floor of the living room, and spent most of her time watching television with the lights dimmed while I sat in one of the armchairs and suppressed the impulse to tidy up. I usually made sure I left early in the morning before Ros returned.

That night we were watching a documentary about poverty somewhere when we heard the front door open and close. Ros was back. Jane's panic was wonderful to watch. She jumped to her feet, looking around, unsure what to pick up first. She still hadn't made a decision when Ros walked in.

Jane went straight for apologies, 'I'm sorry, Ros, I didn't expect – '

She stopped, as if she'd noticed something different about Ros. I thought she looked just the same. Her clothes were the same peasant costume of thick blouse and wraparound skirt. True, her hair had been cropped even shorter and the nose stud replaced by a ring, but these didn't seem to be enough to account for Jane's surprise. The first clue I had was when she looked around the room and smiled, as if she was pleased to find her room a mess and me in it.

'Beth and Margaret are arguing,' she announced. 'Beth wants everybody to stop talking to Adam. Margaret wants to stay in touch…' She crossed to the chair opposite mine. Jane's sweater was wedged behind the cushion. Ros didn't seem to notice. She closed her eyes, sighed faintly, then fell into the chair. For a moment I thought she was unconscious. Then she opened her eyes again, and grinned at us.

'Ros.' Jane found her voice. 'Are you OK?'

Ros giggled. She waved at me, a regal droop of her right arm. 'Hello, bailiff.'

'Hi, Ros.'

Jane frowned, a signal that she didn't want me to find any of this amusing. She started tidying things away. Ros watched her blankly, as if she had an important message she couldn't quite remember. Then she turned to me again. 'Nice suit.'

'Thanks. Interesting ring.'

She touched the tip of her nose. 'Think so?'

'All the better to lead you by.'

'Not me.' She yawned and stretched, like someone waking from a deep and peaceful sleep. 'Not me.'

Jane went into her own room with an armful of clothes. Ros watched her go. There was doomy, reproachful music from the television. The credits for the documentary ran. Ros watched, fascinated.

I decided I preferred her like this. You could almost believe Jane's claim that she was a nice person. I thought it was a shame about the nose ring, but she had the kind of

55

looks that could survive a few bad fashion choices. I didn't know why I cared so much. It was her face, she'd say, and she could do what she liked.

Ros noticed I was looking. She grinned over at me, then got carefully to her feet and began fiddling with the buttons on her blouse. She worked clumsily, like someone wearing mittens. I didn't pay much attention. In the dim, flickering light from the television she was mostly lost in shadow, and I assumed she'd be wearing something underneath – a T-shirt, or a body, possibly another blouse. I didn't realise she wasn't until she reached the last button. 'Ros,' I said, as casually as I could manage. 'I am still here.'

She hadn't forgotten. That was the point. She laughed the kind of laugh with which people spoil the punchline of their own jokes, and held open her blouse in the traditional flasher-with-mac pose. 'What about these?' The small rings attached to each nipple glinted as they caught the light.

I didn't say anything. There was a problem of etiquette here. If I was too enthusiastic she might think I was leering in an immature, stereotypically male way. Admittedly, in other circumstances, I might have. But the rings made me feel slightly queasy. Nipple rings are commonplace now; back then they were a bit hardcore; they were a statement, usually that the wearer didn't care what *you* thought. Ros, I guessed, was out to shock, and I didn't want her to know she'd succeeded. So I nodded gravely, as if studying nothing more provocative than her holiday slides, and struggled to think of something to say that would not sound stupid.

To make things more difficult for me, Ros took a step forward. 'Well?' There was no friendliness in her voice now. 'What do you think?'

There was a trailer for a sitcom on the television. Her question was greeted with a recorded guffaw.

Jane came out of her room, giving me an excuse to look away. Ros smirked and dropped her hands to her sides. Jane guided Ros back to the chair. 'Fucking hell, Ros, and you accuse me of leaving things out.'

Ros only laughed. 'I was just showing the suit my rings.'

Jane glared at me. She seemed to think Ros was vulnerable and I'd been taking advantage. I decided it was best to shut up. If I said the right thing, Ros would forget; if it was the wrong thing, she'd remember forever. The chances were I'd say the wrong thing. Ros sprawled in the armchair, her blouse still open. She closed her eyes and seemed to lose consciousness again. After the first shock I decided the rings were fascinating objects, in a grisly way. I wondered what it had felt like having them done: I'd never had so much as an ear pierced.

Jane stood over Ros wearily, like a babysitter at the end of a hard night.

'I'll go,' I offered.

Jane didn't look at me. 'I think you'd better.' She didn't say, *You've caused enough trouble already*, but the implication was there. She waited a few seconds, until she was certain Ros was asleep, then tried to fasten the blouse. Ros stirred. She pushed Jane's arms away impatiently. Jane stopped trying. She was prepared to touch Ros only when unopposed. Even at her slowest and least reasonable, Ros was the authority in that flat.

She was awake again, and still dippy. 'He still hasn't said what he thinks.'

I stood up. 'And he isn't going to.'

Ros waved Jane aside. It wasn't a push. Ros was too relaxed to push anybody. She simply moved an arm. Jane offered no resistance beyond saying, 'Ros,' very quietly. She stood back as if everything possible had already been tried. Ros was intent on proving her point, a personal liberty thing she probably thought of as political. It was clear she saw me as an ambassador from the conventional classes.

'Why don't you like them?'

'Because they're ugly.' Evasion hadn't worked, diplomatic silence hadn't worked, and Ros didn't like me anyway. What did I have to lose? 'I don't understand why you do it.'

Ros stood up again. There was a triumphant swagger about her: having beaten me to my knees, she was now going to tread my face into the dirt. 'So what do you think of this?' The skirt was less trouble than her blouse. She removed it with a flourish and held it at arm's length, like a matador goading a weak, half-blinded bull. The effort was too much for her. She sat down again. 'Oh, fuck, no,' said Jane, helplessly. Ros drew up her knees. In the bad light all I could see was a glint of metal. On television, an audience cheered.

Ros smiled. 'Next, my eyebrows.'

Jane seemed to get over her dismay; she crouched to have a closer look. 'Ros, it's beautiful.'

'Beautiful?' I made for the door. 'It's barbaric. Have you ever heard of septicaemia?'

Ros was delighted. This was the result she'd hoped for: *Look, Jane, Mr Self-Control has just checked into the Neurosis Hotel.* Jane didn't say a word. She was entranced, cuntstruck.

I stopped at the door and took a last look back. Jane was on her knees, gazing raptly between her flatmate's legs, as if Ros had a kaleidoscope in there. Ros herself seemed to have passed out again.

'Jane, I'll call you.'

Jane looked up, the spell broken. She came to the street door with me. 'I'm sorry about that.' It was the first sign that she didn't think it was my fault.

'You should find a landlady you don't have to keep apologising for.'

She frowned. 'Maybe. Perhaps we could use your flat for once.'

'Yeah, why not.'

'Why not tomorrow night?'

58

I remembered, 'I'm going to a fight with Brian.'

'I didn't think you were interested in that sort of thing.'

'I was once. Friday?'

'I'll be working late...'

We arranged a date for the following week.

I told Mike about Jane. Or rather, I sat on the end of his bed and talked about her. It made a change to have something new to say: when I talked about Jane I was able to stay for longer than my usual half-hour. Mike paid no attention, which made him easier to talk to than our parents. Poor Mike. He might have been insane but he wasn't judgemental. He might forget everything you said, but at least he never told you you were wasting your life.

I also told him about Ros, 'She seems to hate me...' I rambled on, as Mike craned his neck or hunched his shoulders and stared out of the window, just the way he always did. 'You should see her, Mike. She's beautiful and she's ruining herself with all that piercing shit.'

'I haven't seen anybody for two days.' Mike shifted his weight. The chair creaked. He must have weighed nearly thirteen stone. Soon, I thought, his sense of balance wouldn't be enough to keep him up there. 'I reckon they might be inside,' he said. 'They let anybody in here.'

'They can't be, Mike, whoever they are. The doctors keep them out, remember? And anyway, this Ros – '

'They let anybody in here.' He sounded more agitated than usual. What he said was his usual rubbish, but the tone was different, closer to the way he'd sounded in his last days at home, just before he'd stopped going out at night. 'People come in off the street, and they walk right in – electricians, they reckon. I don't go to the TV lounge. The TV lounge is full of them. And what if some of them *are* doctors?'

'Who, Mike?' I tried to sound calm. His tone disturbed me. 'What if some of who are doctors?'

'You can't tell if they are. They might walk in off the street. All kinds of people.' And then he climbed down from the chair, two easy steps.

Another time I'd have been glad to see him do that. It made me realise how much I'd relied on him not changing. As long as he stayed on the chair, I'd thought, he was safe. Not well or normal, just safe.

He stood in the middle of the room and looked in my direction. 'I don't go to the TV lounge.'

'Who walks in off the streets, Mike? You mean Kevin Taylor?'

He laughed. 'Six other people. They come in all the time.'

It was the first time I'd seen his face properly for nearly two years. Once we'd looked so much alike people thought we were twins. Nobody could make that mistake now. His face was puffy from doing nothing and the frown lines were there to stay.

'What's going on, Mike?'

He looked in my direction but gave no sign of seeing me. When he spoke it was as if he was talking to himself. 'They haven't been out there for two days. They're clever. They know I'm in here. The car park. They're always there, always...'

The car park was on the other side of the building. It couldn't be seen from his window.

'Who, Mike? You're always talking about these people and you never say who they are. Who are they?'

As if for an answer, he waved at the walls of his room. 'They know I'm here. There's signs.'

He turned his head slowly. You'd have thought he was making an inventory: bed, table, chair, empty shelves. It was impossible to know how much he was taking in. Whatever he saw seemed to calm him down. He began to breathe more evenly, the way he used to after a hard sparring session.

'They're clever. They're cleverer than we think.'

'Who's cleverer? You're not being helpful, Mike.'

'Something's *planned*. How do I know they're not here? People coming in all the time. Coming and going. Nobody checks anything.'

'Who, Mike? Nobody comes here.'

He shivered, and took a step forward. For the first time I was certain he had seen me; I still didn't know if he recognised me. I didn't know if recognising people was even a skill he still possessed. He'd lost so much else. 'They do. They're always fucking there.'

'Maybe they've given up on you. Maybe they've gone away.'

He shook his head impatiently, and took another step forward. He was now only a few inches away. He looked at my face as if it was the photograph of someone he'd been asked to identify. He said, 'You've seen them.'

'No, I've never seen them.' I didn't know if he was responding to what I said or if it was just that our monologues had coincided. 'That's it, Mike, that's the problem. You're the only person who's ever seen them.'

Mike took a step back. For a moment you'd have thought he was about to offer a reasoned objection. Then his expression became blank, the deliberate blankness of someone withholding information. He climbed back on to the chair, muttering.

A nurse looked in. 'Everything all right, sir?'

'He seems anxious today.' *Anxious*. Such delicacy, such tact. 'Is something happening?'

The nurse nodded, as if this was a question he'd answered several times already. 'Yes, sir. We're – er – modifying his treatment.'

'His treatment?' The idea of treatment was unexpected. I knew the place was nominally a hospital but I'd assumed they could only treat the minor ailments, the reasonable fears. I'd assumed they were like Elding Collections and could only find what hadn't been lost.

The nurse corrected himself. 'His – er – medication.'

'Why?'

'To – er – see if there's any change in his – er – condition.'

'Is that the only way you can tell?'

The nurse ignored me. He looked at my brother, now once again staring out of the window, and made a clicking noise with his tongue, like a man trying to lure a kitten out of a tree. He didn't seem to be aware he was doing it.

'I mean,' I said, 'aren't there more sophisticated methods?'

The nurse shook his head. 'That's the best we can do in this case. Mike, your – er – brother, isn't the most serious case we have.'

'What does that mean?'

He answered like a man with more pressing concerns elsewhere. 'It means we don't think he's dangerous.'

'What about the danger to himself? I've never seen him this agitated.' Though I had, in his last weeks at home.

As if to prove me wrong, my brother now appeared perfectly calm. He looked out at the grounds without so much as a twitch.

'That's perfectly normal, sir.'

'Normal?' But of course it was. *Normal* had a different meaning here, the way *accidental* or *sensible* had different meanings in Mr Sullivan's classroom. 'And how is he, now you've modified his medication?'

I tried, I really did, not to sound sarcastic. My brother stood only a few feet away and we were discussing him as if he was in the next room.

The nurse saw nothing strange. 'He's – er – no different.'

'He looks different to me.'

The nurse looked at me calmly. 'He's – no, he's no different.'

'What does "no different" mean? Is it good or bad?'

Mike was muttering under his breath. It was faint, audible only when nobody else was talking. I hadn't noticed this on earlier visits. Every few seconds he made a sudden movement with his head. He seemed to be following the movements of something outside, birds probably. Whatever it was, it made his head turn so rapidly he seemed to twitch.

'It's hard to tell, sir. I'm not an expert.' The nurse had noticed the movement as well. Every time my brother's head moved, he nodded, like someone acknowledging an old friend across a crowded room. 'I can see for myself, though, that the... the – er – delusional structure is still intact. Your brother is – is what they call a paranoid schizophrenic. It's a loose category, and what it means is we don't really know enough about him.' He had lost his usual hesitancy. Maybe the jargon gave him confidence. 'We don't even know if his condition is process or reactive. All we can really do is suppress the more obvious symptoms...'

That was the truth about the place. They didn't offer a cure. All they could do was keep Mike quiet, using discreet, modern methods. He wasn't gagged or strapped to the bed, but the results were the same. He was kept out of the way in a well-meaning, underfunded oubliette, and every few months they modified the treatment or updated the jargon. I couldn't keep up with it, or, rather, didn't want to. I'd learned about all sorts of things because of girls, the little interests you want to share: kickboxing because of Shona, and now, thanks to Jane, what Erin C. Burke called 'non-naturalistic sciences'. But I couldn't bring myself to read up on Mike's condition. There were books in the library about understanding or coping or living with it, slim dog-eared volumes that told you not to be frightened, it wasn't so bad. I'd glanced through them hurriedly, as if they were contaminated. Even so, some information stuck. You'd turn on the radio for the news and hear, 'Some scientists now think...' You couldn't always switch off in time, and you couldn't help remembering some things. The nurse's *process or reactive* was out of date.

Mike went on looking out of his window.

'I think he'll be all right now,' the nurse said.

All right in the sense the phrase had here.

The nurse left.

My brother looked out of the window.

'OK, Mike,' I said, 'where were we?' I told him about Jane, how pretty she was, how clever, how good. He didn't need to know, but telling him calmed me down. 'Yeah?' he said at one point. 'Really?' I wasn't getting his full attention, but I was getting part of it, if only from some residual politeness. Mike had always been the one who said *please* at the dinner table, or phoned aunts to thank them for Christmas gifts. It wasn't that I was rude; I did those things too, when I remembered. But Mike had had a natural grace. He hadn't needed reminders. He listened to me talking about someone he'd never met and when I finished he said, 'So that's good, then,' in his thoughtful, faraway voice, then fell back to his guttural murmur.

I sat for a minute or so, watching him. Gradually the twitches died away, the muttering stopped. I felt it was safe to go.

'I'm off now, Mike. Look after yourself. See you again soon.'

As I opened the door he turned again.

'Paddy,' he said.

I froze. He was the only person who'd ever called me Paddy. I hated the name. Mick and Paddy: hadn't our parents noticed? Girlfriends had always called me Patrick or Pat. Our parents called me Patrick. 'Mike?'

He turned back to the window. 'Give my regards to Shona.'

'Yeah,' I said. 'Sure.'

64

I left even faster than usual. By then I was probably famous for the speed of my exits. I crossed the back of the TV lounge like an Olympic walker on the home stretch.

Kevin Taylor was asleep in one of the armchairs.

Work was quieter than anybody could remember: four or five recoveries each a day, just enough to justify employing us. We spent more time sitting around in the office.

One morning I was in early. Piers and Tony were already at their desks, having one of their conversations. 'No,' Piers was saying. 'You can maintain a distinction between sense and meaning if the reference is indirect.'

Tony nodded, like a man out of his depth, but that might have been for my benefit. 'I'll take your word on that one, old son.' He looked relieved to see me. 'Morning, Psycho. Seen the paper?' He waved a folded tabloid at me. Tony always carried one, as a kind of badge. I hadn't thought he actually read them. If he read anything, I suspected it was the broadsheets, and only when he thought no one was watching.

'What's in it?'

'Your patch.' Tony tossed the paper across. It had been folded at page seven. I read the headline.

'"Phone pervert cut off"?'

'Not that one. Further down.'

Three short paragraphs at the bottom third of the page. '"Devil room mystery probe"?'

'That's the one. Now try reading it without moving your lips.'

My first thought was that the story was filler. Man found dead, the police did not suspect foul play. The journalist made a lot of the room having been painted black: it was mentioned twice in a very short paragraph. A police spokesman denied there was any link with Satanism. There was no picture.

I folded the paper and lobbed it back. 'So? What makes you think it's my patch? There's not an address.'

Tony smoothed it out again. 'What drugs are you taking these days? Didn't you recognise the name?'

'Sod you, Bellman.' I was getting impatient. Tony always tried too hard to make dramas out of trivial incidents. And I hadn't even noticed a name. 'I can't remember everyone I see.'

'Piers remembered it.' Tony nodded at Piers, who sat, back straight and hands clasped, like a schoolboy who knew the answer to the next question.

'So? Piers remembers everything.' This was almost true. There was some information he allowed himself to forget after, say, six months. He always remembered where to find it again. 'So who was it?'

Piers sounded almost eager. 'Peter Bedding. It was a tracer. You couldn't find him.'

'No wonder he stopped answering letters.' Tony broke the silence. 'It was the bit about the room that I noticed. Painted black. I've seen rooms like that. I'm telling you, it's weird. Fucking weird.'

'They probably just belonged to Smiths fans.' I wanted to forget Peter Bedding. 'Hameed saw one too, remember? Maybe it's the fashion.' I pulled a book out of my jacket pocket, another paperback on loan from Jane.

'What, like the mystical crap you read nowadays?' Tony was in high spirits. I wondered if his girlfriend had walked out again, or come back. 'Come on, what's that one called?'

I showed him the front cover: sober white letters on a black background, not a pentangle in sight.

'Joyce Bateman,' he read. '*The Mystical Analogy*. What the fuck is that?'

'Sympathetic magic.'

'And you believe that shit?'

'I keep an open mind.'

'An empty one, more like. Is it any good?'

'It's better than some I've read.'

'It argues for sympathetic magic?' As a rule, Piers didn't ask questions. He gave answers or corrected us on points of detail. 'Do people still do that? Do you mind if I have a look?'

I passed the book across to him. Tony acted astonished. 'Piers, you're taking an interest in something outside work. You're not going to crack up again, are you?'

'No.' Piers gave his full attention to the book. He was open about his breakdown. He had to be, after Tony had circulated the photostat of his personal files. He was reticent about what he'd done before, and about every other aspect of his life, but there was no doubt about the breakdown. Brian claimed Piers had made a lot of money in the City, burnt out, and now worked at Elding Collections as therapy. I thought this sounded too neat to be true. Burnt-out overachievers were something comforting for us to believe in: they justified our rotten jobs and average salaries. Piers couldn't be drawn about his old work, though Tony tried. Tony often attempted to tease him, but Piers never got angry. He didn't even get impatient.

Tony turned back to me. 'I don't go with any of this "ancient wisdom" crap. You do know most of it was made up in the Sixties?'

'So you don't think witchcraft's a survival of earlier pagan stuff?'

'Margaret Murray.' It was a name I'd come across in the books. Tony said it in what had once been his real voice. He realised his mistake. 'All that stuff's bollocks. Bad scholarship.' He reeled off a list of names I didn't recognise. 'Those are the people you should be reading.'

'You should write them down for me.'

'Yeah, but would you read them? I mean, you're not trying to impress *me*.'

We watched Piers turning the pages. He read quickly: a glance down each page seemed to be enough. I envied him; I had to pick my way through every loaded sentence. After five minutes he was halfway through. Tony couldn't hold back any longer. 'Are you actually reading that, Piers?'

'Most of it.' Piers closed the book and passed it back. 'It's quite well written. Of course it's rubbish.'

It was the first time I'd heard Piers express on opinion on something unrelated to the job. I knew about his conversations with Tony, and often caught some incomprehensible snippet as I came through the door. Piers was *intelligent*. A few hundred years earlier he'd have been swapping subtleties with St Bernard of Clairvaux or Peter Abelard. He had nodded at my Five Proofs as if they wouldn't have given *him* any trouble.

I couldn't read the book after that. Instead I leafed through Tony's newspaper until Brian showed up, and then we went out and collected plastic.

Five

Mike continued to change. The next time I visited him he was sitting on the end of his bed, head bowed, gazing at the skirting board. When I closed the door behind me he looked up, startled.

'Paddy. How are you, you're looking well.' He seemed harassed, as if the phone hadn't stopped ringing. There was a newspaper on the bed, a day-old *Mirror* or *Star*. He tried hard to be cheerful. 'How's Shona these days? She OK? Still fighting?'

I stayed by the door. 'I don't see Shona, Mike. She left, remember?'

'I've got to get in shape again. When this is over.'

When this is over. He'd never said that before. He started asking questions. What happened to Paul Kavanagh and Declan and the McDermotts? Was Brian still boxing? Every time I answered he would nod impatiently – this was old news – and start again: how was Mum? Our cousins? How was my job with the travel company? Shona still fighting? He tried to look relaxed – he was rigid with the effort – and laughed at almost everything I said, on the off-chance it was a joke. He didn't talk about any visitors.

I wasn't sure this was an improvement. Mike had been like this in the last few months at home, a jabbering amnesiac terrified of silences and frantically searching for another conversational stopgap. They had been miserable times, with the whole family on edge and pretending nothing was wrong, a houseful of people biting their tongues or talking about subjects nobody found important. And our parents gradually withdrawing, turning to me with their hopeless, 'You talk to him. You understand him.'

I'd tried to, back then. I'd say things like, 'What are you talking about, you mad cunt?' in the hard banter we'd used once.

He'd smirk, like it was a game. 'There were two in the shop. They followed me through Woolworth's. I managed to lose them by the roundabout. They can't know the area.'

I'd say, 'Two of what? Who followed you?'

And he'd say, 'Phil McDermott's hair's too long. He's turning into a fucking hippy.' A normal remark he'd make strange by repeating it twenty times while methodically going through the pockets of every pair of trousers in his wardrobe. I'd hated that voice then, and now I was hearing it again.

But at least he'd said, 'When this is over.' I tried not to let it raise my hopes. Before, Mike might as well have been in suspended animation. Now, with the *new approach to medication*, he was waking up again, just as crazy as before.

I wanted to speak to whoever was in charge of Mike's case. Jane agreed that I should. 'It's obviously upsetting you.' They were trying a new treatment, and nobody had told me anything or asked my permission. She said I had a right to know what was going on. So I went back the next day and asked the nurse, who wandered off to see if he could find someone in authority. I went to Mike's room. Mike was sitting on his chair, facing the wall. From time to time he pushed at the whitewashed plaster as if searching for the panel that opened the secret door.

He didn't turn to see who had come in. He said, 'You're looking well, Paddy.'

'One of us has to.' Mike's face was inches from the wall. He was looking at it carefully. 'You look terrible, Mike.' His skin was pale and dull, whether from drugs, nerves or lack of exercise or some combination of all three hardly mattered. His hair was thinning. When he turned to look at me there were dark rings under his eyes. 'Mike, you look fucking awful.'

He shrugged, or twitched. 'Down the gym. A few sessions. Twice a week. No trouble.' He abandoned the wall, turned his whole body to face me, and moved from the chair to the bed. 'Have you seen *Emmerdale* lately? It's shit.'

It was the first time he'd ever mentioned television. I asked him what he watched. He kept changing the subject, as if he couldn't help himself. His mind channel-hopped. Yeah, he'd been watching it for weeks. *Emmerdale*. There was an actress in it. The programme was shit, but this actress… So Brian had retired, right? Blonde woman. He liked her, only she wasn't in it enough. You'd watch it, right, and she'd only be on for a few seconds. Shame what happened to Phil McDermott's brother. It was his brother, wasn't it? She should have her own series, this actress. He'd watch that… Mum watched *Emmerdale*, didn't she, back then, when it was on earlier? It was even more shit then…

It was heartbreaking. What he said was normal, but the coherence was gone. He'd taken an ordinary conversation, smashed it to pieces, and reassembled it to suit himself. The parts were all there, only they didn't fit; the machine didn't work.

And it was strange to hear him talking about a woman. When he was sixteen he'd had a crush on Declan's sister. I remembered him coming home from school and saying, 'She's gorgeous, Paddy, she's really pretty.' Declan's sister was supposed to have liked him as well – or so Declan said, though that was afterwards, and he might have been trying to be polite. Whether she liked him or not, nothing came of it. Shortly afterwards we saw the first unmistakable signs that something was wrong. Mike stopped going out at night. He needed daylight. He needed to be surrounded by the people he knew. Then he stopped going out at all.

71

He talked about the actress, asked his usual questions. 'How's Shona?'

'She left, Mike. Two years ago.'

'Where'd she go?'

'Aberdeen.'

'Yeah, you said. You should have gone with her.'

'I know.'

'Yeah, *Emmerdale*, right. There's this blonde woman – '

'What's her name?'

It was the first time I'd interrupted him. He glanced quickly at the wall. 'What?'

'What's her name?'

He picked up the folded newspaper, rolled it, as if to swat a fly, then put it down again. He moved back to the chair. He looked hard at my shoes. 'Her name?'

'Her real name. Or her character's name.'

He shook his head. 'Haven't seen the credits. I don't watch those. Boring, they're just boring. I don't watch them. Seen any good fights lately?'

He didn't really care about the blonde woman. He probably hadn't watched *Emmerdale*; even if he had noticed a blonde woman he wouldn't have remembered her afterwards. No, this was something he repeated in the hope of sounding like the rest of us, or what he remembered of the rest of us. *Blonde woman* fitted straight into that gym crowd's range of desirable types, the half-wistful desires of punch-drunk virgins. *Look over there. Legs on that.* Mike had sussed it was a waste of time talking about what concerned him and was trying to humour us, to give us what he thought we wanted. And this was taken as a sign he'd improved.

Maybe it was.

The nurse came back. His face had the set expression of a man bringing bad news and expecting blame for it. 'I'm sorry, sir.'

'No one's available?'

'Not just now. We're – er – so thinly staffed at the moment. But if you're going to be back the same time next week…'

He trailed off, to save me from having to interrupt. I didn't have the heart to shout at him, though I wanted to shout at somebody. Mike sat on his chair, staring at nothing. Unless he was watched or spoken to he slipped back into his own convoluted thoughts. I made an arrangement to see a doctor the following week. As I was leaving, Mike said goodbye. He remembered Jane's name.

Jane called me at work. 'Come over tonight.'

'Is Ros going to be there?'

Jane laughed. 'She's the one who invited you.'

'I thought she despised me.'

'She does. But she feels guilty about the way she behaved. She wants to apologise.'

'So she can feel better about herself afterwards?'

'Probably. Will you come? We'll go for a drink afterwards.'

'In that case, yes.'

An apology from Ros, however grudging or insincere, was something to treasure. I was looking forward to this.

Later that day I met Joshua again.

As there was no driving that afternoon I went for a pub lunch with Brian at the Sceptre. Sue was already there. Brian described the fights we'd been to see a couple of nights earlier and Sue listened exactly as if she was interested. I went to the bar. Sue seemed to have taken to heart all that old advice about attracting a man by faking enthusiasm for his interests. She faked it well, but listening to her say 'He didn't!' and 'No!' over and over again soon became hard work. Besides, I'd had enough of boxing. The night had been a succession of predictable scraps, with Brian's old opponent stopped in the second by a rising prospect. I'd been bored and uncomfortable: the audience had made me think of Mike, who should have been there. Afterwards, as we'd left, a man had actually called out, 'Hey, Mike!' I stopped and turned round but didn't see who it was. It might have had nothing to do with me, but it was another reason not to go again. There was always the chance I'd meet someone from that old crowd who didn't know what had happened or might even mistake me for him. 'Close,' I'd have to say. 'I'm Patrick, the brother.'

Joshua Painter was at the bar sipping a half of bitter. I associated him with bedsits and shabby flats and didn't recognise him at first. The Sceptre wasn't his natural environment, though he'd made a partial effort to adapt. His clothes – a shapeless black sweater that hung like a robe over his narrow shoulders, black drainpipe trousers – were new, or at least clean. His long hair was tied back. I stood next to him long enough to be served before realising why he looked familiar. He recognised me at about the same time.

'This is your local, I suppose.' He spoke quietly, with a tone he probably thought was ironic. 'You drink here all the time.'

'That's right.'

'I won't come here again, then.'

I shrugged.

'Now that I know the kinds of people that come here.'

'Oh?'

'Scum.'

I didn't even shrug.

'I'm surprised you're not in the police.'

'I failed the exam.'

'I don't know how you can live with yourself.'

'I've got a rota for the cleaning.'

The drinks came. I went back to Brian and Sue. Joshua followed me part of the way, as if he wanted to say more, then changed his mind, contenting himself with, 'You're not worth it.' He went back to the bar, and left shortly afterwards, though not before giving me a lingering stare that was probably meant to express moral superiority. Brian was still describing the final bout. When he finished, Sue turned to me with well-concealed relief.

'How's Jane lately?' She said I was good for Jane, or at least an improvement on her previous boyfriends. 'She's had some bad times. I don't trust that flatmate. She's weird, isn't she? All that magic and stuff. I wouldn't have her in my house, I'd be scared to. And what with Adam and some of those others...' I told her Ros was a lovely, approachable person, and that we got on terrifically. 'Oh, don't!' she said, laughing.

I reached Jane's flat exactly on time. I didn't want to give Ros any excuse for avoiding me.

Jane answered the door. 'Hi, Patrick.' There was a subdued formality about her: an apology from Ros was going to be a ceremonial occasion with a rigid protocol. I wished I'd put on a more formal suit. Jane led me through to the lounge. I half expected to find the room in darkness, lit only by a few carefully arranged candles, with Ros at the centre of them, in sackcloth and ashes.

No such luck.

The room was the same as before. Ros sat at her computer, tapping angrily at the keyboard. She looked at me as if I was the latest unwelcome interruption. 'Oh. You.' She turned back to the screen.

'Ros,' Jane prompted.

'I know. Just a moment.'

Ros was still hostile. I decided to annoy her by showing a friendly interest. I leaned over her and looked at the screen. 'Is that a chart you're working on?'

'No.' Her heavily ringed fingers hit the keys hard. 'Personal accounts.'

I turned to Jane. 'Any chance of a coffee?' I sat in one of the armchairs, angling it so it faced away from the television. Ros flinched. She switched off her screen and swivelled on the chair to face me. There was a new silver ring an inch in diameter through her right eyebrow.

'I may have behaved badly to you last time you were here. It may have seemed rude.'

'It did.'

'Well, I was upset at the time.'

'Upset?'

'Yes, upset.' Ros was determined to stick with the euphemism. 'I may not have seemed it. I was going through a difficult time. I'd had a bad night. If I said or did anything that might have offended you, that wasn't necessarily my intention.'

This was even more grudging than I'd expected. 'Do you feel better for having apologised?'

'My feelings are not your concern.'

'Fair enough.'

Jane handed me a half-empty mug of coffee. 'Ros, what was it you mentioned earlier?'

Ros ignored her. 'In fact, I don't really think I did anything I need to apologise for. I was in *my* home. If other people are narrow-minded, I can't be blamed for their prejudices.'

'*Ros*,' Jane repeated. She sat on the arm of the chair and leaned against me.

'Oh, that.' Ros looked at me ferociously. 'You're sceptical about all this, aren't you?' She tapped the wall chart. 'You think I'm wasting my time on it.'

'Not at three hundred quid a throw.'

'There's more to it than that. There's more to it than you think. I can prove it to you. As a token of goodwill I am prepared to cast your horoscope. For no charge.'

'It's a good offer.' Jane rested a hand on my shoulder, possibly to stop me from laughing. 'She wouldn't even do that for me. I'd take it.'

'OK, then. What do you need to know?'

'The time and date of birth. The exact time.' Ros looked disappointed. I wondered if she'd expected me to refuse. 'You'll have to find it out.'

I finished the coffee. 'I know it already.'

Ros was doubtful. 'Are you sure? Not many people know the *exact* time.'

'I'm sure.' This was true. When we were younger, our mum used to repeat the times and dates of our births. As far as she was concerned they'd been the first in a series of deliberate injuries, all of which she'd enumerate in her Saturday-morning monologues as she watched us dust and hoover. Every trip to the hospital, every cup we'd ever dropped, every present we hadn't appreciated properly – she was precise and unforgiving. The times of our births were part of the litany. I'd been the difficult one, apparently, finally delivered at 3.15 in the morning after thirty-nine hours of labour. And eighteen months later there was Mike, at 2.27 in the afternoon. 2.27! She used to talk as if we'd chosen the times that would be least convenient. And everything we'd done since – or, once she stopped talking about Mike, everything *I'd* done since – had been to cause her more pain. It made visiting her difficult, so I didn't visit often. Mum could get by without me. Mike couldn't.

Ros wrote the figures down on a little spiral pad, nodding thoughtfully, as if I'd confirmed her darkest suspicions. Jane squeezed my shoulder in congratulation. I thanked Ros and told her I'd be interested in the results. We left her to her charts.

After a drink at the Half Moon we went back to my flat. Jane sat on the pale leather sofa and looked at the bare white walls. 'It's tidier than most blokes' flats,' she said, once she got over the initial surprise. 'Like a show flat. Ros would feel at home here.' She was intrigued by the bare walls: there were no pictures on display, or prints or photographs. 'Don't you find it impersonal?'

'That's why I like it,' I said. 'It's the self as Other.'

She was amused. 'You don't even know what that means.'

I'd never kept photographs, somehow thinking I wouldn't need them, that things would never change. The one photo I had of Mike had been given to me by the manager of his old club. Mike had left by then, but I was still there, holding the pads for Shona. Wes had been clearing out his filing cabinet. 'Give this to your brother when you see him.' Casually, keeping up the club's pretence that Mike had stopped coming because he was bored. The picture had been taken when Mike was fifteen. He'd just won a bout and was still wearing the headgear and sweaty vest. I had my arm around his shoulder and we were both grinning. I kept it in the bottom of the wardrobe, where I'd once kept a blurred one of Shona I'd cut from the magazine that carried a report of her first fight. It showed her still wearing her gumshield and with a cut over her eye. She hated it, and not because the cut made her look like the loser. Shona had hated having her photograph taken even when her face was unmarked. I used to think what kept us together was that we didn't like ourselves. I ran, and she trained. It was as though we were both trying to become someone else. I threw the picture away when she went back to Aberdeen. I didn't need mementoes.

I hadn't told Jane about Shona. She hadn't asked. We were both old enough to have a past.

I hung my jacket and tie in the wardrobe, put my shoes on the shoe rack, then sat next to her on the sofa. 'I didn't think much of your mate's apology.'

She rested her head against my shoulder. 'It's worth three hundred quid.'

'Maybe. But it's not like I can sell it to somebody else. And I'm not too keen on what she's doing to her face.'

'She's going too far.' Jane conceded. Loyally, she attempted a defence. 'But she's had a difficult life. She used to be anorexic.'

'That figures.'

I told her I'd seen Joshua Painter again. She shivered. Her visceral dislike made me suddenly happy. 'What did he do that was so terrible?' I didn't think it could be much. Jane had mentioned drugs. Maybe he'd stolen somebody's stereo to pay for them. Maybe he just got on people's nerves.

'Ask Adam.' She brightened. 'There's a party at the weekend. To celebrate his promotion. You can ask him then.'

'You think I'd be welcome?'

'Course you will. They're not bad people. Even Ros is OK when you get to know her.'

'Even Ros.'

'She'll surprise you with your horoscope.'

'Yeah?'

I wondered if she would. I expected her to provide a flattering version of her idea of me. It would be full of words like 'careful', 'controlled' or possibly 'conservative', all adding up to a picture of someone who needed to relax. The joke would be on her. The time and date of birth I'd given her had been Mike's.

Six

Adam had a flat on the other side of town. Promising not to drink, I borrowed Brian's car and set off to collect Jane. Ros was once again staying with Beth-and-Margaret. She would make her own way to the party, if she went at all.

Adam's flat was in a new development, a walled-off park of neat little blocks in two-tone brickwork with tiny windows, the kind of flat you're supposed to stay in for two years before moving somewhere larger. I'd been there twice before, for Elding Collections, once to Adam's own block.

Adam greeted us effusively, as if now the party could really begin. The plaits, I noticed, had gone, replaced with a ponytail. 'Jane, it's great you could come.' He kissed her gently on the cheek. I wondered if he greeted all women in the same way. He offered me his hand. 'Patrick, it's good to see you again. Ros is casting your horoscope, isn't she? Jane told me.' His fixed grin softened at her name.

Jane had no time for this sentiment. 'Who else is here?'

'Lee, Daniel, Sonia...' He ran through a whole list. 'There's drink in the kitchen, and Daniel may have left some of the food.'

We went through to the living room. Apart from a sofa and a small table, all the furniture had been moved out, leaving only indentations in the carpet. A small black hi-fi rested in one corner, playing a tape of dance music with the volume set low. Three women sat on the sofa, talking, two of them easily identifiable as the sort of women Jane would know. The third, in blue jeans and a pale mauve top, seemed to be at the wrong party. Jane went over to the women in black and exchanged greetings, ignoring, and being ignored by, the third woman. I made a note to ask about this later.

Two men stood by the table with the food. They introduced themselves as Marcus and Daniel. I recognised Daniel from the cellar; Marcus announced he was a neighbour. Daniel slipped away quickly, my arrival giving him the chance he'd been waiting for.

'Glad to see I'm not the only normal person here,' Marcus said, probably because I wasn't dressed entirely in black. 'Have you come straight from work?'

'They look normal enough to me.' I wondered if he was about to give me some examples of Adam's strangeness – chanting at midnight, the smell of incense.

'Computer people. No social skills.' He seemed about to say more, so I chewed a soft sausage roll and waited. Finally he said, 'So what do you drive?' I told him I didn't have a car. He backed away, ever so slightly. 'So what do you do for a living, then?'

'Ever heard of Elding Collections?'

He had: he put down his paper plate, muttered something, and went to the kitchen.

A woman from the cellar came to the table. I made conversation.

'How did that thing go that you were planning?'

She was one of the older women in the group: mid-thirties, dark hair pulled back, full complement of arcane jewellery. She looked at me warily. 'What thing?'

I told her I was a friend of Jane's and she relented. 'She brought you that night, didn't she? I was sure I'd seen you before. Didn't you stay to the end?'

'Jane had to leave.'

'So you didn't hear? We had to abandon it for this year. Not that we ever really started. No subject, you see.'

'No subject?' Once again, the word made me think of Elding Collections.

'Yes. Without someone suitable it wouldn't work. Somebody has to make themselves the vessel, and we just couldn't find the right person.' She laughed. 'It's all very boring. Ros is casting your horoscope, isn't she?'

'You've heard.'

'She did mine. She's a genius. Do you know if she's coming tonight?'

It was a conversation I had several times over the next two hours. Every time Jane introduced me to somebody in black they asked about the horoscope. They seemed envious. I presumed they'd had to pay for theirs.

The living room filled up. Adam moved from guest to guest, offering food, telling them how good it was to see everybody together. Marcus appeared to be avoiding me. He spent most of the evening alone in a corner, holding a drink and stubbornly avoiding eye contact. I asked Adam about him.

'He's my neighbour,' he said, with a grimace, 'so I had to invite him.' There was no sign of Ros. The music grew louder. Some of the women started dancing in a half-hearted, dutiful sort of way. Jane and the woman in the mauve top ignored each other. Daniel, eyes glazed, started talking to me about, as far as I could tell, operating systems – OS/2 against UNIX.

Jane was amused, 'You were nodding as if you understood him.' She pointed out Beth and Margaret. At first I couldn't tell them apart. In a room full of similarly dressed women they were *identically* dressed. They were also a good ten years older than anybody else in the room. They stood to one side, absorbed in their own conversation, occasionally looking at the rest of us with a kind of indulgent approval. 'They're here because it's only a party,' Jane told me. 'If it had been one of the important dates they wouldn't have come.' Adam, she explained, was a moderniser; Beth and Margaret were traditionalists. On the important dates – Beltane, Candlemas

– they'd be out on some common ground or dancing naked round Margaret's living room. These respectable-looking people really danced naked in each other's living rooms and told themselves it wasn't just for fun.

I asked Jane, 'Could you do that?'

She glared at me. 'At least they're not as bad as some.'

'Some what?'

'Some of the idiots out there.' She told me there were people who really believed in black magic. They decorated their council flats with symbols learned from horror films and kept domestic pets for ritual sacrifice.

'What, like hamsters? Goldfish?' I thought of the room Peter Bedding had been found in, empty of furniture, the walls painted black.

'Dogs and cats,' Jane said, seriously. 'Mainly cats.' Beth and Margaret, she said, despised Satanists. I said they probably thought Satanism was too working class for them, a kind of Blackpool of the spirit. 'No,' Jane said, 'it's because as vegetarians they didn't approve of animal sacrifice. And as for dancing…' A slow record started, and she pulled me into the middle of the room. Every other couple in the flat had the same idea, so we stood, crammed together and almost motionless, until the record finished. A not bad, perfectly ordinary party.

At around one o'clock, as the first couples started to leave, I was alone in the kitchen pouring myself the last of the orange juice. There were books stacked on worktops next to the plates of bread and vegetarian sausage rolls. Framed prints of dolphins leaned against the washing machine. Adam came in, arm in arm with the woman in the mauve top. They argued in intimate whispers until she said he'd had enough and walked off sulkily. Adam opened another can of bitter, muttering to himself. He noticed me and gave his odd smile. 'Glad you could come. Is Jane still here?'

'On the sofa.'

'She doesn't think I should drink.'

'Jane?'

'Fiona.' He upended the can and gulped, splashing the front of his T-shirt. 'Still, it's my party. Have you seen Ros?'

'She's not here yet.'

'Isn't she?' He looked down at his T-shirt. 'Good thing it's black.' I had the impression he'd been spilling drinks all night. 'I doubt if Ros will come. She never comes to these things.'

'Jane says you know Joshua Painter.'

His face twisted. 'Don't talk to me about him.'

'It's just I've met him a couple of times.'

'Yeah. He gets about.'

There were empty bottles on the draining board and floating in the sink. Adam seemed to notice them for the first time. They absorbed all his attention. I gave up on Joshua Painter. There were some videocassettes stacked on the fridge, all from the Disney animated range. I pointed at these. 'You've got kids?'

Adam's smile didn't waver. 'They're mine.' I must have looked unimpressed. 'People have the wrong idea about those films. They think they're just children's entertainment.'

'And they're not?'

He looked straight at me. 'Those films are the repositories of a core of mystical knowledge.'

I didn't laugh. 'You mean, the witches and the magic?'

Adam was encouraged. 'It's deeper than that. It's at a more symbolic level. I mean, do you know *Pinocchio*?'

'Not very well.'

'But you know the plot?'

'It's about a wooden puppet, isn't it? In the end it becomes a real boy.'

'Right. Now that's obviously an allegory.' Adam was suddenly sober. He put down his can and smiled as if he was pleased with my answer. 'A created being moves on to a higher plane of existence, and does it through a series of trials and initiation rituals. There are some people who think that's just an accident, as if Walt didn't know what he was doing, as if it was instinctive. I think the man was cleverer than that. In fact, I *know* he was. The proof is in the intervention of the Blue Fairy.'

I couldn't think of anything to say. 'The Blue Fairy?'

'That's right. I mean, it's obvious, isn't it? The Blue Fairy is an avatar of the Triple Goddess in the form of the Virgin Mary.'

I must have looked surprised.

'The clues are everywhere! Even in the colour. What colour does Mary wear in the traditional iconography? Blue! It's always blue! Of course, the Marian cult is merely a debased form of the earlier cult of the mother, just as the Catholic Trinity is a debased form of the Triple Goddess. *Pinocchio* alludes to the myth of Artemis, and Pinocchio is a Dionysius-Christ figure.' He warmed to the subject. 'It's amazing these things aren't more widely known. Of course, it's in the interests of established religion to suppress this kind of knowledge. Those films are Walt's way of smuggling that information back to the people. They are all allegorical fables about the early matriarchal fertility cults. Take *Sleeping Beauty*. It's the same as the Greek myth of Persephone. She can only be woken from her sleep by the kiss of a prince, and her palace has become a forest. A forest! The meaning of that is clear enough. And right up to the last century there were midsummer kissing rituals celebrated in England, and of course we still have mistletoe at Christmas. Now, I'm not saying that Walt made the stories up. He took them from folklore or whatever. The point is, he knew which stories to take. The Sleeping Beauty is obvious. And *Snow White and the Seven Dwarfs*!' He made a sweeping gesture with his right hand, hitting a spice rack. 'There's a film that's absolutely steeped in astrological symbolism! I mean, seven dwarfs! Seven! That's exactly the same as the number of the planets in traditional systems. And the really interesting thing is, in the original version of the story *none of the dwarfs had names*. They're just dwarfs. But Walt realised the true significance. He gave them names – names that corresponded to the traditional qualities assigned to the seven planets. And that number seven is so significant. The Hebrew god rests on the seventh day. Look at the musical octave. That's based on the frequency of vibration. Look at the periodic table.'

I counted in my head. I was thinking: the seven wounds of Christ, the seven Beatitudes, *Seven Brides for Seven Brothers*... 'But aren't there nine planets? Or is it ten?'

He nodded vigorously. 'Ten of course is the ideal number. But I think this just illustrates another aspect of the man's genius. When they found the ninth planet, what did they call it? Pluto, after the Greek god of the underworld. Now the Egyptian equivalent of that is Anubis. Anubis the jackal-headed god. In the Greek myth, hell is guarded by a dog – a *triple-headed* dog. And in Northern mythology we have the Gabriel Hounds who roam the heavens gathering the souls of the dead. In fact they're geese, but it's significant they're called hounds. So there has always been a connection between dogs and the underworld. And what does Walt call his most famous cartoon dog? Pluto! Now, can that be a coincidence?'

I wanted to say yes. I wanted to ask why he called a mouse Mickey, or a duck Donald, and which of the planets were associated with Sleepy or Doc. But I didn't say anything, and Adam didn't really expect an answer. His pause was only so he could swig his beer.

'Snow White herself is the moon. This is the Triple Goddess again, as Artemis or the Roman Diana. She still has the Marian iconography. Look at the colour of that dress. She's killed by a poisoned apple but revives, so it's another fertility myth. Just like Sleeping Beauty. Just like Persephone.

The wicked queen is an impostor, possibly even a man in drag. That could be a reference to the movement from matriarchal to patriarchal cults. The myth of the revival – it's so potent! When it was stolen by the Christians, they took over so much. Christ rises after three days. Three! And who finds him first? The women. In the original version they would have been priestesses, and Christ would have been a Dionysian or Orphic figure. Even that poisoned apple is significant. It represents the harvest, the end of the season when things grow. Look at Greek mythology. Avalon was an orchard.'

'The tree of the knowledge of good and evil?'

'A corrupted later version, written to legitimise the patriarchal usurpation. Walt deals with that more fully in *Cinderella*. The two Ugly Sisters and the stepmother. It looks like a parody of the Triple Goddess, but Cinderella is the real incarnation. It's no accident that in modern pantomimes the Ugly Sisters are always played by men or that pantomimes are always shown around Christmas. The men are pretending to be women in order to fool the goddess. That's the origin of the myth of Hermaphrodite, who was supposed to be the son of Aphrodite. It marks a transitional phase in early religious history. *Cinderella* is about the struggle between matriarchal and patriarchal systems. The name contains an obvious reference to sacrificial rites. And it's about resurrection. Except instead of being asleep or dead, Cinderella is in thrall to a false male principle, like Persephone. Of course, the male principle won in the end. Have you ever read Virgil? He's very good on this. As a gay man he was alienated from the materialist ethos and attracted to the worship of the mother. The tension he experienced gave him wonderful insights. They make him a great teacher, a real shaman. Do you know the fourth *Eclogue*?'

'We did it at school.' From some abandoned corner of my memory, a line came back. '*Ultima Cumaei venit iam carminis aetas.*' Dazed, I said it out loud, wishing I could remember what it meant.

Adam nodded solemnly, as if I'd just given him a secret sign. '*Tuus iam regnat Apollo,*' he whispered. 'You can't tell me that isn't irony.' He seemed lost in wonder at the profundity of it all. He stared at the spines of the cassette boxes, blinking away tears. 'Virgil and Walt,' he finally said, his voice thick with reverence. 'Those men *knew.*' He remembered he was at a party. 'Do you want a drink?'

'No, thanks.'

'Sure?'

'Driving.'

'Right. Sensible. Have you ever heard of the *sortes Virgilianae*?'

Erin C. Burke had mentioned it. 'Is that where you open the book at random and – '

'That's right! That's exactly right! It's a kind of western I Ching. You use chance to focus your mental energies. Did you ever try it yourself?' I shook my head. He nodded. 'I've tried it a few times. I remember once I was doing some research into Celtic tree lore...' He trailed off into a blissed-out nostalgia. I wondered what he meant by research, and if it had involved watching *Bambi*. He faded back in. 'And I couldn't understand it. I just couldn't make sense of it. So I turned to my copy of Virgil. And do you know where it opened? You know, the bit that means the subject you're asking about isn't obscure. '*Rem nulli obscuram nostrae...*' Everything fell into place. I saw the connections. The ring finger, the willow tree, the sacred alphabets. Everything.'

Suddenly, he stopped. I didn't know if he was waiting for me to ask a question, or if the drink had finally caught up with him.

I didn't ask a question. Margaret came into the kitchen. 'Someone called Marcus has passed out in the bathroom.'

Adam's mind was still on higher things, and took a while to descend. He furrowed his brow, his smile as fixed as ever. 'Get Lee and Daniel to put him in the spare room.'

'But he's locked himself in.'

Adam thought about this. He looked very tired. 'I've been talking to Patrick.' He nodded in my direction. 'He's an enlightened guy.'

Margaret smiled. 'Isn't Ros casting your horoscope?'

'Yes.'

'Ros is a genius.' Adam leaned against the tiled wall. 'Jane is wonderful, isn't she?'

Margaret touched his arm. 'Adam, what about Marcus?'

Adam closed his eyes. 'Leave him there.'

'Other people want to use that bathroom.'

Adam murmured what might have been 'kitchen sink' and slid down the wall. Margaret showed no surprise. She turned to me. 'Are you any good with locks?'

As we drove back Jane asked, 'Where did you learn to do that? Do you have a criminal past?'

'Brian showed me once.'

'Brian? How does he know something like that?'

'Used to be a locksmith.' It was a humdrum explanation. Back when Brian had been trying to be the next John Conteh ('I used to worship that man') he'd also learned a trade. 'Years ago. It was a family thing. He just got bored.'

Jane sounded as if she didn't believe me. 'So it's not something you use on your job?'

'God, no. It's just something Brian showed me how to do once. A party trick.'

'Did he show you any others?'

'A few. We have these quiet afternoons at work.'

'Your job is strange. What else can you do?'

'That's about it. That's the only kind of lock I can beat. I haven't the patience for the rest.'

'Brian isn't *patient*.' Jane had never understood him. 'He's just slow.'

'He puts up with Sue.'

'My point exactly. Anyway, Adam was grateful. When he came round. What were you talking about?'

'This and that. His theories.'

She nodded. 'Adam and his theories. What do you think of him?'

'Of Adam?' I considered it for a bit. Adam was a bit of a crank, but he was harmless enough, and friendly, and he thought well of me, which meant a lot. 'Actually I liked him.' I really did.

Seven

There was a day when we finished work just after one o'clock and agreed it wasn't worth going back to the office. Brian went home to watch a Joe Frasier video and cook Sue's dinner. I decided to see Mike.

The TV room was noisier than usual and crowded. The hard-edged blare of an afternoon talk show was drowned by three or four excited conversations taking place simultaneously. A nurse stood by one of the doors, watching them all and pretending to listen to the complaints of one of the lifers. He nodded as I walked through, one sane person acknowledging another. The corridor beyond him was quiet. I marched towards my brother's room without passing anybody. I knocked on the door and walked in. 'Hi, Mike.'

The room was empty.

I'd never seen the room without him in it. I stared dumbly for a few seconds, as if all I had to do was wait for my eyes to adjust. He didn't become visible. I went back to the TV room. I thought maybe he was there, and I hadn't recognised him in an unfamiliar place, the way I hadn't recognised Joshua Painter in the pub.

Mike wasn't in the TV room.

It was too early for panic or anger. He might have been in the toilets or wandering in the grounds, though that was unlikely. As far as I knew, he never left the building. I went back to his room. Empty. I sat on the end of his bed for a few minutes. Even though it was a dark afternoon the room seemed brighter than usual. This puzzled me, until I realised Mike wasn't there to block the light. On an impulse I climbed on to the chair and looked out across the grass, at the bare trees and the walls. There was nobody outside. I wondered what it was Mike saw out there. Did he just misinterpret real people – visitors, patients – walking in the grounds, or was the shadow from a tree or a stain on the wall enough to suggest the figure of someone there, watching and waiting? I felt a chill as I looked out, imagining how, if I looked for long enough, I would start to see the branches and shadows as camouflage for – for what? Slowly, and then heavily, it began to rain.

Somebody said, 'Can I help you, sir?' I turned. It was a nurse – not one of the friendly, hesitant ones. This one was surly, a tired man at the end of a bad shift.

'I'm looking for my brother.' I climbed down from the chair. 'Mike Farrell.'

'I see.' He sounded as if this was the one question he'd hoped no one would ask. 'Michael has moved to another room.'

'Moved? Why?'

'You'll have to speak to Dr Cortevalde.'

'Can I see my brother?'

'That won't be possible. He's resting.'

'Well, can I see Dr Cortevalde?'

'That's not possible.'

'Why isn't it possible?'

'She's not in the building at present.'

'Where is my brother?'

'He's resting. In the Marigold Wing.'

The fight went out of me. 'Thanks.' There was no point arguing with the nurse. 'I'll be back tomorrow.' I already had the appointment booked.

Jane was out when I called. I left a message on her machine. I didn't want to stay in and brood. I needed to go out and talk to someone. I'd have been pleased to see Adam. Or even Ros.

While I waited for Jane to call back I tried to read Joyce Bateman's sensible book. I'd got as far as chapter three, the one on dowsing and rainmaking. 'It seems plain, then, that these ceremonies, though based on a logic that is avowedly unscientific, are none the less valid. The so-called primitive might not have been burdened with the dubious benefits of our technological obsessions: she would have had a more direct perception of physical phenomena. Just as country people even today can predict fluctuations in the weather with more accuracy than our meteorologists, the so-called primitive would have had a clearer picture of actual conditions than the reductive cause and effect model provided by science...'

It wasn't enough of a distraction. I couldn't forget Piers's 'of course it's rubbish'. I couldn't tell if Joyce Bateman was clever or stupid. She *sounded* sane enough. There were no obvious clues, such as being wrong about Aquinas. But then, what did I really know about *him*? A few definitions learned parrot-fashion: the unmoved mover, the first cause, the chain of necessity, the source of perfection, the purpose of everything, blah blah blah.

I waited until seven-thirty. When Jane still hadn't called I went to the pictures. I chose a thriller, hoping the big screen and the noise would be enough to stop me thinking about the Marigold Wing.

I tried to like the film. There were guns and car chases, and a Mafioso's daughter was kidnapped and kept in a cellar while the good criminal and the bad cop tore around Los Angeles shouting questions and discovering they had a lot in common. It was fast-moving and stupid, but I still walked out halfway through. My thoughts kept going back to the Marigold Wing. I decided to go to a pub. I chose one I used to go to with Shona. I didn't plan to stay long. One drink, no more. Standing at a bar and drinking alone isn't comfortable.

You might as well carry a placard saying 'Friendless social failure'. You find yourself listening carefully to music you once hated, envying people's conversations about football or bus routes, beginning to fancy the woman behind the bar. You keep checking the time, as if it's important, as if you're either waiting for someone or you have somewhere to go, a stratagem that fools nobody because nobody is paying any attention.

There was no barmaid and no music playing, just six other drinkers in a big empty room. The barman stood at the other end of the bar. He looked at me and didn't move.

I sorted through a handful of coins. 'Quiet night.'

'Yeah.' The barman was in his twenties, fair-skinned, fat. I recognised him from somewhere. St Augustine's? A punter from that month in Tenerife? He didn't pretend to be happy to see me. 'It gets busy, though.'

'Same in my line of work.'

He walked to the other end of the bar. 'I know about your line of work.'

Then I remembered him. Three months earlier. The name had gone but I still had the face and the circumstances. Bank card, three thousand pounds. It had taken two visits and the threat of court action to get the card back. He had been aggressive, convinced he had rights. An averagely difficult subject. I must have spoiled his whole week. The name came back: Timothy Muller, twenty-seven, a house-painter, stuck at the end of a season when nobody wanted anything painted. He might have served me if I'd insisted, but facing hostility wasn't the diversion I was looking for. I walked to the Drover, half a mile down the road. The Drover was a small pub, noisy with talk. I hadn't drunk there in years. Ideal. I stood at the bar and drank.

Mike was in the Marigold Wing.

I didn't know anything about the Marigold Wing for certain. I'd never seen it or read any official documents. All

I had to go on were the chance remarks of the nurses and a local tradition. Even so, I thought I knew what the name meant. It was one step from Broadmoor, the place where they kept nutters who hadn't killed yet only because they hadn't had the chance. It seemed unfair that Mike should be shut away while I was outside, enjoying all the advantages of freedom. Agreed, I had a rotten job, and no clear idea of what I wanted to do with the rest of my life. That was ordinary. That was what you'd expect. But I had Jane. And what did Mike have? Drugs and fear, and, once or twice a week, me jabbering at him about the full and interesting life I led. What had he done to deserve that?

I hadn't wanted to stay in and brood and now here I was, standing against a bar, brooding, as the same few songs were played over and over until I found myself looking forward to them. 'Take It To The Limit'! 'Lying Eyes'! 'Desperado'! There was an Eagles fan in the pub, possibly one of the two middle-aged men on my left talking about Fulham's bad start for the season and the best way to get from Penge to Haydons Road. And the barmaid – the barmaid was familiar. She was a thin woman, about my age. Pretty, in a soulful, highly strung way, the kind you suspect still has a room full of teddy bears and will introduce them to you by name. I couldn't place her. You only remember the subjects' faces when they make trouble, and she didn't look the sort to have made trouble. Now and again she'd glance in my direction, as if she couldn't place *me*. At about half past ten, during a lull in trade, she came over when my glass was still half full.

'I know you.' She sounded uncertain. 'You're Mike Farrell.'

It was as though I'd expected this. 'That's right.'

She smiled. 'You haven't changed much.'

'No?'

'Do you know who I am?' She didn't give me time to look confused. 'Sally Mercer, Cazales as was.'

Of course. Declan's sister. I'd only really noticed her after Mike had started mentioning her. Before that, she'd been no more than a small, nervous girl flitting across a hallway as we waited for Declan to decide what boots he was going to wear. Mike, hanging around at the back of the group, had been the first to notice she was pretty. And now here she was behind a bar, still pretty, and much less nervous.

'Sally Cazales.' I nodded. 'I've lost touch. It's years since I last saw Dekko.'

'Months since I've seen him myself. What are you doing these days?'

'I'm in computers.' I managed to sound casual. 'Programming. Troubleshooting. That sort of thing.'

'Really?' She was impressed. She looked at me the way Sue sometimes looked at Brian. She glanced down. 'Not married yet, then?'

I realised she was looking at my left hand. I held it up and showed her both sides, like a magician about to pluck a coin from the air. 'I am. I just don't like rings.'

She laughed. 'Then how come you're here on a Wednesday night alone?'

'My wife's staying with her parents.' The story came readily. 'Her mother's sick. Like I said, I would have gone with her, but what with work and everything…'

'Oh, that's terrible. Is it serious? Did she have to go far?'

'Aberdeen. We don't think it's serious, but it's hard to tell…'

'That's terrible.' She showed her concern by gazing at me and nodding slowly. 'I'm separated myself.'

'Yeah?'

She shrugged. 'Things don't always work out. It's a shame how we lose touch. I haven't seen Dekko for months. He's out of the army now.'

'Really?' I hadn't known he was ever in. 'So what's he up to now?'

'Nothing much.' She gave a wry smile. 'How's your brother?'

'Patrick? I see him now and then.'

'Was that his name? What does he do now?'

'Are you working for the DSS? I don't know. He gets by.'

A customer stood at the bar, tapping the bottom of his glass against a plastic ashtray. 'Nice to see you again.' Sally backed away, smiling. 'Sorry to hear about your wife's mother. Hope she gets better.'

I left. Back at my flat, there was a message on the machine. It was Jane. 'So where the fuck are you?' Her voice sounded cheerful. I was sorry for having gone out and missed her, and for having given Mike that fleeting, fictitious existence. It didn't do him any favours and could only make it awkward if I ever met Sally again, Sally Cazales as was. It was gone eleven, too late to return Jane's call. It seemed I was no good to anyone.

Work the next day was quiet. I was sitting in the office, waiting for Brian to come back with the sandwiches, when the phone rang. Tony reached it first. 'Elding Collections.' Then he nodded at me and smirked. 'It's your mad tart again.'

Jane sounded concerned. 'So what happened? Is something the matter with Mike?'

'I'll tell you later.' I didn't want anyone in the office to hear the details. 'The Half Moon?'

'No. Come over. Ros has finished your horoscope.'

'Yeah? I thought she'd forgotten about it.'

'She had trouble with it. Are you going to see Mike again?'

'This afternoon.'

'Do you want me to come?'

'No.'

'OK. Tell me about it tonight.'

'Sure.'

The horoscope wasn't important; I wanted to see Jane.

That afternoon I had the appointment with Dr Cortevalde which I'd arranged the week before. She was a pale woman in her forties, dressed in the same pastel shades as the walls of the institute. She began by telling me she had only a few minutes to spare. She didn't say her other work was more important, or that I was wasting her time. Instead she kept looking at her watch, as if she couldn't believe how quickly the minutes passed. There was nothing on her desk, not even a phone or a notebook. I wondered if she wasn't one of the patients, sitting behind an empty desk, pretending to be an expert.

'There is really no cause for concern.'

'So why was he moved to another wing?'

Her tone was calm. 'Michael became a little overexcited. He was moved to a more secluded wing so that he wouldn't upset the others. We have to take the wellbeing of all our patients into account.'

'What do you mean by overexcited?'

It was a second before she answered. 'Exactly that. Over-excited.'

'But it's working, this treatment?'

'I feel that it is, yes. You must try not to become too anxious about processes you possibly don't understand.'

'If I don't understand, it's because – ' I stopped myself. Losing my temper wouldn't help anybody. 'What processes?'

She stayed cool. She was a professional. 'I don't feel it would be helpful to go into too much detail at the moment.'

'Can I see him?'

'Your brother is resting. It really isn't a good time. I know you usually just walk in here whenever you want and see him whenever you feel like it. But do you know what we do here?' She didn't give me a chance to answer. 'We are trying to help your brother. Remember, we have to work with him during his every waking hour. We have to see that he eats properly, keeps himself clean, and has some sort of social contact with the people around him. It is a full-time responsibility. You will have to learn to trust our judgement.'

We were both angry now, and both trying not to let it show. 'What *is* your judgement?'

'I don't want to go into specifics just yet.'

'Then give me some general information.'

For a moment, I thought she was going to shout. Her left hand clenched into a fist. Then she relaxed. 'The general information I can give you is this. Your brother is responding to treatment in a way that had been anticipated. You must have some idea of the nature of his condition. Our best course of action was to keep him apart from the other patients, for their sake and his.'

'Can I see him?'

'Not now. He's resting.'

'Tomorrow?'

'That may be too soon.'

'When?'

Finally, reluctantly, she agreed a time. I was still angry when I left. The way she had said *resting* made me think of forced restraint. They probably hadn't gone as far as a straitjacket, not while they had drugs, though I'd have bet the door to his room was locked from the outside. That was his life. He wasn't a card collector, like me or Brian, or just out of the army, like Declan, or married, as in the lies I'd told Declan's sister. He was resting. He had no history, he'd done nothing since he was sixteen except retreat and grow stranger. It was no life at all.

I was still in a bad mood when I reached Jane's. Uselessly preoccupied, all I noticed was that Ros had two new rings through her lower lip, which looked swollen and tinged with purple and black. The rings annoyed me. What was the stupid woman doing to herself? It wasn't until she offered me coffee that I realised she was trying to be polite and that the strange twist in her mouth was meant to be a smile. Not the dreamy smile I'd seen the night she decided to show me her piercings, or even a businesslike greeting for a valued client. No, Ros was smiling as if she was pleased to see me.

She sat by her computer and began.

'Your chart took much longer to interpret than I'd expected. The first results were so surprising I had to recheck them just to make sure. Sit down. Put your coat anywhere.'

Jane stood by the kitchen door, beaming. I almost regretted the trick I'd played. Giving her the false date began to feel like unnecessary cruelty, like telling a four-year-old there is no Tooth Fairy or that Santa Claus is only their dad. I sat there, feeling vindictive and cheap.

'My first surprise was your birth sign. Of course, that's only a very approximate guide to character, and not really scientific, but I really didn't think Mercury would have such an influence. I'd assumed it would be Saturn or Neptune. You have a lot of characteristics associated with Saturn. That's on the surface, though. A person's true nature is not always apparent...' The introduction finished, she became more serious. She picked up a sheet of paper from the table next to her printer, studied it for a few seconds, then came over and placed it on my lap. It showed four concentric circles, like the chart on the wall, like Jane's tattoo; inside the circles were numbers and small symbols linked by broken lines. Ros sat on the arm of the chair, leaning against my shoulder, and began to explain. Her voice was warm, affectionate.

'The sun signs aren't important things, despite all the traditions. Aries, Cancer – nobody takes that stuff seriously any more. These days we know it's more to do with the alignment of the planets... See this triangle here? That's Mars. It's more prominent than I would have thought. After

100

Gauquelin's research it's usually taken to denote athleticism or leadership qualities.'

I found myself wanting to agree with her, to appear convinced. 'Well, I run.'

'Do you? I didn't know.' She snuggled closer. I was surprised. Ros wasn't supposed to like me, and now she was almost sitting in my lap. 'But look. Here you have Saturn in opposition to Mercury. That's what I had to recheck. The angles are strange. That usually means somebody is receptive. It didn't seem to fit. And the alignment of Venus is unusual as well.'

I knew from Erin C. Burke how astrology was embedded in everyday language: Saturn meant saturnine, Mercury mercurial. It wasn't hard to work out the significance of Venus. From the kitchen, Jane laughed. Ros ignored her.

'The moon is more decisive than I expected. This chart gave me a lot of trouble.' There was no reproach in her voice. If anything, she was pleased with the challenge I'd presented. 'Anyway, that's the chart I had to work from. I've prepared a fuller report I can give you now.' She pulled herself away, and went back to her computer.

Jane smiled at me. 'Receptive? I've got to read this.'

Ros tapped some keys. The printer started to buzz. The report was two pages long. She handed it to me with a flourish. Small type, narrowly spaced. I would have preferred to take it away and read it in private. Ros wanted to see my response there and then. She stood over me, expectantly. I looked at Jane, who grinned and nodded encouragingly. The best I could do was pretend to take it seriously.

Your chart presents some striking contrasts. The first paragraph rephrased what she'd already told me. I skimmed through. *Mars suggests qualities of aggression, yet these are balanced by a concern for order and control.* That was expected. A conjunction of Saturn and Mercury, producing a combination of both deliberation and quick-wittedness...

A good, if unlikely quality, one anybody would be proud to possess.

The second paragraph went into more detail.

These conjunctions suggest the presence of internal contradictions and tensions. A sense of indecisiveness may be masked by the forceful adoption of certain attitudes, perceived as more socially desirable... Here we go, I thought. This is where she tells me to relax. *On the positive side, this can lead to creativity and a sympathetic attitude to the problems of others. On the negative side, however, if these tensions are not resolved, there is a possibility of real unhappiness, perhaps even to the extent of mental disturbance.*

Perhaps even to the extent of. It was as if somebody had punched me over the heart. Ros smiled, unaware of the jolt she'd delivered. Of course, I thought, it's just another warning to relax. I read on.

The saturnine element suggests a tendency to dwell obsessively on a single thought, whether an idea or a memory. In some cases this may be aggravated rather than relieved by the mercurial component. It may lead you to invent difficulties where none exists, or imagine you have enemies when those around you want only to help. In the worst cases it can lead to an intense preoccupation with things of the moment, leading to a failure to make adequate plans for the future, or a tendency to say things you don't mean or to make promises you are unable to keep.

I could feel both of them watching me, waiting for my response. I kept my head down and my face straight, and tried to stop my hands from shaking. The final paragraph was easier to read.

Moving from general principles to your present situation, it seems that, although you have experienced many drastic changes to your living conditions, your underlying circumstances remain unaltered. You may feel confined by this, and the good intentions of those around you may be hard to appreciate. Nevertheless, you must be patient. Your current situation is intrinsically unstable, and there are bound to be further upheavals ahead. It will be only when you have resolved the underlying tensions of your personality that you will reach a period of relative tranquillity. Family, or those close to you, may find it hard to understand you during this period, and you may well misunderstand their attitude towards you. Your unusual receptivity may lead you to pick up the wrong signals or concentrate too much on details that are, in retrospect, unimportant. You must try not to be distracted by trivial incidents and imaginary dangers, however real they seem. You must trust those around you more. It is only by taking things calmly and putting them in perspective that you will be able to shake off your feelings of confinement, and it is only by acknowledging your uncertainty that you will achieve any contentment or inner peace.

My first thought was that Ros had somehow found out about Mike. *Think you can trick me, bailiff?* Some of what she'd written – about the need for patience and putting things in perspective – were no more than routine good advice, but the rest... There were two more paragraphs, one praising my spiritual awareness, enjoining patience when those around me did not acknowledge what appeared to be obvious, and another that ended: *Remember that some of what you see might be no more than a projection of your own anxieties.* I looked up from the page, my chest and arms damp with sweat. Never before had I felt so uncomfortable in a suit.

Ros grinned at me through her bruised lips. Whatever this was, it wasn't a trick. Ros was incapable of deception. 'Well? What do you think?'

'There's a lot to think about.' I turned to Jane. 'Have you read this?'

'No.' Jane was pleased. 'Ros never lets me read anything. What does it say?'

'It's not what I expected.' Jane would know it wasn't me. I decided not to let her read it. 'Do you always go into this kind of detail?'

Ros nodded. 'It wasn't what I expected either. I had to put out of my mind everything I knew, and trust only what the chart told me. To begin with, I thought I must have got something wrong.'

'Right.' I struggled for something to say. 'And you can tell all that from a chart?'

'The chart is easy.' Ros was still delighted with the effect she'd produced. 'I've got a program to generate those. The hard part is the interpretation. That's what took me so long. The results I was getting just didn't square with what I knew about you. With what I *thought* I knew about you. And then it dawned on me that I was simply wrong about your character. I thought you were negative and materialistic, but now I see you have a spiritual side you haven't yet learned to respect. It's there, and you shouldn't offer so much resistance. Only the other day Adam was telling me he thought you were enlightened, and he's a good judge of character.'

All I could say was, 'You've given me a lot to think about.'

'Can I read it?' Jane seemed to feel left out. 'I'd like to hear more about these spiritual qualities.'

'I'm not sure if I should.'

'Oh, come on.'

I folded the report away in my jacket pocket. 'I want to think about it first.'

Ros touched my shoulder. 'A wise decision.'

Jane didn't argue with Ros. We went to the Half Moon.

'Is it accurate?' Once there, Jane repeated the question. 'Was it you?'

'It was accurate.'

'So why don't you let me see it?'

'I want to think about it.'

'But you recognised yourself? You were impressed?'

'I was impressed.'

'More than you expected?'

'I didn't expect to be impressed.'

'So you've changed your mind about astrology?'

'Well, about Ros.'

'Ros has really changed her mind about you as well. She said you were welcome at the flat at any time. You know what she was like before.'

'What, you think the horoscope told her I'm her type?'

'Of course not. Ros isn't like that. It's what she was saying about your spiritual side. If she respects that in you, maybe you should learn to accept it.'

'I'll try.'

There was a pause. Jane became serious. 'Did you see your brother?'

'They wouldn't let me.'

'What?'

I explained. I told her what Cortevalde had told me.

Jane looked grim. 'I'm not sure they can do that.' She spoke as if from experience. 'I mean, it's not like he's a prisoner. It's not a Regional Secure Unit. Presumably he's there on some kind of voluntary basis.'

'I don't know.' I'd never thought about it in terms of rights. We'd handed Mike over to an authority and the authority had kept him. Surely that was best for everyone? 'I'll find out.'

Jane was surprised. 'You don't know? Look, I'll find out for you if you want. You can't trust these people with anything. I've dealt with them before, I know what they're like. I can make some calls tomorrow. Did they tell you what they're doing to him?'

'Not exactly.' I always found talking about Mike difficult, even with Shona. Out of all the people I had known, Jane was the most matter-of-fact. *I've dealt with them before*. 'As far as I can tell, they took him off the tranquillisers and he scared them. Whether he became violent or whatever, she – the doctor – wouldn't say. Now they've got him quiet again.'

'Sounds like standard practice. I could tell you a few stories.'

She only wanted to be asked. Her stories would probably have been moving and instructive but I didn't want to hear them. I didn't want that kind of experience to be shrunk to an anecdote, a story passed on in a pub. I asked about her day.

'The usual shit. Easy stuff. You could do it.'

'As easy as that?'

'It's better paid than what you do. And you could still wear a suit. Don't look now, but there's a man by the door staring at you.'

I looked. It was Kevin Taylor. He *was* staring at me, with an expression somewhere between diffidence and panic. He wore the same ripped coat and dingy jeans as ever, and half his face was still red from the rash. When he saw I'd noticed him he came over.

'Hi, Patrick, haven't seen you for a while.'

'Hi, Kevin. How are you?'

He didn't question the name. 'I've found somewhere to stay, yeah. A proper house, a room, this bloke's sorting it all out for me. Gonna get some new gear for me as well, yeah. Good, innit?'

'Yeah. Good.'

He glanced shyly at Jane. 'You a friend of Patrick's, then? He's a good bloke, isn't he, yeah?'

'He's OK.' Jane smiled at him, the way you'd smile at a child. 'So who's putting you up, Kevin?'

'This bloke, yeah. It's part of a scheme. Was seeing him here tonight. My local, see. New clothes. He was going to get some new clothes for me as well.'

'That's good.' If anybody could benefit from a scheme, it

was Kevin. That a place had been found for him somewhere was almost enough to restore your faith in the system. It was odd – given his history – that he'd been asked to come to the Half Moon rather than an office, but maybe that was how they worked. Or maybe they didn't know he was an alcoholic.

Kevin didn't move from our table. I guessed he was waiting for me to offer to buy him a drink. Close up, he looked sicker than before. I asked, 'So where is your room?'

'In a house, yeah.'

'Not a hospital?' Jane was matter-of-fact. 'That's good, then. I'm surprised they've found places.'

'Why should I go to hospital? I'm OK, most of the time.' Kevin started to cough, a phlegm-ridden, hollow-chested hacking that doubled him up. He clutched the back of Jane's chair and convulsed for a few seconds. When he looked up again the whole of his face was bright red, as if the rash had taken over. Gradually the usual sickly colour returned to one half. 'Sorry,' he said. 'That's not serious, yeah, the cough and that. That'll soon clear up. It's part of my present situation. When I get the room, yeah.'

'I thought you'd got it already.'

'I get it tonight. To see this bloke. That's what I'm here for.' The door of the pub opened. Kevin turned expectantly. 'There's the bloke now.' He didn't look pleased, though. He looked as if he'd done something wrong and expected to be told off for it. The man at the door marched straight towards him. It was Joshua Painter.

I didn't recognise him at first. It was the suit. Dark grey, single-breasted, £140 off the peg I'd have guessed, and still new enough to look presentable. His own bad skin had cleared. He even looked healthier.

'You made it, then, Kevin. Jane.' He seemed surprised to see her there. 'I've wanted to speak to you for a while.'

Jane turned away from him.

'I don't want to talk to you.'

Joshua sighed. It was clear he was more interested in her than in Kevin. 'Jane, there are a lot of things I need to talk to you about.'

Jane gave me a look I interpreted as meaning: *Stay out of this, I can look after myself*. She looked coolly at Joshua. 'I don't want to talk to you.'

'If I could explain…'

'I wouldn't be interested.'

'What happened – it's not what you think.'

'I don't care.'

Joshua seemed to realise he was pleading, and that this put him at a disadvantage. He changed tactics. 'I'm surprised to see you in *this* company.'

Once upon a time, this would have been fighting talk. Thanks to my experience at Elding Collections, it was now only the lead-in to fighting talk.

Jane asked, 'What kind of company is that?'

For the first time, Joshua looked at me. 'That. Him.'

'Patrick's OK, yeah.' Kevin was having trouble following this. 'He's a mate.'

'What do you know about this situation, Kevin?' Joshua snapped. 'You do *not* know *anything*. Please do *not* get involved.' He reached into his jacket pocket and pulled out a key ring with three keys. He held it to Kevin's face, an inch from his nose. 'These are the keys, understand? Take them and go. You still remember where to go?' Kevin nodded. 'Good. I'll talk to you about the rest later.'

Kevin took the keys and backed away. I expected Joshua to follow him. He didn't. He leaned forward, resting his hands on the table, his back still turned to me, to cut me out of the conversation altogether. 'Jane, there are some people you should not associate with.'

Jane leaned back, as if to avoid his breath. 'You're one of them. Leave me alone.'

'You don't understand. I'm surprised you don't understand. I expected more from you, Jane. I thought you'd have more, more *insight*.'

'Just fuck off, Joshua.'

'You mustn't believe the stories.'

I was interested. 'What stories?'

'Keep out of this.' He wouldn't look at me. 'This isn't your concern.'

'It might be.'

He finally turned, just far enough a sideways glance. 'I've told you this is no concern of yours. You couldn't begin to understand. You haven't got the – the – the *moral imagination*.'

Jane glanced at me, to see how I took this. She pressed one of her feet against mine. I smiled at her and shrugged. I was calm, though I might have been angrier if I'd known what Joshua meant. Moral imagination? What was that, exactly? And if Joshua thought it was good, maybe I was better off without it. I let Jane do the talking.

She was terse. 'Fuck off, Joshua.'

'Jane, I respect you. I don't want to see you making a mistake.'

'Oh, well, you'd know about mistakes.'

This went home. Joshua straightened up and stepped back from the table.

'That was necessary. That was all according to the projection.'

It was my turn to interrupt. 'Projection?'

Joshua kept his gaze fixed on Jane. 'Why are you still here? This is a *private* conversation.'

I'd had enough. 'Why are *you* still here, Joshua? You've already been told to fuck off.'

'I don't take orders from you.'

'Then take them from me.' Jane's weariness was turning to anger. 'Fuck off.'

Joshua didn't move. It was time to provoke a crisis. I would have liked to hit him, just once or twice, if only because he obviously didn't expect it. He'd moved in the wrong circles, and had grown used to insulting people who didn't respond. I stood up.

'Come on, Jane, let's go.'

'He can go.' Joshua placed a hand on Jane's shoulder and pushed down as hard as he dared. 'We still have a lot to talk about.'

'No, we haven't.' Jane brushed his hand aside and stood up. 'Can't you understand that?'

Joshua turned to face me, staring. It was a wild-eyed effort, the sort you get in films where the psychopaths are obviously mad in every way possible and still don't get caught till the final reel. It wasn't convincing. Joshua was jumpy and arrogant, but he didn't look remotely dangerous.

He kept up the mad axe-man expression for exactly two seconds, then stepped aside huffily. He followed us to the door and a little way down the street, still talking.

'You don't understand. You shouldn't believe everything Adam tells you. In fact, you shouldn't believe *anything* Adam tells you. He has his own reasons for telling you things. It *suits* him to tell lies about me. Have you ever stopped to ask what it is he's so afraid of?'

Jane stopped walking. I had never seen her so angry. 'I don't need to rely on Adam, I've got the evidence of my own eyes.'

'There is an explanation...'

'I wouldn't be interested. I *saw* you at the hospital. "What am I going to do, what am I going to do?" You're lucky you're not in prison.'

He overtook us, blocking our path. 'I'll tell you what the difference is between him and me.' He pointed at me, his thin arm extended and his fingertip almost touching my forehead. I noticed the nails were long and specked with white. Zinc deficiency. 'Kevin calls *him* a friend, a *mate*. I don't know how long he's known *him*, but *his* so-called friendship is worthless. I don't *know* Kevin. I wasn't his *friend*. I simply saw him in the street and realised he was someone I could help. I'm giving up my own room and my time to help him. And I'm not doing this because I expect any reward. I'm doing it because I regard it as my duty to a fellow human being. And what has *he* ever done to help anybody? Nothing. *I* am the one who's making the sacrifices. *That's* the difference between us.'

He retracted his arm and spun away from us, keen to end on a note of triumph. Jane called after him, 'Is that the same way you helped Avril?'

Another direct hit. Joshua stamped once, like someone trying to put out a small fire, then hurried on without turning back. We went to my flat.

'I thought you said you didn't really know him.'

'I don't. Not as well as he likes to think.'

'So what was all that business about Avril and hospitals? And prison?'

'Ancient history. He was pretty fucked at one time. Avril was a friend of mine. She got involved with him. There were drugs. It was a mess.'

'And this "projection"?'

'Adam knows more about it.'

'You keep saying that. He didn't want to talk about him when I asked.'

'He will now he thinks you're enlightened.' She said it without a trace of irony. 'Anyway, why should you care about Joshua? He's just a fucked-up paranoiac.'

'He hates me. I want to know if he's a *dangerous* fucked-up paranoiac.'

She laughed. 'Josh? No way. All that crap he gave about helping your friend – he's not running anything. He's probably on the same programme. They're just sharing the refuge.'

I laughed, but I didn't think she was right. I thought it was just about possible Joshua had cleaned up and found a job with a charity, something that fed his burning sense of self-righteousness and gave him an excuse to bully people. He was bad news for someone like Kevin, but then, for someone like Kevin, most of life consisted of bad news. Whatever Joshua had done in the past, I didn't think he was a threat to me.

Eight

Mike was back on his bed, leaning against the wall. It was another dark afternoon, and the light was off. Now and again he'd glance up at the small window. The rest of the time he stared at the wall the way the others stared at the television. He didn't look at me.

'How do you feel, Mike?'

There was a pause before his answer, as if it was drawn from a confidential file and needed triple-checking before release. 'OK.'

'What's been happening?'

'Not much.'

I hadn't expected a lucid account. I hadn't expected him to be so casual either. 'How was the Marigold Wing?'

'Not bad.'

'What did you do there?' It was like asking a reluctant child about their day at school. *And did you make any new friends?*

He glanced up at the window, turned back to the wall, sighing. 'Not much.'

'Why did they move you there?'

'Dunno.'

'So how do you feel now?'

'OK.'

'What have you been doing since you moved back?'

'Not much.'

'Is there anything you want to do?'

'Not really.'

I didn't know what to ask him next. As ever, I felt I had missed something significant, that I should have been there an hour earlier. He wasn't standing on his chair any more, and he tried to answer questions. A few months earlier this would have counted as an improvement, and maybe it was.

'Mike, how would you feel if I brought Jane to visit?'

He frowned, as if I'd disturbed him in the middle of one of his favourite thoughts.

'Who's Jane?'

'The girl I told you about.'

'Her.'

'So how would you feel?'

'OK.'

'Soon. Is that all right?'

'If you like.'

'No, not if I like. What do *you* want?'

He didn't answer, or give any sign that he'd heard the question.

'Mike, I saw Sally Cazales again.'

'Yeah.'

'Declan's sister. Remember her? She asked about you.'

Nothing, not a flicker. Once he'd talked about her for minutes at a time. It was almost the last rational thing he ever did. Years had passed since then. What did all that time feel like to him? Months? Weeks? Decades?

'She was married. Now she's separated. She's working in a pub. If I see her again, what should I tell her?'

'I'm OK.'

'OK? Is that enough?'

He glanced up at the window. 'I've seen them outside. By the trees. Sometimes I hear them in the corridor. They'll work it out. It's only a matter of time.' Her voice was flat, as if after all these years he was bored by whatever was following him, half resigned to their dogged and incompetent pursuit.

'Nobody's after you. Whoever you saw, whatever you heard, nobody's after you.' I knew it was a waste of time arguing with him, but it was a habit I couldn't break. 'If you left here, what would you do?'

'Stay at home.'

'Just stay at home?'

'At home.'

'What about the gym?'

'Yeah, the gym.' He said *gym* like a foreign word he'd learnt by rote, without ever understanding what it meant. 'A few sessions.'

'You're getting fat.'

'Yeah. Getting.'

'Mike, do you remember any of your fights? Brian remembers his. Blow for bloody blow.'

'Brian.'

'You remember Brian.'

'Course I remember. He stopped, didn't he – boxing. You told me.'

'Do you remember any of your fights?'

He wasn't interested. 'You work with him now. I know that.'

'Yeah, I work with him now.' I could sense him slipping away. 'I'll go now. Get some sleep if you want. Do some exercise, for fuck's sake. Soon I'll bring Jane.'

'Yeah. Jane.'

I went to see Dr Cortevalde.

'Michael has made better progress than we hoped.' Her delivery was flat. She might have been reading from a press release.

'How can you tell? He's tranked out of his skull.'

She took this well, like a politician deflecting a familiar, difficult objection. She probably had me marked down as awkward and made an extra effort to stay calm. 'Superficially, he may give that impression. The use of drugs is a necessary part of his treatment. This may sound callous, especially if you are unfamiliar with the range and purpose of the treatments now available. But it must be remembered that what we are trying to achieve is something more sophisticated than simply keeping your brother sedated. We aim to give him a chance to function in society. We want to give him a chance to do something with his life.'

'Function in society?' I still had doubts. I didn't like the word *function*. It made us sound mechanical, replaceable. Change a circuit board here, plug in a new component there. Sorry, mate, this one'll have to go back to the suppliers. 'Do you mean normally?'

She didn't so much answer my question as go straight over it, like a steamroller over a cardboard box. 'That of course would be too much to hope for, at least in the sense in which *normal* is generally understood. Your brother is, as I shouldn't need to remind you, an extreme case. With an illness like his, there is often a good prospect of an eventual return to relative social viability. Your brother developed the symptoms of the disease early, and in quite a severe form. Sadly, these cases are always the hardest to treat effectively, especially when neglected in the early stages. If the symptoms had not appeared until he was in his late twenties or thirties, there would be a greater chance of a full recovery. In Michael's case, we have to face the fact that, with our present state of knowledge, his condition is unlikely to show much more than minor improvement.'

I'd feared this, or known it. Or rather, I'd been frightened of openly admitting I knew it, in the same way the family had avoided saying anything when he'd lived at home. All I could do was mumble, 'You mean, no cure?'

'Not in the sense that there's a cure for...' She paused, as if she couldn't at that moment remember any curable diseases, then shook her head. 'We can *alleviate* your brother's condition. I need hardly say that, in a case such as his, this will involve a combination of the right environment and the right medication. This is not the right environment for Michael. It is not really the right environment for anybody. A place like this is a last resort, when a person has either become a threat to themselves or, without proper supervision, risks becoming such a threat. We have recently taken in such an individual, a seventeen-year-old girl who has twice attempted to eat glass. She requires constant attention. Obviously her parents are not equipped to deal with something of this nature. Although the case seems difficult, not to say distressing, I am certain that the girl in question will soon be able to return to a normal family life. Similarly, I feel that in due course your brother will be able to return to the outside world. He will still require supervision, particularly in the early days. The initial movement out of a sheltered environment will be traumatic. We will of course provide all the support we can.'

So leaving was no longer a remote possibility. It was going to happen. I asked when she thought this would be.

'Not until we're certain he's ready. It would be dangerous to release him prematurely.'

'He said he wanted to go home.'

'I know. It is a wish he has expressed several times. That of course would depend on you. A return to a familiar environment, one where he does not feel threatened, might well have a beneficial effect. I take it that you're in full-time employment? Unless you have a partner prepared to devote time to him, I really don't think it would be fair to you to burden you with that kind of responsibility. Your parents, how are they situated?'

'They've retired.'

'Do you think they would be able to offer any help in this respect?'

'I don't think so, no.'

'I see. In that case, once we are satisfied with his condition, and once a place becomes available, we would move your brother to shared accommodation. We may even be able to find work for him. Once in the accommodation he would be with people who understand his problem, and he would benefit from regular visits from our staff to ensure there is no... that he is happy.'

She might have sounded as if she was reading from an interdepartmental memo, but she meant every word. She really believed that Mike could have his own room and responsibilities, and work. It would be menial and undemanding work, and if he was sharing a kitchen with the likes of Kevin Taylor I could see it getting stressful, but it would be an improvement to what he'd had so far. His life was changing. It might even become a life.

And when, a week or so after Ros delivered the horoscope, Adam invited me and Jane out for a meal, this was something else new. Apart from the occasional Chinese with Brian and Tony, I didn't get invited to meals.

'Nothing formal, just a few friends. There's so much we have to discuss.'

I wasn't sure about a *discussion*, but Jane wanted to go. 'Come on, Adam's OK. It can't hurt.'

OK. We seemed to say OK about everything. How's your brother? OK. How's Ros? OK. How's your life? OK. Adam was OK. Beth and Margaret were probably OK. The only person nobody seemed to like was Joshua.

They didn't have an opinion about Kevin Taylor.

We met in an OK Indian restaurant, ate an OK Indian meal. 'Glad you could make it. Of course...' Adam said as we sat down. He'd dispensed with the ponytail, and gone for the hippy look. I wondered how long it would be before he tried dreadlocks, or an alice band, or if he'd already tried them. Perhaps the hair was an emblem of his questioning spirit...

'Of course, the food they serve here isn't really authentic. In India itself...' He went on to explain the differences between the food served in the restaurant and what you ate in India. I have a limited sense of taste. When people talk about food I feel like a tone-deaf man at a concert. I took what Adam had to say on trust. He seemed to know what he was talking about. 'And thanks, by the way, for coping with Marcus.'

'It was nothing.'

'No, it was good of you. I'm afraid I wasn't much use by that stage of the evening...'

Daniel was there: he was OK, in a floppy, good-natured way. And there were two women, both called Sarah, apparently there to make up the numbers. Daniel occasionally tried, tentatively, to flirt with one of them, but that seemed to be for form's sake. They were OK too. Everybody wore black. Adam did most of the talking.

He talked about magic, politics, computers, old traditions, new developments in science, his travels in India and South America, and how they were all connected. He was a good talker, in the way that marathon runners are good runners. They may not be dramatic or fast, but they'll keep going long after you've been stretchered to the oxygen tent. He knew how to tell a story, when to explain important points, and he could even be funny, though I was always wary of being the first to laugh. I didn't get all the connections. One moment he'd be telling you about London's underground rivers, which was *fairly* interesting, then, somehow, he'd have moved on to alchemy, which wasn't, or the latest interesting internet site, which wasn't either (the internet was more specialist back then), and you had to wait until he came back to a subject you understood. There were worse ways to spend an evening. Standing alone at a bar, for instance, and telling lies about my brother.

At what felt like a suitable break in the conversation I mentioned Joshua. Adam looked mournful.

'Joshua Painter? I don't know what he's doing now.'

Daniel chipped in. 'I hear he's found a new medium.'

Jane said, 'Let's hope it's watercolours.'

Adam shook his head sadly. 'Joshua and his mediums.' Then he turned to me., 'What did you think of your horoscope?'

The others seemed to lean forward slightly. Except for Jane. 'Don't bother,' she said. 'He won't talk to you about it.'

'I wouldn't expect him to.' Adam looked faintly disappointed. 'It's not unusual for people to be sensitive about the results of such a close reading. A consultation with somebody like Ros – it can touch nerves. Some people fail to recognise themselves at all. It can take some getting used to. In your case, I hope you don't mind me saying, Ros told me the results were not what she'd expected.'

So they'd talked about me. I couldn't imagine the conversation lasting more than a minute. 'Did she say what she did expect?'

'Oh, she didn't go into the details, and of course I didn't press her. She values her clients' confidentiality. She wouldn't give up that kind of detail without their permission.' He looked at me hopefully. 'Not, of course, that I'm trying to press *you*. But it's interesting, don't you think?'

I agreed it was interesting. Adam realised he wasn't going to get any more out of me and started talking about how church architecture reflects the influence of the lunar cycle.

At work our clients followed their own cycle, as arcane in its way as any of Joshua's. Instead of Candlemas or Beltane, they had Quarterly Accounting Periods. One came to an end at the beginning of December, a good time to clear their books of hopeless debts. That meant tracers. Two weeks before, Piers had said, 'We're entering a busy period.' An understatement. At the same time there were a lot of collections, thanks to the Christmas rush to overspend.

Piers already had a stack of requests eight inches high, two weeks' work, with more expected the next day, and more again the day after that. 'You wanted Wednesday afternoon off, didn't you?' he asked as soon as I came through the door Monday morning. 'Well, you can't have it. I'm sorry to have to take this line. But you'll be able to visit your brother in the evening.' Piers was trying to be tactful, in his remote way. I wished he hadn't said this in front of Tony, who was standing nearby, waiting for his chance to offend. 'There shouldn't be any problem,' Piers went on. 'I checked the visiting times.'

Tony's response was muted, for him. 'You had to check? Piers, I thought you'd remember.'

'I wasn't at that one.' Piers didn't care. 'The hours vary.'

He handed out the worksheets. Dozens of names, addresses, amounts owed. Tony said he wanted to make a start right away. I decided to wait for Brian. Tony put on his overcoat. Instead of leaving he stood by the window, humming 'Winter Wonderland' and looking up at the sky.

'Waiting for something, Bellman?' I asked.

'Life to begin.' He pulled himself away from the window. I didn't blame him. It was a depressing sky. 'Fancy going for a drink tonight, Psycho? Unless you're visiting someone.'

'I'm seeing Jane.'

'The witch? She can come. It'll be a laugh.'

Tony's idea of a laugh. 'What about your Chrissie?' I asked.

'Angie.'

'Whatever. She not available?'

'Fuck knows. No, she isn't. She walked. Two weeks ago, if you must know. I'm getting fed up with eating takeaways and watching her old videos. If I have to watch *Smiles of a Summer Night* one more time I'll go barmy.'

Piers looked up. 'The Bergman?'

'No, Piers.' Tony rapped on the desk with his knuckles. 'The hardcore version. Lots of splash and two-on-one action.

121

Of course it's the fucking Bergman. Well, Psycho, you coming or what?'

'Maybe. Where will you be?'

He named a pub I didn't know. 'About nine. We can talk revenge. And I'd like to see this tart of yours.'

He left.

We followed a plan. We'd divide an area between us, park the car in a strategic place, then head off in different directions, with our little leather cases of paper and our wallets for the recovered cards. That day I drew the short straw: eight cards from the same estate, one of those places you're not supposed to visit alone. Daft rule anyway. If it were that bad, nobody there would have any cards. The job wasn't dangerous. It was just dull and repetitive and you usually came away empty-handed. Occasionally somebody shouted at us. At the first hint of trouble we left, quickly. Besides, on that day it was raining. I always felt safer in the rain.

From subject number three, who lived in a seventh-floor flat in one of the blocks, I got a threat of violence and, for once, some actual violence. I was standing on the balcony, looking down at a grey-haired man in a Kevin Taylor-style jacket who crouched by the edge of a churned-up patch of green. He skipped along sideways, his chest against his knees, like a commando approaching a machine gun emplacement. He didn't seem to notice it was raining. I turned away and knocked on the door. From the grime on the kitchen window I wasn't expecting an answer. The door opened, revealing a little black guy whose age seemed to match the one on my worksheet. He wore a woman's red housecoat with a fluffy pink collar and clutched a plastic broom handle. He didn't waste words. 'Fuck off!'

'Mr Alexander Murphy?' I said this politely, as if 'fuck off' had been no more than his version of good morning. 'I'm from Elding Collections. Your – '

He swung the broom handle at me, then jumped back, slamming the door.

He'd aimed at my head, but miscalculated. The blow caught me on the shoulder. The broom handle weighed maybe a few ounces. I barely felt it through my coat. That was the violence. Rather than ring on the bell again I took the walkway to the next building, where Miss Isidora Turranos told me that if I bothered her again her boyfriend would kill me. This was a step up from the usual vengeful mutterings or loud wishes that we die of cancer. Miss Turranos said that we were bastards, bloodsucking scum, and her boyfriend would soon sort me out. He'd been in the army.

'Fine,' I said, as the door closed. 'We'll be back tomorrow.'

When I got home that night the phone was ringing. I intercepted it before the machine could answer for me.

'Jane?'

'It's Margaret.'

'Margaret?'

'I'm a friend of Ros. Jane may have mentioned me.'

Of course. This was Margaret as in Beth-and-Margaret. The priestess.

'We're going to have a little gathering this Sunday. We'd be glad if you could come.'

A gathering? What did that mean? 'I'll have to see.'

'Jane is welcome.'

'I'll see.'

'Will you let me know?' She gave me her number. I didn't bother to write it down. 'We *do* look forward to seeing you.'

'I'll see.'

When Jane came by, angry at having had to work later than expected, I mentioned it to her. She wasn't impressed. 'That's just flattery. I'll probably get a call tomorrow saying

I can bring you.' She told me about her day. A deadline had been brought forward; her current boss had become hysterical. 'It was bedlam. I want to go somewhere. Where shall we go?'

I told her about Tony's offer. She was intrigued. 'The one who pretends to be hard? We could see him. It can't hurt.'

'It might. I work with him. I know what he's like.'

'But have you ever seen him outside? Come on, he can't be as bad as Brian.'

We took a minicab to the pub. It turned out to be narrow and smoky and filled with men over forty shouting at each other over loud rock 'n' roll. Tony must have looked long and hard to find a pub with exactly that mix of fatalism and menace. Apart from the barmaid, a redhead with a cancerous tan and a throat like old leather, Jane was the only woman there. Heads turned as we walked in.

Tony had kept a table, presumably by the threat of physical violence. He'd swapped his working suit for a black sweater and overcoat. Next to all the sweatshirts and frayed bargain-bin suits he stood out.

When he saw us he got to his feet, holding out a hand to Jane. 'So you're the witch.'

'What?'

He sat down again. 'The one who lends Psycho here all those books.'

She laughed, and sat down. 'You call him Psycho?'

Tony told her about our last disagreement. He made it sound unprovoked. Then he told her about the one before that, then the one before that... He came over as good-humoured, magnanimous. I came over as a hate-crazed thug with a four-second fuse.

'Psycho here thinks all problems can be resolved through violence.'

Jane laughed. 'He can't be that bad.'

'Do you want to see the scars?'

'I'm not that bad.' I wasn't going to let Tony have all the running. 'Anyway, you're the one with the record.'

'Long time ago.' Tony looked pained, as if for once he wished it hadn't been mentioned. I saw no harm. Jane already knew. 'I was younger then.'

'So? I'm only young now. And I've got you winding me up.'

'You're not that bloody young. And you don't know what I had to put up with. Besides, I've repaid my debt to society. Psycho here hasn't been caught yet.'

Jane smiled. 'Don't you have to be hard in your job?'

'Doesn't hurt. We're not, you know, supposed to use violence, despite what Psycho here might tell you. *Looking* hard is the main thing.' It was the key to Tony's success. 'Me, I'm soft. I'm like that puppy with the toilet rolls.'

I said, 'You wanted to talk about revenge.'

'Did I? Yeah, s'pose I did. Thanks for coming, by the way.' He leaned forward, lowered his voice. 'Soppy tart walked out two weeks ago. Said she couldn't stand the drinking and the rows. I told her to stop visiting her mother…' He went into a routine about living alone: '…the only good thing is you can take a crap with the door open. Means you don't miss the football.' And the downside, by his account, all bad food and physical neglect. It was a slick performance. If he'd been on stage I might have laughed. 'I found a cockroach in the fridge last night.' A pause for the punchline: 'I was pleased.' Pause. 'I thought I'd eaten the last one.' Boom, boom. Then he told us about his ex. She hadn't just left him, she was on a vendetta. She'd taken his car and deliberately wrecked it, reversed it into a brick wall: 'She never did like that back seat.' He hadn't liked the car either, a boxy little Sunbeam with iffy brakes and altered mileage. At first, thinking it meant money, he'd been glad it was wrecked. But the insurance company refused to pay and there was still the loan to cover. Tony retaliated by printing two hundred fluorescent green cards with her telephone number under the legend 'Hot new talent' and left them in phone boxes across North London from Kilburn to Manor Park. 'It cost, but it was worthwhile. Her number was permanently engaged for a week, until she changed it.'

'That's terrible.' Jane was amused. Then she had second thoughts. 'If it's true.'

'It's true.' Tony looked happy, as though he wanted people to think the worst of him. 'Anyway, aren't you a witch? Doesn't that mean you're credulous?'

Jane recognised Tony's game. She didn't lose her temper. 'It doesn't mean I believe everything I hear.'

'So what do you believe?' Tony winked at me. 'Is it the secret wisdom of the east or the Margaret Murray rubbish?'

'And how much do you know about it?'

'More than you think.'

'I bet. The Old Religion – '

'You'd lose. And don't call it the *Old* Religion. It's not that old. I studied the stuff. Do you know what my subject was? (By the way, Psycho, when I say *subject* I mean a topic I once studied, not some shit with an overdraft.) The myth of the Illuminati in the nineteenth century. Bloody good subject. With a sideline in Masonic conspiracy theories.'

Jane was cautious. 'You studied that?'

'In detail, sister. Primary sources, four different languages. Conspiracy theories are one of my hobbies. All those fucking ranters and dreamers, from Philippe le Bel right down to the latest JFK nut. That's how I know about your Margaret Murray revisionist crap.'

'You can't say it's crap.' Jane finally rose to the bait. 'Her scholarship is central.'

'It's central to a lot of rubbish.' Tony tried to keep the glee out of his voice. 'Nobody serious gives it the time of day. You should read Norman Cohn.'

'There's work that's been done since.' Jane rallied. 'We don't just rely on Margaret Murray, you know.'

'No, you just find other ways to reach the same conclusions. It's not history, love, it's ideology. It's worse than Foucault.'

'At least Foucault questions the assumptions – '

Tony snorted. '*Questions the assumptions*. I never thought I'd meet somebody who actually believed that. So what if he does? Foucault's a bad historian because he ignores evidence. And that's what your dozy witch cult tarts do. Their problem is they don't question their own assumptions. And why is it always tarts who believe in these spurious counter-narratives? Your round, Psycho.'

Jane was unmoved. 'So what about Butler?'

'Joseph Butler? You're asking me about Joseph Butler? It wasn't his field, darling. And that was fifty years ago.'

I left them to slug it out. This was a contest I couldn't score. Jane might have lent me the books but she didn't seem to like discussing them with me. The bar was crowded. I stood there for what felt like hours, waving a ten-pound note until the barmaid finally served me, showing the same contempt she showed the regulars. I walked back with my usual thought that barmaids must see the worst of people, and found that Tony had changed the subject. 'The walls had been painted black. Usually they've just been wrecked. This one was fucking redecorated. Why should someone do that?'

Jane laughed. 'How should I know? All sorts of reasons.'

'Hameed found one too,' I said. I was surprised Tony was still going on about the black room. He must have thought he'd gone too far with Margaret Murray, and was trying to make up by telling a story he thought she'd like. 'It doesn't mean anything.'

'I know that.' Tony retreated. 'Just puzzled me, that's all. Sort of a *News of the World* thing, isn't it? Devil cult. Wondered if it was something you knew anything about.'

'Why should I?' Jane was amused. 'I'm not a Satanist. I don't even believe in the Old Religion myself.'

'So what kind of witch are you?'

Jane actually laughed. 'Who says I'm a witch?' She turned to me. 'Have you told him I'm a witch?'

Tony looked dumbfounded. 'So what about these books you keep landing on Psycho here?'

'I'm just interested in different approaches to what we call reality. I think modern science is too restricted.'

'Oh.' Tony was still at a loss. He tried to drag me into it. 'You had a black room too, didn't you? That tracer you couldn't find, remember?'

'Peter Bedding?'

'That's the one. The paper had some Satanist angle on that, didn't they?'

I shrugged. 'That was just wishful thinking. Some journalist jazzing things up.' I could sense this was leading up to something. Tony was always leading up to something. It was best to give him as little encouragement as possible.

'Mind you, they're only keen on it for the sex and drugs angle. All those fat bastards dancing round fires. Exclusive pictures.' He laughed. 'Actually, that's the only reason I'm interested. I was hoping you'd know someone who could get me into an orgy. Ever been to one?'

'No.'

'Are you open to offers?'

Jane laughed. 'Not with you.'

'You're no bloody fun. How about a black mass?'

'*Nobody* goes to those.'

'You're right, they are a bit 1890s. So what's the point of all this magic, then? It can't be just love potions and blighting the cattle. I thought the sex was why people did it. It's why people do most things.' He slumped back into his chair. 'And you haven't even brought a friend. You could have had the decency to bring a friend.' He finished his drink. 'Whose round is it now?'

'Yours.'

He got to his feet and pushed his way through to the bar. There were a few half-hearted complaints, but no trouble. The regulars weren't as aggressive as they looked, or maybe they were just impressed by his appearance. Jane watched him.

'Strange, isn't he? He's bought the whole establishment angle.'

'Yeah?' For some reason I didn't like the way she said *establishment angle*. 'Do you want to stay?'

Jane didn't hesitate. 'This'll be the last one. What was that name you said?'

'What name?'

'The man in the black room.'

'Peter Bedding.'

'What was he supposed to have done?'

'He killed himself.'

'I used to know a Peter Bedding.'

Tony came back with the drinks before I could say anything. 'So much for the double date. Fancy a fight?'

'What, with you?'

'No. Be serious. Down at the Ferret and Trousers. Yeah, I know, stupid name. It's a teen pub. Always get a bit of aggro down there about closing time.'

'Looks like you could get it here.'

'Here? You must be joking. No trouble here.'

'They look rough enough.'

'They're not rough. They're just badly dressed and unhappy. The Ferret and Trousers is the place. What do you reckon?'

Jane wasn't impressed. 'A fight? And what am I supposed to do?'

'You can watch. Or take part. I haven't seen a good catfight since I introduced Angie to me mum. Come on, get there about ten-thirtyish, just as things are beginning to loosen up.'

'Sorry – I've got work tomorrow.'

Tony gave up. 'Me too.' He sighed. 'Work. Fuck it, don't you ever get fed up with Elding fucking Collections? Those crap little flats, all black ash shelf units and Cézanne prints, and you know they're Cézanne because it fucking says so in big letters underneath. Or council gaffs. Fucking hell, some of them are holes. I'm not fussy, but I come out of some of those places feeling like Harold fucking Nicolson. And those fuckwit fucking students – '

'I used to be a student.'

'Me too, darling. Bunch of know-nothing wankers. Smoke a couple of joints and they think they're Sardanapalus. Then there's the money scum, and the businessmen, the self-righteous bastards. Tell me, if they're so fucking clever what am I doing there? And they look at you as if you're treading shit into the carpets they haven't paid for yet. Christ, I'm thirty-six. I don't want to be doing this job in five years' time.'

Jane was unsympathetic. 'Then don't.'

'It's not that fucking easy. Don't ask me why, it just isn't.' Tony studied his glass, turning it in his hands. If this was meant to be another routine, he seemed to have strayed from the script. 'You ever want something to happen? Just once I'd like to, you know, stumble across something. Drugs maybe, a body – anything. And not just some forgotten granny who pegged out three months ago. I've had one of those; that was nothing but trouble, and nobody thanked me for it. I want a bit of drama. Something more than taking cards off people.'

Jane looked at her watch. 'What else are you good at?'

'I've been doing this for six years. Before that, I was a security guard. Before that… well, never mind. This is the best job I've had. I've got a second-class degree and a record. I might as well try to live up to it.'

A long silence followed. I finished my drink. Jane had already finished hers. 'We're off.'

'You don't fancy trying the Ferret, then?'

'What for?'

Tony shrugged. 'A man has to do something with his life.'

'Suit yourself. I'm not tempted.'

'Well, fuck off, then. See you tomorrow, Psycho. Nice meeting you, Elvira. You were exactly how I imagined you. Beautiful and crazy.'

In the cab Jane said, 'Sad bastard.'

'He liked you too.'

'I didn't know Peter had killed himself.'

'That's what it said in the paper.'

'He was a friend of Joshua's.'

Joshua had answered the door when I'd called at Peter Bedding's flat. It hadn't seemed significant at the time. People like Joshua were always moving. It wasn't uncommon to see the same faces as you tramped through the income support zones where they seemed to end up. 'Joshua had friends?'

'Sort of. A drug thing.'

'Peter owed money as well.'

'Doesn't surprise me. The black room. That was in the paper? Sounds like the sort of thing Joshua would do. Sensory deprivation. You sit in a dark room, curtains drawn, lights out. The less you can see, the easier it is to focus.'

'Easier to focus on what?'

'Who knows? Joshua was crazy then. And Peter was crazy long before he met Joshua. He'd tried to kill himself at least three times already, and he'd OD'd twice by accident before I knew him. He wasn't exactly someone you could talk to. He heard voices. That's how he got involved with drugs. He was on medication he didn't like and started taking other stuff.'

'Poor bastard. And then he meets Joshua.'

'And then he meets Joshua.'

I remembered Daniel saying Joshua had found a new medium. I wondered if he was talking about Kevin Taylor.

I couldn't imagine Kevin as a medium. I wouldn't have relied on him to contact someone in the phone book. Still, I thought, if I ever saw him again I'd ask what was going on. I might even warn him to be careful.

Nine

Tony showed up for work the next day, hungover and unscathed.

'You didn't go, then?'

'I went all right. Place was full of weedy student types, all up on passive resistance. Where are the bricklayers and hod carriers of yesteryear, eh?' And so on. Another set piece. More work arrived. We still hadn't finished the previous day's. Piers drew up the worksheets. They were so long we had to laugh.

'There are five requests here for non-existent addresses,' Piers announced. 'And two more for someone we couldn't find last week.' He was in his element.

We went out and knocked on doors. This time Brian did the estate. Mr Murphy, he reported, was a lamb. Isidora Turranos apologised and handed over the card straight away. The usual thing. If somebody different makes the second call the subjects assume he must be harder, more dangerous. It also gives them a false idea of our resources. I visited a few shops, well-meaning people so committed to their business that they'd borrowed from everywhere rather than admit defeat. You couldn't help feeling sorry for some of them, even the ones who shouldn't have been allowed to run a business in the first place. They'd struggle to keep their shop open another month, they'd swear the Christmas rush was about to solve all their problems, and then a letter would arrive to say I was coming. It wasn't the end; they might still make that money. But I'm not a favourable omen. My appearance at their door means another line of credit has crystallised into debt, and a happy new year to *you*. Plus the usual run of punters, the mugs who should never have been given cards, their little rooms filled with pricey tat. Unemployed warehouse operatives with fax machines and SETI standard satellite dishes, redundant insurance clerks with a small fortune in *Star Trek* collectibles. And they all watch television. They can be roadsweepers or office managers or lecturers forced into early retirement, but they all seem to watch television. You walk in, if you're allowed in, and the television will be on the whole time, and always too loud, the way it was too loud in the TV lounge, as if getting into debt affects the hearing. And they watch such rubbish. Dramas on cardboard sets, general knowledge questions even I can answer. If nothing else, Elding Collections gives you a good idea of the daytime schedules.

We recovered all but three of twenty-eight cards and couldn't find six out of seven tracers.

Brian's new word was 'parameter'.

I did see Kevin Taylor again, that same week. As usual it was in the street, though this time it wasn't a street I expected. I was in Deptford, at the very border of my patch – anything from Deptford to the English Channel belonged to the East London office – and I was halfway between a ruined boutique and another possible runner when Kevin Taylor stepped out of a bank right in front of me.

I didn't recognise him at first. His patch was supposed to be a few back streets between the Half Moon and his local Kwiksave. It wasn't Deptford. The only reason for the Kevin I knew to be in a bank was to keep out of the rain. It was another dark morning, but it hadn't rained yet. Kevin had also had a change of clothes, presumably the new gear Joshua had promised: a burgundy jacket, grey polyester slacks and black plastic shoes with the shine already gone. It was smarter than anything he'd worn in months. He skipped down the steps of the bank – the one that didn't employ Elding Collections – like someone who'd finished business there and now had the rest of the afternoon free. I thought, 'That bloke looks just like…' I thought it was no more than an uncanny resemblance until he saw me and froze. That expression of ingratiating panic couldn't have belonged to anyone else.

'Wotcha, Patrick.' He was agitated, as if he would have preferred to run. 'You doing OK?'

'Fine.' His rash had faded. Instead of covering half his face it had retreated to the edges, giving him one red sideburn and a raw throat. 'You're looking better, Kev.'

'I am, yeah.' He reached up to scratch his neck. There was money in his hands, a few ten-pound notes. Instead of passing on his latest good luck story, he crushed them, as if he didn't want me to notice. 'Much better.'

'You working now, then?'

'Joshua's arranged it. He's got me a cheque book and everything.'

'What do you do?'

'For Joshua, yeah. A bit of, you know, running around.'

'In Deptford?'

'Around, yeah.'

'Money good?'

'Good.' His answer didn't seem to satisfy him. He tried other formulations. 'It's OK. Yeah, the money's good.'

'Good. And how is Joshua?'

'He's…' Kevin struggled with this. I might as well have asked him to define being and essence according to Aquinan principles. All he could do was grin. 'You know Joshua, yeah.'

'So what do you do for him?'

'This and that.' He backed away and looked across the road. 'Here and there.'

'Well, good luck with it.' He was now out of arm's reach. 'And be careful of Joshua. I don't trust him.'

Wasted advice. Kevin didn't seem to be listening. 'Gotta go, yeah.' He walked away quickly and crossed the road, turning to look back at me every few yards.

The next day at work. The same stack of paperwork. 'Always our busiest time of year,' Piers said.

Tony agreed, 'Must be, what, five times as much work?'

'Four point seven,' Piers corrected. 'Our average for tracers has fallen again. It's now one point six nine. The only one of you who ever finds anybody is Hameed.'

'He's just lucky.'

'There's no such thing as luck.' Piers sounded as if he had this on good authority. 'There are only averages. If you were doing your job properly you'd find just as many.'

'You're assuming an even distribution of temperaments.' Tony winked at me. 'Maybe they have less initiative in his patch. They sit there waiting for him.'

'You should still find the same number.'

'Piers is right,' I said. 'Law of averages.'

'The law of averages isn't a law,' Tony said. 'It's more of a guideline. How's your mad tart?'

'She was impressed by you too.'

Tony sighed. 'We really need to talk about her.'

'You can do it in your own time,' Piers said, but only because it was expected of him. He seemed to enjoy being overworked. The paper covered his desk and stacks were growing on the filing cabinet. He was getting to work at seven, leaving at nine, and loving every minute of it. Me and Brian sorted our jobs into order and worked out a route. Start in Kennington and move out, or follow a figure of eight based around Norbury? We settled on Norbury.

I visited Mike straight from work. I left my wallet of recovered cards and folder of 'Not Found' forms with Piers and walked there. It was the first time I'd seen the place at night. I didn't like it. The unlit path from the gate to the main door reminded me of too many horror films, the sort where the hero arrives at the research establishment to find the laboratory wrecked and the staff missing... The building was dark, with only a few yellowish lights showing, all on the ground floor, like somewhere under temporary occupation by people who didn't need all the rooms. I walked along the path with a growing sense that something was wrong. It wasn't just because I wasn't used to seeing the building at night: I wasn't used to seeing Mike then, either. Maybe he was different in the evenings. Maybe he always had been...

Inside, there were more people around than usual, which only added to the sense that something had gone wrong. Two men, dressed like visitors, waited at the empty reception desk. The TV room, now sparsely hung with faded paper chains, was crowded, the conversations once again drowning out the television – some sitcom: the staff didn't allow anything as disturbing as the early evening news.

Mike's door was open, and the light was on, giving the impression that somebody else had just left. Why would Mike bother with a light? Didn't he prefer to sit in the dark? But he was sitting on his bed, reading or at least looking at a *Daily Mirror*. He put it down as soon as I came through the door.

'Paddy.'

'Mike.'

'Wasn't expecting you.' He ran his left hand over his hair, and made a gesture like a shrug.

'I meant to come this afternoon. Couldn't get the time off.'

'Yeah.' He looked more relaxed than before, healthier. 'You said.' More relaxed, that is, by his standards. He twisted, as if trying to stop me from seeing his left side. These were slightly more than the contortions of someone trying to find

137

a comfortable position. They looked like embarrassment. I might have been our mother, catching him with a dog-eared copy of *Knave* or *Club International*. I blamed the medication.

'Must get busy,' he said, more to himself than me. 'This time of the year.'

'Off my feet. How are you?'

'OK, I'm OK. It's pretty quiet here. Where's this Jane, then? You said you were bringing this Jane I've heard so much about.'

'Couldn't come. I'll bring her next time maybe.'

He nodded vigorously. 'She busy too, then? Off her feet. Always is, this time of the year. And Mum and Dad, they OK?'

'Same as ever.'

'Bad as that?' He smiled. He knew I hadn't expected a joke.

'I'm seeing them at the weekend.' I hadn't seen them for months. 'Anything you want me to tell them?'

'I'll be able to see them soon, Mum and Dad. They've said. Do you think they'll like that?'

'They've said you can go?' Cortevalde had mentioned it as a possibility. I was surprised they'd mentioned it to Mike – and that he'd remembered. 'Have they said when?'

He twisted away from me and looked up at the window. 'That Cortevalde's a stuck-up bitch. I've been sleeping. I've been asleep for two years. A vegetable, a mushroom. Is a mushroom a vegetable? Keep you in the dark. Door opens and they throw shit on you. She's a stuck-up bitch but it's OK, it's like the things I thought I saw, it's like the wrong frequency – you know, reception. A bad fucking picture. You think it's *Emmerdale* and it's fucking *University Challenge*. I know what's there, it's just learning what I know.'

He said this carefully, like someone trying to repeat a lesson. I wondered if the television analogy was Cortevalde's.

Was she trying to talk to him in a language she thought he'd understand? She probably thought he was stupid as well as sick, but then most people did, and always had. Even at school Mike had never been good at giving answers. He wasn't stupid or dyslexic; on paper he was no worse than average but, when he was put on the spot and asked to talk, his nerves took over. You had to know in advance what he was talking about before you could understand him. It was in all his reports: *Michael seems to be intimidated by the classroom environment.* He didn't like too many people around him: he would stammer, tie himself in knots, or say nothing at all.

He only used to be calm when he was in the ring. Then he was relaxed, no matter how many were watching. In the ring he seemed to know what to do instinctively. He was a good fighter, better at it than I ever was at running. When we'd sparred I'd never been able to touch him, time and again punching the air where he'd once stood, then walking on to a jab. If I could have run as well as he'd boxed I might have come third in my races, or even second. In the ring, Mike was gifted. Once outside, he was average, a duffer. He couldn't even fight. He needed the ropes, the bell, the rules, and somebody telling him when to stop. When he said, 'It's just learning what I know,' I thought I knew what he meant. He was trying to reason with himself. They call it taking a reality test. I'd have given him a D+, and that was generous.

'She said it'll be in two or three weeks,' he went on. 'Not till the new year, February or March or April.'

He was talking rubbish again. 'Is that what she told you?'

'No. I overheard her.' He had his back to me by now, his shoulders rolling as if loosening up for a fight. 'She didn't think I was listening.'

'How do you feel about going?'

'I don't like it here.'

'Nobody likes it here, Mike. It's not a holiday camp.'

'Cortevalde likes it here. She fucking loves it.'

'What does she say?'

'What she likes. She doesn't say much. Talks a lot, doesn't say anything. Not to me. Out of the room, when she thinks I can't hear.'

'You sound OK, Mike. Better than last time.' He did, too. He might have been twitching like a nervous wreck on an amphetamine rush, but he sounded no more than mildly aggrieved. I couldn't blame him. Spending a few years under sedation must really piss you off.

'I've always been OK.' He pulled himself away from the window and studied the backs of his hands. Then he lost his temper. Instantly. One moment he sounded fed up; the next he was screaming. 'Always! There's never been anything wrong with me! Have you seen them, those wankers watching the telly? They're sick, the fucking sick wankers! I've been a good boy, I've been fucking good. Taking my medicine.'

'It's all right, Mike.'

He brought his fist down on the bed. 'What would you know about it? You're never fucking here. You said you'd come yesterday, and you didn't. Too busy with that Jane cunt you're always going on about, you cunt. Never worry about me, do you, bastard, you bastard cunt.'

'I'm here now.'

He ignored me. 'I could be killed in here. They could kill me in here. Nobody would fucking know. Nobody would fucking know. *Nobody.*'

'Who'd kill you?'

'You don't know. Nobody. You don't know what they're like here. I know. I fucking know.'

'You don't know, Mike.' I was reminded of all those evenings at home, sitting in his bedroom, listening to him rave. Oh, after a few minutes I'd get up, take the bus down to the high street, catch up with Andy Longman's crowd in Charisma and dance with the underage girls from Assumption and Herbert Morrison, flush with the earnings from my Saturday job at Britomart. Great days. What happened to them? 'If you think you know something, tell me what it is.'

He threw himself face down on to the bed. 'Fuck off.' His voice was muffled by the pillow. 'Fuck off.'

Hopeless. 'I'll be back next week.'

'Fuck off.'

'Just as well I didn't bring Jane.'

I left him muttering into his pillow.

In the TV room I saw one of the hesitant red-faced nurses. He stood off to one side, alert, waiting to be needed. He recognised me immediately. The suit. 'Mr Farrell, no – er – I've had some time off.'

'It must get a bit much working here.'

'Oh, no, it wasn't that. It was an injury.'

'Not here I hope.'

'Yes, actually. In fact, it was related to your brother.'

'Mike? How?'

He paused, as if being hurt was an embarrassing professional lapse. 'Your brother, he – er – broke my jaw.'

'He did what?'

He looked to make sure nobody else was listening. 'He – er – became quite agitated. I tried to calm him down. Usually he has these... they're like panic attacks. Usually he just needs reassurance. This didn't go quite like that.'

'What did he do?'

'I'm no expert, but Stuart said it was a right cross. We were – er – surprised. We thought his own hand would have been broken, but it was hardly bruised. I had to take some time off because obviously I can't work if I can't talk.'

'I'm sorry.'

'It's all right, sir. You can't blame him. And he did apologise when he saw me again.'

'That's when he was moved to the Marigold Wing.'

'We had to. You see, it wasn't just me. Lloyd was caught as well. Stuart said it was one of the fastest combinations he'd ever seen. Stuart's a fight fan, see. Lloyd was badly winded and his nose was bleeding for nearly an hour.'

'I'm sorry.'

'It happens, sir. Really, we do see worse sometimes.'

'He was talking about going out.'

'Returned to the… yes. He's better now than he's ever been. We all feel he would benefit if he was outside. It's just a question of waiting for the accommodation to become available. There is a waiting list, you see, though your brother is quite high on it.'

'I bet you'll be glad to see him go.'

'For his sake, yes. But I like your brother. He can be a bit aggressive, but he doesn't mean any harm. And he's quite funny. Excuse me.' On the other side of the room a thin man in a Megadeth T-shirt was weeping uncontrollably. He was about forty, with a greying beard and long dark hair which he knotted with his hands. The nurse crouched by the side of his chair. I waited for a few minutes. I wanted to talk to him again, to find out what he meant when he said Mike was *funny*. The man in the T-shirt was too upset for the usual consolations. The nurse led him away, an arm round his shoulder.

I left. There was nothing else I could do.

Ten

Jane eventually got her invitation from Margaret. It came when we were at her flat. Ros was out. I didn't know if she was with Beth and Margaret again or getting something else pierced. I didn't ask. Jane sat cross-legged on the floor, watching *Seinfeld*, which she liked more than she'd admit. When it finished she said, 'It wasn't so good this week.'

It was a few seconds before I realised she meant the sitcom. 'Sorry. I wasn't really watching.'

'Is anything wrong?'

'Nothing really.' I'd been thinking about Mike, or, rather, brooding about Ros's words. *Your current situation is intrinsically unstable, and there are bound to be further upheavals ahead.* Had she been being deliberately vague, or did she know something? 'I was thinking about Ros.'

'She has that effect on men.'

'Not that. The horoscope.'

'Really?' Jane was intrigued. 'I'd like to read it, when you're ready.'

'Maybe.' The horoscope troubled me. I didn't know how Ros had done it and suspected she didn't either. 'It's personal.'

The phone rang. Jane answered. 'Yes,' she said. She looked amused. 'He did say. Yes.' It was a short conversation, ending with, 'See you then.' Jane looked at me in triumph. 'That was Margaret. She's invited me to that dinner on Sunday. I told you she would.'

'Dinner? She told me it was a gathering.'

'With Margaret that means a dinner. She's invited everybody. It's politics. She must have heard about Adam's Indians...' Jane explained that the group had been divided for years, but had somehow managed to drag along, at least until what she called 'the Samhain fiasco'. Samhain was one of the important dates, and they'd planned to celebrate it with a Great Rite – a phrase that made me think of Brian – but Margaret and Adam hadn't been able to agree about the appropriate ceremony. Margaret had wanted a grand celebration with incense and incantations and dressing up. Adam wanted guided meditation and mood music. Samhain came and went, and they were still not so much arguing as failing, always politely, to agree. According to Jane, missing Samhain was like missing Christmas. The group had never recovered and was heading for a split, reformers versus orthodox, a sort of science versus a sort of tradition. Adam and Margaret, she thought, were sounding people out. Jane talked about them like a neutral observer. I assumed this meant she hadn't yet picked a side.

'It'll be interesting to see who turns up,' she said.

'Yeah, but why ask me? I'm not really part of it.'

'She asked everybody. Everybody except Adam. And you are part of it. Ever since Ros did your horoscope. Do you want to go? Daniel's invited as well, so it won't be too stuffy. It could be fun.'

I hesitated. Adam was OK, but Beth and Margaret? A priestess and someone who read cards? Wouldn't that be like having tea with the bishop and an exorcist? And Daniel was OK in a dim, well-meaning way, but I didn't look forward to spending time in his company.

'I'm not sure.'

'It's only one evening. It can't hurt. Besides, I've gone drinking with *your* friends.'

'Tony's not exactly a friend.'

I agreed to go in the end. I'd never had dinner with a priestess before. There was another reason: it gave me an excuse not to stay overnight at my parents'.

On Saturday morning I took the train to the suburb where my parents now lived. Their station was surrounded by streets of little semi-detached houses and low-rise flats. There was *nothing* else, not even a decent park. It was an OK place to live, no fun to visit.

My parents lived in one of the semis. After Mike had been taken in, they had waited for exactly a month before deciding to move – or before telling *me* they'd decided to move. We'd lived until then in a house bought off the council with Mum's savings from her job as a part-time dental receptionist. The house had been a three-bedroom terrace, bright as a button. Mike was taken just after house prices started to get silly. They sold for a ridiculous profit and moved out to the edge of town, buying their new place outright and with enough left over to retire. They didn't look back, not once.

Mum opened the door in her gardening clothes: an old red tracksuit of mine, a fifteenth birthday present I'd outgrown without ever wearing. It was big on her, and faded, and there were black stains on the knees that would never wash out. She glared at me, as if I'd come about the gas and was two days late. 'Your father's upstairs.'

'Yeah?' That was all the greeting I was going to get. 'How are you?'

'I don't change much.' It was hard to tell if she was proud of this, or resented it. 'You should come more often.'

'I'd like to. But there's work…'

She closed the door and followed me into the living room, with its leather suite and shelf unit where photographs of her relatives were packed alongside plastic madonnas and sub-Murillo crucifixions done in three colours. 'So you're still with that company,' she said. 'I don't see how it can take up

145

all your time. You get weekends off, don't you? And it's not even a good job. How far can you get in that line of work? Maureen's son has been promoted again. He's an assistant manager now.'

'Everybody's an assistant manager these days.' I'd never met Maureen's son, I didn't even know his name, but for as long as I could remember he'd been setting the standards I never reached. Good job (either Nationwide or NatWest), nice home (in the same street as his mum), family man (four kids), went to mass, worshipped his mother. Other people's sons were always better, and Maureen's son was the best of the lot. Sometimes I wondered if he really existed, or if he was just an inspirational fiction. 'We deal with people like that all the time.'

'He does have a nice house.' She didn't give up. 'And his wife's expecting again.'

'How many does that make? Six? Seven?' As I looked around the room I already knew what she was going to say next.

'You can laugh, but when are you going to settle down?'

Always the same question. And the same temptation to answer: *I have settled down. This is as settled as I get.* Instead I said, 'And Dad's upstairs?'

She nodded. 'Decorating.'

No surprises there, either. They had the most made-over semi in Kent. After Dad had retired from decorating as a profession he had taken it up as a hobby. He enjoyed the work. If it hadn't been for his back trouble he'd have still been looking for jobs, even though he didn't need the money. So he redecorated at home, moving seamlessly from one little project to the next. Whenever I visited, there was always a room draped in old sheeting or a door you couldn't touch.

They had three bedrooms. Two of them were supposed to be for the guests they never really had, though, as a rule, only one of them was ever available. I found Dad in the smallest one, crouching over an open two-litre tin of emulsion, rose white according to the label. He didn't move. This might have been absent-mindedness, though from where I stood it looked like veneration. I knocked at the door, and noticed it was still tacky. Tiny specks of white came off on my knuckles. He looked up, smiled, and clambered to his feet. 'This is a surprise.'

If Mum had said this, it would have been sarcasm, the only kind of humour she could handle with any confidence. Dad meant it. He really hadn't expected me, which meant he hadn't been told I was coming. Mum was always keeping things back from him, then claiming she'd forgotten because of all her other worries.

'Nice to see you.' He slapped me on the shoulder, then crouched again to put the lid back on the tin. 'What brings you here, then? You staying tonight?'

I told him I had to see some friends for dinner. I wasn't seeing them until the next day, but he didn't have to know that.

'That's a shame. Let me get out of these and we'll go for a pint.'

'It's only ten. They won't be open yet.'

He shook his head. 'Still only that? I must be working quicker than I thought.' He gestured at one of the walls, where, under a scrappy cover of rose white, the original magnolia was still visible.

'Undercoating?'

'That's two coats.' He peered at the wall, as if noticing the unevenness of the tone for the first time. 'Doesn't look finished, though, does it? I'll go over it later.'

The more I looked, the worse it seemed. Even for an undercoat it would have been sloppy. I had to stop myself from volunteering to help. He could be sensitive where his work was concerned. A year before he'd hung some wallpaper in the other bedroom. It was £16-a-roll stuff, with an intricate pattern that needed to be matched just so. He'd hung half the sheets upside down – a fact Mum would remind him of whenever she got tired of reminding him it was her house, bought with her money. Dad took it well. After thirty years he knew what to expect. I didn't want to add to his troubles.

I turned away from the wall. 'You should wear your glasses in this light.'

'It *is* a bit dark.' He stepped out of his overalls. 'But I don't really need them for this, only the reading. Let's go down and have a cuppa.'

Have a cuppa. It was something *his* dad used to say. It was supposed to be funny, a young man like himself using the words of an earlier generation. He said it in an old man's quavering voice, probably copied from his dad. The joke was wearing thin. These days when he said: *You didn't have that sort of thing in my day*, or *Hanging's too good for them*, you couldn't always tell when he was joking.

We went down to the kitchen. From the window we could see Mum pottering about in the back garden, wearing a black leather jacket over the track suit. Beyond the neatly trimmed lawns the flower beds were choked and black with twisted branches. It looked as if a vanload of dead shrubs had been dumped there for burning. Dad plugged in the kettle. 'Gardening at this time of year. I don't know what she thinks she's doing out there.' He wanted to tidy the beds, clear them out properly. He had no sympathy for Mum's ineffectual tinkering. Whenever he looked it was clear he was making plans to uproot the lot and start all over again. Concrete, or gravel. Planning was as far as he was allowed to go; his sphere of influence ended at the edges of the lawn. 'I don't see what difference she makes. I ought to go out there one night and get rid of it. Tell her it must have been foxes...' He smiled at the idea, and pulled himself away from the window. 'So, what brings you back this time?'

'Just to see how you're doing. Find out what's news.'

'There's not much.' He told me anyway: one of his old friends was in hospital. Heart attack. 'Only fifty-three.' He was fifty-one. 'I mean, that's no age at all. And one of your aunts has died.' *One of your aunts* meant someone on Mum's side. I felt like saying, *Another one?* We had lots of aunts and great-aunts, and we only seemed to hear about them when they died. They all lived to incredible ages: ninety-seven, ninety-nine, a hundred. I couldn't imagine living that long, stuck in a home full of addled and pious contemporaries, and neglected by the middle-aged grandchildren who thought you were already dead.

I told him about my job, how safe it was, how easy, how it hadn't changed since my last visit. Then I mentioned Mike. He didn't ask about Mike, but then neither of them ever would. I always had to mention him first, and it had to be done casually, as if it was just another piece of humdrum news. Whenever I visited I planned what I was going to say in advance. That day I'd rehearsed before I left, practising the necessary offhand intonation as I shaved.

As soon as he heard the name he looked out of the window, making sure Mum hadn't overheard. She was at the other end of the garden and the window was closed but he still lowered his voice. 'You can tell me about it in the pub.'

He knew I wouldn't embarrass him by mentioning Mike in front of his friends. 'There's not much to tell. I might as well say it here.' My own voice had sunk to a whisper. 'He seems to be improving. They're talking about letting him out.'

Dad looked out to the garden. Mum knelt at the edge of the lawn, pulling at something heavy or stubbornly rooted. 'The ground's too hard,' he said, then added in his older man's voice, 'She'll just do herself a mischief.' Then, himself again, 'Look, if he does come out, where's he going to stay? He can't stay here, it wouldn't be fair to your mother. And

149

he can't stay with you because it wouldn't be fair to you. They can't let him out.' He already saw what it would be like: Mike crouched in one of the spare bedrooms, interfering with the rhythm of the decorating, embarrassing them in front of visitors, imposing his own awkward silences on mealtimes…

'He wouldn't have to come here, or to me. I've spoken to the doctor. They have special accommodation now, in normal houses. And they have regular visits…' I talked about these houses I hadn't seen as if I was trying to sell him one.

He didn't believe a word. 'If he's let out, he'll end up here. I'll put money on it. And I'd win, for once in my life. We haven't got room for him here. We haven't got the time.'

'He won't end up here. It's not even definite he's going to be allowed to leave. But if he does – '

Mum came in from the garden, announcing, 'I've done enough for the day. I've been working since eight. I see you've given up already. If you were making tea you could have offered me a cup, or don't I matter any more?'

'I'll make you one if you want…'

'No, don't bother.' She stood back while Dad poured her a mug. 'You've done enough for one day. You ought to lie down, build up your energy for when you go to the pub.'

'You can come if you like.'

'I've got better things to do than waste time in pubs.' She accepted the tea from him as if it had been placed in her hands by an impersonal force, one that didn't require thanks or acknowledgement. 'I don't see the attraction of the place.'

'It's just a bit of socialising.' Dad topped up his mug, smiling. 'Got much done?'

She peered into her own mug. 'Bit strong, isn't it? Done where?'

He gestured at the chaos beyond the lawn. 'In the garden.'

'A lot, if you must know.'

'Really?' His tone was perfect. An outsider would have thought he was showing a polite interest. 'Where?'

Mum was about to answer when the penny, visibly, dropped. 'Why do you care? You don't know what to look for.' She barged out of the kitchen, calling as she went, 'You probably wouldn't see it anyway.'

This was Dad's weak spot. He grinned. 'There's nothing wrong with my eyesight. Nothing serious. Have I shown you what I've done to the loft?'

Two hours later we were sitting in his local, drinking. Once out of the house, he became a different man. He chatted to Geoff, the manager, a thin, miserable Welshman. Dad teased him about an incident I didn't begin to understand, eventually drawing out a grudging smile. He was the life and soul of the place. I envied him. The other drinkers, most of them only five or ten years older, referred to him as 'the boy Farrell'. At home this would have sounded ludicrous. At the bar, it fitted. He joked with everybody, even the strangers who came in to ask directions. The other customers laughed. I didn't know most of them, so the hour we spent there was mostly taken up with introductions. *How old are yer? Elding Collections? Never heard of 'em. Great bloke, your dad. Did me kitchen. Reminds me, wanna word with him about one of the doors.* Just as he intended, we never got back round to discussing Mike.

Mum had reheated a stew from earlier in the week. We ate in the usual uncomfortable silence. Mum didn't like people talking while they ate, claiming it wasn't polite, and Dad was subdued, almost guilty, as if his hour in the pub was something he'd suffer for later. When we finished, he collected the dishes and carried them out to the kitchen. Any excuse to get away from the table.

Mum lit a cigarette and leaned back in her chair. 'So then. Why have you come to see us? To what do we owe this pleasure?'

'It's about Mike.'

She glanced at the door to the kitchen. We could hear the sink being filled.

'What about him this time?'

'They're talking about letting him leave.'

'They? They?' She swung forward, resting her elbows on the table. 'Who are *they*, then? What do *they* know about him? He can't be let out. It's impossible. Where is he going to go?'

'It's not definite yet.'

'If they're talking about it, then it's definite. I think it's immoral. They've no right to let him out. Where is he going to go?'

'Accommodation. They have these shared houses...' I repeated what I'd told Dad. I hadn't got very far before I noticed she wasn't listening. It was an old trick she had, one I'd got used to long before I learned it was strange. You could be talking about your day or asking about the garden, and you'd realise she just wasn't there any more. She always denied it afterwards, and if you pressed her she'd insist she had been listening. These abrupt withdrawals of attention had been a regular feature of our childhood. She had shouted at us freely enough when we were young, but never at Dad. Silence had been her favourite weapon against him, and, when we were old enough, against us. You'd think you were having a normal conversation, and suddenly find she'd stopped listening. We called it 'drifting'. 'Where's your mum?' Dad would say, as he came back from work, covered in paint or a layer of dust. 'Drifting,' we'd answer. She was drifting now. She could drift for hours if there was a subject she wanted to avoid. She stared at the kitchen door, as if expecting Mike to walk through at any moment. Mike, the unmentionable.

I went to the kitchen. Dad was wiping the dishes. He read my expression. 'How is she?'

'Drifting. I told her about Mike.'

'You never learn.' There was a radio on the windowsill. He switched it on, catching the end of a country and western song. He didn't like country and western. For reasons I never understood he preferred trad jazz: Bechet and pre-war Armstrong. He left the radio on. On another day he'd have turned it off and made his joke ('What cowboy wrote that, then?'). This time he just wanted something on in the background. 'And did she say anything?'

'No.'

'So why mention it?'

'It might help if you saw him again.'

The song faded out. 'Bloody rubbish.' He meant the song. There was a pause before the news bulletin. 'What good would us seeing him do?'

'I don't know.'

'You know she won't go near the place.'

'You could go.'

'I don't see it would make any difference. They would have asked us, if they thought it would.'

'He hasn't seen you for years.'

'I know that. And do you remember what that was like? He didn't even recognise us.'

'He'd recognise you now.'

'I'm not going there again.' He stacked away the dishes. 'And that's final.'

'And what do I tell him, the next time I see him? The next time he asks me?' This was bluff. Mike had never asked. 'That you won't be coming because you're scared of him? Or do I lie again and tell him you're too busy?'

He closed the cabinet door slowly. Slamming it would have only roused Mum from her dreams of perfect borders and successful, married sons. 'You always bring this up. We're pleased to see you, and then you go and spoil everything.'

'What am I supposed to do? He's family. And I'm the only visitor he gets.'

'And what good does that do? Maybe you should see less of him. You're getting obsessed. It doesn't help anybody. You're just doing your head in.'

'I can't just leave him.'

'It does no good at all.'

'He's changed. There are new treatments now.'

'Changed.' He folded the tea towel and placed it in the washing machine. Even by my standards this was fussy, unless he'd meant to put it in the drawer. 'We saw him for long enough. We lived with him too, remember. If there was anything we thought we could do that might help, we'd do it.'

'Yeah, and as soon as he was out of the house you moved. You stopped visiting – you never really started. You stopped even talking about him.'

'What good does talking do?' He rubbed at his eyes and yawned. I remembered it was time for his nap. 'And we always had you to remind us. Every bloody time.'

He turned off the radio, a sign the conversation was over. We went through to the living room. Mum sat in her chair, holding her *Daily Express* as if it was a prop. Dad stretching out on the sofa gave her a cue.

'That's it. You put your feet up. You've deserved it.'

He ignored the sarcasm. 'Very kind of you to say so.' He closed his eyes.

I sat in a chair facing her. She pretended to read until Dad's low snoring convinced her he was asleep. In a low voice she asked, 'So what were you arguing about?'

'We weren't arguing.'

'The radio was on.'

'Doesn't mean we were arguing.'

'What was it about this time?'

'The usual thing.'

'Why do you always have to come here and start arguments?'

'I don't know.'

'I don't understand you.' She rested the newspaper on her knees. This was usually the sign a big speech was coming. When it came, it was as quiet as before. Dad asleep in the same room meant that neither of us would raise our voices. 'You've had so many chances and you've wasted them. You had a good job with that travel company. You could have gone all over the world. And you gave it up to work for those... debt collectors. You were getting along fine with Deirdre's girl, and then you leave her for that Scottish thing. At least you saw sense about her.'

'That was years ago. And the company collapsed.'

She ignored this. 'You meet a good girl like Susan, and throw it all away because of a girl like that...' Mum had loathed Shona from the first, and still disliked her so much she couldn't bring herself to mention her name. Shona was a girl *we* didn't know, and Protestant to boot, of a dour, Calvinist kind. I could barely remember 'Deirdre's girl'. I'd taken her to the cinema twice when I was fifteen. Mum considered this an engagement. 'It's not even like she was pretty...'

'There's nothing wrong with Shona.'

'She ditched you soon enough.'

'She didn't ditch me.'

'Then why did she go back to wherever it was she came from? What do you call that?'

'I've told you why. It's over, ancient history.'

'You can't accept I was right, can you?'

'Look, she didn't walk out. She wanted me to go with her.'

'So why didn't you, if she's so perfect?'

'Don't bring this up. You know why. Who else would have looked after Mike?'

She picked up the paper, holding it high enough to cover most of her face. 'We did what we could.' She pretended to read, turning the pages swiftly, as if looking for a particular story. Newspapers, housework, gardening, drifting – she always had an excuse for not talking to people. We sat there, the silence broken only by Dad's snores and the tearing sound she made every time she turned a page. When she reached the last one she folded the paper in two and let it fall by the side of the chair. 'He can't come here.'

'Nobody says he has to.'

'You can't trust these people.'

'They seem OK.'

'I don't care what your father says.'

Dad snorted. I wondered if he was only pretending to be asleep, in the way Mum pretended to read, or the way I pretended I wasn't angry. 'He hasn't said anything.'

She picked up the paper again. 'He's not coming here.'

'He won't be coming here. But you could visit him.'

She didn't answer.

'Did you hear me? I said you could at least visit him.'

Again, nothing. I stood up. 'I'm going.'

Now she heard me. 'You're not staying?'

'No. I told you I wasn't'

'I didn't think you would.' She spoke as if this was the final disappointment, the one she'd seen coming for years.

I left her sitting there. She didn't say goodbye or follow me to the door. Another Saturday wasted. I seemed to spend so much time doing things I didn't want to do, or going to places where I wasn't wanted or useful. I came away telling myself it was the last time, that I wasn't going back. I knew that a week later I'd blame myself for having given up so easily, and that a month after that I'd have half convinced myself it would only take one more effort. And then, another month later, I'd be there again, appeasing Mum and being introduced to Dad's drinking friends, and being shocked all over again by the way they ignored Mike. I felt cheated.

After that, Margaret's party could only come as a relief.

Eleven

Before we set off, Jane told me a little more about our hosts. Margaret was the older of the two, the one with the authority. Daniel sometimes called her the Earth Mother Superior. 'She's calm and patient and all that, but you can't help thinking that deep down she pities you.' She was blunter about Beth. 'I've never really liked her.' The way to tell them apart was by their hair: Margaret's was pulled back, severe; Beth looked as if she'd been caught in a storm on her way to a Louise Brooks convention.

They had a flat in a nice block in Tulse Hill. 'Bet you've never been to this one,' Jane said as we were buzzed in. Margaret greeted us as if we were old and trusted friends. Her flat was like a larger version of Jane's room. Jane's friends not only dressed alike, they seemed to furnish their houses from the same shops. Margaret's flat was full of antique-looking clutter, and there were pictures on every wall, mostly of naked women with their arms raised to the moon. There were waist-high statuettes in the corners and wooden amulets hanging from hooks on every door, as well as the usual Christmas decorations. There was even a tree in the main room, hung with lights and pink ribbons, and with a little silver Seal of Solomon on the top. A long table was set with twelve places. I wondered if the number was significant.

I sat facing Jane. There were still two empty chairs. One, Margaret said, was for somebody called Owen, who was expected at any moment. The other was for Ros, who had been invited but was unlikely to come. I recognised some of the other guests from the basement. After some polite nods they went back to talking about their holidays. It seemed harmless enough. And then Beth announced that next year she was going to Russia to investigate Shamanism.

Something about the way she said *investigate* annoyed me. I knew what Shamanism was, sort of. Corinne Hardwick's *The Healing Traditions: Alternative Therapies For Free Women*, which Jane hadn't lent me but which was on her shelves, had a chapter on it. I said, 'What are you hoping to find?' I tried to sound polite.

Beth smiled, as if my question was an idiocy she'd laugh at later. 'Shamanism is an authentic survival of the Old Religion.' Her voice was heavy with condescension. I could see why Jane didn't like her. 'It takes us closer to the Great Mother.'

I must have looked doubtful. Lee, an older man I remembered from the basement, leaned towards me. 'Of course, there'll be some, you know, distortions. Do I mean distortions? But you'd be surprised at how much is, what is it, authentic? The oral tradition is, it's like, it's a lot more, I don't know, it has… more accurate than, than the written. It's more real.'

'Right.' I'd been in houses where you were judged by how you treated the family dog, some treasured old Doberman or stinking terrier. When it pissed on your shoes or went for your throat, did you stroke it, or flinch? I wondered if Lee's conversational openings were a test along the same lines. 'I'm new to a lot of this.' I didn't look at Jane's face. I was certain she was laughing.

'Some people can be very closed-minded,' Beth announced. She had one of those voices. She couldn't just *say* anything: it had to be announced, if not proclaimed, so that everybody in the room could hear. 'And these people – many of them have lived outside of our civilisation for generations…' She talked for a while. I smiled through clenched teeth. 'It's a matter of looking at what different practices have in common. Those will be the most ancient parts. It's really just common sense.'

There was a murmur of agreement from the others. I couldn't help myself. 'Wouldn't that be like looking at cities and deciding the oldest parts were the airports?'

Beth stared at me. Her mouth moved without saying anything.

A blonde woman I recognised from the basement said, 'Beth, have you made any contacts there yet?'

Beth turned to her with relief. 'Agnes is going to send me names. They have a lot of contacts out there. There's so much to be done now the Wall has come down...' They began to talk about people I didn't know. I looked at the furniture again. When they talked about theory I could understand them; Jane's books always seemed to cover the same ground, the same names turning up to prove the same points. If Beth and the blonde woman had talked about Murray, Crowley, Gardiner or Dion Fortune I might have been able to follow them. When they talked about their friends I was lost. Agnes, I gathered, managed some kind of important archive ('They have to be careful,' Beth told us. 'The paper itself has power.') The other guests listened indulgently. Jane studied the tablecloth and occasionally kicked me under the table. I wondered how long the dinner was going to last.

A phone rang in the hallway. Margaret excused herself. She soon returned. 'That was Owen. Says he's not going to be able to make it. Car trouble, apparently.'

'Car trouble?' Beth was scornful. 'Does he really expect us to believe that?'

'I think we should give him the benefit of the doubt,' Margaret was conciliatory. I suspected she spent a lot of time calming Beth down. 'But there's no point waiting any longer. Beth, a hand?'

The two women went to the kitchen. Lee hadn't finished with me yet. 'I was, it was, was listening to what you, to Beth, to what you were, you know, about the cities, saying. I'm not saying you might not have, you know, a point, but it's not, it's not – it's like I didn't, I didn't quite follow.'

'It doesn't matter.'

'I'm not saying that,' he began boldly, then faltered. I waited for him to gather his thoughts. It was like watching a baby preparing to totter across a room for the first time. My heart was in my mouth. 'I'm not criticising you in any way, but I do want to say Beth is, she's an expert on this, this, this, all over the world she's been. The country.'

The effort left him breathless. I shrugged. 'Really? I'm just a beginner myself.'

I hoped that would end it. Lee seemed about to say more, but all he could manage was, 'Here, here comes the soup.'

Beth brought in bowls. Margaret followed with a tureen. The talk stopped for about five minutes.

The blonde woman broke the silence. 'You've got a lovely flat, Margaret.'

'Thank you, Liz.'

'So many lovely things. You must have been collecting for a long time.'

'Since I was a girl. But a lot of them belonged to my mother.'

'Your mother collected?'

'She certainly did. She was one of the earliest to become involved with the great revival in the Thirties and Forties.'

'Margaret is second-generation,' Beth said.

Margaret smiled serenely. 'Born and raised. I was named after the great Margaret Murray, and my father was initiated by Crowley himself.' She looked sternly up and down the table. 'Well, it seems clear how far we can rely on Owen. I must say, I thought when the time came he'd side with Adam.'

Daniel asked, 'How do you know he really doesn't have car trouble?'

'It's too convenient,' Beth proclaimed. 'Besides, he was part of Adam's clique from the beginning. I can see the division being along lines of gender. It's a classic case.'

'Not necessarily.' Lee's face turned bright red, though that could have been from the effort of speech. I noticed a crease like an old operation scar across his right temple. 'It's not, it's unfair to assume, stereotypical... it's not.'

'No, no, no.' Beth smirked, as if she thought this was going to be a walkover. 'It's a clear-cut distinction between sterile analytical thinking and intuitive modes of perception.'

'I think Lee has a point.' Margaret was magnanimous. 'I don't expect everybody here to follow me, and I don't expect them to make the choice because of their chromosomes. I don't know which way Ros will go.'

Jane immediately became more attentive. Seeing her suddenly look up from her bowl revived my own flagging interest.

'She'll be with us, surely.' Beth seemed to think doubt was impossible. 'Adam once told me he didn't think the zodiac mattered.'

'Neither does Ros,' Daniel said. 'Isn't she neo?'

Beth laughed, the same I-know-that-already cluck. 'Adam's problem is that he thinks he's a scientist. And you know what's wrong with science? It doesn't believe in experience.' There was a general murmuring from the other guests. Margaret began to collect the bowls. Lee, still red-faced, stood up and offered to help. Beth hadn't finished. 'They call themselves scientists, and the joke is they're not even scientific. Just because it can't be reproduced in a laboratory they say it doesn't exist. There are so many things you can't reproduce.' She turned to me. 'I mean, can you reproduce love in a laboratory?' I wanted to say *Yes*, just to annoy her, but the question was rhetorical. She turned back to the table, her voice rising with emotion. 'After all, the only evidence we have for that is what they call anecdotal, and according to them that means it can't exist. According to science there's no such thing as love. That's what science means.'

It was a strange, embarrassing outburst. But she recovered. She even smiled happily. 'And that's all Adam is, as far as I'm concerned. A scientist. He's nearly as bad – ' she paused, like a comedian holding back a punch line ' – as Joshua Painter.'

Some people laughed; a few groaned. From the other end of the table Daniel said, 'That's unfair.'

'Who to, to Joshua?' Beth laughed again, surprised by her own wit.

Daniel shook his head. 'You can't compare them.'

There was a crash of china on linoleum from the kitchen, followed by the sound of Lee's flustered apologies.

'Lee!' Beth muttered. 'Do you know what Margaret once called him? She said he was a walking disaster area.' I expected some elaboration, but that turned out to be the whole joke.

Daniel tried to change the subject. 'Does anyone here know the latest on Joshua?'

'I heard he was in care,' a woman said. 'Really?' said another. 'I heard he was working for the council.' Everybody had heard something about Joshua: that he had left London, that he was living in Cornwall or Amsterdam, that he'd gone back to university. That he had found a new medium.

'That's what I heard.' Daniel sounded peevish. I guessed he would follow Adam, if he didn't walk away from both groups. 'Mediums, though. It's so Dark Ages.'

'But the spirits exist.' Beth once again had the facts, or her certainty about the facts. 'Whatever we choose to call them. And I see nothing wrong with attempting to make contact with them.'

'With Joshua it wasn't just contact, though, was it?' Daniel said. 'It was control.'

There was a murmur of disapproval: control was clearly a bad thing. Erin C. Burke, I remembered, had complained about 'misrepresentations of "magic" as a means of control.' Magic wasn't about subjugating the natural world – that was the doctrine of the Judeo-Christian scientific tradition – but of living in harmony with it. 'Your desires will be fulfilled not through coercion or violence but because they coincide with the desires of the world.' I was uncomfortable with this doctrine: it sounded too much like put up and shut up. I'd seen what the natural world wanted for Mike and thought it needed all the coercion it could get.

But Beth was bored with Joshua. She wanted to talk about herself. 'Of course, I've had my own experience of precognition.'

'We all have,' Jane said, her tone meaning: *shut up*.

Liz was more diplomatic: 'Perhaps we can share them after we've eaten.'

Beth didn't take the hint. 'It was about five years ago,' she began, as if it was going to be a long story. She was stopped by the return of Lee, carrying an armful of plates, followed by Margaret with a trolley. On the trolley was what I first took to be a large black stockpot with some fancy patterns on the side. The others laughed when they saw it. Then I realised: Margaret had prepared the main course *in a cauldron*. She acknowledged the applause.

'Nothing if not practical. You'd be surprised how useful it is when cooking for large numbers.' Lee dealt the plates, Margaret served. A stew. Out of politeness, or possibly caution, Jane asked what it was. Margaret smiled. 'Eye of toad, wing of bat.'

Whatever it was, it kept Beth quiet for a few minutes. While we ate, Margaret did most of the talking. 'On this question of gender. We can make general assumptions about female and male attitudes, but we must beware of accepting stereotypes created by a patriarchal society…'

I stopped listening, and settled down to watch Jane eat. This always amused me. Finesse, delicacy, discrimination –

these had no place in her life when she ate. She ate to beat the clock. Anything placed in front of her was pawed into her mouth and swallowed with the absolute minimum of chewing. She ate carelessly, messily. I liked this about her. I would have hated her to be as finicky as her sister. And, despite the way she dressed and the things she claimed to believe, I didn't think she was like the other women at the table.

My thoughts had wandered some distance when Margaret suddenly asked me, 'You agree, don't you?'

I didn't know what she was talking about. 'Agree with what?'

'About the projection. You'll help us, won't you?'

'Projection?' I guessed they weren't talking about a film show. I also wondered if this wasn't the point of the evening. They hadn't invited me just because I was Jane's friend. 'What sort of help?'

And then, before Margaret could explain, Ros arrived.

She walked in like someone bringing urgent news, then dropped into the empty chair next to Jane without saying anything. There were no new rings on her face, though she'd added chains linking the ones already there, three from each ear, to her eyebrows, nose, and lips. It looked like some improvised procedure to hold her face together until the proper treatment was available. There was no slack on any of the chains. Any tighter, you thought, and they would have torn her skin. Her hair was like worn felt, and her eyes were ringed with black. Jane leaned in. 'Are you OK?'

Ros didn't answer. Nobody else said anything to her, almost as if they weren't sure it was really her.

'Well,' Beth said brightly, 'as I was saying, it was about five years ago…' If she had noticed the change in the mood of the room, she wasn't going to let it stop her telling her story. It was a feeble story, too: how she had come across this letter from an old and forgotten friend while clearing out some papers, then, later that same day…

'And do you know what she told me?' Beth concluded triumphantly. 'She said that only that very morning she'd found an old letter from me. And do you know what was written on that letter?'

Ros had heard enough. 'That you hoped to see her soon? Come on, Beth, that's only coincidence. It doesn't *prove* anything.' Her voice was higher than normal, and dry, as if she'd crossed a desert to be there.

Beth was surprised. 'I think it does.'

'But it's not precognition. It's not anything like precognition.' Ros's face was expressionless. 'That's the kind of story that gives us a bad name. It's *idiotic*.'

Beth looked to the rest of us for support. It was plain she felt she hadn't done anything to deserve this. Jane had trouble hiding her smile. Ros went on, talking now to the whole table, 'We're tolerant, but we can't believe in *everything*. We have to draw the line *somewhere*. Foretelling the future is one place to do it. It can't be done.'

There was a gasp of surprise at this. Liz said, 'But you're an astrologer. You look into the future.'

Ros clenched her teeth. The chains from her lip shifted slightly. You could still tell she had once been pretty, but she had gone beyond that now. 'I do not *look* into the future.' Her voice was hard, angry. 'Nobody can *look* into the future. I make reasoned assumptions based on what I *know*. It's *impossible* to look into the future and *anybody* who thinks they can is fooling themselves.'

There was another gasp. Even Daniel and the unflappable Margaret looked surprised. Beth found her voice first. She was always going to find her voice first. 'What about Cindy de Souza?'

'Cindy de Souza is an idiot.' More gasps. It was hard to tell if Ros was enjoying the effects of her intransigence. She didn't sound amused. 'She's not even a real astrologer. She uses a tarot pack.'

'But what's wrong with that? The cards are traditional.'

'No, they're not. They're playing cards. That's all they ever were. She might as well use Happy Families.'

Beth was still the only one who dared say anything. 'They have centuries of tradition...'

'Oh, grow up, Beth!' Ros snapped back. Jane kicked me under the table again. I must have been grinning. 'That tradition was made up, the way most of your traditions were. The whole mystical tarot business is crap. It's as bad as reading tea leaves.'

'My mother reads tea leaves,' Liz said brightly.

Ros glared at her. 'Really?'

Liz backed down. 'I never thought there was much in it.'

'There isn't. How can there be?' Ros turned back to Beth, who was at last speechless. She had, as Brian would say, nothing left. Following a good fighter's instinct, Ros pressed on. 'As for Cindy de Souza, she's a fraud. She's still touting that zodiac crap. And then she uses tarot cards. If she had half a brain she'd use one or the other. You can't use both.'

Margaret stopped the contest. 'I think you're being very harsh, Ros. And I don't see why you can't use both.'

Ros made an effort to calm down. 'Because they are based on different principles. Astrology is a scientific discipline dealing strictly with cause and effect. At least, that's what it's *meant* to be. Otherwise it's no more than guesswork and promises. The zodiac is rubbish. As for people like Cindy de Souza – she might as well be writing for the tabloids. And the tarot is garbage, along with palmistry, the I Ching, casting runes – ' at each one of these somebody winced ' – *anything* that claims to foretell the future. It's garbage. You might as well spin a roulette wheel.'

Margaret nodded slowly. 'I think that that,' she said with the careful emphasis of someone used to having the last word, 'is a rather narrow outlook.'

Ros's tiny hands were clenched on the table, their knuckles white. Her voice cracked. 'Divination by chance. Do you know what that assumes?' She looked at me the way a teacher looks at a favourite pupil, the one who can usually be relied on to know the answer. I didn't say anything. 'It assumes that the future is fixed,' she said, more quietly, still looking at me. 'Otherwise how could you foresee it? How can you see something unless it already exists? And it isn't fixed. So many things depend on chance.' Her voice dropped almost to a whisper. 'So many things depend on choices other people haven't made yet. Choices they don't know how to make.' She turned back to Beth. 'Relying on chance is *stupid*. And, if it wasn't, then astrology would be false. You can't have both.'

Margaret intervened. 'I think we should keep an open mind. I don't think we can dismiss these things out of hand.'

'Margaret.' Ros stood up. 'It isn't a question of keeping an open mind. It's a question of right and wrong. You can't see into the future because the future hasn't happened yet. People who say they can are lying. If it were possible – ' she shuddered ' – life would be horrible. It would mean we had no choice. All we can do is use astrology to make sense of it. That's all.' She stepped back from the table and turned to Margaret. 'I'm sorry. I have to go.' She touched Jane on the shoulder, nodded at me, and left. Nobody said anything until the street door closed.

'Well, that was unexpected.' Beth sat back, pleased with herself. She seemed to think she'd won the argument. '*Somebody's* had a bad day.'

Jane stood. 'I'd better see if she's all right.'

I stood up as well. Margaret followed us to the door. 'I'm sure she'll be fine.' She implied we were wrong to waste time on such a fruitcake. 'You really ought to stay. There are so many things we need to discuss.'

'Later, maybe.'

Margaret didn't give up. 'Please don't think it's always like this, Patrick. We're usually much more balanced. Ros is very clever, but she can be disruptive sometimes. I wouldn't want you to have the wrong impression.'

Jane answered for me, 'We'd better go. She might be unwell.'

On the street I asked, 'Unwell?'

'She might not have eaten lately. She doesn't eat for days sometimes. She can get a bit irrational then.'

'If she doesn't eat, she's irrational already.' I'd assumed anorexia was a teenage thing, something Ros had outgrown. I thought of the girl Dr Cortevalde had mentioned, the one who ate glass... 'Anyway, she sounded more rational than anybody back there.'

'Ros isn't like them. But she's not always rational herself.'

'You mean she might flash her piercings at some other mug?'

'You're the only one she's ever done that to. I don't know why she did it.'

'Maybe she hadn't been eating.'

'It's not funny. There she is.'

Ros was leaning against a little green Škoda. She stood as if she'd been about to open the door before succumbing to exhaustion. Jane put an arm around her shoulder.

'Ros, are you all right?'

Ros looked at her blankly. She was crying, the black stuff under her eyes streaking her face. Jane took the car keys, guided her into the back seat, then got in beside her. She handed me the keys. 'You'd better drive.'

All the way back, she said only one word, 'Thanks.' The rest of the time, not even a sniffle.

When we reached the flat Jane said, 'She's asleep.'

'So? Wake her up. She's not a baby.'

Jane shook her gently. 'Ros.'

Nothing. Jane tried again. Nothing.

'Shit, she's passed out.'

I got out of the car, pushed down the front seat. 'Go and open the door. I'll carry her in.' Jane got out. I leaned across and picked up Ros. She was light, much lighter than I'd expected. She felt empty, as if there was nothing under her skin. I stood there, on the pavement, amazed. 'She must have hollow bones.'

Jane was impatient. 'What did you expect? I told you she doesn't eat. Take her through to her room.'

There were no surprises about her room. A single bed, more like a child's, a wardrobe, a chest of drawers. Her room was as anonymous as a hotel, missing only the fire regulations taped to the door. I put her down on the bed. Even unconscious she had a pained expression. With the mess she'd made of her face she looked like an accident victim, a tragic and ludicrous casualty.

'Does she pass out often?'

'Not often. Only when there's somebody to catch her.'

'You mean she does this for attention?'

'When she's sure she's got it, anyway. Come on.'

'We have to be sure she's all right.'

'She is, now.'

'Are you just going to let her sleep?'

'She's OK. It's exhaustion. She doesn't eat enough; she goes without sleep.'

I leaned over closer. Her breathing was faint, and her expression had gradually softened; the anxious twist of her dark pierced lips had begun to relax. 'Should we take these chains off?'

Jane shrugged. 'If you like.'

'She might twist in her sleep. These rings.' The chains came off easily enough. They were surprisingly heavy for such slight things. She didn't stir as I unclasped them. I would have liked to take the rings out as well, if only to remind myself how her face had once looked, but that was a job that needed more delicacy than I could manage. Then I would have washed away the ruined make-up...

'That's enough,' Jane said softly. 'Unless you want to loosen her clothing as well.'

'It's loose enough.'

'Come on, then, and let her sleep. The last thing she needs is to wake up and see you standing over her.'

I gestured at the room. 'We've more in common than you think.'

'Don't you believe it. Ros doesn't have anything in common with anyone.'

Twelve

Jane phoned me the next day to tell me Ros was feeling better. She'd eaten some soup and a piece of celery and thanked us for driving her home. Soup and a piece of celery! In an earlier age she would have been a saint, one of those desert holies canonised for the rigours of their self-denial, like Rosa of Lima or Elizabeth of Hungary: the sort who are heard mumbling prayers in the womb, refuse their mother's breast at two months, flagellate themselves through childhood, and then turn their backs forever on their wealthy families – because this kind of saint always has a wealthy family; there's no point embracing poverty otherwise. It was easy to imagine Ros leading that life: living on rotten vegetables, sleeping in a ditch, cutting her arms and bathing the wounds in milk, all to the respectful applause of a bishop who knew the tourist value of a full set of relics. She should have lived then, when an eating disorder was recognised as a vocation. These days her sort has a harder time. Ros could starve and pierce herself to blazes, but it wasn't the stigmata, the authorities wouldn't care, and if she had visions of angels they'd only recommend a course of antipsychotics, the way they had for Peter Bedding. Poor Ros.

Meanwhile Elding Collections received a recovery request marked 'Urgent'. A subject had been cashing cheques in different branches and had run up a two-thousand-pound debt in three days. The card belonged to a Mr Kevin Taylor and hadn't been reported stolen, so it was probably their customer, on a spree. For some reason, I didn't think it was the Kevin Taylor I knew. He didn't have the nous for systematic fraud. And then I thought, Of course, *that's* what he was doing so far from his usual streets – *that* old scam. *That's* why he was so keen to get away when he saw me. And of course Kevin hadn't dreamed this up himself: Joshua had probably worked out the details and told him what to do and kept most of the money. The request went straight to the top of my list.

Brian offered to go in first. 'If this Painter bloke knows you, he might cause trouble.'

'He won't. He's all talk.'

I went alone. I wouldn't even let Brian drive me there. I wanted to see the look on Joshua's face when he opened the door.

It was another tenement divided into flats. Disappointingly, the door was opened by a pale, red-haired girl with a ring through her right nostril. She grinned up at me as if she knew me from somewhere.

'Can I help?' West Country accent.

'I'm looking for Kevin Taylor.'

'You'd better come in.'

She didn't ask to see any ID, and didn't seem to care what I wanted. She was clearly the kind of neighbour who would tell you the worst.

'A Mr Painter lives here as well, doesn't he?'

'If you can call it living. He's out now, though.'

'Shame.'

She led me up the dark stairs (no window, no lighting) and into the flat. A worn brown carpet in the hallway, a stack of newspapers serving as a telephone stand. She knocked on one of the doors. 'Kev.' There was no answer. She looked at me as if to say, *See what I have to put up with?* 'He's in there.'

The door opened slowly. Kevin peered out, blinking nervously, like a small nocturnal creature with a lot of natural

172

enemies. 'Hello, Patrick.' The room behind him was as dark as a cupboard.

The girl went through to the kitchen. 'Want some coffee?' I could see unwashed plates on the floor, next to discarded burger cartons and a litter tray. I refused.

'It's business this time, Kevin.' I spoke softly, so the girl wouldn't hear. 'Can I come in?'

Kevin stepped back from the door. He slumped on to his low bed. The ragged curtain had been drawn and the wall behind the bed was black. The room was too dark to be sure of much else.

'Can I put the light on?'

He made a noise I interpreted as 'Yes.' The forty-watt bulb threw most of the room into shadow. I noticed the smell of incense. Kevin sat on the bed, elbows on his knees, blinking. 'Haven't seen you for a while, Patrick.'

'Five days.'

'No, longer than that, yeah.'

'It was five days ago.'

He didn't argue. He just sat there blinking, even after his eyes should have adjusted to the light.

I said, 'I'm with Elding Collections.'

He looked up at me blankly, waiting for me to say more. The name meant nothing to him. Ros had looked more thoughtful when she was unconscious.

'You should have had a letter.'

'Haven't had a letter.'

I reached up to the shelf above the bed. 'So what are these?' Four envelopes, all from the bank that employed me. 'You haven't opened them.'

He shook his head. 'Not mine.'

Of course. Today he was Jerry. That was why he'd been left at home. I said, 'Then Kevin should have opened them.'

'Kevin's out.'

I put the letters back. 'Where's Joshua?'

He gulped. 'With Kevin.'

For a moment I could almost believe him: Joshua and Kevin, the odd couple, marching briskly towards their next scam, Joshua complaining, Kevin apologetic and out of breath. I dismissed the image.

'Did Kevin leave his card behind?'

'No.'

'Mind if I look?' I kicked aside the discarded socks and chocolate wrappers. Dust, a few splashes of black paint. A notepad left open at a doodle.

Kevin put his hands up to his head. 'Not mine.'

'It's not Kevin's either.' I went on moving things. 'That card belongs to the people I work for.'

'It's with him.'

'No, it isn't.' There was a black plastic wallet lying half under a grey trainer. The card was in it, along with four others, including one for the bank I'd seen him leaving. I held them in front of Kevin's face. 'Did Joshua get these for you?'

'Mr K. Taylor.' He read his name from them, miserably, as if it was a test he expected to fail.

There was something else in the wallet: a wad of the back pages from cheque books, the ones cashiers were supposed to mark when you cashed a cheque. That was how the fraud worked, back then. All you had to do after drawing money was take out the marked page, tip in a clean one, and go to the next branch. The cashier would turn to the back page of the book: if it was clean and the cheque card wasn't on a list they would hand over £50. They'd mark the page. You'd leave, take that page out, put in another clean one, and off to the next stop. It didn't matter if there was nothing in the account because they couldn't check the balance (networks were different then). Besides, it was only £50, which wasn't going to sound any alarms, and, if you used it when there was a queue, they'd be even less attentive to detail. Usually it was done with stolen books and cards and Elding Collections wouldn't be involved, but sometimes people used their own accounts and then we'd get a letter. The subject might have lost their job and decided to grab what money they could, or they might have been deliberate fraudsters who'd spent a few weeks seeding their innocent-looking account with cash from their last scam. If they were fraudsters they'd have to disappear afterwards, but they'd have a few thousand in cash, and, when that ran out, they could start all over again. Or, if they were Joshua, persuade somebody else to start for them. As criminal activity went it wasn't exactly Colombian drug cartels, but it still required too much organisation for Kevin. I didn't think Joshua had produced the fake pages himself, but he was probably smart enough to know where to get them.

I took all the pages, and the card I was supposed to collect. Kevin watched me, alarmed.

'You can't take those. They're Joshua's.'

'Well, he shouldn't have them.' I flicked through them. They were printed on coarse paper, but they looked good enough to pass for real if you were in a hurry. 'I'm going to give these to the police.'

'Joshua said – '

'Forget what he said. Do you know where he got these?'

Kevin looked at the floor. 'Doesn't tell me.'

That was plausible. I wondered how Joshua had reacted when he'd found out about Jerry, assuming he'd noticed.

'When Joshua comes back, tell him I took these.'

Kevin shook his head. He was frightened. I felt sorry for him. How bad did you have to be to feel frightened of someone like Joshua?

I gave the pages to the police. They joked about major crime syndicates and said they'd pay Mr Painter a visit. Back at the office I phoned the banks where Kevin had opened accounts.

It was part of the scam. You took a few hundred pounds and moved it from one account to another to make it look as though there was regular money in all of them. Then, once they decided you were an ordinary customer and gave you a cheque card, you went on your spree.

The banks hadn't noticed anything wrong. 'The account seems to be operating normally.'

'Has he been paying in cash?'

A long pause, then, 'I'm not allowed to give out that information. But thanks for drawing this to our attention.'

I was triumphant. My only regret was that I wouldn't see Joshua's face when the police called.

Tony, in the office to make some calls himself, was envious. 'Jammy bastard. All I've got is a few weepy pissheads.'

Piers disapproved. 'It's very civic-minded, Patrick, but it's not what we're actually paying you for. And it seems to have taken most of your morning.'

'It's good for business, Piers.' I was elated for the rest of the day, and had to stop myself from smiling at the subjects. We were supposed to be discreet and professional. We weren't supposed to enjoy ourselves. When I went back to the office Piers told me the police had left a message: they'd called at the address I'd given. Mr Painter and Mr Taylor had already gone. I thought that was the last I'd hear of them.

I had another invitation from Adam, this time to a Thai restaurant. There were 'still a few things I want to discuss'. When I went to the flat to collect Jane, Ros opened the door. She looked gaunt, but healthier than she had at Margaret's dinner. 'Jane's going to be late,' she announced. Her rings were still in place, that night without the connecting chains. 'She's had another deadline brought forward.'

She led me through to the living room, which was as spotless as before, and more or less pushed me into a chair. 'She'll be about half an hour. Coffee?'

'Er – thanks.' I was surprised, as much by her friendliness as the offer of coffee. 'If it's no trouble.'

'I was about to make some for myself.' Her voice had a light quality I'd never noticed before. 'It's no trouble.' She wandered in to the kitchen and came back almost immediately with a cafetiere and some mugs. 'The kettle had just boiled.'

'I didn't think you drank coffee.'

'For a long time I didn't.' She stood so close to me that our knees touched. 'But that was just a prejudice. Sometimes you can dislike something on principle, and it's a mistake.' Her tone – the expression on her face, even the way she stood – was scarily flirtatious. She stepped back, just enough to put the tray down on a low table. 'I thought it was an artificial stimulant, and it was supposed to be bad for stress. But then I thought maybe stimulants were what I needed. And stress can be quite creative.' She lowered herself on to the arm of the chair and leaned against me, her hand resting on my shoulder.

'Ros,' I said, or maybe, 'Ros?'

She slid on to my lap, squirming as she turned to press her face against mine. 'Jane won't be here for at least twenty minutes,' she said, and put her hand on my crotch.

'Twenty minutes?' I pushed her away as gently as I could. She weighed almost nothing. 'Ros, you're so romantic.'

She grinned. 'Come on, it won't matter.'

'Ros…'

She pulled herself away and stood up. 'Coffee's nearly ready.' Her tone had changed again: friendly and remote, as if nothing had happened. I was relieved and faintly disappointed. She depressed the plunger on the cafetiere and poured the coffee into the mugs. 'Hope this is strong enough for you.' She moved to the chair opposite and watched as I drank. The coffee was bitter, stronger than I'd have made it myself.

'Has Margaret said anything about Candlemas?'

'She mentioned a projection.'

'Will you take part?'

'I don't know. I don't know what a projection is.'

'It's the word we use.' Her voice was distant, impersonal, as if translating a message from somebody in another room. 'For what we want to do. Margaret has projections. Adam has them. Jane, even. It's just a word. We mean different things. This – ' she touched her face ' – is my project. My projection.'

'And Margaret's?'

'It's nothing to be scared of.' She pressed her hand against her jaw as if it ached. 'I think you should say yes. You don't know what you are.'

'I've got a good idea.'

'The horoscope – ' she began, and I thought she was going to tell me something new when we heard the front door open. 'Jane's early,' she said, blankly.

Five minutes later I was on my way to a Thai restaurant.

'Some of the sacred sites – the Temple of Dawn, say, or the Little Tiger Cave...' We hadn't yet looked at the menu and Adam, ponytailed again, was already in full flight. He'd got as far as the significance of the sites of East London churches before he remembered why he'd invited us. 'I wanted to ask you about Margaret's dinner.'

'Can't tell you,' I said. 'I left early.'

Daniel brushed hair from his eyes. 'Same here.'

'But what happened? Jane?'

Jane gave a brief account of events. She ended with, 'Beth *really* doesn't like you.'

'I knew that already.' Adam shook his head in wonder. He made such an effort to like other people. How could they not like him? 'It's a shame, a real shame. Margaret is such a positive person...'

'But you disagree about so much.' Daniel looked at Adam with something close to pity. 'You'll never be able to work together. Forget them, move on.'

Adam wasn't prepared to give up so easily. 'If magic is about anything, it's about reconciliation and healing. It must be able to contain contrarieties. We don't want to go down the Christian route of schism. We can't afford to be dogmatic.'

'But we can be sensible,' Jane said. 'Besides, I thought you wanted to get rid of Margaret.'

'It was wrong of me, I see it now. Though *get rid of* really isn't how I'd put it. I should have worked harder at settling our differences.' Adam seemed pained at the trouble he'd caused. 'Our *apparent* differences, I should say. Too much of Western thinking is based on opposition. It's the legacy of Manichaeism.' He looked at me for support. 'Even scientists are starting to talk about the value of fuzzy logic. What appears to be a contradiction can be an affirmation. Perhaps if Beth is going to be out of the country I could approach Margaret again...'

'"Apparent differences"?' Jane was scornful. 'Adam, you disagreed about everything. From the beginning.'

'Come on, Adam.' Daniel tried to lighten the mood. 'You'll be telling us you want Joshua back next.'

Adam nodded. 'If he changed, I might.'

Jane almost spat out her wine. 'You've *got* to be joking.'

'In principle. If he *really* changed.'

I had to ask. 'What was he like?'

'Joshua?' Adam glanced at Daniel. 'He was a disappointment.'

'But what did he do?'

Adam looked around the restaurant, as if he expected Joshua to suddenly appear, possibly disguised as a waiter. He lowered his voice. 'It's all ancient history now. Joshua was – well, he was too extreme for us. He was clever, and he had some fascinating ideas regarding sacred sites around South

London. You know, how places are supposed to be haunted because something bad happened in them?' Adam began to cheer up. He was happier with theory than gossip. 'Well, Joshua thought people had this all backwards. He thought there were places that caused bad things to happen. The spectral activity – what people think of as ghosts – was there first – an emanation, you could say, of this negative energy. I thought this was an interesting theory, but Joshua couldn't leave it at that. He was just too extreme.' I had the feeling this was as much as Adam was going to tell me. 'It's a shame. He had some good ideas.'

'I came across him recently. Through work.'

'That doesn't surprise me.' Daniel seemed heartened. 'I never trusted him.'

'He had some good points. And he's gone now. There's no need for us to be negative.' Adam clearly wanted it to be the last word. 'Is Ros OK?'

No, I felt like saying. *She's not OK.* I thought it was best not to say anything.

'She's fine.' Jane was guarded. 'You know Ros. Are we going to order, or what?'

We ordered. Adam told us some more about sacred sites in Thailand. He planned to go, next year, or the year after. Somehow this turned into general chat about holidays. It wasn't until we were on the main course that Adam said, 'To go back to Ros. I think she may have found the key to heal the rift.'

Jane was so surprised she almost dropped her fork. 'Ros? I'm sorry, Adam, but I don't see her as a unifying force.'

'Not Ros personally.' Adam turned to me. So far, I was the only one who hadn't disagreed with him. 'Listen, Candlemas is coming quite soon. I want us, the group, to take advantage of that. Would you like to help?'

'Me?' First Margaret, now Adam. I wondered what they meant by *help*. 'How could I? I don't know anything.'

'What's got into you, Adam?' Jane was amused. 'You've been arguing for months about the need to break away, and now you want to unify everybody again. And Patrick's right. He doesn't know a thing. Besides, Candlemas is months away. We've got to get through Yule first.'

'Candlemas is more significant. The energies of Yule have been leached away by that *other festival*.' There was something comic about his refusal to mention Christmas. Adam, though, wasn't trying to be funny. 'I think we should be planning for Candlemas early.'

'After what happened at Samhain...' Daniel nodded. 'What did you have in mind?'

'I haven't decided yet.' Adam had his faraway look again. 'But I want it to mean something. I want it to bring people together.'

There was a few seconds silence. Then Jane said, 'You're beginning to sound like *Thought for the Day*.'

'I know, but...' Adam's sincerity was painful – to everybody else. He wasn't the leader because he was charismatic or resourceful; he was in charge because he was surrounded by decent people who didn't want to hurt his feelings. When he asked if I could help he was almost quivering with vulnerable friendliness. 'I really think your input could be helpful.'

'Really?' My input. What was the phrase Jane used? *Garbage in, garbage out*. 'What would I have to do?'

'There are details we still have to finalise. But it would be nothing too onerous. Have you ever tried meditation?'

'Once.' Years ago, with Shona. We'd sit cross-legged on the living-room floor and try to empty our minds. After five minutes we'd have to turn on the television. 'I'm not sure I'm the person you need.'

'I think you underrate yourself. Candlemas is one of the most powerful days. One of the things I hope to prove is that what we do is for ordinary people. Not – ' he corrected himself quickly ' – that I think you're ordinary. My point is that it won't require specialist training, or even any particular skill. You just have to approach these things with the right attitude…'

'It won't last, you know,' Jane said, on the way back to my flat. Jane was spending more and more time there. Thanks to Ros, her own place was becoming uncomfortable. 'Adam might be all over you now but it won't last. He's like that. You're his latest enthusiasm. And do you really think you have the right attitude?'

'Probably not.'

'But you'd help him if he asked?'

I suspected I'd give in eventually. Because I didn't want to hurt Adam's feelings. 'As long as there's no nudity or animal sacrifice.'

'With Adam?' She laughed. 'That would take too much planning.'

I hadn't seen the last of Kevin Taylor. A few nights after the Thai restaurant Brian invited me to a card game in the sticks with a few of his old sparring partners. Jane was busy again, and Brian had sworn Sue wouldn't be there, so I went. I soon wished I hadn't. Brian's friends drank heavily, were serious about cards, and told stories I was fairly sure were not true. *He was on the ropes, and that bloody ref stopped it. Low blow? It was never a low blow.* Once I might have enjoyed that kind of talk. I might even have made up some stories of my own. But that night I felt out of place. I belonged with a different crowd now. I told myself I'd leave as soon as I was fifty pounds down, and did. By then it was after midnight. Brian wanted to stay. He had status in this group, and was drunk enough to think he was doing well. He let me have his car keys, saying he'd make his own way back. I drove away thinking that kind of evening was something I'd never do again.

I was three turnings away from home when a man ran into the road in front of me. I braked sharply, grateful there was nothing following. I didn't want to put a dent in Brian's car. The man staggered back on to the pavement, oblivious, veering from side to side as he went. Another stupid drunk, I thought, though this one walked faster than most stupid drunks.

Then I recognised the coat. There was no mistaking those rags.

I reversed up the street until I was level with him. 'Kevin.'

He stopped for long enough to look straight at me. There were black lines down one side of his face that made me think of hair-dye. He was out of breath.

'Kevin, are you all right?'

Stupid question. He turned away and carried on down the street. I realised he hadn't recognised me. I could have driven on and left him. Afterwards I wished I had.

I parked the car. It was easier to follow him on foot. He zigzagged on, not looking back. He was wearing his old clothes and back on his old streets. I guessed that Joshua, for all his talk about fellow human beings, had disappeared, leaving him with just enough money to get stewed. 'Kevin,' I called again. 'It's Patrick.'

This stopped him. He looked around, as if not certain where the voice came from. He shook his head and went on walking. I tried calling, 'Jerry.' No effect.

I overtook him. I stood right in front of him under a street lamp so he could see me clearly. Close to, he looked worse. The streaks of black weren't dirt or shadow: the side of his head was cut, probably where he'd fallen or walked into a wall.

He tried to walk straight through me, as if I wasn't there. The impact almost took me off my feet. Kevin realised he'd come into contact with something solid and alive. He panicked, flailing his arms and tripping over his feet as he backed away. 'Relax,' I said, or, 'Don't worry,' or,

'Calm down.' Kevin groped along the wall, hissing through clenched teeth. He moved like a blind man, or someone who didn't trust what he saw. He didn't relax or calm down or stop worrying. He was out where words couldn't reach him.

That was the second moment when I could have left him. After all, what could I do to help? I didn't know how to restrain him. And, even if I did, what would I do next? I can block and punch as well as the next man, but I'm not subtle: my arm-locks, when I can be bothered with them, are meant to hurt. All I could do was follow him and try to stop him hurting himself while I looked out for a police car.

Kevin set off again. He seemed to know where he was going. We turned another corner. He bounced between walls and parked cars, stumbling and gasping. It reminded me of when you come home drunk and think you can find your way around the house in the dark. And these streets had been Kevin's home for months. He knew them the way I knew my kitchen or bathroom.

We came to the wooden gate that led to the road behind the shops, a dirt track with a few lock-ups and rubbish bins. It was closed. Kevin put his shoulder to it and pushed. The hinges creaked and squealed, and it opened. Of course. If the streets were his home, this was his bedroom. He headed for one of the lock-ups and tugged at the handle of the rusting door. He'd told me before that one was left open for him – charity by one of the shopkeepers. If this was the one, I told myself, everything would be all right. If he'd only go in and lie down, everything would be all right. I could go home and forget him.

It was locked. Kevin pulled and twisted at the handle. There was no movement. He whimpered. I stepped up to him. 'Let me have a go.'

Before I could even try he threw himself at me. I wasn't ready for the suddenness of the attack, or its strength, and landed noisily between two half-filled dustbins, knocking one of them over. My right elbow felt hot and wet, but the embarrassment was worse than the pain. To have been knocked down at all was bad enough; to have been knocked down by *Kevin Taylor*...

Kevin hardly seemed aware of what he'd done. He looked hard at the dark metal door, lowered his head, and charged. The crash of his head against the door was followed by a howl. He staggered backwards and steadied himself for another attempt. This time I caught him before he reached the door. He struggled more violently than I would have believed. His arms were slippery with sweat and mud, and he tried to twist his way free, his muscles tense, his thin elbows jabbing into my ribs and chest. It was a mismatch. I was stronger, but, while I was trying not to hurt him, he lashed out in all directions. After a few seconds he managed to throw me off again. This time I didn't hit the dustbins. Skidding on the churned mud at the entrance, I went through the gate and out on to the pavement. He reached the garage door again before I could stop him. This time he made less noise, and fell to his knees, his head resting against the door.

This was my best chance. I hooked my arms under his and tried to drag him away. He kicked, feebly at first, digging his heels into the mud. I lost my balance. The rest was a confused, sliding tussle. We scrabbled on, until suddenly the yard filled with light and we were pulled apart. The police.

It could have gone badly for me. At first it was bad enough. In the glare of their headlights we both looked terrible. Kevin was covered with mud and his face was bloody, and by then I looked no better. At first they treated us with equal contempt. Then two things happened: Kevin went on struggling, and one of cops recognised me.

'You're the bloke from Elding?' It was the officer who'd taken Joshua's forged pages and joked about major crime syndicates. I almost cried with relief. 'Are you all right? What's going on?'

I didn't have a chance to explain. Kevin broke free of the other man's grip and ran straight at the garage door. They stopped him just in time and pulled him out on to the street. I gabbled something about him being disturbed and needing a hospital. They wanted to take us both to the station first; they'd get a doctor to look at him there. I was too exhausted to argue. Kevin, pressed against the wall, still struggled on, but feebly, without conviction. Another fight he couldn't win. Eventually he quietened enough to be forced into the car.

We headed for the station. I sat next to the driver while his partner held Kevin down on the back seat. I told them how I knew Kevin and what I'd seen that night. The one in the back joked that this could look like police brutality. Kevin stopped struggling. I began to calm down; there was some scrappy conversation. Work still heavy? Found any more fraudsters? So you'd been to a card game? Any good?

The bloke in the back said, 'Fuck, he's passed out.'

'Hospital, then.' Siren howling and lights blazing, we roared through the quiet streets like the worst news imaginable. We reached the hospital inside five minutes. There was a trolley waiting for us. I stayed in the car as the bloke in the back repeated, 'Fuck, this looks bad, this looks fucking bad,' over and over again.

Kevin was wheeled in. We followed him as far as the emergency bay, then waited, along with the drink victims and domestic accidents. The one who'd recognised me explained the situation to a doctor. I was too far away to hear. He came back to us, frowning.

I couldn't bear it. 'Now what?'

'You go home. There's nothing else you can do.'

His colleague had other concerns. 'We'll need a statement.'

'We'll get it tomorrow.' The one who'd recognised me had seen it all before. 'Want a lift?'

It was nearly two o'clock before I got back to the flat. Jane was asleep. I had a shower. This, I thought miserably, was what came of being a Good Samaritan: bruises, a ruined suit, a sense of uselessness. And I couldn't remember where I'd parked Brian's car. I was annoyed Jane didn't wake up. I felt a childish need for sympathy, for someone to tell me I'd done my best and made a difference. I didn't have the heart to wake her.

The next day, when I went to make my statement, they told me Kevin hadn't come round.

'What are his chances?' I asked, then realised what they meant. They told me they felt bad about it as well. They told me not to worry, I'd done my best. It was no consolation. My best hadn't been good enough.

Thirteen

When I next saw Mike he was nervous and bad-tempered and did most of the talking. It was as though he was trying to make up for three years of missed conversation. I didn't tell him about Kevin Taylor, but then I hadn't talked about him to anybody since making the police statement. I'd translated the whole experience into Standard Cop English ('Mr Taylor showed signs of mental distress') and heard their unofficial reassurances ('Nobody can blame you for this. You were only trying to help.'). There was a chance I'd have to appear at the inquest. ('But I wouldn't worry about it. You tried to do the right thing.') I hadn't mentioned it at work (Tony would have had a field day) or told Jane (Kevin had been my problem; no need to involve her). Once I could have told Mike, confident he wouldn't remember a thing. Kevin's death would have meant no more to him than made-up stories of Dad's DIY. But Mike was changing and that day he wanted to talk, so I listened as he tried to tell me about the other patients. His stories were confused and dull; even Mike found it hard to pay attention. And then he told me he'd be out, just as soon as a room became available. In February, he said again, or March or April – soon, he didn't really know, but soon. He had a sudden flash of temper. 'Not like you care, you cunt.' Just as quickly, he forgot, and slipped back into a rambling anecdote – not even rambling, *jaywalking* – about what Nathan said to Alex when Alex lost the remote control.

I found Dr Cortevalde at reception. She confirmed that Michael was better than expected and would soon no longer need round-the-clock institutional care. He could be put in a general ward now, she said, but, out of consideration, they would let him have his old room until a place became available.

I still found it hard to believe. Then, a few days later, as I waited for Brian at the office, Tony transferred a call from Dr Cortevalde.

'Please tell your colleague I do not appreciate being called a "posh tart",' she began, before telling me what she said was the good news. A place had unexpectedly become available. Michael would be able to take up residence the following day.

Caught off guard as I was – this was the first time they'd ever phoned me at work – it took me a second to translate this. It meant Mike was coming out.

It was a room in a house, originally meant for someone else. Lloyd, one of the nurses Mike had hit, met me at reception.

'The other guy killed himself,' he told me. 'He'd been waiting for months, and then the week a place comes up...' He sounded bitter, as if he thought Mike didn't deserve this chance. 'It got me, you know? I liked the guy.'

I didn't have to be there. Mike wasn't expected to cause any trouble. Lloyd was supposed to drive him to his new home. There was no need for family. But I didn't want Mike thinking he'd been abandoned, though it was possible he wouldn't notice I was there and would think he'd been abandoned anyway.

Lloyd pulled himself together. He walked into the TV room like an actor stepping on to a stage. Mike was waiting for us, slouched in a chair in a parody of a teenage strop. He glanced up at me, then went back to looking at the carpet.

'You came, then.'

It wasn't clear if he was talking to me or Lloyd. I pretended he was talking to me. 'Of course I came.'

'Cunt.'

Lloyd winced. 'Ready, then, Michael?' There was a suitcase by the side of his chair, an old one of Dad's. It gave me a jolt to see it, to find any trace of our parents. I picked it up. It felt half-empty. Years of his life, and there wasn't even enough to fill a suitcase. Mike knocked my hand away, grunting.

'OK, then,' I said. 'Carry it yourself.'

'Will.'

Lloyd sighed, the grown-up. 'Come on, then.'

He led us to reception. I walked behind Mike, like a bodyguard or a police escort. Mike started briskly enough. And then, as he got further from the TV room, he began to slow down. At the main door he came to a dead stop.

Lloyd carried on walking towards the car park. After a few paces he turned. 'Coming, Michael?'

Mike was looking at the trees in the other direction. They were bare now, the wall behind them visible. 'The car park,' he said. He took a step back. I felt sick. It wasn't going to work. Mike wasn't going to leave, or we'd have to drag him out. The world was too much for him.

'That's right, Michael,' Lloyd said. There wasn't a trace of annoyance in his voice. There wasn't a trace of *anything*. 'That's where the car is.'

'Yeah.' Mike went on looking at the trees. They were the same trees he'd seen when he stood on the chair in his room. He seemed surprised to find them there.

'Well?' Lloyd was calm. He gave me an I've-seen-this-before look. If he felt any resentment towards Mike he disguised it well. 'Are you coming?'

'Yeah.' Mike stepped out on to the gravel. He tried hard to look casual, but he took careful steps, as if he was walking across ice. He kept looking back at the trees.

He sat next to Lloyd in the car. I sat in the back with his case. Once the doors were closed and locked, he started to talk. He talked softly. I couldn't catch everything he said. Maybe that was his intention.

'Glad to see the back of the place... rotten shithole.' We pulled away, along the drive, out into the streets. Mike seemed to feel he had to say something about everything we passed. 'There's a bus stop... what a wreck... look at that cunt with the green hair... that place burnt down... there's another video shop. Fish and chips! If that's near, we'll have fish and chips...'

It took half an hour to get to the house. It seemed too far away, a small terraced house in a street full of the same, a shabby, treeless street I'd never had to visit.

'Is that it? Don't think much of that... give me my case... number twenty-six, H or BF... look at those fucking curtains...'

'There are three other people sharing this house,' Lloyd explained. He talked to Mike, but it was as much for my benefit. 'It's a good one, one of the best. Not far from the DSS. That's important, you know.'

I knew. I'd been briefed by Dr Cortevalde.

We sat in the car for a few seconds, like robbers nerving themselves to enter a bank. Mike's commentary became a mumble.

Lloyd handled him well. 'What was that, Michael?'

'Wasn't saying anything.'

'You going in, then?'

We got out and followed Lloyd to the door. He rang. I'd expected him to have a key. The house was an outpost of the institution. But Dr Cortevalde had used phrases like 'autonomy' and 'personal responsibility'. She meant the inmates could lock their own doors.

'Hope they're not all out,' Lloyd said, deadpan.

'Is that likely?'

Lloyd shook his head. 'Roger's always in. Always.'

Mike stood back from us, looking up and down the street. 'Don't see anybody.' He sounded disgusted, as if he'd been promised crowds, a brass band.

After some scrabbling with bolts the door opened.

'Good morning, Lloyd.' It was a tall, fair-haired man in his forties in a black shell suit. He held out a hand towards me. 'And this must be Michael.'

'I'm Patrick, the brother.'

I stood to one side. Mike stepped forward, grinning sheepishly.

'I should have guessed from the suit. Pleased to see you anyway.' Roger had the kind of smooth voice Mum would have loved. She never forgave us for sounding like Dad. 'I'm Roger. Well, you'd better come in.' He led us through. 'Welcome to our humble abode. I'm afraid the hallway is a bit of a tip. This is the living room.'

Everything looked ordinary. A three-piece suite, a little television, a small bookcase with a few books and magazines. I noticed *Auto Trader* and *Penthouse*.

'And through here is the kitchen.'

Again, ordinary. A typical family home. Roger showed us around, pointing out the desirable features like an estate agent. Next to Mike, who muttered and hummed, he appeared normal. You wondered if he was there by mistake, or malingering. Frank and Leonard, he told us, were out at the moment. I hoped Frank and Leonard were the other occupants and not figments of his imagination. Mike seemed to trust Roger. He followed him around, nodding and saying, 'Nice,' about everything. Lloyd watched them both carefully.

The bedrooms and bathroom were upstairs. All the rooms were small. Mike's looked out over gardens and the backs of other houses. It was as bare as his last room, but brighter, and clean.

'What do you think?' Roger asked.

Mike nodded. 'It's nice.'

It was. It was better than most of the gaffs I visited.

After the tour we sat in the living room drinking tea. Roger told us more about the others. Frank spent most of his days at the local library, when it was open. He read all the newspapers, cover to cover. 'You'll like Frank,' he told Mike, who was absorbed by a price list in *Auto Trader*. 'He's a helpful sort of bloke. Can't do enough for you.' Leonard did temp work for an agency. He was a chartered accountant, recovering from a breakdown.

At this, Mike looked up. 'I know Leonard, you don't have to tell me. Pissed me off, crying all the fucking time.'

Roger looked at him benignly. 'You'll find Leonard's a changed person these days.'

Mike put the magazine down testily. 'Tired. Going to sleep.' He walked out. We heard him clump up the stairs.

'He'll be all right.' Roger began collecting the cups. He seemed to have expected bad behaviour. 'The first day away can be a bit of a strain even when you've only been in for a couple of weeks, let alone years. Fear not, I'll keep an eye on him.'

Lloyd stood up. 'Thanks, Roger. Do you want a lift back, Mr Farrell?'

Roger came with us to the door. He seemed sorry to see us go. With only my brother for company I couldn't blame him.

'I'll drop by one evening,' I said. 'What's the number of this place?'

Roger laughed. 'The money doesn't run to a phone. But don't feel you have to give us any notice. I'm always here, and I don't think Michael will be going out for a while. Come by any time.'

As he drove back Lloyd said, 'That was better than you expected, wasn't it?'

'Much better.' I felt light-headed with relief. 'Roger seems dependable. What's he like?'

'You mean, what's wrong with him? Roger's OK. He gets depressed. I mean, *really* depressed. You and me, we get a bad day, only our friends notice. When he gets depressed it shows on a cardiograph. He just sits there, he isn't able to do anything. But he's OK most of the time.'

I decided Lloyd was OK too.

He drove me to Elding Collections. 'Don't worry about your brother. I'll call round tonight and check how he's doing.'

He meant well. They all meant well. And the move had taken much less time than I'd thought. Piers got an afternoon's work out of me.

I went back the next night. I needed to see if Mike was settled.

Jane understood. 'The first days are always the hardest,' she said. Conventional wisdom, but somehow she made it sound like personal experience. She asked if she could move in for a while – 'Just for a week or two.' Ros was going through a difficult patch; it had started before the dinner at Margaret's. Her moods had become unpredictable. 'I don't think she knows what she's doing half the time.'

I thought of the way she'd fallen into my lap. 'Only half the time?'

'She's not usually…' Jane began the ritual defence of her friend, this time without conviction. 'She's getting worse. She's had something done to her teeth.'

I felt a sympathetic ache in my own jaw. 'How does she look?'

'Like someone's beaten her up. She can't open her mouth properly yet.'

'She's mad.'

Jane agreed, sort of. 'Disturbed. I'd need to bring a few things over. My computer…'

I didn't see a problem. In two days the whole shape of my life had changed.

Roger answered the door. 'Patrick, good evening.' He still wore the black shell suit, or perhaps it was another, identical one. 'Michael's in his room at the moment. I'll introduce you to our fellow residents if you like.'

Frank and Leonard sat in the living room. Frank watched the news while Leonard filled in some forms. They were both in their thirties, frail white-collar workers with orderly pastimes. They looked OK, if jumpy. Neither was interested in talking.

Mike was stretched out on his bed. The light was on. He jerked to attention. 'Hi, Patrick, I was just... This is a good bed. It's better than...' He lost interest in the comparison. He sat on the crumpled duvet looking at the window. All he could see was the room reflected back at him. I thought I understood why he wasn't sitting with the others. He was the odd one out in this household, the youngest one, the only one who had never been anything.

'How are you, Mike?'

'I'm OK. Been reading.' I couldn't see any books in the room. 'Taking my... I'm OK.'

'Good. Seen Lloyd?'

'Yeah. He's a prick. He came yesterday.'

'Say much?'

'Not a word. He's a prick. Just looked around. Fucking know-all.'

No point asking about Lloyd, then. 'Mike, remember you used to talk about going to a gym?'

'Yeah.' He hunched his shoulders and threw a slow left jab. 'Yeah. A few sessions.'

'There's a gym not far from here. Had a look at it on the way over. Nothing flash, but they've got all the gear. They've even got a heavy bag. Want to join? I'll pay.'

'No gear.' He clenched his fist at his side. I soon grew used to these abrupt changes of mood, the way his temper would suddenly flare and fade. 'All my fucking gear's at home.'

He meant with our parents. He was wrong. Mum had kept his clothes for a year, then thrown them out. A year to the day. She didn't discuss it. There had been a row when I found out. I hadn't visited them again for months.

Nobody had told Mike.

'So? What good's your old gear? None of it would fit you now, anyway. I'll buy you some new stuff. Do you want to join or what?'

'Yeah, OK.'

'Try not to sound so enthusiastic.'

He started swearing. It lasted about a minute.

Finally, he relaxed. 'How are you, Paddy? How's the old job going? How's Jane?' This was becoming familiar. After each outburst, polite questions. They were the closest he came to an apology.

After a few minutes, he said he was tired again. In the living room Leonard was still working on his forms and Roger was reading a book. There was football on the television. Frank was in the kitchen, making himself a sandwich. He filled the empty hours between news programmes by preparing food. I wondered if he ever ate any of it, he seemed so frail. As I passed the kitchen door he asked me if I knew anything about the Japanese market. He thought I worked in finance. The suit.

Later, I tried to describe the atmosphere of the house to Jane. It was so different from what I'd imagined. With four people like that, living without supervision, it could easily have been tense or hysterical. As it was, the house was calmer than most of the houses I visited for Elding Collections. Jane told me this was normal. She'd seen these houses before; they worked, given a chance. It was what I wanted to hear. Still, I visited the house every night for the first week. One night

I took him some sports gear and walked Mike to the gym. I was glad to be occupied with him. It took my mind off Kevin, and gave me a sense of doing something useful.

As we walked along the street Mike kept up his muttered commentary on everything we passed. In the house he was surly. He still couldn't hold a conversation. Anything beyond a simple question and answer was beyond him. Outside of the house he muttered to himself. He didn't stop until he reached the gym. When he walked into the room with the equipment he became almost bashful.

It was a stark, functional place, unashamedly macho, if not industrial. You half expected to find the regulars machining or spot-welding between reps. Fortunately we were there at a quiet time. The only other people were the in-house trainer and a thin guy pounding one of the treadmills. The trainer spent most of his time at one of the big mirrors, apparently trying to stare down his own reflection. At first Mike was reluctant to use any of the equipment. I had to go on first, show him what to do. It was harder than I remembered. I hadn't been to a gym in years, and even then had mainly worked with free weights. I could run for miles and walk for hours without getting tired, but this was different. My exertions only made Mike laugh. The trainer glanced in our direction, then went back to the mirror. I didn't want to involve him. I'd taken one look at his heavy arms, slab face and swollen torso and formed a low opinion. I knew the type: a four-hour-a-day workout man, with a system full of steroids and a wall chart for a brain. A word like *schizophrenia* would go straight over his head, or make him laugh.

After he got started, though, Mike did better than I'd expected. He was strong, even after all those years of standing on a chair. On his first visit his favourite equipment was the rowing machine. On the second visit, he needed less encouragement and tried everything except for the heavy bag that hung in one corner. He kept looking over at it wistfully, as if, one day, he might summon up the courage to use it.

On the third day the trainer asked me if this was some sort of therapy. I told him Mike had been ill.

Mike was on the rowing machine, absolutely intent on maintaining a steady pace. It was set at the slowest possible speed. The trainer watched him.

'Mental illness, yeah?'

I nodded. It was still an admission I found hard to make in front of strangers.

'Thought so.' He told me he'd once worked in a day centre, teaching basic fitness to people with a history. He'd learnt a lot. Exercise, he said, was good with depressives – once you got them started – but you had to be careful with the body-image cases. The class was cancelled, budget reasons. There'd been complaints that keep-fit classes were a luxury wasted on nutters. 'Your brother, he hasn't done this for a while, has he? Keen enough, though. He'll be OK, long as he doesn't overdo it.'

We chatted for a while about weights and reps and the proper diet. It was the kind of conversation I used to have all the time with Shona's friends. He knew more about the subject than me, or was more up-to-date. My ideas about complex carbohydrates were no longer the orthodoxy.

'Look,' he said finally, 'you're not really into this, are you? If your brother wants to come in by himself, I'll keep an eye on him.'

'Would you mind?'

'Course not. The place is always quiet about this time. Gives me something to do, saves you having to come here.'

'Thanks.'

'No problem. I'll soon have him in shape. Name's Kent. by the way. Yeah, as in the county.' He went over to Mike, who was still rowing furiously, and suggested he try another piece of equipment. Mike, overawed, did as he was told.

When we walked back to the house all he could talk about was Kent. 'He's got a funny name. He told me what to do, all the settings and everything. He knows everything about that gym.' And so on, and on.

'Kent said he'd train you if I can't make it. Would you like that?'

'That'll be great; he really knows what he's doing.'

'You'd have to make your own way to the gym.'

'OK. That's OK. It's not far.'

It was further than he'd walked for years. 'Tomorrow?'

'OK.'

Jane was pleased to hear about Mike's new interest. It meant I'd get home in time to cook now and again. She had her own plans for me. 'You're going to learn about computers. It's easy money. Even you can do it.'

My flat was changing. Jane was moving in slowly. Her arrangement with Ros was informal. Even if Jane didn't want to live with her, they were still friends and, as Ros wasn't about to take in a new lodger, Jane was able to move at her own pace. One week she brought clothes. Soon afterwards she decided it was time to move her computer. There was a second bedroom I didn't use, even for storage; Jane thought it was ideal as an office. She went from calling it 'the spare room' to 'my room'.

Mike began going to the gym by himself. The short walk there became as normal for him as it would have been for anybody else. I still went every other night, supposedly to exercise, but mainly to watch. Kent was gentle, encouraging. Mike worshipped the man. His talk was still disconnected, but he lost weight and stopped twitching.

Lloyd was impressed. 'If Michael carries on like this, we can start to think of finding a job for him.' Not a real job, of course, not even temp work like Leonard, but still something he'd never had before.

Roger noticed another improvement. Kent didn't like swearing, so Mike made an effort not to swear. Roger was the oldest, the head of the household. He'd been a teacher once, German, one of the exams I'd been told not to bother sitting. Frank and Leonard were OK, just dull. Leonard only seemed to become animated when trying out his conversational German on Roger. The rest of his time was spent filling in forms: he belonged to a consumer group that kept him supplied with questionnaires. He reminded me of Piers: a Piers who was ten years older, with another breakdown behind him. Frank was more actively boring. He worked at it, conscientiously. His interests were current affairs, world markets and, by a progression that looked natural to him, supermarket prices. He knew the price of every product in every store within a mile of the house. Some of the discrepancies – he always said 'discrepancies' – were, he claimed, 'fascinating'. He couldn't have been more wrong.

I was glad they were dull. Mike didn't need excitement. His growing attachment to Kent was enough. The trainer's name intrigued him. 'That's where dad lives... coincidence.' At least he said coincidence rather than conspiracy. 'Wonder what the rest of his family are called.'

After ten days, he was going to the gym by himself even on the days I visited. I'd turn up at the house and find he'd already gone. Under Kent's guidance he progressed from light fifteen-minute sessions to hour-long workouts that left him drenched with sweat and aching. He started saying things like 'muscle group' and 'definition'. I wondered what he found to do there; the machinery bored me after twenty minutes. Mike walked away from the gym exhausted and eager for the next visit. He wanted to get fit, he said, so he could spend even longer in the gym, with Kent. I'd always regarded bodybuilding as a fool's game, but, if it was what Mike wanted, well, at least it was an ambition. Maybe he'd get a better one later.

I borrowed Brian's car to collect Jane's computer. Jane came with me, though she wasn't really needed. I was grateful. I didn't want to face Ros alone.

She opened the door. She didn't talk or smile. She couldn't. Jane had been right: even weeks after whatever she'd had done, Ros still looked as if she had been beaten up. The bottom half of her face was puffy and greenish. She'd taken the rings out of her lips, though the rest of the ironware was in place. She'd shaved her head again.

Jane found it hard to look at her, and she'd seen her two days earlier. 'I've come to pick up some things, Ros.' She said 'Ros' hesitantly, as if she doubted whether this was the right person. It might not have been. With her bare skull and pear-shaped face she no longer resembled the woman I'd met a few months earlier.

Ros nodded, and stepped back to let us in.

Jane went through to her old room. Ros, apparently exhausted, sat by her computer and stared at me. She looked terrible. Her eyes were half closed and her face was gaunt where it wasn't swollen. I wondered if she could eat at all through that damaged mouth. She went on looking at me, not making any sign. There was something inhuman about her attention. It was like being studied by a dolphin.

'Are you all right, Ros?'

She pointed to a bottle of pills by the keyboard, and nodded.

'Is there anything we can do to help?'

Jane came out of her room. 'Are you going to give me a hand with this or not?'

We left Ros sitting on her chair, with the blank screen and a bottle of pills. On the way back I asked, 'Do you think she's going to be OK?'

Ros had frightened me; she just made Jane impatient. 'She's never going to be OK.' For once, she didn't defend her old flatmate. 'She doesn't want to be OK. Some people don't.'

'And that's all right, then?'

'It's her life.'

Jane installed the computer in her room. She started to teach me the basics. Over the next couple of days I wrote a 'Hello World' program and learned how to build a database. It wasn't hard, or interesting, but I persevered. I thought it was the kind of thing that could be useful when I left Elding Collections.

The mood there was changing. Tony's complaints about the job became more strident. Even Brian was affected. He'd always treated Tony's outbursts as jokes. Now, as we drove from the office he'd say things like, 'Old Tone's got a point. I think it's time I did something else.' Night school might be a start. He was thinking about a new job, or Sue was thinking for him. Counselling, he said. Drug rehab, young offenders, something useful. Or a pet shop. We collected cards. I began to feel as if I'd already handed in my notice and was working out my last few weeks.

And every other day I'd visit Mike at the gym on the way home. I wasn't really needed; Kent had everything under control. He'd turned out to be better with Mike than the trained nurse. Lloyd was offhand, as if he still hadn't forgiven Mike for taking another man's place. He delivered the medication, asked routine questions, and left. Mike claimed to hate him, though it was hard to tell how much of this was bravado, the way schoolboys claim to hate teachers when they don't really care. Mike was twenty-three, but a lot of those years didn't count. He'd missed out on so much. He'd never worked, or looked for work, or lived by himself. He'd never kissed a girl, let alone slept with one. And he wasn't likely to do any of those things. All he had ahead of him was his own room in a shared house and, maybe, some time, the chance to work in an Industrial Rehabilitation Unit. Yet this was the best time of his life, a *period of relative tranquillity*.

I would watch Kent watching Mike. They'd talk about a television police drama. It was Kent's favourite programme, so now it was Mike's favourite too. Mike became so relaxed he even took some swings at the heavy bag: efficient jabs, sudden flashing crosses. He'd been faster once, a dancer. He still wasn't bad, considering where he'd been since. I used to walk away wiping my eyes, pretending it was sweat.

So I was in a good mood for Adam's Yule party. If he'd asked me to take part in his Candlemas ritual I would have agreed without a second thought.

The party turned out to be more like an ordinary party than I'd expected. People stood around, drinking and talking. There was music playing – ordinary chart stuff. And then, at ten o'clock sharp, Adam turned off the music and announced it was time to bring the Yule log in from in the kitchen. There was applause, cheers.

The Yule log was a piece of wood about two feet long and a foot thick. It looked like something you'd find washed up on a beach. After clearing the centre of the room, Adam balanced a metal tray on two half-bricks, placed the log on top of this, and gave a short talk.

'Some of you may already be aware of the significance of this ritual…'

I whispered to Jane, 'I thought a Yule log was chocolate.'

She laughed. 'Just be grateful you didn't go to Margaret's party.'

'I wasn't invited.'

'I'm surprised you weren't. She's still interested in you, you know. And do you know why?'

'Because of you?'

'No. They don't care about me. It's because Ros thinks you're *it*. She was so impressed with you she showed Margaret the chart.'

'What happened to client confidentiality?'

'That's only for interpretations. The chart's fair game.'
The chart, she said, was all Margaret had needed. She knew enough about astrology to remember the important details; then she went to Cindy de Souza. Cindy de Souza, whom I didn't know and would never meet, had told her I was a deeply spiritual person. 'And that's why Adam's keen as well. They think you're the man.'

'The man? Like the chosen one?'

'I think you're better than you think you are.' She shrugged. 'But it's still hilarious.'

She turned back to the centre of the room, where Adam, having run through the history of the Yule tradition, was ending with a warning.

'There will probably be some smoke from this. Don't worry! It's not as harmful as cigarette smoke. I've turned off the smoke alarm and I'll be opening the windows, so it may get chilly. If you want to, you can get your coats now...'

He struck a match with a sacerdotal flourish. I remember wondering if he'd ever been an altar boy. I could picture him staring enviously at the officiating priest, longing to wear those robes and roll those sonorous words off his tongue. Then he'd grown up and his heart wasn't in it any more. Like me, he had stopped believing. Unlike me, he had found something else.

'The log should only be lit by wood. The match is a compromise as we haven't got time to rub two sticks together. Here goes. Make sure the extinguisher's ready, Dan.' He touched the match to the log. People stepped back, as if they expected it to go off like a firework.

The match burned out without the log catching.

'Typical,' Jane whispered.

'Sorry, everyone.' Adam struck another match, and once again held it to the base of the log, muttering softly. I couldn't tell if he was praying or swearing. This time he stepped back triumphantly, extinguishing the match with a flick of his wrist. A line of smoke rose from the log. It thickened and dispersed at chest height, caught by a current of air from the kitchen window. There was a ripple of applause.

Daniel stood by the log, rapt. I couldn't tell what pleased him more: taking part in an immemorial rite or being allowed to hold the fire extinguisher.

Smoke started to fill the room. Jane retreated to the hallway. I was about to follow her when Adam buttonholed me, asked what I thought of the log and, before I could answer, started talking about Margaret. 'Essentially, she's religious. I've always seen that as a problem…' When *he* talked about the Goddess he was using the word as a shorthand for a source of power ignored by conventional science, whereas Margaret believed the Goddess was an actual person who liked prayers and rituals and her birthday to be remembered. 'I thought we'd got over that kind of thing when we expelled Joshua. Have you seen him lately?'

'Not lately.' Adam didn't need to know about Kevin Taylor. I doubted he'd care. 'I think he's lying low.'

'Probably just as well.' Adam considered the log. The smoke was getting thicker. Adam turned away and muttered to Daniel, who stood dutifully by the log, fire extinguisher in one hand, a can of lager in the other. Daniel nodded, carefully placed the extinguisher next to the log, and left the room.

Adam turned back to me. 'It's not working as well as I planned. But I don't want to put it out just yet. My last flat had a double-aspect lounge, so I could open a window on each side. Much more effective.' He nodded at a woman by the kitchen door. 'Do you mind? I haven't seen Sarah for months.' He left me at the edge of the smoky room.

Daniel came back with some tea towels. 'Could you give me a hand with this? Adam isn't going to be any use at all.' We took a towel each, folded them over our hands, and carried the hot tray with the log through the kitchen and

205

out into Adam's tiny garden. The air was sharp and cold. Daniel asked, 'So how do you know Jane?' He tried to sound casual.

I told him about Brian and Sue. He seemed relieved. 'So you didn't know Avril?'

'Jane mentioned her once. That's all I know.'

'Really? I thought she'd have said more. It was pretty significant. Jane met her after her – you know – suicide attempt.'

'Last time we ran into Joshua she mentioned the name. That's all.'

'Avril and Joshua. A real can of worms. You know what Joshua's like. Avril was one of his first mediums. She was a bit disturbed, but then, you know, that's how he likes them. But that's because *he's* a bit disturbed.'

After Adam, who described almost everybody he knew as intelligent or bright, Daniel's bluntness was surprising.

'That was when he was doing the drugs, as well. Plus he was in some sort of trouble over stolen cheques or something. But Adam still put up with him. Right up until the business with Avril...'

It was about time I heard the full story. 'What happened to her?'

'Well, you know Joshua had theories?'

'Adam said.'

'Adam makes it sound better than it was. Joshua believed that everything we see is only part of the story. You know, like the visual range is between ultraviolet and infrared? Well, Joshua thought the things we can't see go beyond the – you know – visual spectrum. And you know that idea about how mad people are really the sane ones?'

'That bollocks.'

'Well, Joshua believed it. He thought we were held back by conventional thinking. That's where the drugs came in. A whole derangement-of-the-senses thing. Mind you, he wouldn't take them himself, Instead, he talked Avril into taking them. And she OD'd.'

Like Peter Bedding, I thought. Maybe like Kevin Taylor. People seemed to OD a lot around Joshua. Maybe he was as bad at counting as he was at reading small print.

'For a while after that Joshua just flipped. He claimed he'd actually seen something. *Elemental personifications of force*, is what Adam calls them.'

'Adam believes in them as well?'

'Not the way Joshua does. Adam believes there's some kind of energy. Joshua believes it's sentient. He thinks you can talk to it.'

'Like conjuring spirits.'

'Exactly. Joshua believed in that shit. Anyway, Avril was wrecked, ill for months. She had to go into *long* long-term care. Joshua claimed that it was because she got too close to something. Jane never forgave him. I can't say I blame her.'

'OD'ing *and* a suicide attempt. What a life.'

'Avril didn't…' Daniel was surprised. 'I mean, she had a shitty time but she never tried to kill herself.'

'But you said Jane met her – '

'No, it wasn't like that.' He looked down at the log. 'Jane didn't tell you?'

I couldn't think of anything to say.

Daniel backed away. 'If she hasn't told you…' He shivered. I'd forgotten how cold it was. 'I'm sorry. I thought you knew. If she hasn't told you, I shouldn't have said anything. We'd better go back in.'

I followed him back into Adam's living room. The smoke had driven most of the guests into the narrow passageway. They had put on their coats, which gave the impression they were about to leave. The music had been turned up. A few women gamely attempted to dance under the dimmed light. Jane came back and sat on the sofa, watching them.

I stayed in the empty kitchen, watching the last grey traces of smoke drift across the ceiling.

She looked over and smiled at me, one of those smiles that cut out everybody else in the room.

Daniel's story couldn't be true. I must have misheard, I told myself. Or he was repeating something *he'd* misheard. What he'd said nagged at me, like a line from one of the *Eclogues* we'd studied at school, where you remember the words, and can even recognise some of them, but can't say what it means. I tried to smile back. The smile felt stiff, the kind I'd offer a subject after taking their cards.

Jane got to her feet and joined the dancing women. They formed a rough circle, dancing and chatting, occasionally stopping to blink away the tears from the remaining smoke. She seemed happy. I felt an ache in my chest, as if I'd been running for hours.

Adam reappeared at my side. 'About Candlemas.'

'I'm still up for it.'

'That's not what I was going to say.' He hesitated, like somebody about to give bad news. 'I've been giving this some thought. Perhaps it is a little too early to involve you in this kind of thing. Please, *please* don't take this as any kind of reflection on you personally. In other circumstances I would have liked to involve you…'

'So you don't need me.'

'Not this time. Next time, maybe. The preparation – it's been more complicated than I'd anticipated. I hope this isn't a problem.'

'It's not a problem.'

'Good.' He grinned with relief. I wondered if he'd expected me to be upset. 'Have you seen that Lebanese restaurant in Streatham? We should try it. Not next week, sure, but maybe the week after?'

Just to show he wasn't abandoning me altogether. I half expected him to say, *But we can still be friends.*

I felt faintly disappointed, but also relieved. The party dragged on. Scrappy conversations with different people, a slow dance with Jane. I wanted to ask her what had happened, and couldn't. Instead I told her what Adam had told me. She laughed.

'See? I knew the infatuation wouldn't last. Your novelty value's worn off. He must have made a new friend.'

The smoke cleared, leaving no more than a faint smell. Ros never showed up. Someone asked if it was true she'd had all her teeth taken out and replaced with stainless steel. Someone else said Candlemas looked promising this year.

Fourteen

I went to the gym and Mike wasn't there. Kent was unconcerned. 'Is it as late as that? I thought he'd be coming with you.'

I went to the house. Roger answered the door wearing, as usual, his black shell suit. 'Good evening, Patrick. Nice to see you again.'

'Is Mike in his room?'

'He is, yes.' He sounded surprised I had to ask. Where else would Mike be? 'You're the second visitor we've had today.'

Not much happened in their household. A visitor – any visitor – counted as news.

'From the hospital?'

'I think it was the DSS.'

'You think? What did they want?'

'He didn't tell me.' Roger must have asked. The visitor's refusal to answer clearly still rankled. 'I expect they're looking for an excuse to cut back his benefits. Some change in their definition of disability.'

I had the idea Roger could talk about this at length. 'They can't!'

'Oh, they would. Believe you me, they would.' He said something in German and smiled, possibly hoping I would ask for a translation. But I was already halfway up the stairs.

Mike's room was dark. He stood by the window, looking out. Just from the way he stood, with his hands clenched at his chest and his back slightly bent, I could tell he'd been standing there for hours and probably hadn't noticed how dark it had grown.

I placed my finger on the light switch. If I turned on the light without warning it might frighten him, so I spoke quietly first. 'Why aren't you at the gym, Mike?'

He didn't answer.

I switched on the light. 'Roger tells me you had a visitor today. Who was it?'

'The gym. The fucking gym.' He stepped away from the window, shuddered. He was angry. 'They're there, aren't they? Gardens of England, they're there. It was in the numbers. Fifty reps at one-fifty. Wait a bit, until you're ready. The right house. Two of them.' He looked at my shoes. 'What you come for?'

'To see how you are.'

'How I am. How I am *isn't*.' He turned back to the window, resting his forehead on the glass, his head angled so he couldn't see his own reflection. I wondered how he shaved. Strange, I'd never thought about that before. 'What I see is, it's not through the walls. It's next to them all the time. And they said they're not, that bitch Cortevalde.'

I went over to him and put my hand on his shoulder. 'What's happening, Mike?'

He pushed my hand away, scowling. 'You wouldn't believe me. You didn't believe me. All the time I was saying – ' And then he said a lot, suddenly, very quickly, more than I could understand.

'Come on, Mike,' I said, over and over again. 'What's brought this on?'

Finally he got fed up with trying to explain. 'Look at that, at that.' He stared down at the garden. Looking through our own reflections, all I could make out was the kitchen lights from the facing houses. There was nothing moving down there, not so much as a cat. 'Next to the walls,' he insisted. 'A place we don't fucking recognise. It all changes.'

211

'I can't see anything, Mike.'

'Don't try and tell me.' He pushed me away roughly. I stumbled back on to the bed. 'What *I* see. What *I* see. It isn't that cunt Lloyd. You turn every corner and they're fucking there. They think and they don't know. They must have looked in the phone book.'

'You're not in the phone book.' This was as bad as he'd ever been in the hospital. Worse, because I couldn't leave him to the nurses after half an hour. 'You haven't even got a phone.'

'Cortevalde's a bitch. Watching all the fucking time.'

'Mike, she's not here.'

'Someone who believes me.'

'Believes what, Mike?'

'I saw them. There were two of them.'

'Mike, stop fucking about and come to the gym.' I was talking to him the way you talk to a kid when they've fallen over, and you think if you can distract them they'll stop crying. It didn't work. Mike wasn't a kid. He was confused for other reasons. 'Come on, Mike.'

'Paddy!' he shouted. When he shouted his voice quavered, like an old man's. 'I can't. There were two of them today.'

'*Two* people? From the DSS?'

'You think that's where they're from? You don't fucking know.'

'What did they say?'

He moaned. It was like the moan of those mothers you see in supermarkets, as they sink to the level of their uncontrollable children. *What did I tell you? Next time it's a slap.* And what follows is either resignation or violence. In Mike's case it was a combination of both: he began to beat his head gently against the glass. 'Two of them. They're not from there. I talk and you don't listen. Fucking cunt.'

'What did they say, then?'

He stopped beating his head.

'I can't go to the gym.'

'Fine.' I got up from the bed. 'Take a day off if you like. Why not just sit here and relax? You've got nothing to worry about; they haven't found you yet.'

The wrong thing to say. I hadn't counted on Mike's ability to add two and two and make a hundred and twenty.

'Who hasn't found me?'

'Whoever, Mike. Nobody.'

'You've seen them?'

'I haven't seen anybody, Mike.'

'You wouldn't say that if they weren't there.'

'I don't know what you're talking about, Mike.'

'You fucking know.'

I was scared. If he carried on like this he'd have to go back to the hospital, and if he went back he'd never come out again... Slowly, thankfully, Mike calmed down. The next day, he was back at the gym, listening to Kent, and practising combinations on the heavy bag. Everything seemed to be back to normal. When I said this to Jane she replied, 'It's just a blip. You have to expect this sometimes. You shouldn't let yourself get too wound up by it.'

If anyone else had told me this I'd have resented it. Coming from Jane, it sounded like sweet reason.

The new year began quietly. Adam seemed to have forgotten me. I never heard anything more about the Lebanese restaurant in Streatham.

'Admit it,' Jane said, when I asked if she'd heard from him, 'you *are* disappointed. Anyway, you wouldn't like Lebanese food.' Adam was all talk, she said. Candlemas was going to go the way of Samhain. Jane seemed to be drifting away from her old friends. Now that she was no longer living with Ros she stopped urging me to read books and rarely mentioned her old interests. I was beginning to wonder if I wasn't a good influence.

213

Margaret seemed to have lost interest as well. I wasn't sorry about that.

And Mike seemed to have found a new pastime: reading. There would be four or five paperbacks from the library on his bedside cabinet – thrillers. I'd ask if they were any good, and he'd try to explain the plots, which all seemed to be about ordinary people getting mixed up with the Mafia or the Yakuza or the Triads. I wondered about the significance of this until Roger told me the books were Leonard's choice. There was one about a kidnapped Mafia heiress. There was a note on the cover: *Soon to be a major film.*

'I think I've seen this,' I told him. Or rather, I'd walked out, halfway through, on the day he was moved to the Marigold Wing. The night I'd met Sally Mercer. 'Or something like it.'

'I've read it.'

'Any good?'

'It's OK.'

'Think I'd like it?'

'It's OK.'

It was unfair to push him. At school he'd never willingly read a book. I couldn't remember him listening to any particular music or having a favourite film. Until he'd met Kent he hadn't even paid much attention to the television. A lot of playground conversations – the ones beginning 'Did you see…?' – used to leave him cold. Instead he'd talked about the people we knew. Mike's enthusiasm for the gym was only the second real one he'd ever had, after Sally Cazales, and he looked better for it. With Kent's patient tuition his back became straighter and he wasn't short of breath after climbing the stairs. Outside the gym he still looked preoccupied, sullenly intent on some problem he'd never solve and couldn't abandon, but the only person to get anything like his full attention was Kent.

And then the infatuation began to wear off. One day Kent asked if I realised Mike now only came on the days when he knew I would be there. I didn't think this was necessarily a bad thing. Perhaps it meant he was becoming more independent.

I asked Mike about it as we walked back one night. 'Kent tells me you didn't go yesterday.'

'Go every day.'

'That's not what Kent says.'

'So? Can't go every day, can you? There's always a replacement.'

'Replacement?'

'Don't have to. Fucking questions.'

'Calm down, Mike. We're in the street.'

'Fucking know we're in the street.'

He muttered to himself the rest of the way back. When we reached the house he ran up the stairs and slammed his bedroom door. Roger suggested I stay away for a few days. Jane thought this was good advice. I ought to let him have some space. What right *did* I have to keep asking questions? So I stayed away from the house for a week, enjoyed it, felt guilty about enjoying it, wondered if it was safe to stay away for a fortnight, and discovered I couldn't. On the day of his birthday I organised my worksheet so I had an excuse to be in his area, and took him a present, a little radio.

Roger answered the door. 'Good afternoon Patrick, this is unexpected. Your brother already has *one* visitor.'

'He's there now?'

'Yes. He's always dropping by. They don't visit *me*.'

'Maybe you need them less.'

'Perhaps not. All the same…'

I went up to Mike's room, expecting to find Lloyd, or some other representative of concerned authority. His visitor was Joshua Painter.

It was like a meeting in a dream. Mike was lying on his bed. Joshua stood with his back to the window. He wore a long black coat over a grey suit as businesslike as my own.

I dropped the radio. Joshua was just as surprised to see me.

He recovered first. He said, 'I knew you'd come.'

I thought of Kevin Taylor, and the others, Avril and Peter Bedding.

'Get out.' I said. 'Now.'

'Who do you think you are?' Joshua smiled at Mike, inviting him to share in his moral superiority. Mike was a bad audience. He looked up at the ceiling, the naked bulb. Joshua turned back to me. 'I think *you* should leave.'

I took a step forward. Elding Collections employees were supposed to use the minimum of force, and then only when it was unavoidable. The rest of the time we were meant to run. I thought the minimum of force would be enough, at least to begin with.

'I'm not arguing about this, Joshua. Get out.'

'You can't do anything.' Joshua had all the arrogance of a man who'd never stopped a real punch. 'I have as much right to be here as you. Isn't that right, Michael?'

'Fucking right.' Mike didn't look at either of us.

'You don't know this bastard, Mike,' I said. 'You don't want to know him.'

'Fucking know who I like.' Mike didn't take his eyes off the ceiling.

'That's it, Michael.' Joshua hadn't realised Mike's presence was the only reason he was still standing upright. 'I'm the real friend here. I want to help you. All *he* can do is destroy.'

'Yeah? Then tell me about Kevin Taylor.'

'Kevin?' Mike said. 'What a wanker. That party he had. Six people.'

'That's the one. Ask Joshua about him. And about Peter Bedding. And Avril.'

'That has nothing to do with this.' Joshua lost some of his composure. 'That was long ago. This is about Michael's future. What do *you* want, Michael?'

Mike sat up. He stared into the space between us. 'You want him to go.' It wasn't clear who he was talking to. 'You never did anything about the others.'

'What others, Mike?'

Joshua felt so safe he took a step towards me. '*You're* the one who *should* get out.' He jabbed at the air between us, as if throwing psychic darts. '*You* have no right to tell Michael what to do. You've lost that right. You're part of the same system that tried to destroy him. Do you realise that? Did you *ever* stop to consider that?'

His finger struck me on the chest, and I hit him. I don't usually lead with the fists. Hands are fragile, heads hard. Better to trip and kick or twist arms. But the jab on the chest was more than I could stand. I threw a punch without thinking, a straight right into the middle of his face. Joshua fell over, his hands limp at his sides, his mouth open. Blood started to flow.

Mike laughed. Slapstick.

Joshua dug a handkerchief from his pocket, held it to his mouth. There were tears in his eyes. 'You're going to be sorry you did that.' A would-be sinister threat, muffled by the bloody cloth. 'That's assault. I can get you for that.'

'It's battery. And you hit me first.' I looked carefully at his thin, twisted face. I'd reached the stage of wondering not *if* I should kick him, but *where* and *how hard*. He didn't try to protect himself. He didn't draw up his knees or attempt to crawl away. He sat there, making threats. Some people have no idea. But I didn't kick him: if I started I might not stop. 'Maybe I should take you to the police now. See what you have to say for yourself.'

Joshua shifted away from me, pushing back against the wall. When he thought he was out of reach he pulled himself to his feet. 'What have you ever done to help him? I'm the one who's tried to help. I'm the one who understands. All you've ever done is try to take his – his birthright.'

This was so bizarre that I glanced at Mike to see if he responded. He was still smiling to himself. 'Birth.' His sarcastic voice. '*Right.*'

I was encouraged. Joshua hadn't impressed Mike at all. 'Just get out.'

'You see, Michael?' Joshua didn't give up. 'He admits it. He tried to take your place. He was jealous and tried to take your place.'

I grabbed him by the lapels of his coat, pulled him towards the door. 'Come on, let's go.'

'Michael! Remember who your friends are!'

Joshua's appeal was wasted. Mike had stopped paying attention to anything in the room. He sat up straight, his knees drawn to his chin, his expression blank. 'What is it, Michael?' Joshua asked softly. 'Are they here?'

Mike lowered his face into his hands. There was nothing in the room, but I still felt a chill.

Joshua twisted out of my grasp. 'You see? This is what you've tried to deny.'

I kicked his feet out from under him. He fell heavily. 'You can't – ' he began, and yelped when he saw my foot drawn back. This time he curled up, covering his head.

'There's nothing here, Mike.' I steadied myself for the first kick.

'Fucking right.' Mike jumped up from the bed and stumbled the two paces to the window. At first I thought he was after a better view of the fight. Then I noticed he was more interested in what was happening – or not happening – outside.

The moment of anger passed. I stepped back.

There was a shout. 'What the hell's going on?' Roger was at the door. 'What do you think you're doing?'

'It's all right.' I stepped back. 'He's just leaving.'

Joshua writhed on the carpet like a footballer hoping to be awarded a penalty.

'All right? All right?' Roger was angrier than I'd have believed possible. 'It most certainly is *not* all right. If *you* don't leave *now* I'm going to call the police.'

Bluff. The threat must have been a reflex, a survival from the days when he had a job and a phone.

At the mention of the police Joshua jumped to his feet. 'There's no need to involve them.' He went over to Mike, who was still looking out of the window. 'I'm prepared to overlook this. I'm going now, Michael. Don't worry, I'll be back tomorrow.'

Mike was intent on the garden. Once he'd stood on his chair, looking out at the trees in the same way. Joshua pretended Mike had given him a sign of acknowledgement, something too subtle for an outsider like myself to notice. He edged by me, warily.

'You're not coming back here,' I told him.

'You can't stop me.' Joshua limped out of the room, and positioned himself behind Roger. 'Michael can see whoever he likes. You don't control him any more.'

'I don't want you near him again.'

'You don't have the right.' Joshua backed down the stairs with as much dignity as he could manage. I wanted to follow him, take him by the throat and drag him to the nearest police station.

Roger blocked my path. 'Let him go, Patrick.'

Joshua was out of sight. The street door opened and closed.

'I don't want that man to come here again,' I said.

'You're not in a position to demand anything.' Roger had already jumped to his conclusion. 'It's appalling that you can behave like this, in this house of all places.'

'I did it for a reason.'

'I'm sure you did. Only I don't want to hear it.' Roger had never sounded more like a teacher: for a moment I felt like a schoolboy dragged from a scuffle in the corridor, with that same mix of swagger and embarrassment as when you stood in the head's room, shirt tails out and still sweating, ready for the questions it was always a mistake to answer. 'I saw for myself what was going on. I don't doubt you could give all sorts of reasons. Frankly, it would be in the interests of all of us if *you* stayed away for a while. I don't care what excuses you've got. To put it bluntly, I don't want to see you here again. I won't tolerate this sort of behaviour, and if you call here again you shan't be admitted. After all, your brother can see whoever he chooses.'

'Except me.'

'For the time being, yes.'

'And what if he makes a bad choice?'

'That's his right.' Roger's temper began to ebb. 'That's the whole point of houses like this. I don't want to see you in this one again.'

'But you'll let *him* in again?'

'If Michael doesn't object.' Roger clung to his principle. 'What Michael does and who he sees is no longer up to you. He has to live for himself now.'

Mike climbed back on to his bed, blind and deaf to us. Roger talked about Mike making his own decisions, but spoke as if he wasn't there, the way the nurses had in the hospital. Mike couldn't work, or hold a conversation, but he was expected to make his own decisions.

'What if Mike wants to see me? That's his decision as well.'

'You can see him at that gym. I don't want you here.'

'Mike.' There's a tone of voice I have that sometimes gets through. Maybe it reminds him of Dad. 'Get your things together. I'm taking you home.'

I didn't give myself time to think.

'You can't take him away,' Roger said, weakly. 'He has to stay here.'

'Watch me.'

The only obstacle would have been if Mike refused to go. But he didn't have an opinion. At the word *home* he sat up, as if it was a familiar tune, some forgotten hit from his childhood. I packed his clothes into Dad's old suitcase.

'You *can't*.' Roger's authority had slipped away. All he had left were the riled tones of someone who would write a strong letter afterwards.

'I'm not letting him stay here. Not with that...' I didn't finish.

Roger stood at the bedroom door, repeating his one argument. 'Michael must be allowed to make his own decisions...' Pitiful. Mike was in no state to decide anything. He had to be told to stand up, what shoes to wear, when to follow me.

Before I let Mike walk through the front door I made sure Joshua wasn't waiting outside. We walked to the minicab office. Mike clutched the suitcase to his chest. Once in the street I noticed just how insane he looked, nervous of every lamp-post and passing car. Nobody could have mistaken him for normal then.

I started to think only after reaching the cab office. I'd meant to deliver a radio, and here I was planning another disruption to my routines.

'You'll like my flat,' I told Mike. I tried to sound casual, as if this wasn't a kidnapping. 'You'll have your own room there.' Jane's computer would have to move. The only other furniture, a chair that folded down into a bed, would at last have a use... My mind raced, in no particular direction. 'We can still go to the gym if you like.' Take the bus there, or join another one, or just give it a miss for a few days...

Mike didn't say anything until we were in the car. He described the things we passed: Look at that... see those... legs on that... she's all right...

We reached the flat. It was the middle of the afternoon, too early for Jane. I was supposed to be at work. I still had my list of names and a wallet of recovered cards. They hardly mattered now. I showed Mike around.

'It's nice,' he said, in his seen-it-all voice. 'Very nice. You've got yourself a nice little flat here, Paddy.' He made *nice* sound like a deliberate insult.

'This will be your room. Don't worry, the computer's coming out.'

'When do I go back?'

'Soon.'

'So you want me to stay here now? I know about you. Keeping an eye on me.'

'It's not that.'

'I know. So what am I meant to sleep on – that?'

'It folds down.'

'I know that.' He knelt at the computer, examining the dusty screen. 'Whose is this?'

'Jane's.'

'What's on it?'

'Jane's stuff.'

'What's on it?'

'I don't know. It's personal.'

'It's about me.'

'Don't be daft.'

I carried on talking. I congratulated him, like a salesman closing a crooked deal. 'You'll like it here, Mike. The food's better, I bet. The television's bigger. You won't have Frank talking to you at all hours…'

'Frank's a cunt.'

'It's a good job Jane's not fussy about language.' I still had to square it with Jane. I relied on her understanding. After all, she knew about Joshua; she'd hated him before I did. Squaring it with Dr Cortevalde and Lloyd might be harder. All I really had against Joshua was hearsay. Two people dead, one damaged. For me, this was damning. Cortevalde might hear it and decide Joshua was just unlucky.

I didn't even think about involving our parents.

Mike wandered from room to room, as if looking for one he'd missed, a hidden chamber he'd have to catch by surprise. 'It's tidy, it's tidy.' At least he noticed that. 'What is there to eat?'

I made him some sandwiches. There was an envelope by the breadbin. From the shape I could tell it was a birthday card. There was no stamp and the *Patrick* on the envelope was in Jane's handwriting. She'd remembered the date I'd given Ros.

Mike ate the sandwiches messily, dropping crumbs and bits of crust into the chair. I realised I hadn't seen him eat for years.

'Jesus, Mike, what happened to your table manners?'

He laughed.

I tried a different question. 'What did Joshua tell you?'

He shrugged. That is, it was more than a shrug, less than a spasm. It looked voluntary. 'You don't like him, do you?' He grinned. 'I could tell. The way you punched him in the face. Dead giveaway.'

The hardest part of talking to him was always the moments of sanity. You realised what was lost, like an archaeologist finding a shard rather than the whole vase, knowing the rest is irrecoverable. And maybe he only seemed to make sense because you wanted him to, and it was coincidence, not a shard at all, just a random piece of clay…

'Yeah,' I said, trying not to make too much of it. 'I don't like him. Do you want to know why?'

'What time's she get back – Jane?' He stood up, brushing the crumbs from his lap on to the carpet. 'I want to see this Jane.'

'She won't be long now.'

'Good. That's good.' He seemed eager to meet her. I was touched. 'When's Lloyd get here?'

'I haven't told him yet.'

'You've told him.'

223

'Mike, I haven't had a chance yet.'

'He knows already.'

'How?'

'When you...' He smiled to himself, as if he'd realised I was trying to trick him. 'Lloyd's a cunt.'

Living with him was going to be harder than I'd imagined. Between my earlier short visits I'd never given much thought to what he was like when I wasn't there. Didn't he just stand quietly on his chair, waiting for me to bring him my news?

'Lloyd's not so bad. Why don't you like him?'

'Why should I? He doesn't like me.'

'You hit him.'

'Yeah.' That grin again. 'A combination. The business. He didn't see it coming. No defence at all.'

'Aren't you supposed to be sorry?'

'For that cunt? He was always trying to tell me – ' He became incoherent for a few minutes, zapping through his preoccupations without finding one he liked. It wasn't like one of those outbursts you get in films, full of significant clues for the brilliant analyst. Mike's disease was nowhere near as obliging. All you could do was wait for the fit to subside. I never found out what Lloyd tried to tell him.

The worst was over by the time Jane came back. At the sound of her key in the door we both jumped to our feet.

'Jane.' I met her in the hallway. She had to have some warning. 'Mike's here.'

'Is he?' She marched into the living room. Mike crouched over his chair, not sure whether to stand or sit. She looked at him neutrally, then smiled. 'Hello, Mike.'

Mike stared at her, open-mouthed. Normally he didn't look directly at anybody – not Kent, not the people in his house, but he was staring at Jane the way people watch a match on television: completely absorbed.

'You can sit down if you like.' Her smile held. 'So, why the visit?'

Mike didn't move. He remained halfway between sitting and standing, his mouth hanging open. I put an arm round Jane's shoulder. I wanted to draw her somewhere out of earshot.

'Mike's going to be staying with us for a few days.'

'Is he?'

'Only for a few days.'

'Right.' Her body stiffened the way it had when I'd first touched her tattoo. She held out a hand towards Mike. 'Pleased to meet you, Mike.'

Mike tried to back away. 'Jane.' He fell into the chair, then stared off to his left.

Jane turned to me. 'Kitchen.'

We closed the door behind us and talked in whispers. She wanted to know what I was doing. I told her how I'd found Joshua in Mike's room. I was sure she would understand.

She didn't. 'So?'

'I don't want Joshua anywhere near him.'

'Why not? What danger is there?'

'You of all people should know. After what happened to Avril.'

She frowned. 'Who told you about that? You don't even know what happened.' And anyway, she went on, Mike was in no danger. He wasn't like Avril or Peter Bedding. They might have been weak, susceptible, but Mike wasn't coherent enough for Joshua to have *any* influence, good or bad.

I told her Mike was staying.

'Until when?' How was I going to look after him? Was I prepared to take time off work and spend the whole day with him? That was what it would take. That was what Roger at the house did. Would Elding Collections let me take the time off? 'Get sacked by them, and then where do you go?' And if I went to work, what happened to Mike? Who'd stop him letting Joshua in, if he wanted? And if Cortevalde and co. knew I'd taken him away, they might choose to consider him cured

225

and give his room to somebody else. There was demand for those rooms. Mike had been lucky to get it, considering his condition. If he lost it, I might be stuck with him for years. 'And where would that leave you? Have you thought about that?'

'I'm not debating this. It's only for a few days. Mike's staying.'

'So what are you going to do?'

'I don't know yet.'

'You've really thought this through, haven't you?'

'It's only for a few days.'

'You keep saying that. I don't think you've thought about this at all. What's going to change so much after a few days?' She tried to read my face. There was nothing there to read. 'I can see you've made up your mind. Well, I've made up mine. If he's going to stay here, you can't expect me to stay as well. It isn't fair of you.'

'So what are you going to do? Go back to Ros?'

'Yes. Until this insanity is over.'

'Don't use that word.'

'I wasn't talking about him.'

She left five minutes later with an overnight bag. There were still clothes at her old flat. They were all black, so there wouldn't be any trouble making things match...

Mike didn't understand what was going on. He watched her leave with the same gawping, speechless attention. He stared at the door. 'Jane.'

'She's gone to stay with a friend.' Cheerfully, again. This was just another part of the plan. 'Until we get this sorted.'

'Sorted.' Mike lay down on the sofa. 'She's the one. I know why. Joshua.'

'He's a bad influence.'

'I'm not a kid. Not stupid.' He spoke in a low growl, and I was glad Jane had left. 'Why can't you leave me alone?'

'I know what he does to people.'

'You don't know. I know.'

'Yeah? What do you know, Mike?'

'He said – ' Mike stopped himself again. 'I know why I'm here.'

'Really?'

'I *know*.'

'It's for your own good. Don't you want to see how I live?'

'I know how.'

'You think I'm doing this for my benefit?'

'Know you are.'

Jane's absence began to sink in, like cold water. 'Doesn't feel like it, Mike.'

He lowered his hands from his face, looked straight up at the ceiling. 'The gym.'

'Not tonight. Watch television.'

'Fucking television. I want to call.'

A kid. He'd ask for a drink of water next. 'Call who?'

'Don't have to tell you.'

'You do in this flat.'

He curled up, foetal position, mumbling.

The first evening wasn't too bad. Institutionalisation, his habit of obeying orders, helped. He ate when I told him to, watched television when it was on. He even went to his room when I told him to go, though he didn't stay there for long. I lay in bed and couldn't sleep, listening as he wandered round the flat, making noises: the click of light switches, the sudden blare from the television in the living room or the radio I keep in the kitchen. Around two o'clock I started to worry about the silence. I found him in the living room, hunched over one of Jane's magazines. *Network* or *Computer Weekly* – pages of jargon and technical spec.

'You should go to bed.' He didn't answer. I deadlocked the front door and took the key back to my room.

The real problems began the next day. I reconnected the phone and begged some time off from Piers. Mike had finally gone to his room a little before four. At seven o' clock he was still asleep. I got dressed as quietly as I could. The card was still by the breadbin. I opened it as I sipped coffee. Blank except for the handwritten: *Happy birthday, Pat. Promise you'll never grow a beard like this*. The picture showed a man dressed as a bishop pointing at some snakes. I wondered if there was another joke I hadn't got. But no: there was no amusing caption, just a straight image of St Patrick. Jane had probably gone to some trouble finding it. When I left, I locked the door from the outside. I took the card with me and dumped it in a bin outside the station. I'd have to admit the truth to Jane soon. As soon as Mike was safe...

I took an early train to Tulse Hill. I counted on finding Margaret at home. I knew she worked locally, and guessed she wasn't as devoted to her job as Piers.

She sounded wary on the entryphone. 'What do you want to talk about?'

'Joshua.'

She greeted me at the door to her block. She was dressed for work: a dark blue suit, the corporate colours of her employers. She looked like any other woman in her late thirties with a responsible job. She wore more jewellery than most – two neck chains, an elaborate brooch – but she was still not someone her colleagues would take for a priestess of the Old Religion. 'What about Joshua? What's happened?'

'Do you know his address?'

'I have *an* address.' She was suspicious. 'Why do you want it?'

'I want to talk to him.'

'Talk? Is this to do with your work?'

'Sort of.'

'I'm not sure I should...' She backed into her building and closed the door, returning with a scrap of paper. 'That's the last one I have. But he might not be there. He moves all the time.'

The address was within walking distance. All of Joshua's addresses had been in the same small area. This one was for a small flat over a boarded-up shop. Fifteen minutes later I was there, without any clear idea of what I was going to do. Nobody answered the bell, so I hammered on the door a few times. There was a café over the road. I took a window seat and had a slow fried breakfast. An old man in a donkey jacket sat at my table. 'Rough night?'

'Yeah. Terrible.'

'Tell me about it.' Meaning: don't.

Joshua didn't come out or go in. I didn't really expect him to. The surprise was that Margaret had such a recent address when she wasn't supposed to trust him. Had he given it to her, or had she found out from other people? Why had she kept it? I waited another hour. There was still no sign of Joshua.

Fifteen

Piers found Joshua's previous addresses in seconds. Whatever I was doing, though, he disapproved. 'You're supposed to be looking after your brother.'

'I am.'

At the first address nobody remembered Joshua. 'That was, like, *months* ago.' At the second house, where Peter Bedding had died, it was the same story. They hadn't heard of Joshua or Peter.

At the third house, the red-haired girl with the ring through her nose remembered me. 'Still haven't found him, then?' She regarded the police raid – she called their visit a raid – as an amusing incident. She hadn't seen Joshua since, but remembered how he'd talked about having lots of money. 'He was always flashing tenners about.' She'd never been impressed by him. She didn't go for his 'malign forces' bullshit either. She thought the universe was essentially a nice place, and that everything was for the best in the long run. 'What about the other one?' she asked, meaning Kevin Taylor. 'Did the police ever catch him?'

'Yeah, they caught him.'

'It's for his own good, though, isn't it, someone like that?'

'Yeah.'

By noon I'd run out of ideas. For all our claim to professionalism, tracing was one talent we didn't have, one area where we were no more skilled than any other mug with an *A–Z* and a suit.

What made it more frustrating was that I'd never had to look for him before. I'd turn a corner, knock on a door, idly kick a stone, and there he was. Now, when I wanted to find him – nothing. No sign of him in the flat over the shop. It still looked as if nobody had lived there for months. I called it a day.

On the way back home I stopped at a chemist's.

'I haven't been sleeping too well,' I told them. 'What can I get without a prescription?' They recommended Dormatan. I came out with two packs.

Mike wanted to know why I'd locked him in.

'You don't know the area. You might get lost.'

'I want to go out. You haven't got the right to keep me here.'

'Stop whinging.' I still hadn't told the hospital he was staying with me, and now I wondered if it was wise to tell them at all. I wasn't sure how to explain Joshua to an unprejudiced audience.

Mike went on complaining in a muffled, half-hearted way. He was bored; he wanted to go out; he wanted to make a phone call; he wanted something else for dinner; he wanted to see Jane again. And when he got to the bottom of the list he started again, or complained the flat was too cold; the microwave was too complicated; there was only rubbish on the television.

I held out for an hour. Then I handed him the telephone. 'You want to make a call, Mike? Make one. Ring somebody.'

'Not while you're listening.'

'Who are you going to call?'

He shook his head. He was close to tears.

'OK, then.'

I went to the kitchen and turned on the radio so he wouldn't think I was listening. I could still see him, though, in the metal side of the bread bin. He held the handset to his ear, his other hand resting on the buttons. After a few seconds he replaced the handset, and pushed the phone away. Just as I thought: he'd wanted the phone because it was forbidden. He didn't have anybody he could call. When I walked back to the room he hid his face. I was vindicated. It felt terrible.

The phone rang.

He jumped back, panicked and helpless, still not looking in my direction.

I answered. It was Jane.

'What's going on there? I've been calling all day.'

'There were no messages.'

'I left three.'

'Mike must have wiped them.' I could picture him crouched over the phone, listening to Jane's voice and not daring to answer, then pushing at the buttons until something happened. 'Nothing's wrong.'

Mike slouched to his room, shoulders loose, head down, the recent glow of athleticism gone.

Jane asked questions. Had I told the hospital yet? Had I decided how long this was going to last?

I gave all the wrong answers and asked a stupid question of my own. 'Do you know anyone who might have Joshua's address?'

'Why?' Immediate suspicion. 'What are you planning?'

'Nothing.'

'That's worse. Forget him. Joshua's not a problem.'

'Are you coming back?'

'Be reasonable. I know it's your brother, but I don't want to live with him. I really don't.'

Mike came out of his room when I started cooking. He didn't live in the flat, so much as hang around, like a vagrant expecting to be moved on. He ate what I gave him without complaining or showing any interest.

'So what do you want to do now, Mike?' I hated the fake cheeriness in my voice. 'Do you still want to go out?'

He didn't take his eyes off the window. 'It's dark.'

'We could see a film. Go to the pub.'

'No.'

'Have you ever been to a pub?'

'Alcohol is poison.' He began to get agitated again. 'What month is it?'

'January.'

'Summer?'

'Not for a while yet.'

'I know that.'

He reached for the remote control. The television clicked on. I realised how he'd spent his day: like a *subject*. Mike might not know where he was, but he knew how to use a remote control. He hopped from channel to channel until he found the end of a news programme. He nodded at the summary of the main stories and leaned forward slightly for the weather forecast. He didn't change channel after that, even though the only thing that seemed to interest him was a segment on a nature documentary about greenfly. Whenever a ladybird appeared he hunched his shoulders and muttered under his breath. 'Ah,' he said, when the segment was over, 'that's it.' I asked what he meant. He said it was too dark to go out. At half-past ten I gave him a Dormatan and a glass of water. He didn't quibble. He was used to taking pills. They were as good as promised. After fifteen minutes he felt drowsy and went to his room. He slept heavily the whole night. I lay awake, listening.

The next morning I once again tried the address Margaret had given me. This time someone answered. An Indian kid, faded jeans, Home Counties accent. Yes, he knew Joshua Painter. No, he didn't live there any more. And why was I interested? I showed him my Elding Collections card, and told him I was

233

looking for Mr Painter in relation to a fraud. He said that was no reason for him to help me. I told him I'd soon be giving my file on Mr Painter to the police. It would have to include a note saying that the present occupant seemed to know his whereabouts but had withheld the information. That did the trick. Even completely innocent people don't like talking to the police. He came back with an address scribbled on the back of an envelope.

'He told me to redirect any mail to him there.'

'Thank you, thank you very much.' I overdid the thanks. Typically, the new address was nearby. Joshua was unadventurous. I couldn't understand him. If I were engaged in fraud I'd have moved further away.

It was another flat over another boarded-up shop. He wasn't there either. There was a newsagent's next door. I asked the girl at the till if she'd seen anything.

'That dump? People use it, but they don't *live* there.'

Mike was still dazed from the Dormatan.

'Any visitors?' I asked breezily. He ignored me. Most of the time he ignored me. He was hunched on the sofa, deep in thought. I wondered if I should slip him another sleeping pill, and ended up giving him his usual medication instead. When I tried to talk to him he walked into the next room, swearing under his breath.

I sat down, closed my eyes. I was woken by the phone ringing. It was early evening, dark. Mike was watching me from behind the door of his room. I grabbed the phone.

'Yes?'

No answer. A click.

I slammed the handset down, dialled 1471. I didn't recognise the number, and dialled it. It was picked up; I could hear breathing.

'Is that Joshua?' Whoever it was hung up. It occurred to me that Mike hadn't erased Jane's messages by accident.

234

'That was for me.' Mike came out of his room. He moved sideways along the walls, as if trying to avoid sniper fire. He reminded me of the man I'd seen just before Alexander Murphy had whacked me with the broom handle. 'That was mine. You can't do that.' He wouldn't cross the room directly. He had to edge around it, until he stood next to the phone. 'It was fucking mine.'

'There was nobody there. It might have been a wrong number.'

'It was for me.'

'How do you know, Mike?'

'How do you know it wasn't?' He was angry. I saw why Jane had doubts about living in the same flat. If you stood next to someone like him at a bus stop you'd expect trouble.

'There was nobody there.'

'I bet.'

'I can talk to who I like.'

'Of course you can.' I yawned. I was still tired and I'd fallen asleep in my suit. Fortunately it was only a work suit. The shirt felt clammy. 'I'm having a shower.' I went to my room for a change of clothes. As I switched on the light I stumbled on something on the floor. The wardrobe doors were open and my suits everywhere, on the floor, the bed, the chest of drawers. The lining of every jacket had been ripped. 'Mike.' I suddenly felt very tired. 'What have you been doing?'

'I can talk to who I like.'

'My clothes, Mike.'

That wiped the smile off his face. 'I was checking.'

Right. Of course. The pockets, I now noticed, had been turned out. A waste of time; I never leave anything in my suit pockets. 'Checking for what?'

'To see what you've got of mine.'

'I haven't got anything of yours. What makes you think I have?' A stupid question. After all this time I couldn't get

235

out of the habit of reasoning with him. 'There's nothing here that belongs to you.'

He'd found the photograph, the old one of the two of us. One half of it, the part showing him, was on the bed. The other half had been screwed up and left on the floor.

I uncrumpled it and showed it to him. 'What did you do that for?'

He glanced at it. 'You changed it.'

'What?'

'You changed it. You made us look the same.'

'We did look the same. Remember?' Only in photographs, though. Nobody had ever confused us in the flesh. We moved differently, dressed differently. I was a few inches taller and started conversations. 'Why would I want to change it?'

'You're with them.'

'With who?'

'You know.' He kicked over the low table, sending the telephone crashing into the wall. 'I know it. All along I've known it. You wanted me out of the way, so I wouldn't tell.'

'Tell what?'

'I know what you are. I know what you're planning.' He waved his arms jerkily, as if trying to catch the words from the air. 'You kept me there. You made them watch me. You only came to make sure I was still there.'

'That's crap, Mike.'

'You have friends, all these friends. How many of them did you tell about me? So where were they? Why don't I see them? You wanted me out of the way. That's why you brought me here, cunt.'

'I brought you here for your own good.'

He stamped. 'For my own good!' He was shouting now. 'For my own! And that's why you kept me here. First time I'm allowed out, and you followed me.'

'Why should I want to do that, Mike?'

'Because of them. They tell you what to do.'

236

'Who are *they*, Mike?'

'Don't have to tell you.'

'Is one of them Joshua?'

'Why did Jane go, then? Isn't it! She can't face me, she changed the photo. Next time she sees me I'll be dead...'

He became more and more confused, finally settling into a resentful silence, crouched with his arms folded tightly across his chest, frowning at the blank television screen. He forgot his arguments enough to accept a second Dormatan. The last thing he said was, 'I want to go out.'

'Fine. We'll go out. We'll go to the park.'

'Not going now.'

'Tomorrow, then. Tomorrow.'

When he was asleep I disconnected the phone.

The next morning we went to the park. I'd chosen the park because I thought there would be too much air and space for a rat like Joshua. We went early, as people were still leaving for work.

Mike was still groggy when we left. I couldn't tell if this was the Dormatan or one of his bouts of confusion. He didn't say much, and followed instructions when I repeated them carefully.

The park wasn't far. Until recently it had been part of my early-morning circuit. I wondered if Mike would recognise the place. We'd played football there as kids.

As we walked he mumbled under his breath. He walked quickly, shoulders hunched. 'This is where they'll be waiting...'

'What was that, Mike?'

'Didn't say anything.' He stopped walking. 'When's Easter?'

'Two months away.'

'That's when. Why are we going to the park?'

'You wanted to get out.'

'What's the park like?'

'OK.' A bit of green, some flowerbeds, fenced-off swings and the paddling pool that only ever held rainwater. What did he expect it to be like? 'It's just a park. You've been there before.'

'What are you going to do?'

'With what?'

'You know.'

'I don't know, Mike. I can't know until you tell me. Or do you think I can read minds now?'

We reached the park. It was a bright, cold day, not many people about. A young mother hunched over a pram, two old people with dogs. Mike hesitated at the gate.

'I know this.'

'Of course you do. We used to come here a lot, remember?'

He shook his head. 'Where are we going?'

'Nowhere special. Wherever you like. We're just going for a stroll round the park.'

He smirked. 'Yeah, OK.'

We hadn't gone ten paces before he started to run. He made a bad start, putting too much effort into the first dash, panting and swaying before he'd gone a hundred yards. I could have caught him easily. I let him run: it was obvious he wasn't going to get far, and I wasn't dressed for a sprint. He turned a corner, disappeared from sight behind some bushes. I followed him at a steady walking pace. If he left the path it was only a short way to the road. Once across the road it would have been easy for him to lose me in the surrounding streets. It was what I'd have done. But somehow I knew he'd keep to the path.

He did. He kept to it as if it would take him where he wanted to go. He threw himself forward desperately, stumbling and getting slower with every step. Eventually, next to a convenient bench, he stopped altogether, and sat down heavily, leaning forward until he was bent double over his knees. He was still wheezing heavily by the time I caught up.

I sat next to him, and gave him some time to recover. When his breathing became more regular I asked, 'So what was that about, Mike?'

I didn't expect an answer. He made an effort. All I heard was '…beat me.'

'That's what happens if you don't pace yourself. You always had trouble with that, remember? I always had to go the whole way with you, saying, "Not too fast, not too fast".' I was rambling. 'It was why nobody wanted you on their side in football, remember?' He didn't answer. He just sat there, panting like a dog. 'You'd play like a lunatic for ten minutes then be too shagged to move.'

Actually, this wasn't the reason. They'd never wanted him because he'd never been any good at any team sport. You'd create openings for him, pass the ball so that it stopped at his feet in front of an open goal, and he'd fall over or gently tap it straight to the keeper. At first I put it down to lack of practice. I didn't have any influence in his year, so he was always left out of teams or picked last as a sub. The only chances he had to play were in four-a-sides with my friends in the different parks and commons. They let him play as a favour to me, careful not to complain too much every time he conceded a corner or missed a penalty. Eventually even I had to admit he was hopeless. We left him minding the coats, which he seemed to prefer.

'We used to play in this park.' I kept talking. 'Dekko lived just over there. Him and us against Paul, Andy, and the McDermott twins.' Or some other combination. Nostalgia. The McDermott twins! They looked alike in the flesh, not just in photographs. They were always made to play on the same side, otherwise it just got confusing: you'd pass to the one you thought was on your side and he'd score against you. I talked on. Did he remember that penalty shoot-out that went to sixteen-all until Andy couldn't save because Paul Kavanagh was sitting on him? The attempt at a cricket match that ended with Dekko needing stitches? They were funny, weren't they? The sort of event you came away from knowing you'd remember it forever...

Mike had forgotten them all.

It was too cold to sit on a park bench reminiscing.

'Come on, Mike, let's go.'

'Go where?'

'Wherever you like.'

He got to his feet. 'I want my room back.'

'You'll get it back. I just want you to stay with me for a couple more days.'

'I know what you want.'

'Oh, that.'

'My place.' He was getting angry. 'You took it. They wanted you to take it.'

Them again. 'There isn't any *they*, remember? You've got to sort yourself out.'

'Cunt. Cortevalde's a lying bitch...' And then he was raving again. It was those moments that made me want to dump him back at the house and let him take his chances with Joshua. It was like listening to Adam, only speeded up and with none of the sentences finished. At one point he said he was going to be eaten, and then stumbled at *transubstantiation*, a word I'd never heard him attempt before.

He talked as if I was the enemy.

'If I'm so bad, Mike, why are you telling me all this?'

He scowled, resenting the interruption, maybe not making sense of it, and went on muttering about me wanting to take his place. 'It's important. They need someone who isn't me.'

'Even if I do take your place...' Mike flinched. I kept forgetting he wasn't up to hypothetical cases. 'Even if I was, who'd take mine?'

He was emphatic. 'Jane.'

'Really? How?'

'They're watching us.'

I stopped walking. We were in the middle of a stretch of open ground that sloped gently down to the high street. A cold wind blew across, rippling the grass. There were some trees and benches, nothing else. Some way off, a woman was walking towards us. Further still, in the other direction, a man with a dog was moving away.

'Mike, are any of them here now?'

He didn't look up. 'No. Yes. No.'

'Good answer.'

He sank on to one of the benches. 'Her.'

'Jane?'

He was looking at the woman walking towards us, a small young woman still too far away to see distinctly. He looked at her hard, the way he'd looked at Jane. 'Her.'

'What about her?'

'I know her.'

'You've never seen her before in your life.' I looked at her myself, just to make sure. She was now close enough for me to see her face. She looked familiar, but then she had one of those pleasant faces that always look familiar. You think they're people you know, when all they do is serve your chips or work behind a bar.

She came closer. She looked at us warily. I didn't blame her: Mike could look threatening if you didn't know him. Then she looked again, and smiled.

It was Sally Mercer. Cazales, as was.

Poor Mike's face lit up. He probably couldn't name her, but her smile meant something to him. He beamed back, a winner's grin, as if he expected to be handed a prize. Sally ignored him and skipped over to me.

'Mike! What are you doing here? Fancy seeing you again!'

It was too late. Mike heard this and his expression changed, then went on changing.

'Sally,' I said, not sure what else I could say. *I'm Patrick, the brother*? Not likely. I felt sick.

'So what are you doing here?'

I found a voice. 'Taking a walk.'

She looked at Mike, noticed the resemblance.

'Hiya, Patrick, how are you? How's – what was it – computers?'

Mike turned away. A dog ran across the far end of the green. He watched that instead. 'Jane,' he said aloud.

'Sorry?' She turned back to me, mouthing something like: *Is he all right?* I made one of those hand gestures that are supposed to mean: *Don't worry*. She made a face indicating sympathy. She knew what computer people were like. 'How are *you*?'

I shrugged. 'OK. You?'

'Still looking for Mr Right, you know.'

'Well, good luck with that.' I wanted to get her away from Mike as quickly as possible. 'Give my regards to Dekko.'

'Dekko? Haven't seen him for months.' She stood grinning at me for a few seconds longer. 'We'll have to get together some time, Mike. Talk about old times.'

'Yeah, maybe.'

'Well, you know where I work.'

'Yeah.' From where we were standing I realised you could see the Drover. 'Sure.'

She walked away, occasionally turning back to wave or smile. Now she wasn't paying any attention to him, Mike watched her as she went. He looked disgusted.

'Jane,' he said, loudly.

'Come on, Mike.' I didn't know what else to say to him. 'Let's go.'

'That's not the name.'

'We'll talk about it later.'

Sally was still visible, marching to the place where she worked. She was too far off for me to be able to tell if she was looking back. Mike started to follow her. 'Not that way, Mike. Let's go home.'

'It's not *Mike*.' He didn't take his eyes off her. I felt suddenly resentful. Why did I waste my time with him? He'd driven Jane out of the flat and put my job on the line, not to mention what he'd done to my suits. And was he sorry? For a moment I wanted to turn and walk away. Then he put his head down and charged off again, this time heading for the Drover.

After that, I had to stay with him. Once again, he kept to the path. I didn't know if he was chasing Sally or simply trying to get away from me. As I watched him panting and gasping along the narrow grey strip of the path I knew I couldn't abandon him. The way he ran reminded me of Kevin Taylor.

He didn't get as far the second time. He still hadn't recovered from his first attempt. He stumbled and collapsed halfway between two benches and stayed hunched on the grass until I helped him to his feet. We walked home slowly. He made no more attempts to escape. Once back at my flat, as well as his usual medication I gave him another Dormatan. Mike looked at the pills as if he knew what I was up to, but took everything I gave him without saying a word. I sat with him for a while, and tried to explain why Sally Mercer had called me Mike. He was too tired to listen, or care. When I was sure he was asleep I left quietly, locking the door behind me.

I went back to the office. Piers was working by himself. He wasn't pleased to see me.

'If you've come here to work, you're late.'

I told him I wanted more time off. To the end of the week, maybe some of the week after that.

243

'We're quiet at the moment,' said Piers. 'It shouldn't be a problem. Unpaid.'

'Fair enough.'

I thought that would be all. 'One more thing. I disapprove of what you're doing with your brother.'

'You don't know the full story.'

'Perhaps not. Having him stay with you is not necessarily in your brother's best interests.'

'I think it is.'

'Or yours, for that matter. You look exhausted.'

'I'm OK.'

'I don't think you are.'

He opened one of the drawers of his desk. I thought he was going to offer me a pill: *When I can't sleep I use Dormatan...* Instead he handed me a piece of paper.

'About this Painter person. I asked the banks if they knew anything. I thought you might want to see this.'

It was a letter from one of the banks. *Re your request of the... while we are unable to confirm anything definite... believe there is a possibility he might now be found at the following address...*

'Piers, it worked! How did they find out?'

'I don't know. Perhaps somebody saw him leaving. Notice how careful they are. They only *believe*.'

I took the letter. 'Thanks.'

'What are you going to do?'

'See if Joshua is there.'

Piers frowned. 'And then?'

'I'll tell the police.'

'Is that all?'

'I'm just going to see if he's there. It's routine. A day at the office.'

Piers didn't smile. He produced another sheet of paper. 'A company like Elding Collections can't afford to be associated with any sort of trouble. One mistake, and we're out of business. See this? It's a letter of dismissal, dated two days ago. If there's no trouble, I'll tear it up. If there's trouble, you're sacked already. Do you understand?'

'Understood.'

'Try not to do anything illegal.'

I didn't make any promises.

Back at the flat, Mike was still asleep. I stood over him for a while, watching while he snored. Even asleep he frowned with concentration, as if dreaming was hard work.

'Don't worry,' I told him. 'With luck you'll be back home this time tomorrow.' I reconnected the phone, adjusting the volume. Almost immediately it began to ring.

It was Jane. 'What's going on? I've been on redial all afternoon.'

'I disconnected the phone.'

'Siege mentality, Patrick. You should hear yourself.'

'Can you do me a favour?'

'What kind of favour? I don't issue blank cheques.'

'Can you keep an eye on Mike for a few hours tonight? I need to go out.'

'No. No way. If you'd left him where he was – '

'I know what I should have done. Are you going to help me or not?'

There was a long pause. 'You're completely fucked-up.' There was nothing friendly about the way she said this. 'I'll be there at six.'

Mike woke up towards four o'clock, dazed and hungry. He was in a bad mood and made a point of calling me 'Mike', dwelling on the name almost triumphantly. Occasionally he talked about me as if describing me to somebody else in the room.

I told him Jane was coming.

He wouldn't look at me. 'Jane's not coming.'

'She's coming.' It was a quarter to six. I wasn't convinced myself. 'If she doesn't, I'll just have to stay in.'

'I know the reason. She'll take your place. I know, don't fucking say I don't...'

At six o'clock, as soon as the news on the radio began, he clapped his hands together. 'See, you cunt. You can't fool me, I know what's hiding behind you. You're fucking part of it.'

'Did you get this crap from Joshua, Mike?'

He was buoyant. He jumped to his feet, grinning, the backward boy who at last knows the answers. 'It's not Joshua, Mike. *He* didn't tell *me*. *I* told *him*. It was *me*. That cunt Cortevalde – '

The doorbell rang. He dropped back into his chair, suddenly miserable. By the time I reached the door Jane had let herself in.

'What's going on?'

'I told you. I need to go out.'

'Couldn't you have got your parents to babysit for you?'

'I've told you about them. They don't even know he's out yet.'

'Let's see him, then.'

Mike was still in his chair, arms folded across his chest, pretending he couldn't see Jane. He knew she was there though: when she said his name, he winced. 'How are you, Mike?'

He looked down at his wrists.

Jane took her handbag through to the kitchen and began to make herself at home. 'By the way,' she said, above the clatter of cups and saucers, 'I phoned the hospital. I knew you wouldn't. They think he's just spending a few days here as a treat. We had quite a talk about your attitude. The woman I spoke to said you were overprotective.'

'It's the kind of word she'd use.'

Mike had bent his head in our direction. I put an arm round her waist. She didn't pull away.

'I'm glad you could come,' I said.

'I'm beginning to wonder why I did.' She searched for the coffee. It was in the usual place. Had she forgotten already? 'I've never had to deal with...' She saw Mike was listening and lowered her voice, 'How is he?'

'He gets agitated sometimes. He didn't think you'd come, and that upset him.'

'He's upset because he's here.' She found the coffee. And the Dormatan. 'My God, when did you start taking these?'

'He makes a lot of noise at nights.'

'You don't want to take these. They're addictive. Haven't you read the papers?'

'I don't read papers. They were recommended.'

'Recommended?' Jane knew better. There was a campaign to have them banned. A crowd of sorry housewives and mid-ranking executives had stumbled forward claiming their lives were ruined. They weren't just addictive: they also caused mood swings, weight gain, continual drowsiness, and constipation. The links with respiratory problems, bad skin, sore throats and motion sickness were still denied by the manufacturers.

'I've read the instructions.'

'Christ, I leave you for two days and you've become a junkie.' She didn't push it any further. She might even have guessed the pills weren't for me. 'I don't know why you want me here. Can't he be left to himself?'

'I'd sooner he wasn't.'

'So what are you going to do about Joshua? Sort him out?'

'I'm just going to find where he is, and tell the police.'

'Are you sure?' She wasn't sure whether to joke or get angry. 'It's really easy to dislike you sometimes, Patrick. I thought you weren't a flake.'

'I'm not.'

'Well, I came back this time.'

'Thanks.'

'If I get any trouble from your brother, I'm leaving.'

'Fair enough.'

We sat with Mike for an hour. He didn't say a word.

The latest address was for a basement flat in another divvied-up terrace. There was nobody in. The street was all houses, so there was nowhere I could sit and keep a discreet watch. Joshua would see me whichever direction he came from, if some local snoop hadn't called the police first. I took a walk around the block. It saved me from hanging around, plus, I reasoned, there was a faint chance of meeting him in the street.

As I walked, I tried to think what I'd do next. Find Joshua, tell the police. And then? Once he was in custody I'd take Mike back to his room. And then? I had no plans beyond that. What happened next would depend on Mike.

It seemed I'd always drifted through life, borne along by other people's wishes. I had never wanted to be a middle-distance runner. I'd just happened to be the best in my year and, when I was told to train properly, all I thought was: why not? I'd started going to a boxing gym after a teacher had guessed Mike was talented. I'd trained as well, to keep him company, even though I was rubbish – no lateral movement, not enough defence. Shona had been there; she'd asked me to hold some pads. It was through her that I'd got the job with the travel company. I worked as a rep because I had to, came home after a month because of Mike, and moved to admin. When Shona went back to Aberdeen I'd carried on working there. It wasn't what I wanted, but there was nothing else I wanted more. All I'd asked was to be able to visit Mike and wear a suit, because a suit is a sign you're in control. Then the firm had collapsed, and it was Brian – once a star at Mike's gym – who had pushed me into Elding Collections. It was because of Brian that I'd met Jane, or maybe Jane had said to Sue, *I'm looking for someone with X qualities, who do you know?* And Sue had answered, *I know just the person.*

If it had been left to me we'd never have met.

Tony called me 'Psycho'. He couldn't have been more wrong. Psychopaths have problems, but at least they know what they want.

I turned a corner back on to the street with the address Piers had given me. Joshua was walking towards me from the other end.

We were both in a trance, our thoughts elsewhere. He snapped out of it first. I suddenly noticed the thin man in a long black coat at the other end of the street who'd stopped walking. He seemed to be weighing up his chances of reaching his front door before I did.

He must have decided they were bad. He turned – a neat about-face – and walked back the way he came. Once round the corner it would be easy to lose me among those streets. I started running, an easy jogging pace at first. I was wearing walking shoes, and the hard rubber soles spanked on the pavement like a muffled ricochet. He turned, saw I was gaining on him with every step, but didn't walk any faster.

Then, when I was only seconds away, he started to run. A long, loping stride, his pace matching my own. I thought he'd slow at the corner and then I'd catch him. Again, though, Joshua didn't behave as I'd expected. He didn't slow down. He threw himself round the corner as if attempting to rugby-tackle someone slightly ahead of him. I turned at the same comfortable jog I'd started with, expecting to find him face-down on the pavement, only to see that he was halfway down the street, sprinting like a greyhound. I accelerated. Over a distance I was still sure I could catch him. Wrong again. The distance between us increased.

Here was a feeling I'd not felt for years: the gut feeling of hopelessness you get on the last lap when the three good runners break and you realise the result has been decided from the start. The good runners ran because they wanted to, because they enjoyed it, because they cared more about winning than you, or, as in Joshua's case, because they were more frightened of losing.

Joshua disappeared round the next corner. By the time I got there, seconds later, there was no sign of him, and three different streets to choose from. I'd lost.

I went back the way I came and waited by his door, not caring who noticed.

I loitered there until ten. At first I was disappointed: I'd been beaten at something I was supposed to be good at; I'd failed again. Then, as I walked back, I started to think that maybe the evening hadn't been a complete waste. Joshua now knew I was on to him. He'd stay away from Mike, or, if he didn't, I'd give the police his latest address and let them find him. Mike could go home, I could go back to work, and Jane would move back in. Everything would work out for the best.

It was a long walk.

The front door of the flat was open, the hall light off. The door to the living room was ajar, and I had the immediate sense that something was missing. I stepped through jauntily, still glad to be back.

The something missing was the sound of the television. Jane always watched television when I wasn't there. I'd get home from work and she'd pretend she'd just turned it on and wasn't really interested. If it was just Mike, I expected silence. With Jane, there should have been noise.

There was nobody in the room. The television lay on its back, a jagged hole kicked into its screen. One of the chairs was on its side, the table lamp had been thrown against a wall, and the telephone was face-down on the wrong side of the room.

'Mike?' I felt sick, and suddenly exhausted. I held on to the door frame for support. 'Jane?'

There was a click. The bathroom door opened. Jane stepped out. Her hair was dishevelled, her dress was torn at the shoulder, and her bottom lip was cut.

'You bastard.' Her voice was low and dry, as if there was no breath behind it. 'You even ask for him first.'

Sixteen

'What happened?'
　　She shied away from me. She didn't just have a cut lip, I noticed. Her left cheek was bruised, or, rather, it had that high colour that comes before a bruise. It would look worse tomorrow.

'Your fucking brother.'

'Where is he?'

'That's right, show concern for him.'

'Jane, he's sick.'

She was hoarse. 'You think I didn't notice?'

'What happened?'

'What does it look like happened? What do you fucking think happened? What do I look like?'

It was like a dance. For every step I took forward, she moved back. 'Jane.'

'I should never have come.'

'Jane, he's not well. You can't blame him.'

'I don't blame *him*.'

'I didn't...' What do you do? You drift along, hoping nothing terrible will happen, but somehow believing that if it does you'll rise to it. And when it does you stand there, empty-handed, and say the first stupid thing that comes into your head. 'Where is he?'

'I don't fucking care.' She leaned against a wall, head bowed. All I could see was her hair. 'As long as he's not here.'

All I could do was repeat my stupid question. 'What happened?'

I righted the chair. She let herself be led to it.

'Your fucking brother,' she said again. She was determined not to cry, or had cried already. Her eyes were red. She trembled with anger. 'He seemed to get upset. He was raving.'

'What about?' Another stupid question.

'Do you think I was taking notes? I put my hand on his shoulder, like this.' She demonstrated, touching me for the first time, a light, reassuring pressure. 'To calm him down. To reassure him. And then he hit me. And then it started.'

'It?'

'He started smashing everything. I locked myself in there.' She gestured at the bathroom door. 'He was smashing everything and ranting. Then it went quiet. I didn't want to come out in case he started again.'

So she'd let him go. It was understandable, but Mike was still out there, a thirteen-stone baby with a persecution mania and good reflexes. It was nearly eleven o'clock. Chucking-out time. Before too long the streets around pubs were going to be taken over by lads with a few beers in them. 'I've got to find him,' I said.

'Is that all you care about?'

'Of course it isn't. But if he gets hurt – '

'I don't care. If he does, there's only himself to blame. Or you.'

'Jane.'

'Let me tell you something.' From the way she began I knew this was something she'd thought about since locking the bedroom door. 'I want him committed. Sectioned. If you won't do anything about it, I will. It's not safe for him to be out. He's dangerous.'

'Joshua – '

'Joshua has nothing to do with it! Look, your brother isn't like this because of Joshua. You can't blame anybody for that.'

I stood up. She didn't know the whole story. 'I can.'

'Where are you going?' She screamed at me. I'd never heard her scream before.

I came back. 'Closing the front door. I don't want everybody to hear.'

'They've heard the worst already. If you want someone to blame, try yourself. Mike was better off where he was. You didn't have to bring him here and keep him locked up. You didn't have to appoint me as your warder.'

I didn't say anything.

She said she wanted to go. She called Ros (the phone still worked). Ros was told enough of the story to make her fear the worst. She had made her own plans for the evening, and now they'd have to change as well. Jane called a cab, and went to the bathroom, not coming out until it had arrived. I sat next to her for the ride. She didn't want to make the trip alone.

On the way to her old flat I examined the stragglers evicted from pubs. Old drunks, singing boys, or the quiet, purposeful ones with the set faces of people who've been cheated once again, just when they thought they were ahead. There was no sign of Mike.

We were almost at the flat when Jane broke the silence. 'I read your horoscope.'

As if that mattered, now. 'When?'

'Yesterday. Ros is getting careless with security. I found the disk. She's got you down to a T.'

She cared enough to read it, then. 'It's not mine.'

'You could have fooled me.'

'I gave her Mike's birthday. It's Mike's horoscope.'

'Bollocks. It's you.' Then she asked, 'Why did you do that? Was it meant to be a joke?'

'Something like that.'

'Big joke. Ros was still right. About both of you.'

We reached the flat. 'Come with me,' she said. 'Please.'

I paid the cab. I meant to walk back. I'd take a long walk.

Ros was shocked at Jane's appearance. I wasn't too impressed by hers. Her face was its normal shape again; her lip rings and chains were back in place. I tried to see if there were any additions. Ros had that kind of fascination, like a building site you pass on the way to work. You look over the fence and wonder what they've done lately and when they'll be finished. How far had Ros got? What would she consider complete?

Ros led Jane through to the living room. Jane allowed herself to be led. I followed dumbly.

The room had changed. It looked neglected. There was dust on the flat surfaces, bags of rubbish spilling in the kitchenette. Ros had become careless about more than security.

She reached up and placed a hand on Jane's shoulder. She was wearing brown leather gloves, several sizes too big. What had she done now? Fingernails removed? Plastic joints inserted? Stupid, stupid woman.

She guided Jane over to a chair. Jane seemed to become more helpless by the second.

'She'll be all right now,' Ros said. She meant I wasn't needed.

'I'll be back tomorrow.' I was glad to leave. All I wanted was to start looking for Mike. Yes, I was sorry he'd hit Jane, of course I was. But Jane, I thought, could look after herself. She might be upset now, a long way from the cheerful, confident woman who'd once quizzed me about politics and wanted to organise my life, but that would pass. She would understand. She was a good person. The important thing now was that Mike was missing.

I walked back. I took a long, circular route, random at first, then following a pattern: these streets, then these streets, then these streets. It was late. The steady drinkers had gone home, the rowdies had found somewhere else or already had their fights. Almost the only people left were the total drunks, inching back to their slummy rooms or stalled in shop doorways. There was no sign of Mike.

It grew cold, and then colder. I tried our parents' old street, places he might know: the walk to school, to the bus garage, to different pubs or friends' houses. Places I hadn't visited in years because I already had one source of painful nostalgia. There was no sign of him.

At around three o'clock I gave up.

I woke up to the sound of the phone. I was sitting on the sofa. The first thing I saw was the smashed television.

It was half-past ten.

At first I ignored the phone. It buzzed softly, an accidental adjustment from when it had been thrown across the room. Still half asleep, I assumed its quiet beeps meant the message was unimportant.

It went on. Five, six, seven times. Whoever it was really did want to talk to me. My first thought was it must be bad news about Mike.

It was Brian. 'Are you all right?'

'No.'

'Sue said you'd had some trouble.'

Sue! Jane must have turned to her for support as soon as I was out of the door. 'Yeah, some.'

'Tell you what, I'll come round tonight.'

'Thanks, but don't bother. I'll probably be out.'

'Yeah? Where's your brother now?'

'Fuck knows.'

'Stay where you are, then. I'll come round now.'

'You don't have to.'

'A car might make things easier.'

'What about work?'

'No problem. I'm on my way.'

He reached the flat five minutes later. He noticed the television. It was hard to miss. 'Was that you or Jane?'

'Mike.'

'Ah. There is a lot of rubbish on these days.' He looked around with the deliberation of an insurance assessor, taking in all the minor damage: chipped paint from the doors, the broken glass from the lamp, the broken slats of Jane's magazine rack. 'You haven't heard anything, then?'

'Not a thing.'

'Well, let's start looking.'

We drew up an itinerary. It was simple. Everywhere between my flat and the house, and then anywhere else we could think of. For all I knew, Mike might have made his way safely back to the house and we'd find him lying on his bed, listening to the little radio. A dream. On the way to the house I asked Brian how he'd managed to square the time off with Piers. It meant there was nobody working for Elding Collections south of the river that morning. Piers couldn't have liked that.

'I told him I had a headache.'

'Yeah. Just after he heard you talking to me.'

'You think he realised, then?' Brian didn't care. 'Is this the place?'

There was a bit of a scene on the doorstep. If there was a way of asking about Mike without arousing Roger's suspicion, it hadn't occurred to me. Roger guessed what had happened before I had a chance to say anything. He opened the door and began his lecture at the same instant. I listened for just long enough to suss Mike wasn't there, then backed away smiling: nothing to worry about, everything's under control. I didn't need his reproaches. I had enough of my own.

Brian asked questions like, 'So what was Mike wearing?' There was a world of consideration in what he didn't say. We drove around that knot of streets like criminals casing the joint, facing over and over again the awful sameness of those Drives and Crescents and Avenues when the person you're looking for isn't there, those interchangeable little runs of shops: the newsagents, the launderette, the video store, Indian restaurant and chip shop or Chinese takeaway. The split bags of uncollected rubbish, derelicts with scrawny dogs by the off-licence, pensioners with a week's food packed into ancient handbags. We had a fried breakfast in a café grey with smoke. Brian said, 'It's not looking good, is it?'

'No.'

'Any other ideas?'

I had one, dismissed it. 'He hated the hospital.'

'But it's what he knows.'

'He won't go back there.'

'OK, then. Does he have any friends?'

'Outside the house, only Kent.'

'And the gym was closed.' Brian's thought processes were not just obvious, they were audible. 'Now, Jane said he got sort of agitated. Do you think the telephone call had anything to do with it?'

'What telephone call?'

Brian thought I knew this. 'Just before Mike lost his temper there was a telephone call. Didn't Jane mention it?'

'No.'

'She told Sue.'

'She didn't mention it to me.'

'She was still pretty shaken, I expect. Sue told me you were worried about this Painter guy. What about that?'

Sue and Jane must have had a long conversation. 'I don't know.' I could imagine Joshua calling Mike. He might have called him after he ran away from me, when he knew I wouldn't be home. What I couldn't imagine was how Mike would respond to his call. Perhaps Jane was right, and Mike was too fucked-up for Joshua to be a threat. Perhaps the call had been a wrong number. Perhaps a wrong number had been enough. 'It could be.'

'Why are you worried about him?'

'He's a bad influence.' Was he, though? Peter Bedding, Avril, Kevin Taylor – none of them had been going anywhere special in the first place. Perhaps Joshua really had swooped into their lives with promises of friendship and help, and been unable to save them. 'He's dangerous, sort of. I wanted to keep him away from Mike. Once the police had him, I meant to take Mike back.'

'What does your brother think?'

'I haven't a clue what Mike thinks.'

'You've got an address, though? For this Painter?'

'I think so.'

'Let's try that.'

We went there, parking a little way up the street so he wouldn't see us coming. Brian knocked on the door. I waited in the car and tried to read the paper, but kept remembering the sound of Kevin Taylor's head when he hit the garage door.

Brian came back, signalling for the window to be wound down. 'Nobody there.'

'He's usually out during the day.'

'Want to go in and look around?'

'In where?'

Brian rattled a large bunch of keys. 'His flat. One of these might work.'

'Where did you get those?'

Brian grinned. 'Memento from an old job. Well?'

If nothing else, it was worth a look.

'Technically,' Brian explained, 'we're not actually doing anything much wrong. We've gained admittance without the use of force or damage to the property.'

The flat was a cluttered one-bedroom number in permanent shadow. The furniture was a faded mismatch of hand-me-downs and leftovers, wood effect and Formica. It could have belonged to anyone with no concern for their surroundings. The only immediate sign that it belonged to Joshua was the jacket hanging from a hook on the wall. It was the one Kevin had worn the day I saw him coming out of the bank. Joshua obviously hadn't let him keep it.

There was a table next to the window with a black plastic ring binder and some envelopes. I opened the binder: pages of lined paper covered with neat handwriting. I looked closer. On the first sheet was a date I didn't recognise. There were dozens of pages, lot of dates.

Brian was at the bedroom door. 'What's that?'

'Looks like a diary.'

'Anything racy?'

'I doubt it.'

The first entry read: *It is important to keep a detailed record of my progress. I have to train my powers of observation.* I skipped until I came to a name. *Peter reported sighting on Bensley Road. I went there myself in the afternoon. Sensed a presence, but nothing definite. The foci of appearances do not correspond. If I can substantiate this it will be further proof that the maps are deliberately misleading. I questioned Peter further, but he denied hearing anything. Experimented myself but felt a barrier had been erected. No visions.*

Peter had to be Peter Bedding. The next entry seemed to be a week later, and similar. There were two or three entries to a page, dozens of pages. I skipped through, looking for names I recognised. *Slept badly. Someone is trying to influence me through my dreams. Adam?* Joshua wrote the names out in full. He either didn't trust his own memory or intended the diary to be read one day.

'Any good?' Brian came out of the bedroom holding a knife with a long, curved blade. 'Found this in the wardrobe.'

'I want to see if he mentions me.'

'Yeah? Must have a dull life if he does.' Brian balanced the knife in his hand. 'I bet carrying this isn't legal. Nice, though. Nice carving on the handle.'

I found a passage beginning: *There was a financial setback yesterday. The agent was very negative. According to the business card he worked for Elding Collections.*

Brian began to show signs of impatience. You had to know him to recognise them. 'Do you want to wait here till he gets back?'

It was tempting. But we were supposed to be looking for Mike. 'Let's go.'

'Nothing there, then?'

'There might be.' I closed the folder and held it under my arm.

'If you take it – ' Brian began.

'He won't complain.' I wanted Joshua to know someone had visited. There was a full-length mirror next to the bedroom door. 'Give me the knife.'

'I don't think we should take that.' Brian gave it to me all the same. It was solid metal, tarnished and heavy and not very sharp. I held the blade in a handkerchief, then tapped the mirror with the hilt. The mirror cracked without shattering, a diagonal line down its whole length. I drove the blade into the tabletop hard enough for it to stand up. 'Theft and destruction of property.' Brian was amused. 'Do you think you've done enough?'

I hadn't. I wanted to scare Joshua. I'd have written a message in blood on the walls if I'd had any spare blood. The knife, the broken mirror and the missing journal would have to do.

Back in the car Brian asked, 'Where to next?'

'I give up.' There were too many choices. I wanted to read Joshua's diary and I didn't want to stop looking.

261

'Shall we tell the police?'

'About Mike?'

'About Painter. Now you know where he lives.'

We drove around some more. Brian called in at the station and passed on Joshua's address. He came out looking glum. 'It was like they didn't really want it.' There was no sign of Mike. I checked at the Drover. It was Sally Mercer's day off. The bar manager hadn't seen anyone strange hanging around.

We drove around some more. By the middle of the afternoon we felt like kerb crawlers. Brian said, 'We should tell the police about Mike.'

'No. Not yet.'

'OK, then.'

Ten minutes later he asked, 'When shall we tell them?'

'Not yet.' He'd been gone for seventeen hours. No money, no food, nowhere to go. He'd attract someone's attention before too long.

'What about your parents?'

'He doesn't know the way.'

'It's near a station, right? If he's got the address he could ask.'

'No money.'

'It's not looking good.'

'He can't have gone far.'

Brian pulled up in another residential street. 'Sometimes you don't have to.'

'Why are you stopping here?'

'Sue's place. Want a coffee? This driving's giving me a headache.'

I didn't argue, not after what he'd done so far. He led me into Sue's chintzy flat and headed for the kitchen. He made coffee. After ten minutes he stood up again. 'You might as well stay here. I'll check the hospital. Pretend I want to visit and haven't heard.'

I didn't want to stay in Sue's flat. 'Drop me at my place. There might be a message.'

He drove me back. There was no message. Mike wasn't waiting in the street outside. The television was still on its back. I began tidying up. I put the television back on its base (why? – it still didn't work), swept the broken glass into a pan. Dusted, hoovered, then sat down and began to read Joshua's folder.

Seventeen

Joshua was insane. I'd have preferred him to be evil, a criminal who knew what he was doing and used occultists and the mentally ill because they were soft targets. I'd have preferred him not to believe any of the things he said. It wasn't so. One of Mike's nurses had once used the phrase *delusional structure*. I didn't have to read far into the journal to realise Joshua had more than a structure: he had a whole theme park, complete with white-knuckle rides and a ghost train.

I read methodically, from the beginning, pausing over the entries I didn't understand. *Retrograde. The Tower. The tenth house?* References to astrology and the tarot. A little research might have given the significance. But what about *Sixteen, eleven, four?* Where did you start with that? And why not write *16,11,4?* Some of it was plain as day: *Kevin is weak and unreliable. He wants to help but is too timid. He reminds me of Peter, the same ingratitude.* Joshua's written style was pompous, like the grander aliens in bad sci-fi. He always wrote *I have* or *it is* and was scrupulous about apostrophes to indicate possession. His handwriting was neat and legible, as if he expected marks for presentation.

And he was insane. It wasn't just the things he wrote, though they were obvious enough, the kinds of things Mike would have written if he'd kept a diary: *There are pockets of negative energy by the roundabout*, or *Something was hovering over me at the post office. I could see nothing but the sense of presence was overwhelming.* The real proof was that he recorded all of this alongside descriptions of the weather (*Clear, wind south-southeast. It rained at three o'clock.*) and a lucid, perfectly understandable account of how he'd been visiting Mike regularly for months.

I'd led him to Mike. He'd been suspicious of me from the first, I was *negative*. Then I turned up at Peter Bedding's. Then at a pub where he had gone to look *at the junction of three lines*. When he recruited Kevin and discovered Kevin knew me, his suspicions seemed to be confirmed. *Kevin has already been contacted. This is not a coincidence.* Nothing for Joshua was a coincidence. Joshua believed in conspiracies: huge, labyrinthine plots involving half the people on the planet and directed at keeping him from The Truth. *I saw him again this afternoon. He followed me. I noticed him again later, waiting in a car. His 'work' is just a cover.* When he saw me with Jane it was further proof: *Jane has fallen under his influence. I saw them together. I could tell Jane was unhappy, but she wouldn't leave him. He must use force, or hypnosis.* He started following me: *He seemed to be travelling at random. When I plotted his course on a map the significance was obvious. There are lines he cannot cross. If I discern the pattern I may be able to neutralise him.* I'd never seen him following me, but then I hadn't been looking. Until I'd seen him in the same room as Mike, he'd been no more than an irritation, even after what had happened to Kevin.

I followed him to a building that seemed to be some kind of institution. I discovered it was a psychiatric hospital. This confirms the links between psychiatry and the financial system. Both are systems of control, intent on imposing spurious 'norms' to keep us from noticing the reality of the situation... He then added, for his own benefit, a half-page essay recapitulating his own opinion. He was mad all right, but not at an obvious level. You'd have to listen to him for at least twenty minutes before you noticed.

Kevin says he is visiting his brother… Joshua had become intrigued. Here was a man from nowhere, asking for his credit cards, talking to his latest medium and exercising hypnotic control over a woman he fancied. A brother confined to an institution only completed the picture. What if the brother was a child of light, locked away to prevent the world from hearing The Truth?

So he went to find out.

I gained admission (meaning, he walked in – there were no barriers to cross or watchful guardians to dupe; people walked in off the street). *His brother was unwilling to talk. He has been conditioned against accepting his own reality. He is aware of Their presence, but refused to answer any questions. I have to make him trust me, convince him I am not working for Them. His name is Michael.* And that was the name Joshua used from then on. Not Mike, not even M for convenience. Michael.

Progress was slow, but Joshua was optimistic. *Michael thinks his brother is trying to take his place. He talked about someone called Shona, and said she was gone. Possibly an earlier victim?* Mike was crazy, but then Joshua was crazy himself. In his view, Mike wasn't confused or incoherent, he was just being careful. *He mentioned a blonde woman. He said I should watch her. Is this a warning? It could be Liz. Margaret may already know about him. Or his brother is trying to infiltrate Margaret's group.* He recorded what he thought of his old associates: *Margaret's group are a disappointment. They have not developed. Adam is not to be trusted. Some of his theories regarding popular culture are interesting but too much talk.* The surprise came a few pages later: *I showed Michael to Adam. Rosemary was there, but she was too negative and left early. Michael talked about Kent. Adam thought this was significant (Coldrum Stones, etc).* And later still: *We tried again, away from the house. The results were inconclusive. I took Michael back to the house.*

I am sure he made contact, but he refused to tell us what he saw. Adam felt we would have been more successful if we had held the ritual at the proper time. He wants to try again, on a better day.

I didn't have Adam's number. Jane would know it.

Ros answered. 'Uh?' Her voice was small, childlike.

'Is Jane there?'

There was a long pause. There was no sound except a faint hiss that might have been electrical.

'Ros, are you still there?'

'No.' She answered my first question. 'She's not here.'

'Ros, do you know Adam's number?'

'His... number?'

These people. 'His telephone number.'

Another long pause. Then, 'Why?'

'Because I want to talk to him.'

'No. Not that. Why did you lie to me?'

'What?'

'The horoscope.' There was no anger in her voice, just a remote curiosity. 'Why did you lie?'

'Ros, I just want to know Adam's number.'

'I need to know why you lied.'

'Listen, I just want Adam's number. Are you going to tell me or what?'

She hung up. I threw the phone across the room. Amazingly, the thing wasn't broken. I dialled again. Ros must have been waiting for the call. She answered immediately.

'Is that Patrick?'

I tried another approach.

'Ros, you must help me.'

'I will help you. Only you must allow yourself to be helped.'

'You know my brother has gone.'

'Your brother is safe.'

'What do you mean, safe?'

'His chart. What I thought was *your* chart. It's all there. Do you think he has a choice? None of us has a choice.'

I remembered what she'd said at Margaret's party about everything being chance otherwise we'd have no choice. Now she was a fatalist. I blamed the painkillers.

'Ros, Joshua and Adam, what are they planning?'

'They… what they've always planned. From the beginning.'

'Where?'

'Adam. Joshua has nowhere suitable. Adam…' She faded out. It was like listening to a signal from deep space.

'Ros, is Mike at Adam's?'

'Everything is.'

'All I want to know is – '

'Candlemas,' she said, with a sense of wonder. 'The real Candlemas.'

I realised I wasn't going to get anything else out of her. 'Thanks, Ros.' This time I didn't throw the phone across the room.

Brian came back. 'He's not at the hospital. Anything in the diary?'

'A few things.' I told him about Adam.

'That's weird,' Brian said, when I'd finished. 'That's just weird. Jane knows some strange people. Hammer Horror or what? You don't believe any of it, do you? I mean, that it's real?' He shook his head at the strangeness of it all, and then got back to business. 'This Adam, will he be in?'

'I think he works.'

'What sort of gaff is it?'

'Block of flats. New.'

Brian shook his head. 'I won't be able to get in. Not if there's an entryphone. And if he's at work, would he have left your brother in his flat?'

And then it came to me. There was one place we hadn't checked, and Mike might have been there all along.

'I don't think we need to go to this house. I think I know where he'll be. You might as well go home, Brian. You've been great, but I can do the rest myself.'

'Yeah?' Brian sounded sceptical. 'Might be best if I go as well. In case there's trouble.'

'From Adam and Joshua?' I laughed. 'I'm not expecting any trouble.'

He thought about this for a few seconds. 'I wasn't thinking of them.'

'Meaning?'

'Better to be safe. I'll see if I can get Tony to come as well.'

'Bellman? We don't need him.'

'Just to make sure. We'll stop at the office. Tone'll be there. Then we'll get something to eat.' He spelt it out carefully. 'Give us all a chance to calm down. Anyway, I've seen these films. Hammer Horror. Nothing happens till it gets dark.'

Eighteen

'That's the place.'

'Right.' Brian parked over the road from the pet shop.
'Doesn't look much.'

It didn't. A row of shops, cars parked in front of them. It
looked ordinary.

'Another fucking dump.' Tony sounded weary. He'd been
with us for two hours, most of that spent in a Chinese. You'd
have thought we'd been looking all night. 'Not exactly the
Hellfire Club, is it?'

'I thought of running a pet shop,' Brian said.

Tony snorted. 'Rabbits and alfalfa. Are you sure this is
the place?'

'Might be.'

'So what will they be doing in there?'

'I don't know.' I'd tried to explain over the Chinese: what
Daniel had told me about Joshua, what Joshua had written
about himself. 'I haven't a clue.'

'Contacting elemental beings.' Brian was thoughtful. 'You
think there's something in it?'

'Not a chance.' Tony was emphatic. 'There's nothing
there to contact. It's just dead air.'

'You sound pretty certain.' Brian looked at his watch.
'8.16. I prefer to keep an open mind.'

'They might not even be there,' I said. 'We haven't seen
anybody going in.' What if I was wrong, and all this time
Mike was somewhere else?

'We'll check anyway.' Brian got out of the car. 'If he's not here, then we go to the police. OK, Patrick? Ready, Tone?'

'I'll stay here.' Tony slid into the driver's seat. 'Lookout.'

Brian said, 'What if we need you?'

'If it's numbers, come back for me. Otherwise I'll stay here.'

'Always knew you were chicken.'

'I've got my record to think about.'

I'd waited long enough. 'Come on, then.' I crossed the road.

Brian caught up with me at the door. 'Are you going to ring, or what?'

'What.' I pushed at the door. It gave slightly at the top and bottom. 'Depends on the lock.' I stepped back, steadied myself, and kicked. Shona would have been proud of me. The wood around the lock splintered. All it took after that was a shove.

Brian followed me, shaking his head. 'You should have let me try a key first.'

We crept down the dark staircase. Nobody came up to meet us; no guards had been posted. There were muffled sounds coming from the cellar. Whatever was going on was so intense they hadn't heard the front door breaking. The door at the bottom was unlocked. I opened it maybe half an inch before Brian put his hand on my shoulder.

'Let's see who's there first.'

I looked through the gap. At first I couldn't see anybody. The sofas had been pushed back to the walls, leaving the middle of the room clear. Then, still in the same pale grey suit he'd worn at the house, Joshua stepped backwards into view.

'Look, stand in the middle of the ring. Stand in the middle of the ring. That's all we want. It's not too much to ask, is it? Just stand in the middle of the ring.' He was nearly hysterical. There was an answering growl from a part of the room I couldn't see.

271

Mike. Brian tightened his grip on my shoulder. 'We want to make a good entrance,' he whispered.

'What's happening now?' A woman's voice, familiar, also from the shadows. 'What's supposed to happen?'

'Give it time. We must be patient.' Joshua moved out of sight.

The woman's voice again. 'I don't like this. Is he all right?'

Another growl.

A third voice, Adam's. 'The ring is perfectly safe. Trust me.'

The woman again, 'I don't think this is right.'

'Stay in the ring.' Joshua again. 'Look, it's not difficult.'

'Shouldn't we be in a ring as well?' the woman asked. 'What is it supposed to do?'

'*We're* safe,' Joshua sounded as if he'd explained this already. 'They can't see *us*.'

There was a hoarse shout. Brian tightened his grip on my shoulder.

'What did he say?' the woman asked. 'What did he say?'

Mike shouted again. Panicked, the woman backed into my line of vision. It was Beth. I wondered if Margaret knew she was there with Adam. 'What is he saying?'

'Get in the ring!' Joshua was peevish. Then suddenly elated, 'Can't you feel them? They're here.'

Brian let go of my shoulder. I slammed through the door like a greyhound out of a trap. 'We're here, all right.' Beth screamed and jumped back. Mike was sitting on the floor at the edge of an elaborate chalk circle. His hands covered his face. Adam stood behind him, holding what looked like a walking stick. There was nobody else. Whatever they thought they'd summoned wasn't visible. Joshua looked at me as if he'd never seen me before. I hit him so hard my forearm went numb.

Adam backed away. 'Now, Patrick, I think that was unnecessary.'

Joshua crawled across the floor, coughing.

Brian told Beth, 'I think you should leave.'

Mike didn't look up. 'Mike,' I said. 'It's me.'

Mike kept his hands over his face. I couldn't tell if he was laughing or crying.

Joshua climbed up the side of one of the sofas and managed to stand. Blood streamed from his nose. He bled easily. His mouth and hands were covered, his white shirt and grey jacket streaked. 'Look what you've…'

Adam had backed away as far as possible. 'Now, look – '

I moved towards him. 'What do you think you're doing?' I pointed at Joshua. 'With this bastard?'

For Adam there was no such thing as a rhetorical question. 'It seemed there was a good chance of verifying some basic – '

'Don't say anything,' Brian told him.

Beth found her voice. 'What's going on? Patrick?'

Mike said, 'He's not Patrick.' His voice was hoarse. He brought his hands down from his face but kept his head bowed. 'You're too late. He's fucking done it.'

'Done what, Mike?'

'Them.' Mike was rigid with concentration. 'He. They. Me.'

'There's nobody here, Mike.'

'They're here.' Joshua discovered he could stand without holding on to the wall. He took a step forward. 'Can't you feel them?'

Mike sat with his shoulders hunched, wringing his hands slowly, as if trying to rub off an oil stain. 'You should see them,' he said. 'They didn't see it coming.'

'I think you should leave.' Joshua attempted dignity. 'You're not welcome here. We're trying to help Michael. What have you ever done, apart from keeping him locked up?'

Adam looked from us to Joshua and back. 'I think enough has been said already. It's obvious there's been a misunderstanding.'

273

Joshua kept walking towards me. 'Everything you've done has been aimed at destroying what this man – what Michael truly is.'

He stepped into range. I hit him.

My hand went numb and stayed numb. Joshua went down again and sobbed, but he didn't give up.

'See? This is your answer to everything. This is all you can do.'

I felt I was no longer in control, as if this was a film I'd seen once, or a bad dream I should have snapped out of days earlier. 'What did you give him?'

'He has to ask,' Mike said. 'He doesn't know.'

Joshua stayed on his hands and knees. I kicked him in the ribs. 'What did you give him?'

He collapsed on to his stomach.

Beth slipped past Brian and ran up the stairs.

Joshua gasped. 'I helped him become what he truly is.'

Useless. I felt the same sense of futility I'd felt when I ran after him in the street. I couldn't reach him then and I couldn't reach him now. 'Mike,' I said.

Mike looked up. He glanced around the room, all the time nodding as if he was listening to dance music. 'Yeah, Mike.'

Brian crouched next to him and put an arm round his shoulder. 'We'd better go. Leave him, Patrick.'

'Look,' Adam made a final attempt at explanation, 'I think you ought to know that if Joshua gave him any kind of illegal substance, I knew nothing about it.'

'Judas!' Joshua started to crawl away. 'You know as well as I do.'

I turned to Adam. 'Do you?'

Adam clutched the stick. 'I can explain everything.' He held it with all the street-fighting assurance of a Morris dancer. 'But this probably isn't the time. You're obviously very upset. I think we all need to calm down.'

'Yeah.' Mike watched Joshua crawling across the floor. 'Yeah, calm down, *Mike*.'

'Look at him.' I could feel the anger building again. 'What do you think you're doing?'

Adam looked at me warily. 'Your brother is an exceptional person. When Ros told me about your horoscope... Look, normally I wouldn't pay any attention to Joshua. He – his methods are fundamentally unscientific. But when he told me about Michael, and his connection to you...' He trailed off, and took a step back. 'Joshua showed us what Michael could do. I thought it was worth investigating further. Admittedly these aren't ideal circumstances.' He gave a forced smile; it quickly faltered. 'I appreciate we should have informed you. I really do. But we weren't sure how you would react. Look, you have to admit you haven't been open about this yourself.'

'So who else was involved? Margaret? Daniel?'

'Margaret, we didn't... Beth came because she thought Michael could heal the schism.' He glanced at Mike, who was still watching Joshua. 'Margaret didn't know. This was supposed to be... Look, we never intended to harm anybody and nobody has been harmed...'

Mike looked up at the ceiling. 'They're still here.'

'Did Jane know?'

'We didn't tell Jane.' Adam was growing in confidence. 'She isn't – well, she isn't stable. We couldn't be sure how she'd react. What I mean is, people can be too sensitive about these issues. Jane is. And you. I'm sorry, Patrick, but it has to be said.'

'Let's go, Patrick.' Brian sounded less calm than usual. 'There's no point talking to these people. Let's go.'

'They're still here,' Mike repeated, in his bored teenager voice.

'Yeah, we're still here.' I turned away from Adam. 'But we're going now.'

Adam thought he was safe. 'I'm sorry for the way you feel about your brother. But you do have to acknowledge that some of this is your fault.'

It was as if I'd been waiting for him to say it. I moved towards him. He swung the stick and missed. My hand was already so numb I couldn't tell how hard I hit him. Adam whimpered like a pup shut out in a back yard, and slid down the wall, just as he'd done at his party. He crouched on the floor, shielding his face with his arms.

'Leave him, Patrick.' Brian took Mike's arm. 'We've done enough damage. Let's go.' He stood up. Mike pulled his arm free, remained on the floor. I knelt down to face him.

'Let's go, Mike. Back to the house.'

'Damage.' Mike looked hard at the floor. He could have been talking to anyone. 'You're here now. Fucking cunt.'

'Come on.'

Joshua had got back to his feet. He looked a mess. 'You don't have to go with them. Michael, if you go with them you know what's going to happen.'

'Shut it, Joshua.'

'Michael, you know where they'll take you.'

'Careful.' Brian stood between us. 'Don't say a word.'

Adam's resistance had been crushed. 'Stay out of it, Joshua. Let them go.'

I turned back to Mike. 'Come on, Mike. Let's go home.'

'Home.' Mike stood up, slowly. He looked at Brian, without seeming to recognise him. Brian had been one of the stars of Mike's old gym, the only unbeaten pro, and now Mike didn't recognise him. There was an odd moment of stillness, as if Mike was deep in thought and we were waiting for him to decide, as if his decision could possibly mean anything. The oracle, I thought, the oracle of fucking Delphi. The woman and the tripod waiting to receive the message from the gods. The line remembered from Adam's first party came back: *Ultima Cumaei venit iam carminis aetas*. Now has come the last age of the song of the Cumae. No more prophesies, the golden age beginning with the birth of a son. An arse-licking eclogue by a poet twenty centuries dead. Stupid what comes back to you, stupid what people still believe. Two thousand years later Joshua was still waiting for a message. And Mike wasn't just deep in thought, he was lost in it, with no clue where he was and no road out.

Joshua didn't give up. 'You know what's best for you, Michael.'

'Not a word,' Brian said.

'You know what you have to do.'

'Quiet.'

'Come on, Mike,' I said. 'Let's go home.'

'Home.' Mike raised his head, looked at me with an expression I couldn't begin to read. 'Yeah, let's go.' There was a growl from the back of his throat and he hunched his shoulders.

'Watch it, Patrick.' Brian's warning came too late. Mike caught me with a jab-uppercut combination. I didn't see it coming.

He'd never hit me before, *really* hit me. When we'd sparred as teenagers his punches had been no more than demonstrations, the blows that score points and break an opponent's heart.

Other people had hit me: the usual after-hours tussles and reeling scraps. There was a bouncer at the Elite who thought I was lippy; a Scouser at Dino's who claimed I was after his girlfriend (I'd thought he was joking; his hand was already in plaster); two men in Southend who followed me to my B&B from a nightclub and asked for money; a black guy at a bus stop in Tooting who accused me of jumping the queue; an Iranian in a pub in Sutton who kept talking to my girlfriend (what was her name?); a skinhead who claimed to be a friend of Shona and nearly broke my nose. And then there were the people I knew: Andy Longman, when he warned me off his sister and was offended when I told him I'd never fancied her; Dekko, when he forgot I was still holding the cricket bat; Shona herself, when I tried to talk her out of entering a contest I knew she'd lose.

None of them had hit me as hard as Mike did then.

I went down on one knee. Mike stood over me as if waiting for the count, with that intent, unreadable face. I stayed down: it's the bad fighters who get up straight away, who leap to their feet and find they can't control their legs. Brian moved to stand between us. I looked up and saw Mike step back into the shadows. I remember staring at the spot where he'd stood, wondering how the room had become so dark. I couldn't see the sofa, or the walls. Even Brian seemed to be lost in shadow. Someone must have turned off the lights, I thought. I tried to stand up.

Brian helped me to my feet. 'Are you OK?' I nodded. I couldn't speak. I couldn't think of any words. The floor seemed to move like a raft on choppy water. 'Look at me, Patrick. Are you OK?'

I looked at him. My vision was clear. The choppy water slowly stilled. I didn't know how long I'd been out.

Brian repeated, 'Are you OK? Walk towards me.'

I was still in the cellar. I looked around. Adam had moved to one of the sofas. He held one hand against his jaw and sniffed and kept saying, 'None of this is what I intended, none of this…'

Joshua, on his feet again, leaned against a wall, clutching his side. He was watching me warily.

Mike had gone.

I looked around, the way I'd looked around his room the time he'd been taken to the Marigold Wing; as if he might reappear, step out from the shadows or from behind a sofa. But he was gone.

'He won't get far,' Brian said. 'Tony will stop him.'

'Why didn't you?' I pulled away from him. 'Didn't you notice?'

Brian followed me up the stairs. 'I was worried about you. When I turned around... Tony will stop him.'

We reached the street. Tony hadn't stopped anybody. He was still in the car, waiting. We crossed the road, looking both ways. There was no sign of Mike. I banged on the window. Tony started. He hadn't even noticed us coming out. 'Which way did he go?'

He looked at me blankly. 'Which way did who go?'

'Patrick's brother.' Brian caught up with me. 'You must have seen him.'

'I haven't seen anybody.'

'You must have seen the woman.'

'What fucking woman?'

'Christ, Bellman, were you asleep? You must have seen something.'

Tony climbed out of the car. 'Fuck off, Farrell.' His voice was quiet, measured. 'If anybody came through that door I'd have seen them. I stayed here and I watched, just like I said I would.'

Brian pulled me back. 'Maybe he's still in the cellar.'

So we went back down, Tony following us from a distance. Joshua hadn't moved from the wall. He seemed almost amused to see us again, but didn't say anything. Adam was back on his feet and trying to scuff out the chalk circle. He backed away as soon as he saw us. 'Where's Mike?' I asked him.

'What do you mean?'

'This place,' Brian said, as casually as a prospective buyer checking the details. 'Are there any other doors? Any other ways of getting out of here?'

Adam kept backing away. 'You mean he's gone?'

Joshua sounded triumphant. 'They've taken him.'

I didn't have the heart to hit him any more.

'They? Rubbish.' Brian paced around the room, looking behind the sofas, occasionally touching the bare brick walls. 'He can't have got far.'

Tony stood over the chalk circle. He smiled at Adam: his mobster smile. 'And what's this supposed to do?'

I answered for him. 'Summon demons.'

Adam protested, 'That's not... I mean, *demon* isn't the word...'

'He's not here.' Brian went back to the door. 'Are you sure there's no other way out?'

Adam shook his head.

'If he'd left,' Tony said, 'I'd have seen him.'

'You must have been asleep, Bellman.'

'Fuck off, Farrell.' Tony spat at the floor. 'Check that passage. He could be upstairs somewhere.' He moved to the door. I followed him.

As I was about to leave, Joshua said something. 'You've done it.'

I turned. I expected him to flinch. 'What?'

He was almost serene. 'You've won.'

We walked back up the stairs.

We checked the passage. There was a door apparently leading into the shop at the top of the stairs, but it wasn't just locked, it had been painted shut. Nobody had used it in years.

'He came out of the door,' Brian concluded. 'Are you sure you weren't asleep?'

Tony denied it, but neither of us believed him. He waved at the cars parked in front of the shops, 'If he crouched when he came out, then I might not have seen him.'

'Whatever,' Brian said. 'He can't have got far. And we're wasting time here.' We went back to his car and started all over again.

Nineteen

We didn't find him that night. We drove slowly around the area, expecting to see him at the next turning, shuffling off down a side street or standing absently on a garage forecourt. He should have been easy to find, but there wasn't a trace. Nobody we asked had seen him. I had a sick sense that this time he was gone for good, that Joshua had been right and he'd slipped out of our world forever.

That was my irrational fear. My rational one was a memory of Kevin Taylor running blindly at a metal door.

We'd been driving around for barely an hour when Brian insisted on taking me to the hospital. My hand, he said, was serious.

He was right, but I don't remember feeling any pain. That came the next day. He drove me to casualty and seconded my excuse. Tony waited in the car. They left me there, with nothing to do but watch as each new case was wheeled or escorted in. I wasn't treated for hours, and when I was finally dismissed with my hand in plaster I was too tired to carry on with the search. My fatigue and the growing pain in my hand felt selfish.

I went home because I couldn't think of anywhere else to go.

Brian called at my flat the next morning. They hadn't found him, he said. Yeah, they'd looked, but there were only so many places they could look and if Mike was hiding from them... They'd driven around for another hour, then they'd gone to the police. 'It's down to them now.'

I was exhausted and my right hand was wrecked. I wanted to start looking again, right then.

Brian had had enough. He said he had his own job to do. If I wanted to go on looking, he'd cover for me at work, but that was all. 'Sorry, Patrick, but from now on you're on your own.'

Now Mike was officially missing I expected something to happen. I was, for a while, optimistic. I even went back to work. I should have known better; I knew how easy it was to disappear, to fall out of sight. After all, I spent most of my days not finding people, and Elding Collections dealt with the aristocracy of the missing, the people who'd had jobs, addresses, and credit cards, the ones who existed on company records, and we couldn't find *them*. Even so, I was optimistic.

Jane called me a few days later. She wanted to collect her things.

'OK.' A trial separation, I thought. 'We'll see how it works out.' I thought I was being tolerant, understanding. It wasn't enough.

'I already know how it works out,' she said. She didn't want to live with me again. She didn't want to *see* me again. It was the violence, she said. She couldn't forget what Mike had done to her. She'd heard what I had done to Adam. 'I shouldn't have to live with that.' She didn't come alone: she'd brought Daniel, the wettest man in the group. 'And I'm not going to live with it.' She packed the rest of her clothes, boxed her computer. It was ridiculous how little there was, how quickly it was gone.

I sat and watched as she packed, saying things like, 'You're overreacting.'

She'd say, 'Maybe.'

'We'll have to talk about this.'

'Maybe.' Daniel fetched and carried, looking either smug or nervous.

She didn't come back or phone me again. I called her, and was rebuffed, given excuses. I went back to work. Tony stopped calling me 'Psycho'. There were no more jokes about brothers or mad girlfriends. I collected cards with Brian, as usual. The only difference was that now he didn't let me work alone. He was always standing by, just in case. Once, some stupid unemployed bricklayer asked if I knew, *if I had any fucking idea,* what it was like to have a family. Brian was there, ready to step between us. It went on for weeks.

Back at home, in the once-neat flat with the smashed television, I phoned Jane a few more times. No, she didn't think a drink was a good idea. Ever.

I was sure she'd come round eventually. Optimism, again.

There was one more event, something I'd forgotten was going to happen. I had to attend the inquest into Kevin Taylor's death. His family had 'raised questions'. They soon dropped them. They had lived a few streets away from Kevin and hadn't tried to help him when he was alive. They must have realised they might come across badly. In the end they were barely mentioned. Kevin's death was judged to be the result of self-inflicted cranial damage – severe concussion, haematoma, the works. Traces of a variety of class A drugs had been found in the deceased's blood – hallucinogens and amphetamines. These had no doubt led to the excited state of mind testified to by the witnesses. No responsibility for his injuries attached to the police, who had acted in an exemplary fashion.

I barely had to say a word. Kevin's inquest was routine, over in minutes. Misadventure. Even in death nobody wanted to waste time on him. Joshua Painter was mentioned in

283

passing, as someone associated with Kevin who couldn't be there in person.

Afterwards I talked to one of the policemen. He said he'd seen Joshua a few weeks earlier. They couldn't touch him about the fraud, he said. It was small stuff, not important. The inquest had gone all right, though, hadn't it? There was nothing to worry about. 'At least you tried, mate.' He gave me Joshua's latest address.

The police didn't find Mike. They stopped looking long ago. Why should they waste their time? He's on a record, and if he ever turns up, if they ever accidentally run into him, they'll know who he is. That's all they can do. They won't trawl through the hostels, the huddled doorways, the dismal shanties of cardboard and strong lager. They won't put 'Missing' notices with pathetically out-of-date photographs in shop windows. I did that. I still go out, once or twice a week, looking. It's strange how you can live in a place for years, for all your life, and not notice how many places there are where a man could disappear. All they have to do is climb a fence, walk down a railway tunnel... I still tell myself he can't have got far, though by now he could be anywhere.

There are nights when I lie awake and wonder if Mike hadn't been right all along. He disappeared so suddenly. We lost sight of him for a minute and he was gone. He'd always said there were people following him. Maybe in the end they caught up... But that's insane, something you can't believe in daylight, or when you're fully awake.

The other fantasy is that he's found somewhere to stay and is as happy as he'll ever be, and I'd only spoil it by finding him. Except I can't believe that either. So I go out looking, and I tell myself he can't have got far, that he was too sick and confused, that he can't stay hidden forever. But you don't have to be dragged into a parallel reality to disappear. You don't even have to travel. All you have to do is stop at the first bridge, the first railway track. That's what people like Mike do: they jump from bridges, step in front of trains. Most of the time they're invisible, ignored until they lash out. If they hurt somebody else you'll hear about it. Maniacs in frenzied knife attacks are headline stuff; *Sick Man Takes Own Life* will barely make the local papers.

So I spend a few evenings a month looking, even though I don't expect to find him. Until I know for certain, I can't *not* look, even if it means trudging around the same roads, asking the same questions of the same people. It's futile, but until I know for certain, until the police knock at my door and tell me they're sorry, they're really sorry, it's what I have to do.

And once a week I have dinner with Sue and Brian. It's charity, their good deed. I talk fights with Brian, and occasionally Sue tells me the latest about Jane. The fling with Daniel's long over. Jane lives alone now. She's abandoned magic, doesn't have any connection with Adam or the rest of the group. Adam moved out of London soon afterwards, I heard, maybe even out of England. I never saw him again. Ros went even further. According to Sue, who got the story from Jane, she went to Brazil to have a metal plate inserted in her skull. Her fingernails had been replaced, and the tattoo parlours and piercing shops of South London stopped short of major surgery. She died of a viral infection in a hotel in São Paolo two days before the operation. A stupid accident. Out of all the people in that stupid group, Ros was the only one I'd ever felt sorry for, and with the least reason. She was, after all, doing what she wanted with her life.

Sue thinks I should get back together with Jane. 'Shall I invite her next week?'

Jane never comes. She won't visit Sue unless she's certain I'm not going to be there.

And two nights a week I go for a drink with Tony. He's not so bad these days. He lends me books: popular science, history. We talk about them in the pub, or rather Tony tells me what they mean. It's an education, a bit late in the day and of no real use. I think of that Erin C. Burke stuff I used to yawn over and it makes me laugh. Or not laugh – groan, the way you groan hearing a bad joke for the fifteenth time.

Every few months I take a train out to the sticks. It's a quiet suburb: big semi-detached houses with immaculate gardens and double garages, top-of-the-range cars parked on the drives, and little rows of the usual shops. Half a mile from the station is what looks like a successful private school. There's a red brick wall outside, and you walk up a short path past another immaculate garden, then up the steps to the reception. The woman who works there is local. Her husband's retired. She works on the reception desk at weekends for pin money. It gets her out of the house. She's curious and friendly and once said she didn't understand why I visit. 'Neither do I,' I told her.

Joshua was picked up the day after Mike disappeared. He'd gone back to his flat, found the knife in the table and the broken mirror, seen his journal was gone, and decided to move there and then. He packed his case and left, with no idea of where to go. He was stopped a few streets later by two policemen in a car. They'd seen his bruises and bloodstained shirt and assumed he was a crime victim. He played along with them at first, claiming he'd been mugged. He gave them his old address and told them his name was Kevin Taylor, not knowing these same policemen had driven Kevin to the hospital only weeks earlier. They pretended they believed him, and asked him to come to the station to make a statement. Once there, they told him they knew he was lying about his name. Joshua admitted he had obtained money by fraud, then he told them how credit was a form of black magic, how he was only safe if he kept within the area marked out by the true ley lines, and that within the next five or ten years all the positions of authority in society would be occupied by the former occupants of 'the land wrongly called Atlantis'. When they tried to fingerprint him he became hysterical. He was sent to a small hospital for observation. At first he was kept in a ward with other non-violent patients, until he told them why he was there and one of them attacked him. These days he has his own room.

The first time I visited he called for help. When the nurse came, Joshua told him I wasn't human and that they were all in danger. On the second visit he was calmer. He told me he realised I'd accomplished what I'd set out to do and wouldn't hurt him now. If other people didn't care about the threat I posed – well, he'd tried to warn them. At first he had sent letters – pages of A4 covered with neat handwriting. The Home Secretary never answered; the world's religious leaders didn't even send acknowledgements. He had just as little success with Adam and Ros. When I told him I didn't see Adam any more and that Ros was dead, he laughed.

'Of course. You don't need them now.'

He admires me, or what he thinks I am. You'd almost say he was friendly.

He soon gave up writing letters. These days, he says, he's writing a book. 'Of course it can't be published. They're too powerful.'

There are times when I'm reminded of the old days, when I used to visit Mike. There are differences, though. Joshua has a bigger room, with a small table he uses as a writing desk. He sounds more reasonable than Mike ever did. One of the nurses told me Joshua is a unique case. That's why he's still there. Officially it's because he's a danger to himself, but if that were the only reason he'd have been thrown out long ago. He has no other visitors, though his parents occasionally write. He once showed me one of their letters: half a page on pale blue notepaper, hoping he was well and explaining how busy they were. 'Perhaps we'll have more time in the autumn...' He sees them as part of the plot: 'I learned very early I couldn't trust them.' His mother is a legal secretary, his father a chartered surveyor. 'That's not a coincidence. You only have to think about it.' For Joshua, nothing is a coincidence. He thought his journals had been stolen by a supernatural agency. The lock hadn't been forced; a mirror was broken. The mirror, he told me, was how they'd got in... He thinks he's here because he tried to deal with forces he didn't understand and, in a way, he's right.

Sometimes he asks, 'What did you do to Michael?'

'I thought you could tell me.' That was my hope in the early days: that he might give some clue, mention a place I hadn't yet looked.

'Ah,' he says. 'Michael was gifted. He was special.'

Once, this would have made me angry. Now I just feel tired. I sit in his room and ask questions, while he tells me that the so-called mad people are really the sane ones, that Michael was gifted, and that the others, Peter, Avril and 'whatsisname, that other one', were disappointments. Once I would have been angry. Even now, if I heard it outside, in a pub or an office, I'd get angry. And this is Joshua Painter talking, Joshua Painter who wrecked lives and – shazam! – made my brother disappear. I ought to hate him, but can't. Joshua isn't evil, he's just wrong, and he's wrong because he's ill. You can't hate someone for that, however much you hate what they've done. And nobody else visits him.

Sometimes I ask, 'Why do you think I come?'

'To make sure I'm still here.'

That's all. He doesn't seem to mind being there. 'It's finished,' he'll say. 'You won. I owe them nothing. From now on I've retired.' He talks as if his life is over, and there's nothing else for him to do. He's writing his book to set the record straight, but that's just a hobby, it's not important now. He doesn't expect it to be published anyway, at least not in his lifetime, maybe not on this plane of reality. You'd say he was happy, with his clean room and the medication that keeps him calm, the pages he fills with his neat handwriting. He doesn't want to leave and he's not fit to stand trial. He's happy, and all I feel is tired.

I have fewer suits these days. I have my own computer – everybody does; they're as common as radios once were. My spare room is empty again. I used to think that however things were was the way they would always be. I was wrong, of course. The job has already changed. Everything's connected now: push a button in Northampton, and a credit card in Tooting becomes a worthless piece of plastic. There are fewer cards to collect, and so, although we were never much good at our second string, finding people, it's mostly what we do. Brian and Tony still talk about leaving: Brian's at night school, while Tony talks about becoming a private detective. Hameed left years ago; Piers, who never worked with us for the money, is there two days a week. I go in every day, though I don't know for how much longer. We're paid by the job, and there are fewer jobs. I'm biding my time, waiting for the day Elding Collections goes the way of the crossing sweeper and the night soil man. I still can't think of anything I want to do.

Once, when Mike was in the institution, I'd thought he would be there for the rest of his life. Then, when he moved to the halfway house, I thought the same thing. I thought I'd go on visiting him there, that I'd live with Jane, maybe even eat in restaurants with Adam and listen to his latest theories. It had felt like a normal life; I'd thought it would go on forever. It didn't, but that time is still my standard: what I have now feels like a glitch, a temporary interruption of service. These days don't count, however many of them pass. Joshua has been confined for longer than Mike ever was, Jane has avoided me for more years than we were ever friends – I know these facts, without believing them to be true. And Joshua will be released one day. They'll decide he's no longer a threat to himself – there'll be new drugs, or spontaneous remission, or his room will be needed for a more interesting case. He'll be released, and what then? Mike will be further and further away, unreachably distant. Years will pass; they've passed already and it just feels as if the calendar is wrong.

And it's not as though I cling to the past for my own melancholy pleasure. It's more as if these memories cling to me, haunting me the way Mike was haunted by ideas he could never quite express. *There were two of them today. They didn't think I'd seen them.* The difference is that I know these thoughts are just that: thoughts, the by-products of sleepless nights or having too much time on my hands, that *tendency to dwell obsessively* which Ros once claimed to find in my chart. They aren't Joshua's malign intelligences or whatever Mike imagined was pursuing him. The problem is that knowing this doesn't help.

A memory: I'm twelve years old, in trouble again. The head of year is giving a one-to-one lecture on fighting in the playground. He's also going in for a bit of physical intimidation, probably because he knows this is the last year it'll work. This time next year I'll be the same height, the year after that taller and heavier. He's shouting in my face and prodding at my chest.

'Why is it always you, Patrick? Why is it always you?'

I've been up twice before so I know this is one of the questions you're not supposed to answer. I try to answer anyway. 'Because – '

'There's always a reason, Patrick.' He says something about Mike having to learn to stand up for himself. He says something about coming to the teachers, trusting them to put things right. I look out of the window. If I looked at his stupid face, I'd laugh.

Mike's out at the gate, waiting for me. Everybody who's not on detention has gone home. I could be here another half-hour, and he's waiting. Half an hour's a long time. He could be at home watching television, or playing five-a-side in the park. Instead he's standing at the gates, because he doesn't watch television and nobody wants him in their team, and maybe he ought to go home in case some boys from the next school come by and recognise his blazer. But he waits, and it's as if he knows I'm looking down because suddenly he looks up in my direction and waves.

Acknowledgements

Thanks are due to lots of people: to Martin Agombar, David Hellens, Nigel Hughes, Rob Johnston, James Membrey and Karen Miles, for their encouragement in the early days, and, in the final stages, to Vicky Blunden and Linda McQueen for their attention to detail and the entire team at Myriad for turning this into an actual book. Thanks also to Tony Dugdale, Sue Eckstein, Naomi Foyle, Susanna Jones, John O'Donoghue, Brendan Cleary, Maria Jabstrzebska, Louise Halvardsson, Neil Rollinson, John McCulloch and numerous others for their encouragement and example, and, finally, to Matthew and Nina (and Joe and Sid) for the food and company.

If you have enjoyed *The Schism*, you might like Robert Dickinson's critically acclaimed debut novel *The Noise of Strangers*.

For an exclusive extract, read on...

Denise hated the drive home. At night, driving across town was as bad as driving through the countryside. Once through the security gate at the bottom of Southover Street the only visible lights were the squatters' campfires on the Level. Except at a checkpoint or guard post the roads would be black, the pavements lost in shadow, with only the occasional candle in an upstairs window to show they were passing houses where people lived. Their own house was only a few miles away, but the journey always inspired the same nausea.

And then there was Jack. 'This is the kind of nonsense I mean.' Denise didn't know what he was talking about. 'I mean, this can add, what, ten minutes to the journey.'

She realised he was talking about the new one-way system. 'You can't complain,' she said, although she knew he always would. 'You designed it.'

Jack tutted and turned right, heading towards the Lewes Road. 'Actually, this one was Alan's.'

'But you approved it.'

'That's not the point. Oh, bloody hell.' He braked sharply. At the top of the Level the traffic lights were still working, and showed red. He stopped, even though it was after midnight and there were no other cars on the road. Denise said nothing. The way Jack followed rules when there was no need was one of the things they argued about.

Jack would say that he was maintaining standards, setting an example. Denise thought it was safer to keep moving.

The squatters worried her. She knew they were harmless, that they would drink their moonshine, sing their hymns, and then wait, as they did every night, for the end of the world. In the morning T & E would drive them back into the slums around Russell Street, where they would sit on the pavements until it was dark enough for them to return, when they would once again drink their moonshine and sing their hymns. Denise was not scared of the squatters themselves: what made her uneasy was what they represented. She thought she could remember a time when, except for a few known tramps, the Level had been empty at night.

'Look at them.' Jack glared at the campfires. 'Useless scum.' His anger was at more than the squatters or the one-way system, but Denise was too tired to care about its real object. Jack was always angry at something. Sometimes he pretended it was amusement or scorn or principled outrage; for now it was just anger.

The lights changed. He headed towards London Road, passing the boarded-up windows of Baker Street. 'I suppose you'd prefer it if we lived in Hanover.'

'You know I would.' Hanover was something else they argued about. It was the ward where, somehow, everybody they knew lived. At least once a week they would make this journey to some dinner party or other. 'You have to admit it would be more convenient.' Denise could have said more but was distracted by the stray dogs prowling outside the shell of the old Co-op building. There was supposed to be a nest of them, if that was the word, in the basement. Supposed to be: one of the rumours that, in this town, passed for knowledge. The council had plans for the building: another depot for Transport and Environment, or a holding centre for Welfare – anything to stop the rot spreading north from the Russell Street slums. 'At least we could walk home afterwards,' she offered. 'You'd be able to drink.' And she would need to drink less.

'The houses are too small.' Jack frowned into his rear-view mirror. 'And we'd have to listen to Alan and Margaret arguing every night.'

The tiredness was like a weight behind her eyes. Where did he get this idea? 'Alan and Margaret don't argue.'

'No?' He took a left up New England Road, towards the looming Victorian viaduct on which Denise could remember having once seen a train. She'd been a child; it might have been the first train she'd seen, though sometimes she wondered if she'd seen it at all, or simply been told about it so often she now believed she had. She wondered if dwelling on this kind of uncertainty was a sign of age. Or was it the wine? There had been seven people and five bottles of wine; Siobhan hadn't drunk any, Jack had nursed the same half-glass the whole evening, Alan and Margaret and Tim and Louise... She made the familiar, depressing calculations. Jack sighed through clenched teeth. 'Did you see that graffiti? Couldn't even spell Henderson properly.' Denise looked, but the words were behind them now, and the walls ahead were covered with posters bearing a cross, the sign of the Helmstone mission. There were no words, but then most of the Helmstoners couldn't read, and weren't so different from the squatters on the open ground. They didn't drink, lived in houses and sang different hymns, and most of them had low-level council jobs, but they waited for the end of the world as fervently as any of the derelicts on the Level. Denise almost envied them their hope. She knew the world was not going to end: it would grind on and on until they and all their dismissive taxonomy (Stoner, Scoomer, squatter, scum) were dead and forgotten. 'And how can you say they don't argue?' Jack asked. Denise forced herself to concentrate:

he was still talking about Alan and Margaret. 'They barely spoke to each other.'

'That's not the same as arguing.'

'So you think they're happy?'

'I don't know. But they don't argue.' Denise wondered how Jack could be so wrong. Alan and Margaret were too intent on presenting themselves as a successful couple to disagree in front of outsiders. 'And I don't know where you've got the idea they do.'

'Don't you?' They stopped for more lights. Again there was no other traffic in any direction. 'For crying out loud. This is the kind of thing I mean.' This time she couldn't tell what he was talking about: the pointless lights or her lack of perception, or something else he expected her to guess. His anger was indiscriminate. He turned to her. 'Alan can be such a bastard. The way he carries on with Louise. And Margaret is sitting right there.'

'Tim doesn't seem to mind.'

'Tim doesn't seem to notice. Here's Alan, flirting outrageously with his wife, and he's – I don't know what he's doing.'

'Lights.'

'Right.' He eased across the junction, where, surprisingly, more traffic had appeared: two dirty white Fiats, Scoomer cars, spluttering up from the other direction. The passenger of one was leaning from his window, as if trying to climb out. He shouted at them and waved, laughing. Both cars weaved as they headed away.

'Careful,' Denise said.

'They weren't a problem.' Jack, for once, sounded tolerant. 'They're gone now.'

Denise couldn't relax until the cars were out of sight. 'They're dangerous because they don't care. Henderson voters.'

'If they're Scoomers they're Labour. Besides, I don't think they were old enough to vote.' Jack checked the rear view again. He might have pretended to be unconcerned, but he didn't want those cars to turn round either. They drove on for a few seconds without talking. Then Jack sighed. 'Alan is such a bastard.' So he was back on that hobby horse. 'That's *why* I was talking to him, to keep him away from Louise. I mean, do you think I want to talk about one-way systems all night? I get enough of them at work.'

'I get enough of them at home.'

'I'm sorry. Sorry. It's just such a big deal at the moment. Force the motorists on to the toll roads. Maximise the income.'

'That's Henderson's thing, isn't it? Abolish the toll roads.'

'Henderson's a nobody.' Prestonville Road was empty. Jack, she noticed, was still checking his rear view. There were stories of children in stolen cars driving without lights, for fun. It was supposed to be called 'blinding'. You didn't see them until it was too late. Another rumour that passed for fact. 'He'll never win anything. And even if he did he wouldn't do it.' Jack's voice softened to resigned bitterness. 'Not when he finds out how much money it makes.'

'Jack, I've heard enough about it for one night. It wasn't supposed to be a summit meeting. Alan and Margaret invited us there to eat.'

'I know, I know...' They slowed at the foot of the hill. A Bentley with an escort of four motorcycles swept past them. 'Councillor Goss.' Jack narrowed his eyes. 'Where's he been this time of night?'

'Don't ask me.'

'I thought Audit knew everybody's dirty little secrets.'

'Probably a dinner party. Just like us.'

'Councillor Goss? I doubt it.' The lights changed. Jack took a right. 'Even so...'

'This isn't the way.'

'I know.'

'So what are you doing?' Denise put her hands on the dashboard as if bracing herself for a sudden stop. 'You're not following him, are you?'

Jack grinned at her. It was the first time he'd smiled the whole evening. 'If he's going through the Ditchling Road toll I can tailgate, and avoid Preston Road.'

'You'll add ten minutes to our journey to save five pounds?'

'Seven minutes. And every little helps.' They'd caught up with the councillor's motorcade. Jack slowed to match its pace. One of the motorcyclists glanced back, but otherwise they were ignored; the benefit of having a good car with a blue council badge in the windscreen. Jack bit his lower lip, a sign of concentration. 'I thought you'd appreciate that, being in Audit.'

'Audit isn't about money.'

'Everything is about money.' He glanced in the rear view. 'Looks like somebody else has the same idea.'

She turned. Another car was coming up behind them, headlights full on. 'Scoomers,' she said. 'What are they doing here?'

'You can't say they're Scoomers just because it's a Fiat.'

'It's a good rule of thumb. Shit, they're not slowing down.' Famous last words, she thought: it would be just my luck... When it was inches away the car swerved, overtaking them and the motorcade. 'Maniac,' she said – or possibly only thought. For a moment she wasn't sure.

'Close,' Jack said.

'You should have gone the usual way. This road's a menace.'

'And paid the Preston Road toll? He missed us, didn't he?' He grinned again. Yes, he was amused by her terror.

It probably made him feel manly. 'So, what were you and Margaret talking about all evening? Her miserable marriage?'

'Margaret and Alan aren't married.'

'You know what I mean.'

'Actually we were talking about Doug and Sarah.'

Jack kept his eyes on the road ahead. 'I think that counts as talking about her miserable marriage by proxy.'

The way he said *I think that counts* made her head ache. There were times when talking to Jack was like banging your shin against a familiar piece of furniture. You knew it was there and were still surprised it could make you wince. 'Doug and Sarah aren't unhappy. As far as anybody knows.'

'No.' Jack gave the mirthless smile that usually preceded a witticism. 'But I sometimes believe you lot think they ought to be.'

You lot: the women. 'That's not fair.'

'But you're always wondering how Sarah ended up with someone like Doug.'

'You have to admit it was unexpected.'

'Doesn't mean it was wrong.' Now he was disagreeing with her for the sake of it. 'I know he doesn't have our education. But you talk about him as if he were a Scoomer.'

'So do you, half the time. Besides, he's a Henderson voter.'

'Rubbish.' He glanced at her, suddenly concerned. 'Or do you know something?'

'That's what Sarah says.' She corrected herself. 'That's what Margaret says Sarah says.'

'Then she should leave him. But she won't because he isn't. Here we go.' Ahead of them they could see the barrier beginning to rise. Jack concentrated on maintaining his distance from the motorcade. 'See? That's five pounds saved.'

'I hate going through these.' Denise stared dead ahead as they passed under the barrier. Two guards stood to awkward attention beside the booth, their rifles slung over their shoulders, their faces carefully blank beneath their uniform caps. 'They worry me,' she said, seconds later, when the barrier was down behind them. 'I always think one of them is about to crack up and start shooting at people.'

'You say that every time. There are vetting procedures, you know.' He slowed, allowing the motorcade to pull away. 'Thank you, Councillor Goss. And now...' He had no sooner turned off the road than she heard horns blaring behind them, then a screech and metal crashing into metal, followed a moment later by what sounded like a second, heavier collision.

Jack swore. Denise looked back, but couldn't see anything. 'Don't stop.'

But Jack had already stopped and was reversing back down the street. In the upper windows lights were starting to appear. 'I'm only going to have to deal with this in the morning. I might as well see what it is now.'

'Yes, in the morning...' There were four motorcyclists – council officials – already at the scene. It was their job to handle this kind of incident. 'What difference can you make now? You can deal with it in the morning...'

Jack wasn't listening. He reversed until they were back on Ditchling Road.

The first thing Denise saw, two or three hundred yards ahead of the junction, was a bright orange flare behind a barricade, as if a civic bonfire had been pitched incongruously in the middle of the dark street. She couldn't see the councillor's Bentley. Had it turned off the road? Had the noise they heard been caused by other cars? Then she realised the barricade *was* the Bentley, thrown on to its side, its roof towards them. As her eyes adjusted she could make out two of the motorbikes lying in the road beside it. One of the riders was leaning against a post and tugging frantically at his helmet as if he thought it was on fire. He seemed to be the only person on the street. She couldn't see the rider of the other motorbike, and was surprised how quiet everything seemed. She could hear nothing other than the sound of their own engine: no cries for help, no other cars. The flames seemed to be burning silently, as if they were much further away than they looked. As Jack turned the car to face them they seemed to die down. Denise watched them, fascinated despite herself. Suddenly the rider staggered forward, bent at the waist. He pulled off his helmet as if he had finally remembered how to loosen the strap, then threw it into the gutter with what looked like disgust. He walked unsteadily towards the upturned car. 'You've seen it,' Denise said. 'Now go.'

'They may need help.'

'What can you do? They're not your responsibility.'

'If it's not mine…'

Jack straightened the car. Immediately, Denise heard a popping sound that seemed to come from nowhere in particular. She thought they had driven over something, but then Jack swore. He braked and turned so sharply they jolted against the kerb.

The impact made her nauseous. She clutched the dashboard as he ground them through another wrenching turn. 'What was that?'

'It wasn't the engine.'

She swallowed hard. It had sounded too light for gunfire, unless it was from a sidearm: a bodyguard, terrified and in shock, firing at anything that moved. 'Are you sure?'

'No.' His sense of their danger was finally stronger than his work ethic. 'But I'm not staying to find out.'

They drove in silence for the next two streets. Denise clenched her teeth and took deep breaths and gradually felt better. From far off, and seemingly from different directions, came the sound of sirens. Jack said, 'This is going to be a headache tomorrow. If we have to close that road...'

The job again. She said: 'What about Goss?'

'He's not my responsibility. The road is.' His hands drummed the steering wheel, as if trying to dislodge a thought. 'Shit. I need to talk to Alan.'

They reached their street. The security guard (Paul? Oscar?) let them through the gate after no more than a glance. He seemed to be listening to the noise of the sirens as raptly as a Helmstoner listened to hymns.

Jack eased their car into their allotted space and stopped the engine. Normally he would sigh and sit for a second or two. Now he jumped out of the car and skipped across the pavement as if he thought they were under fire. Denise hadn't seen him move as quickly in years. He was at their building before she could get out of the car. By the time she reached the security grille he had already unlocked the street door and was heading towards the staircase. Ignoring the lift, he bounded up the stairs with Denise clattering unsteadily behind him. When she reached the flat he was already standing by the phone.

'Let's hope the lines are working tonight.' He was panting from the exertion.

She limped behind him. 'What are you doing?'

He picked up the receiver and started to dial. 'I'm letting Alan know.'

'Can't it wait until the morning?'

'It's going to be a lot of work. We'll need to start as early as possible.' He placed the receiver to his ear and listened intently.

'It's two in the morning.' But it was useless talking to Jack when he was in this kind of mood.

'Alan? It's Jack. We've just got in. You heard it? Yes, we saw it. You're not going to believe this...'

She went to the bathroom and threw up with a sudden violence. Her mouth was filled with the taste of red wine. She drank a glass of water and tried not to think about what she'd just seen, but couldn't. For Jack, it was all a matter of one-way systems, but if Councillor Goss had been in that car then there were political ramifications and that would matter to Audit because everything, in the end, mattered to Audit.

It could wait until Monday morning. For now she was tired and her head ached. She wiped her mouth as the cistern refilled. When she came out of the room Jack was still on the phone, talking.

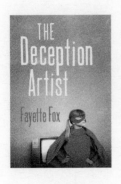

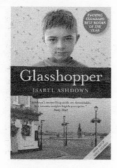

MORE FROM MYRIAD EDITIONS

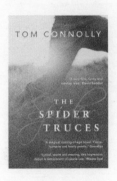

www.myriadeditions.com